Praise for Previous ~~Books in the Series~~
Beyond the Veil and *After Sundown*

'There is no end to the talent Mark Morris has
brought together here. Fans of the genre will be
pleased to see new work from such favorites as
Nathan Ballingrud and Gemma Files, among others.
So if you're ready for a long fall night, pick up a copy
of this massive anthology and fall into the mysterious
worlds *Beyond the Veil*.'
Phantastiqa on *Beyond the Veil*

'I'm impressed with the imagination and variety
coming from the writers. *Beyond the Veil*, from
Flame Tree Press, is another happy clump
of ickiness...and I mean that in a good way.'
The Happy Horror Writer on *Beyond the Veil*

'Beautifully written pieces that lean
into the intuitive and fantastic.'
Publishers Weekly on *After Sundown*

'This rich and masterful collection of horror
highlights both up-and-coming and established
authors in an interesting twist on the standard
anthology [...] Highly recommended for longstanding
horror fans and those readers who may not think
horror is for them. There is something for everyone
in this one.'
Booklist on *After Sundown*

A FLAME TREE
BOOK OF HORROR

CLOSE TO
MIDNIGHT

An Anthology of New Short Stories

Edited by Mark Morris

This is a **FLAME TREE PRESS** book

FLAME TREE PRESS
6 Melbray Mews, London, SW6 3NS, UK
flametreepress.com

US sales, distribution and warehouse:
Simon & Schuster
simonandschuster.biz

UK distribution and warehouse:
Marston Book Services Ltd
marston.co.uk

Thanks to the Flame Tree Press team.

The cover is created by Flame Tree Studio with thanks to Nik Keevil and Shutterstock.com. The font families used are Avenir and Bembo.

Flame Tree Press is an imprint of Flame Tree Publishing Ltd

flametreepublishing.com

A copy of the CIP data for this book is available from the British Library and the Library of Congress.

HB ISBN: 978-1-78758-725-0
US PB ISBN: 978-1-78758-723-6
UK PB ISBN: 978-1-78758-724-3
ebook ISBN: 978-1-78758-727-4

Printed and bound in Great Britain by Clays Ltd, Elcograf S.p.A

A FLAME TREE BOOK OF HORROR

CLOSE TO MIDNIGHT

An Anthology of New Short Stories

Edited by Mark Morris

FLAME TREE PRESS
London & New York

CONTENTS

INTRODUCTION

Mark Morris

Horror fiction, it is said, thrives in troubled times, and whether or not that is true, it cannot be denied that the genre is enjoying a boom period at the moment. The breadth and quality of work being produced in the field, both by seasoned veterans and an influx of exciting new writers, is breathtaking. Stephen King has been a mainstay in the bestsellers lists for almost five decades, but his sometimes lone flag-flying for the genre has recently become a joint effort, thanks to authors such as Catriona Ward, Paul Tremblay, Grady Hendrix, Stephen Graham Jones, C.J. Tudor and King's own son, Joe Hill, whose books are flying off the shelves.

The news that dark fiction is being read widely again is, of course, music to the ears of those of us who work within the field. Whereas we could all do without the real-life fear that comes with a world-wide pandemic and the threat of global conflict, there's nothing more thrilling than losing yourself in an imaginative, tense and scary piece of fiction. Getting the adrenaline flowing, and the heart beating a little faster, makes us feel *alive* – and the sensation is all the better if we can do it from the warmth and security of our beds, or our favourite armchairs, preferably with a fire crackling away in the grate and a mug of something hot and comforting close to hand.

As I've mentioned before, though, horror fiction itself should never be cosy and reassuring. The best horror fiction should be confrontational, challenging, thought-provoking; it should provide us with insights into the human condition, and/or reflect the world around us, and particularly its dark and troubled corners where, in real life, we might be reluctant to tread.

Perhaps not surprisingly, given the past two years, many of the tales in this third volume of non-themed horror stories from Flame Tree Press deal with the subject of loss. This, of course, is something we, as human beings, will inevitably face at some point in our lives, and these stories shine a harsh light on loss in its many forms, exploring not only the physical loss of loved ones, but also the loss of identity, the loss of control, the loss of sanity, the loss of freedom, and the loss of health and security.

It's a grim catalogue, but there's a balance here too. After all, darkness is nothing without light. So where you find despair, you'll also find hope; where you find the monstrous, you'll also find humanity; and where you find depravity, you'll also find the numinous.

All of life, human or otherwise, is here, within these pages.

Mark Morris

WOLVES

Rio Youers

Dawn light, a pale eye opening, looking first on the woodland that capped Deer Hill before taking in the town proper. It was, for all its symbolism, a bleak light, often colourless, which meant nothing; life in First Green was as it should be, and every new day was gold.

Kieran Stork took a seat on the deck and inhaled the morning air. It was scented with mouldering leaves and a trace of skunk. A chickadee landed on the bird table nearby and dipped its beak in three-day-old rainwater. Kieran watched until it took wing. He drank coffee from a mug with BIG WHEEL printed on one side – a gift from Jillian, his companion. She would join him soon.

The light peeled away the last of the stars. It was 6:55. Kieran was still forty-some minutes from seeing the first wolf, eight feet tall with a strip of fire along its back.

★   ★   ★

Jillian came down in sweatpants and a hoodie – not what she'd worn to bed – and took the seat opposite his. She ran a hand through glorious, sleep-tousled hair and smiled.

"Hey," he said.

"Hey." She'd poured herself a mug of coffee and drank now, removing some of the morning husk from her voice. After three or four sips, it was gone. The sleep lines on her left cheek remained, though, and that hair – a confusion of honey-coloured spills.

"You sleep okay?" he asked.

"Hm." A shrug, a crooked smile. "I guess. Got up around four to pee. Took a while to get off again."

"Maybe take a nap later."

"Maybe." She nodded, sipped her coffee. "How about you? How's your head?"

Kieran had returned from his duties yesterday with a sliver of pain – thin as a toothpick – in the centre of his forehead, which expanded over the course of the evening into a blunt wooden stake. He'd taken two Tylenol and gone to bed early.

"Better." He upended the lukewarm dregs of his coffee. "I slept good. That's what I needed."

"Even so, take it easy today."

"I always do."

"Yeah? I'm not so sure about that, mister." Jillian smiled again, nothing crooked this time. With the new daylight in her hair, she looked eighteen, not thirty-eight. "Town meeting later."

"Haven't forgotten," Kieran said. He wiped sleep crud out of his eye and blinked the blurriness away. "Think I'll get Nathan to chair this one, or at least do the lion's share."

Nathan was six years Kieran's junior. They had their father's long nose and cleft chin but these were the only similarities. The younger brother was four inches taller and a good deal wider. He hadn't completely lucked out, though; he'd lost his hair in his late twenties, whereas Kieran still had all of his. Not a thread of grey, either.

"Some say you're grooming him to take the reins," Jillian said.

"Some are wrong." Kieran cleared his throat, then ran a palm across the back of his neck. The muscles there were tight. He could have slept longer. "I do think he should take more responsibility, though. I wouldn't mind slowing down some."

"I wouldn't mind that, either."

"Spend more time with you. With the kids."

"Now you're talking."

Kieran looked at the steady slope of Deer Hill, stitched with milkweed and ferns, and the tangle of fall-coloured trees lining the peak. On the other side, Cotton Road crossed the Muskateni, which marked the edge of town. To the south, Founder Bridge spanned the same river, where it was common to see townsfolk, young and old, hanging a line over the rail, looking to pull crappies and largemouth out of the water.

The Stork family home – an oversized cabin on two acres – enjoyed views of the entire town. This was by design. Kieran's grandfather had constructed the house seventy-four years prior, choosing for himself an ideally elevated plot of land. "Comings and goings," he'd said to Kieran back in the day. They'd been standing at the front bedroom window, looking west over the town and Echo Lake beyond. "You'll want nothin' to escape your eye."

"Where you at?" Jillian asked. She tilted her head. Her eyes glittered. "You're miles away."

"Yeah, well, not that far," Kieran replied, and shrugged. "Just zoned out for a while."

"You want a refresh?" She nodded at his empty mug.

"That I do."

Jillian took their mugs and stepped through the back door into the kitchen. Her scent lingered on the cool morning air for a second or two, so warm and natural, so familiar to him. He could find her in a crowd, blindfolded. Kieran relaxed into his seat and sighed comfortably. Jillian returned a moment later, not with their coffees, but with his cell phone.

"Looks like you missed a call."

"I did?" He squinted at the screen. "Aw, shoot. Ringer was off."

Jillian retreated to the kitchen again, leaving Kieran hunched over his phone. The call had been from Louise Stenner, who lived on the west side of town with her companion, Gary. Louise was one of their kindergarten teachers. Gary was a farmhand, mechanic, and driver. He wasn't bright, but he had his uses.

The call had come in at 6:32. Early. There was one voicemail message. Kieran checked it, holding the phone's speaker a couple of inches from his ear. "Kieran, friend and keeper. It's Louise Stenner. Could you come over when…when you get this message." Her breath hitched slightly and in this alone Kieran heard her emotion. "There's something you need to see."

Kieran waited for more but the message ended with a beep. He put down his phone and looked at the sky, now turned milky blue. Jillian stepped out, a coffee mug in each hand. She handed one to Kieran.

She asked, "Everything okay?"

"If it isn't now, it will be."

"Ever the optimist."

"Why be any other way?" He slurped his coffee, wrinkled his nose, set the mug down on the table between them. "Oh, that's bitter already."

"You want me to put on a fresh pot?"

"No time. I have to go." Kieran got to his feet. "What I would like, though, one day, is a pot of coffee that doesn't taste like dishwater after twenty minutes."

"Impossible," Jillian said. She also got to her feet, but only to wrap her arms around him. "That's probably a metaphor, though. Right?"

"A metaphor? Coffee is a metaphor?"

"Yeah. Nothing good can last forever."

He kissed the tip of her nose. "I don't believe that."

★   ★   ★

The wolf appeared at the edge of Echo Lake. It skirted the shore with the fire along its back reflected in the water, then clambered onto a shelf of limestone and sat looking toward town. Kieran saw it as he turned off Cotton Road, onto Burdock Street. He slammed the brakes and got out of his car.

"No way. There's no way." He cared little for the weakened tone he heard in his voice. It was just surprise – a sudden shortness of breath – but he didn't like it at all. "That can't...that can't be."

The view to the lake was interrupted by the bones of windswept pines, but the wolf was elevated and Kieran saw it clearly. Even at this distance – a hundred yards, give or take – he could tell that it was big. Bigger than any man.

He looked a while longer. The wolf didn't move. Jacob Hillier mooched along Burdock clutching a bouquet of wild asters, probably for Nancy Falk, his sweetheart. She was eighty-eight and he was older still.

Pain skewered the centre of Kieran's forehead – that toothpick-like sliver, same as yesterday. He pressed his thumb between his eyes and it faded.

"Kieran Stork," Jacob called out, raising one hand. "Friend and keeper. What you looking at?"

"Big wolf yonder," Kieran said.

Jacob turned suddenly, following Kieran's gaze. He looked for a long moment, his asters nodding, his white hair blowing in the breeze, before a dusty chuckle broke from his chest.

"You had me for a second there," Jacob said. He flapped a hand in Kieran's direction and kept walking.

⋆　　⋆　　⋆

Gary Jablonski lay sprawled on the kitchen floor with his life's blood all around him. It puddled the stove and countertops. It was splashed across the front of the refrigerator and the sink and the dirty dishes therein. It was even sprinkled across the kitchen ceiling. There didn't appear to be too much blood left inside Gary's body, and there certainly was no life.

The clock on the kitchen wall – and yes, there was a speck of blood on its white plastic casing – read 7:42. It was going to be a long day.

"Thing is," Louise said, and her voice cracked. "Once you start stabbing someone you hate, it's hard to stop."

"I can see that," Kieran said.

Louise sat at the kitchen table, four feet away from her fallen companion, a man she had shared a bed with – a life with – these past eight years. The knife she had used was in front of her. Kieran remembered he and Jillian visiting last Blessing's Eve, and Louise using that knife to chop the vegetables for their dinner.

"Let's, uh…let's move to a different room."

Kieran touched Louise's shoulder. She rose from the chair and they walked together from the kitchen, down the hallway, into the living room. It was a small space, but comfortable. Sunlight streamed through the east-facing window. A cat – Gary's cat, Kieran recalled – dozed on the sofa, bundled luxuriously between two pillows. Louise sat down next to it. Kieran remained standing. He couldn't bring himself to sit in Gary's armchair.

"What's going to happen to me?" Louise asked. There was neither remorse nor joy in her tone. She might have been talking about the colour of the walls or which brand of laundry detergent was her favourite.

"The town will decide," Kieran said.

"They'll want to place rocks," Louise said. She linked her hands and brought them to her chin. She'd washed most of the blood off, but there were still a few dark drops here and there. "Gary could do no wrong in their eyes. Their blue-eyed boy. I was always his companion. Only that. Even when I did things without him."

Kieran had known Louise all her life. He was twelve years her senior, so had clear memories of the big-eyed toddler who'd squealed with delight when they'd decorated downtown for Founder's Day, and of the shivering teenager he and Nathan had rescued after she swam too far across Echo Lake. "I was told the moon touched down on the other side," she'd sobbed, looking at Kieran through a veil of wet hair.

It had only been a few years later when she and Gary had come to Kieran and expressed their wish to be companioned. He'd been hesitant, because they were so new together, but had seen such a fullness in their eyes that he couldn't find it within him to refuse.

Upon this rich soil, where the founders planted their first seeds, I will take root and grow with you.

"He broke me, Kieran, but on the inside, where nobody could see." Louise stroked the cat. It stretched its front legs and purred but didn't wake. "He'd criticise my hair, my clothes, my body. He called me names. He said that touching me disgusted him. It doesn't sound like much, but it was every day, for all these years."

Kieran felt the edge of something, part nausea, part darkness, signalling that pain-needle in the middle of his forehead once again. He looked at the sunlight tattooed across the hardwood floor and it helped, but just a touch.

"Small breaks, little cracks, over time. I didn't know how broken I was until I ran out to Thunder Point – way out, past the old gas station." Louise looked at her hands and touched a speck of dried blood on her wrist. "I sat on the edge of the creek there and felt all the loose pieces inside me. Then I just cried and cried."

"You weren't trying to run away?" Kieran asked. It wasn't the right question, but it wasn't the wrong one, either.

"Run where?"

Kieran shrugged, as if he had no idea what lay beyond First Green (in truth, he had very little idea), and he let the mystery of that hang in the air.

"I just needed distance," Louise said. She stroked the cat again. "Away from the town. The people. A moment to myself. But I don't think I was alone."

"What do you mean?"

"Heard a voice." Louise frowned, considering this for a moment, then she nodded. "Maybe it was in my head…maybe in the sky. Either way, I heard it, and I knew what I had to do."

Kieran pressed his thumb to his forehead but the pain persisted. "This voice...what did it say?"

"It told me to trust in my strength, and make way for salvation."

Kieran opened his mouth to respond but found he had no words, so sighed instead and scratched hard behind one ear. The cat woke but lay barely moving, enjoying being stroked, and with Louise momentarily preoccupied, Kieran went back to the kitchen. He stood for a beat looking down at Gary, who he'd always known to be considerate and polite, but recalled now that Jillian had once described him as having a sour mouth. Kieran hadn't known what she meant by that, but thought of Louise talking about small cracks and little breaks over time, and maybe had a better idea now.

He took out his phone and called Nathan, who didn't trust phones and didn't always answer, but did on this occasion, and on only the second ring. A tick of good fortune.

"Nathan."

"Brother."

"I need you at Gary Jablonski's place. We've got a situation."

"Yeah?" A dry laugh over the line. Kieran imagined Nathan's big chest bouncing. "Nothing Kenny Stork's boys can't handle."

Gary's blood had dried dark as wine. He had struggled, evidently, smearing and splattering his way around the kitchen, until he'd succumbed, and then Louise had finished him off. Kieran wondered how much lighter he'd be without all that blood in his body. Nathan would likely be able to move him alone – wrap him in a sheet and throw him over one shoulder, easy as carrying a downed whitetail from the forest.

"Nothing we can't handle," Kieran echoed. He quickly counted eleven holes in Gary's chest and stomach, another four in his crotch, and that wasn't all of them, nothing like. "Bring cleaning supplies. Rags and such. Bleach."

Nathan drew in a breath and Kieran sensed a question coming. He got ahead of it. "Quick as you can," he said, and cut the call.

He returned to the living room, feeling sick and uncharacteristically nervous; his role often necessitated tough decisions, and he'd never faltered – had depended on the generous strip of calm that ran through him. "Stork cool," his father had called it. A genetic thing.

Louise stood by the window with the cat in her arms, maybe the last living thing she'd ever hold close. She cooed to it, fingers massaging between its ears. The sunlight turned her red hair blonde.

"We'll get cleaned up here," Kieran said. He unbuttoned his shirt sleeves and rolled them to his elbows. "He's your dead, so you're helping."

She nodded but didn't look at him.

"I don't know your fate," he added. There was a regretful inflection in his voice and it was honest. "Until the town decides, though, I have to put you in the cage."

Half a smile and her eyes flashed in his direction. "Know this, Kieran, friend and keeper. You can cage my body, but I am released."

⋆ ⋆ ⋆

Here came Nathan in his pickup truck, coughing diesel fumes as it bounced along the driveway. Kieran stood on the porch steps waiting.

"Brother," Nathan said through his open window.

"Brother," Kieran returned, then gestured with one hand. "Pull close as you can to that side door off the kitchen. Got you some cargo."

Nathan nodded and turned his truck around, then backed up, rear wheels on the lawn, getting to within twelve feet of the side door. The truck's box had in it a leaf blower and garden tools, but there was room yet for Gary and a Hefty filled with bloody rags.

"What's the job?" Nathan said, stepping out of the truck, bumping the door closed with his hip. He carried a caddy loaded with cleaning supplies in his left hand and a jug of bleach in his right. Kieran didn't think he'd brought enough. Louise surely had supplies of her own under the kitchen sink, though, and they could cut up some of Gary's clothes for rags.

"You won't thank me," Kieran said. He took a deep breath and reflected how, just a couple of hours ago, he'd been sitting peaceably in his backyard, watching the morning arrive – a simple pleasure that, now, felt inordinately blissful. "Louise took a knife to Gary and didn't stop. It's an awful mess in there."

Nathan was not a man of many words. His strength was in his shoulders, in his ability to support. You could throw the world up there and he might weaken at the knees but he would carry. Now he just pressed his lips together and nodded.

"We've seen dead before," Kieran added. "Ugly dead. Walt Carver, struck by lightning. That business with Norm and Michael Penny. But nothing like this. You hear what I'm saying, brother?"

"I hear you."

"You need to steel yourself." Kieran held Nathan's gaze a moment, neither man blinking. "But first, walk with me."

Kieran started along the driveway. Nathan set down his supplies and followed. They fell into step as they left Gary and Louise's property and headed north on Willow Avenue, these brothers, different in stature but alike in many ways: their purposeful gait, the stoop of their backs, that unfaltering Stork cool. They turned onto Burdock, both men silent, just the sound of their breathing, then hopped a fence onto tougher country: rocks and roots and trees grown at angles, some near sideways. The ground rose on the other side of those trees, offering an uninterrupted view of Echo Lake, deep blue in the morning light.

The wolf had not moved. It had grown, though, now the height of four men. It sat looking toward town, a calm countenance, regal in its way. Kieran could see the colour of its eyes: amber flecked with black.

"There." The word was little more than a hiss of air from between Kieran's lips.

Nathan palmed drops of sweat off his bald head and said, "Our country. Beautiful. Let us thank the founders."

He took a moment, eyes closed. His lips moved silently.

"What else do you see?" Kieran asked. There was a flutter in his voice but too subtle for Nathan to notice.

"I see strength in the rock, depth in the water. This land echoes the resourcefulness in us all."

The fire along the wolf's back set a haze in the air and the sound of it crackling carried across the lake.

★   ★   ★

The meeting was held in the old town hall, hit by a twister three years previous but standing yet. The windows had been replaced and part of the roof was stapled together with strips of corrugated steel and a tarp covered a hole in the west wall. A new town hall was being built across the way but construction had been halted due to budgetary concerns.

First Green's treasury stretched only so far; the basic needs – food, shelter, warmth – of its people would always be a priority.

Every seat was taken and folks lined the side walls and gathered at the back, three or four deep. Most of First Green's population – 422, as of this day – were in attendance. Word had got around about Gary Jablonski's death, and the people wanted a say in his companion's fate. A sombre business, no doubt, although you wouldn't think it with the buzz in the air: conversation, laughter, salutations, the scraping of chair legs across the floor. The children were mostly orderly but some ran screeching. Such was the way at every community gathering.

Kieran sat on stage with the other five members of the town council, each representing a branch of local government: Nathan Stork, Law and Order; Maurice Weber, Commerce and Trade; Betty Glenn, Treasury; Kirsty Weiss, Health and Education; Eugene Anthony, Public Works and Development. It was Eugene's grandfather who, along with Kieran's grandfather, had cultivated this fair patch of land while the rest of the world was at war.

Kieran, as keeper, would normally steer the meeting, but tonight Nathan took the lectern. It was not an ideal night for him to do so, given the events of the day, but the pain in Kieran's forehead was still present. It had dulled some but not enough. Nathan would be fine.

There were a few surprised whispers when the younger Stork rose from his seat, but he held up one large hand and the room soon hushed. He spoke into the mic and his voice didn't waver.

"Welcome, friends, and thank you for coming. We have several topics on the docket for tonight, including the grim business of which you are all aware. We'll turn to that in due course, but let us begin with a moment of thanks to the founders."

The hall, as one:

For the crops in our fields, we thank you,
For the fish in our waters, we thank you,
For the roofs over our heads and the walls that protect us, we thank you,
May we live by your example and work to make our community stronger.
Now and forever, in all ways.

Nathan nodded and stood tall at the lectern, allowing a moment of silence to descend and draw them all yet closer. That Stork cool was real and on display, but Kieran knew his younger brother had a few butterflies fluttering around in his stomach. He wasn't made of stone.

"My apologies to our friends in the first three rows," he said, patting the top of his head. "If I'd known how badly these stage lights reflected off the top of my bald dome, I would've advised you to wear sunglasses."

Laughter rumbled through the hall and a few friends clapped and others pretended to shield their eyes. Kieran smiled; humour was a good balm for those lingering nerves. Jillian – sitting in the front row – caught his eye and winked.

"We've a lot to discuss," Nathan said, "so let's get it going. Kirsty, you have the floor."

Kirsty Weiss got to her feet and stepped toward the lectern. Nathan adjusted the gooseneck on the mic so that she – a touch over five feet tall – could speak into it comfortably, but she still had to lower it a couple of inches and extend it toward her.

"Thank you, Nathan," Kirsty said. No nerves for her. She'd been on First Green's town council for thirty-two years, and during that time had missed only a handful of monthly meetings. "Some positive news to begin: Hayley Pentlemore recently received her dental hygiene diploma after a year of tutelage with Dr. Elroy, so she'll be joining his practice very soon. Where are you, Hayley? Stand up, friend, and take a bow."

Hayley was in the fourth row and she stood up and took a bow. The applause was warm.

"Oh, you like her now," Kirsty said, once Hayley had retaken her seat, "but wait until she's scraping the plaque off your molars."

Billy Warrington – nary a tooth in his skull – called out, "Chance'd be a fine thing," and this earned a good, hearty laugh from near everyone. Even the tarp covering the hole in the west wall flapped a little louder.

"Thank you, thank you," Kirsty said, raising one hand and settling the room in her expert way. "On to other business…"

An innate mistrust of anything that was not their own made them defensive, and while they strived to be self-sufficient, this was not entirely practical. They depended on the outside world for many things, including consumer goods, medicine, fuel, and technology. For the most part, though, they maintained their distance. It had always been this way.

Two friends – Thomas Stork and Jack Anthony – had returned from the Second World War within months of each other, both under a Section 8 discharge. Thomas's family, disgraced, disowned him. Jack's family was land-wealthy and reckless, and it was on an untapped acreage of Anthony land that the friends decided to start anew. They wanted simple, unspoiled lives. They wanted calm.

The first structure they built was a shelter just large enough for Thomas and Jack to sleep in. The second was a rudimentary lumber mill: a workshop, a drying shed, and a diesel-powered saw that the friends had bought cheap on account of it having taken the hands of three men. They worked the mill, hunted wildlife, and dragged fish from the lake, using only what they needed and selling the rest.

In time they were joined by others, who brought with them knowledge of agriculture, electricity generation, and construction. By 1947, they were thirty-five strong: seventeen men, twelve women, six children. They named this brave, fledgling community First Green. Thomas Stork built his cabin on the hill and watched it grow.

Roads, farms, stores, a school, a hospital, a fire department, sewage treatment, a post office. Taxes were high, but the people were treated equally and wanted for nothing. They followed their own charter – their own laws – and kept their business within the town limits.

Kirsty outlined some of this business now. She had the floor for nineteen minutes – quick for her – then up stepped Eugene Anthony, who appealed for able bodies to help fill in the potholes on Wren Street and give Founder Bridge a fresh lick of paint. He also mentioned that the town's only snowplough was on its last legs, and asked for patience when – in just a few weeks' time, no doubt – they got a drop of the white stuff. Eugene had a few other small things but they didn't take long and he handed the floor over to Maurice Weber, and so it continued...

Kieran sat through it all with his thumb pressed to the middle of his forehead, hearing words but only half-absorbing them. His headache had worsened beneath these lights, and the flapping of the tarp on the west wall bothered him in a way it didn't appear to bother anybody else. He looked down at his boot tops, feigning engagement whenever he glanced up at the speaker or out at the crowd: that blank sameness of faces. He raised his hand when moved to do so. Aye, for the new school supplies. Aye, for adding Uncle Cluck's Chicken Farm in Harrisonville to their list of suppliers. He imagined an open fire and Jillian beside him, her fingers in his hair, her gift of healing.

In time the discussion turned to Louise Stenner.

★   ★   ★

Four and a half years since they'd last decided the fate of a friend. That had been Michael Penny, who'd bought a pint-bottle of bourbon from a gas station in River's Cross (thirty-two miles south, the closest town to First Green), drank it empty, then shot his father in the eye with the .32 ACP pistol he'd acquired on the same unauthorised trip. Alcohol was strictly forbidden in First Green, and guns were issued only to skilled hunters. Kieran hadn't believed the vote would be close, and he'd been right; of the four hundred or so in attendance that night, the vast majority had raised their hand, aye, to place rocks.

Crimes had to be punished. Their way of life had to be protected. This was a fundamental tenet of any society. Still, Kieran wondered if Louise Stenner would face the same fate. She was spirited and fanciful and loved by the children in her Kindergarten class. They called her Miss Lou-Lou and chained flowers for her on Founder's Day. It was hard to imagine those same children standing over her, rocks in hand.

As Nathan started talking, though, Kieran sensed a coldness descend on the room, in a way that made him wonder if bloodlust and justice shared the same DNA. Some friends listened in rapt silence. Others leaned forward in their seats, fidgeting restlessly. At one point a female voice – Kieran didn't see who it was – called out, "Rocks," and there was a clamour of agreement. He was reminded of dogs licking their lips in the moments before feeding.

He hadn't planned on speaking at all but remembered what Louise had said about hearing a voice. *It told me to trust in my strength, and make way for salvation.* Sharing this would likely not sway the decision, but Kieran believed it worth mentioning. Who among them had not felt conflicted from time to time – pulled in two directions by their thoughts and feelings?

Kieran got to his feet and approached the lectern. He wobbled a little but pushed the heel of his hand against his forehead – pushed hard, as if he might force the pain through the centre of his brain and out the back of his skull. He elbowed Nathan aside mid-sentence. Nathan looked put-out but didn't say anything. That was a good thing. Kieran cleared his throat and swept his gaze across the room. His left eye leaked water and he blinked it away. The lights sure were bright up here.

"My father ran this town for twenty-six years and most of you knew him well. What you didn't know is that he spent many a night sitting at the kitchen table having long conversations with himself. We had six seats at that table and it was like every one of them was occupied. This was how daddy...how he..." Kieran trailed off, clean forgetting what he was about to say. He swayed a little, clutched the edge of the lectern with his left hand. More water ran from his eye. "Anyway...I guess...I guess Louise had conversations with herself, too, but her wolves were darker. That can happen when you're broken down."

The tarp responded with a discordant flapping sound and Kieran jumped. His hand jerked across the top of the lectern, brushing some of Nathan's notes to the floor. Nathan retrieved them, stooping awkwardly. Kieran blinked water out of his eye and leaned into the mic again.

"Her voices...her voices were darker, I mean."

Nathan straightened, placed his notes on the lectern and offered Kieran a look that said, *you okay, brother?* Kieran nodded once in his direction and looked again at the townspeople. Jillian stood out, like the shine on an apple. She had one hand pressed to her mouth. He imagined taking this hand and holding it flush to his aching head and in this found Stork cool.

"Gary Jablonski made Louise less of what she truly was." Sure words, each distinctly dropped, as if applying small weights to a scale. "He should have lifted her onto his shoulders, but instead he crushed her underfoot."

Friend Andrew DeBattista – wild hair and lumberjack muscle – stood up and shouted, "I heard she stabbed him over and over with a kitchen knife."

Roars from the townspeople and the tarp agreed.

"Settle down. Settle down, I say." Kieran held up one hand and there was hush. It was brittle, though, apt to break, and Kieran struggled to remember what Louise had said about her companion, something about his incremental abuse – little cracks, over time – amounting to not much more than a bag of loose pieces. The gist of it was there, but the gist alone lacked impact. He looked at Jillian and recalled her analysis. The words jumped from his throat in a rush.

"Gary Jablonski had a sour mouth."

That was all he had. He drummed his palm three times against his forehead and retook his seat among the other members of the town council.

★　　★　　★

Nathan concluded this trial of sorts ably and they went to a show of hands. If it appeared close, they would go to a paper ballot, but it did not appear close.

It was Kieran's duty to inform the condemned.

★　　★　　★

The Keeper's Post was on the south side of Jack Anthony Park, where they held their Founder's Day celebrations and danced beneath the Elder Tree on Blessing's Eve. The old town hall was on the west side. Kieran hoped the short walk, on this frigid fall evening, would blunt the pain in his head.

He could still hear the tarp catching the wind but it faded as he crossed the park. Soon it was just his boot-heels on the cement path and that same wind, in the trees now and soothing. Kieran breathed easier. He reached the Post in six minutes, walking slowly, but took a moment before stepping inside. The night felt good.

The Post was nothing fancy. Two desks, one for him, and one that Nathan shared with Paige Dunne, First Green's other deputy. There was a kitchenette, a bathroom, a storage room that doubled as a weapons' locker. The walls were off-white paint decorated with a map of the town and photographs through the years. There were also photographs of Kieran's grandfather and father, and Kieran himself. Three generations of Storks. The keepers.

Kieran went to his desk, unlocked the bottom drawer, and took from it the key to the basement. Two rooms down there. One was large and dry, used for filing. The other was colder, smaller, and damper. Nothing in there but a cage, four feet square. It had a padlock on the door and a water bottle strapped to the outside. Its nozzle curved downward, through the steel mesh. Louise Stenner drank from it like a rabbit.

★　　★　　★

She looked at him with big eyes, still drinking, then removed her mouth from the nozzle and retreated to the corner.

"You don't have to say anything," she said. "I can see it in your face."

"What you see in my face is tiredness," Kieran said. "But yes, the town has made its decision. They will place rocks."

Louise lowered her eyes for a moment, then looked at him again but said nothing.

"It's not so much what you did," Kieran said, recalling several of the comments voiced by the townspeople. "More that they're afraid you'd do it again."

"And maybe I would," Louise replied with a bitter smile. Her teeth flashed in the room's meagre light. "Maybe all the Garys in this town should pay for what they've done."

"That's not for you to decide."

Louise's mouth twitched. Her smile grew for a second, then disappeared. "There'd be no need to decide anything, if you were a better keeper."

Kieran hooked thumbs into his belt loops. "You don't know what my job entails."

"To protect. To advise."

"That's some of it."

"To be strong where others are weak."

"That's everyone's job, not mine alone."

Louise's eyes flared brightly in the gloom of her cage. She scuttled forward and drank from her bottle again. Her nose twitched as she worked the nozzle.

After a moment, Kieran said, "I keep the wheels on the track, Louise. Every one of them. I keep us moving."

Louise stopped drinking. She wiped her mouth and edged a little closer, looking at him with her pale face pressed against the steel mesh.

"Your nose is bleeding," she said.

Kieran smeared his upper lip and his fingers came away bloody. He sighed and left the basement, flicking off the light at the top of the stairs, hastening to the bathroom, where he wiped his nose with toilet tissue and splashed cold water onto his face.

The door behind him was open and through the mirror over the sink he saw a reflection of the main room and front window beyond. The streetlights shone yellow and clear on Maple Avenue and clipped the southern edge of Jack Anthony Park. As Kieran watched, the wolf stepped into view. Not all of it – it was too large to see all of it – only its legs, extending one in front of the other, then the bushy swing of its tail. It continued past the window in long strides. Kieran reeled from the bathroom and crossed the main room at a rush, out through the door, onto the street. The wolf – taller than the buildings now – proceeded along Maple for a hundred feet or so before bounding over the trees into Jack Anthony Park. The fire along its back painted the night.

"What do you want?" Kieran called after it. His nose was bleeding again.

The wolf paid him no mind.

★   ★   ★

He followed it west through the town, having to run to keep pace with its broad step. It moved surely, lifting its huge paws over power lines and parked vehicles, its tail brushing across buildings, trees, and streetlights. It paused only to sniff at the ground.

Scottie Skelton – one of the town's electricians – drove along Redwood Street in his utility truck, zipping between the wolf's legs like a child's toy between the legs of the family dog. He did not slow down.

The wolf moved faster once it exited the town proper. It padded across open land toward Echo Lake. Kieran could not keep up and fell gasping to his knees. He lost track of the wolf twice behind trees and ridges but even then saw its fire against the sky.

At length it returned to its outcrop over the water and perched there, kingly. Kieran watched it for a stretch, wondering if it might grow large enough to swallow the entire town.

He walked home and kissed his sleeping children.

⋆　⋆　⋆

He saw the second wolf the very next morning. It rose up over Deer Hill – similar to the first, pale-snouted, just as immense – and stepped through the woodland there, its belly passing over the treetops.

Kieran sprang from his seat. He dropped his mug – BIG WHEEL – and coffee splashed his feet. The heat of it registered, but vaguely. All he truly felt in that moment was despair, heavy as a rock on his chest – heavy as a townful of rocks. The dawn light was tepid but the wolf's back burned.

Its bright eyes passed over First Green, tracking from north to south and back again. A tongue the size of a flatbed trailer flopped from its mouth and rolled over its whiskery snout.

Kieran slumped to his knees in tears and that's how Jillian found him.

⋆　⋆　⋆

Dr. Arlo Pryce was ten years older than Kieran but looked ten years younger. He played basketball and squash and ran six miles a day, all over First Green, through the woodlands and across the hills. His stomach was as flat and firm as a hardcover book. The only signs of his age were the crow's feet radiating from his eyes and the strip of silver in his otherwise dark beard.

He pushed a button on his keyboard and the printer on his desk chugged out a single sheet of paper, which Dr. Pryce signed and handed to Kieran.

"What is this?" Kieran asked.

"Requisition for an MRI," Dr. Pryce replied. He took a hand grip strengthener from a drawer in his desk and started squeezing it. The muscles in his right forearm rippled. "We don't have the equipment here, so you'll have to go to Oak Hill Hospital in River's Cross."

"You think I have a tumour?" Kieran moaned. The pain in his head needled deeper, as if to assure him that a tumour was at least a possibility.

"No. What I think is that you're overworked and stressed." The grip strengthener creaked with every quick rep. "You have this worsening headache, but you have no speech or equilibrium difficulties, no blurring of vision. You're functioning normally. You're not especially fatigued…"

"The wolves," Kieran said. He glanced at the window, as if a huge amber eye might be staring in.

"Complex visual hallucinations are linked to temporal lobe tumours, but they're also linked to migraines and sleep disturbance." Dr. Pryce switched the grip to his left hand. "There are any number of possible causes, friend. I'm not overly concerned. Let's just take a look at these imaging results so that we can cross anything nasty off the list."

Jillian drove Kieran the thirty-two miles to River's Cross, the air growing thicker and staler as they neared the city. They sat for three hours in a waiting room in Oak Hill Hospital, its walls painted a flavourless colour, a TV bolted to the wall displaying a loud, vice-like society that they – thank the founders – were not a part of. The people filling the hard plastic seats were dressed in dreary skins and Kieran would not look them in the eye. He went from this room into the machine, which was claustrophobic and loud and invasive, a microcosm of the world beyond First Green.

★　　★　　★

They were home by sundown. Kieran went straight to bed and slept deep into the night, but woke with another nosebleed, his pillow wet and red. He didn't wake Jillian. He threw the pillowcase in the wash but the blood had soaked through to the pillow itself, into its down, and he threw it straight in the trash.

He sat in silence at the kitchen table, head in hands. At some point the wolves circled his house. He heard their great paws coming down on the land, the sweep of their tails through the trees.

★　　★　　★

Kieran didn't have a brain tumour. Dr. Pryce called him that morning. "The imaging results show no anomalies. As I suspected. So take a deep breath, then get some rest. Lots of rest."

Kieran, who'd spent the past hour searching around his property for giant paw prints, said, "I think I may have some form of psychosis. Can you develop schizophrenia, or is it something you're born with?"

Dr. Pryce made a dry, breathy sound. Kieran heard the rhythmic slap of his sneakers and realised the doctor was calling during his daily run. "You don't have schizophrenia, friend. What you do have is too much on your plate. So go easy on yourself. Give it a couple of weeks, and if things haven't improved, maybe we can talk about some kind of anxiety-relieving medication."

No tumour. That was good news. The not-so-good news was that a third wolf appeared shortly after Kieran ended his call with the doctor. It had a shaggy brown coat and green eyes. The fire reached only midway down its back but burned higher.

Kieran watched as it swam swiftly across Echo Lake, greeted its mate – the first wolf – by touching noses, then took up position on the other side of Founder Bridge. The few folk fishing there didn't so much as glance up from the tips of their rods.

*   *   *

Kieran remained the rest of that day, and all of the next, in his bedroom, the blinds tightly drawn. He drank very little and ate less. Every time Jillian came to check on him, he pretended to be sleeping.

The one time he cracked the blinds and looked out the window, he saw that the wolves had grown – fully eighty feet tall when sitting.

*   *   *

A fourth wolf – this one black, not so much a fire along its back, more a full-blown, explosive war – stalked over the hills two days later. It took up position beyond Matt Froch's farm, rising above the two lanes of uneven blacktop that ran north out of town.

There was now a wolf at every point of the compass. Kieran could not look from any window in his home without seeing one towering in the distance.

The next day – the day of the rock-placing ceremony – the wolves started to howl.

They were getting hungry.

*   *   *

For your sins you will feel the weight of the town, the power of the land.

Thomas Stork spoke these words during the first rock-placing ceremony in 1951, after Archie Humber shattered his mother's skull (a terrible nag, apparently) with a ball peen hammer. They had been spoken by Stork men thirty-two times in the years since, which felt like too large a number, but when compared to the outside world…

They only had to watch the evening news to see the decay beyond their borders. The hate crimes and homicides and mass shootings and rapes and assaults, approximately 3,600 violent crimes committed daily across the nation. First Green was not without its incidents – Michael Penny and Archie Humber were proof of that – but, with an average of 4.7 total crimes per year, it was Utopian in comparison.

Punishments were decided by the community (everyone above the age of fifteen got to raise their hand), and included cage time and community service. For the most serious crimes, they placed rocks.

The ceremony would be held at the foot of Bane Woods where, beyond the tree line, the ground was loamy and fragrant, sloping gently to the Muskateni. A shallow grave had been dug between the trees, just large enough for Louise Stenner to be placed in. Wrist and ankle straps were attached to wooden stakes driven into each corner. These would keep her from thrashing around.

Nathan was in charge of preparations. He and Andrew DeBattista were unloading rocks from the back of Nathan's pickup when Kieran arrived, creating a pile not far from the woman-sized hole. There would be 421 rocks in total, one for every man, woman, and child in town.

"Brother," Nathan said, jumping down from the back of his truck. He ran a forearm across his brow, his eyes widening as Kieran approached. "Kieran, oh…" He couldn't keep the shock from his voice. "You don't look well."

"I'm fine."

The cairns of previous offenders were dotted between the trees, shot through with weeds, many of them grown over. The younger children would clamber on top of them during the ceremony, spectating through big eyes. The adults would gather wherever the view was clearest. Some would climb trees.

"You got spotlights?" Kieran asked.

"Scottie's on his way with them," Nathan replied. "We'll rig them up to the trees…here, here, here." He pointed three times. "Genny'll be yonder." He pointed again, deep into the trees north. "She runs loud."

"You don't want folk tripping over the cables."

"Lineup'll be here," Nathan said, indicating a route through the trees southwest. "It's all figured, brother, down to the last detail."

Kieran nodded. He imagined the scene: spotlights at full crank, genny rumbling yonder, Louise positioned in her shallow hole. The townspeople would form a long line, and one by one would select a rock from the pile and place it on top of Louise. Kieran, as keeper, would set the first rock, always the heaviest, and always in the middle of the chest.

For your sins you will feel the weight...

By the tenth rock, Louise would begin screaming. Not shrill screams, but low, laboured cries, and this would continue until the air was crushed from her lungs. The sound of breaking bones would follow. The snare-drum pop of a femur. The crack of a clavicle. Several times, Kieran had heard the entire skeleton collapse, a remarkably unexceptional sound – like treading on seashells – for something so final.

Kieran pressed a thumb to his brow and spat blood and said, "My rock?"

"Here." Nathan showed Kieran a large rock that he'd set to one side, ready to be placed on the top of the pile. "Weighs about sixty pounds, I'd say. Maybe seventy. You going to be okay with it?"

"Why wouldn't I be?"

"You don't look strong."

Kieran had dropped weight these past few days – too much. His clothes hung off his frame. His face was gaunt, cheeks sunken. That wasn't all. He hadn't washed or shaved since the second wolf arrived. Blood caked the insides of both nostrils. There was more dry blood in the stubble on his chin. He stank.

"Maybe you should sit this one out," Nathan said.

Kieran sneered and stepped around his brother. He walked over to his rock, bent down, hooked his fingers beneath it, and lifted. Nathan had said it weighed maybe seventy pounds, but Kieran believed that estimation was way off. He hoisted the rock to thigh-level, arms trembling, then dropped it with a thud and fell to one knee.

Nathan pursed his lips sympathetically and approached Kieran with one hand extended. Kieran opted not to take it. He got to his feet on the second attempt, breathing hard.

"Don't need your help," he gasped.

"Brother." Nathan stepped closer and spoke in a low voice, perhaps so that Andrew – standing beside the truck with a rock in his hands – would not hear. "You're not yourself. I'm concerned about you."

"I'm fine," Kieran said for the second time.

A loud, rising howl filled the sky. It came from the south, and was soon joined by another howl to the west. Within seconds, all four wolves were crying plaintively. Kieran fought the urge to cover his ears. He chewed the inside of his mouth. Sweat trickled down his back.

"Seven p.m.," he said distractedly. "I'll get Louise from the cage, bring her…" The words faded from his lips. He could see the second wolf – the east wolf – through the trees, on the banks of the Muskateni. As he watched, it lowered its head and drank from the river, then resumed howling. Huge drops of water rolled off its muzzle.

"I'll get her," Nathan said firmly. He placed a strong hand on Kieran's shoulder and squeezed. "Let me do this for you, brother. Stay home tonight. Rest."

"Are you keeper?"

"No, but—"

"This is a keeper's duty. My duty." Kieran's left eye leaked as a fresh bolt of pain speared his forehead. He shook Nathan's hand from his shoulder. "Remember your place, brother."

Nathan nodded and stepped back. Kieran brushed past him with a reproachful glare, spat in the dead leaves, kept walking. As soon as he was out of sight, he covered his ears and wept.

*   *   *

He returned home. Nobody there. He and Jillian had fought the night before and she'd gone with the children to her sister's house. She'd be back, of course, but for now Kieran was thankful that he had the place to himself. It gave him time to vent.

The wolves howled. The walls trembled. Kieran stalked from room to room, screaming, pounding both fists against his head. He upended the kitchen table and threw the coffeemaker against the wall and swept every breakable thing off the mantelpiece above the fireplace. The satisfaction this gave him was brief and empty. He took a chef's knife from the kitchen drawer and held the blade to his forehead, thinking he would slice off the top of his skull, remove his brain, and stomp it beneath his heel. The idea alone brought a sliver of relief but Kieran couldn't do it. The knife trembled in his hand before dropping harmlessly to the tiles, shimmering in a band of late sunlight.

"What do you want from me?" His voice was frail, like everything else. He'd been strong once, hadn't he? He'd carried the town. "What... what do...?"

Kieran trudged upstairs and looked out the front bedroom window, where, as a boy, he'd stood with his grandfather, surveying their golden little town. *Comings and goings*, Thomas Stork had said to him. *You'll want nothing to escape your eye.* The west wolf – the first wolf to appear – was now over one hundred feet tall. When it threw back its head to howl, the tip of its muzzle disappeared in a drift of low cloud.

"What do you want?"

Kieran imagined the townsfolk gathered at the foot of Bane Woods, all of them, close-packed, like food in a bowl. In the chaos of his mind, he saw the wolves closing in from every direction, penning them in, feeding well.

★   ★   ★

The black wolf was the most beautiful, its war-accoutrement the most austere. Kieran assumed this was the leader. He drove north on Indigo Road, past Matt Froch's farm, where he veered cross-country, over the raised, rocky ground, and stopped a few yards from the wolf's front paw. Its claws were as curved and long as an elephant's tusks.

Kieran got out of his 4Runner and approached the wolf with his arms open, imploring. The wolf looked down at him – this little thing between its front paws – with its head cocked at a curious angle. Its eyes were amber planets. Explosions raged along its back. Smoke lifted and swirled.

"Take me," Kieran croaked. He kicked off his boots and removed his clothes – first his shirt, then his pants and underwear. "Take me." A little louder. He chose a rounded boulder and lay across it, his back arched, his ribs as clear as prison bars. The wolf cocked its head the other way. "Take me, take me." Over and over, shouting it now, although his voice cracked and wavered.

A deep sound rumbled from the wolf's chest. Its muzzle wrinkled and it lowered its head. Kieran readied himself to feel its teeth, the massive pressure of its jaws, the separation of his body parts. This didn't happen. The wolf sniffed him, then opened its mouth. Beyond its teeth, Kieran saw shooting stars and frothing oceans. The back of its throat was a solar flare.

A voice entered his head. Ancient, powerful, as emotive as whale song. Kieran's spirit lifted immediately. Strength and understanding barrelled through him. He knew what he had to do.

★   ★   ★

Ten of eight and the town was empty. They had gathered, to a person, in Bane Woods, forming a long line through the trees, ready to remove a rock from the pile and place it delicately on top of Louise Stenner. A bluish glow shimmered in the sky to the northeast. Kieran heard the distant blat of the generator.

He drove one silent street after another, absorbing the buildings, the sidewalks, the signs, the trees through new eyes. This town was his entire world, his always-place. As a society, they'd created something perfect, beginning when Thomas Stork and Jack Anthony pulled the first fish from the Muskateni. They had grown over the years. They had loved, and flourished, and for this inviolable existence had thanked only the founders.

"Until now." Kieran pulled up outside the Keeper's Post – brakes hissing, one wheel on the curb. He opened the driver's door, climbed out from behind the wheel, and walked soberly across the sidewalk. "I was blind, so blind. We all were. But I get it now. I can see."

The Post was shut down for the night and dark. Kieran switched on the lights, crossed to his desk, and removed two keys from his desk drawer. With the first, he unlocked the basement door. He went smoothly down the stairs, passed through the room stocked with files and the town's precious history, and entered the small, dank space where Louise was being held. With the second key, he unlocked the padlock on her cage. She huddled in the corner with her knees drawn to her chest, stinking of body waste and pain. He spoke her name.

"Trust in my strength," she mumbled in reply. Her wet eyes glimmered through the tangles of her filthy hair. "Make way for salvation."

"I am salvation."

Kieran held out one hand and she shrank away from him. He dropped to one knee, reached into the cage, grabbed her ankle, and pulled. She was small and light but struggled hard, first kicking with her free leg, then looping her fingers through the meshwork of her cage, holding tight. Kieran retreated, gasping. It took him just a second to think this through. He reclasped the padlock, went upstairs, and returned moments later with a stun baton. Louise was in the same position. Kieran unlocked the cage, opened the door, held out his hand. She shook her head. He triggered the baton and touched the prongs to the cage. 50,000 volts traversed the meshwork. Louise let go at once and curled into a ball. Kieran pressed the tip of the baton to her ankle and triggered for three seconds. She first stiffened, then flopped. Kieran pulled her from the cage and lifted her onto his left shoulder. His strength was not equal to his determination and he bowed beneath her weight, slight though she was. On the stairs she struggled once again and Kieran tried to hold her but could not. She fell clumsily and slid down the steps backward. He gave her another three seconds with the stun baton, the prongs locked to the delicate skin behind her right knee. This took the fight out of her, at least temporarily. Kieran grabbed her ankle and heaved her up the steps one at a time. He stopped at the top for a rest and a drink of water, zapping Louise once again while he caught his breath.

He dragged her across the smooth office tiles, all the way to the main door. Here Kieran lifted her into his arms and carried her the short distance to his car. Her eyes opened once and she looked at him. She was so frightened. In that moment, Kieran saw not the woman who had stabbed her companion thirty-one times, but the shivering teenager he and Nathan had rescued from Echo Lake. *I was told the moon touched down on the other side*. He placed Louise in the passenger seat of his SUV, latching her safety belt to keep her from sliding off into the footwell. She tried to bite him but even her jaw was weak. Kieran slammed the door and went around to the driver's side, pausing briefly to take a big chestful of night air. He started the engine and drove not northeast toward Bane Woods, but north to where the wolves had gathered.

Pulling away from the Keeper's Post, Kieran hadn't noticed his brother's truck pulling into the street behind him. When its headlights appeared in his rearview minutes later, he thought it was the town's distant glow.

★　　★　　★

Louise was part of the reason Nathan's truck had slipped his attention. She had tried to remove her safety belt, perhaps intending to leap out of his vehicle while it was moving. Kieran kept grabbing her hand every time it flopped toward the buckle, placing it back in her lap. This happened four or five times, then she reached for the steering wheel. She grabbed it, yanked it to the right. The 4Runner veered onto the shoulder, throwing up a cloud of grit and dead leaves. Kieran corrected his line, then removed the stun baton from the driver's door map pocket and gave her four seconds. The crackling sound had faded a little, which meant it was running out of battery.

The wolves eclipsed the horizon, outlined by the fires along their backs. Kieran blinked tears from his eyes. The road doubled before him but the wolves remained clear.

"Where...where..." Louise started to speak, then dry-heaved, hacking up nothing but air. She fell back in her seat. Her lips were wet and her eyes rolled. "This isn't the way to Bane Woods. Where are you—"

"It's better you don't say anything."

"Rocks?" she managed.

"Yours is a higher purpose."

As earlier, Kieran went offroad beyond the Froch farmstead, bouncing over rugged terrain toward the wolves. He stopped when his headlights washed over their front paws, their legs rising up beyond the windshield like the trunks of sequoias.

★　　★　　★

She had no fight left. Nor could she walk — could barely stand. Kieran pulled Louise from the passenger seat and half-dragged, half-carried her to the same rounded boulder he'd placed himself on not an hour before. He arranged her, spreading her limbs, tearing her clothes so that her midsection was exposed. The wolves regarded the offering with indifference.

"One of our own," Kieran gasped. He wiped his eyes and looked at the wolves imploringly. "A sinner. Her blood is yours."

"I see no blood," the black wolf said.

Kieran's gaze snapped back to Louise. Her skin was bruised, raw, and dirty, but entirely unbroken. Not even a scratch. Blood, Kieran thought. Of course. The currency of gods. He dropped to his knees, combed through the dry grass around the boulder, and found what he was looking for: a chunk of flint, small enough to wield one-handed, but with a jagged, spear-like point. He clutched it eagerly and stumbled to his feet. Louise's eyes flashed toward him. She groaned. Her ribcage gleamed dull orange in the wolves' firelight. With one strike he could punch through to her heart.

Kieran lifted the flint above his head and was about to bring it down when a voice from behind called his name.

*　　*　　*

He turned and saw Nathan advancing clumsily over the rocky ground, his tall shape backlit by the white of his truck's headlights. Kieran had been so involved in what he was doing that he hadn't seen or heard his brother's approach.

"What's going on, Kieran?" Nathan's silhouette developed definition with every step – the pattern on his jacket, his long nose, the concern in his eyes. "What is this?"

"The way forward," Kieran replied. He felt the wolves behind him, watching keenly, their tongues long and hanging.

Nathan stopped a few feet short of Kieran, one hand on the small of his back, the other wiping a mist of sweat from the top of his head. His eyes drifted from Kieran to Louise, stretched across the boulder, barely moving. Nathan's mouth worked soundlessly for a second or two, then rasped out a few confused words.

"I don't understand."

Kieran lowered the piece of flint but kept it in his hand, then gestured at their surroundings, from the hills and ridges to the trees and lakes, from the roads they'd carved to the electric glow of the town.

"Everything we have," he said. "This land, this life. It's not enough to thank the founders. They were just men. Scared, mortal men. They had a vision, yes, but their faith was shallow."

"Wash your mouth, brother." Nathan squared his shoulders. "That vision paved the way for all of us."

"I'm not denying that, but it's the creators we need to thank. To worship."

"Creators? What—"

"They have glory in their mouths but destruction on their backs." Kieran turned and looked at the black wolf. It was close enough to hear the human misery within the flames – the screams amid the gunfire and explosions. "Don't you understand? We're on the edge of damnation."

"Not all of us. Only you."

"They'll take it all away, with a yawn, with a wink." Kieran looked at each of the wolves in turn. They circled and panted. Their power was immense. "It's always easier to unmake."

"You're not yourself," Nathan said.

"True," Kieran responded surely, turning back to his brother. "I'm broader, fuller, wiser. I'll curate such a place for us, such a shelter."

Louise stirred. She lifted her head and slipped partway off the boulder. Nathan looked at her. He appeared torn. Anguish filled his eyes and his mouth trembled.

"I don't know what you're saying," he managed. His voice was thin and scared.

"I've been chosen, not to keep, but to lead." Kieran spoke as clearly and patiently as he was able, given everything he'd endured. "When you keep something, it remains the same. When you lead, you move forward."

"I don't even recognise you. How can I trust you?"

Kieran said, "This – my truth – is the only truth you need. This is the only life."

Nathan took a step forward, then faltered. He appeared entirely lost in the moments that followed, as if he'd walked a perfectly straight line, only to find himself back at the beginning. Kieran wondered if some of his words were getting through, then Nathan shook his head and motioned at Louise.

"This isn't how we do things. We have structure...respect." He started forward again. "I'm taking her."

Kieran didn't hesitate. There may have been a spark of misgiving somewhere in his soul, but it was too dim and too brief to factor. This man – his brother, yes, but still only a man – intended to obstruct their salvation, and that couldn't be allowed to happen. As he, Nathan, stepped closer, Kieran tightened his grip on the jagged chunk of flint, and with a quick overhand strike, connected it with the left side of Nathan's jaw.

The sound was like an axe meeting softwood – a thud more than a crack. Nathan sagged at the knees but kept his feet. He turned confused eyes to Kieran. Blood spilled from his slack mouth.

"Brother?" he said, not really a word, more a gurgling grunt that Kieran understood anyway. Nathan bent at the middle and coughed up the blood that flooded the back of his throat. Kieran saw his opportunity and struck again, a fierce, looping blow to the back of Nathan's skull. He stumbled forward, dropped to his knees, his scalp unzipped, the bone beneath caved. A smaller man would have been killed outright.

The wolves growled and circled. Kieran turned his attention to Louise, who'd tumbled from the boulder and started to crawl away. He grabbed her ankle, yanked her backward. She dragged her fingertips over the hard ground and twisted her body. Kieran pulled harder. He returned her to the boulder and brought the sharp edge of the flint down in the middle of her chest. Three hammer-like strikes. He separated her rib cage with his bare hands, exposing her heart, then stepped back and watched the wolves feed.

⋆　⋆　⋆

Nathan staggered to his feet. "Brother," he said. "Brother, brother." His head leaked from the front and back, a cracked kettle. It was a wonder he could talk, a greater wonder he could walk, although he did so jerkily, his limbs jangling, his eyes flared and horrible.

Kieran could've let him be. His brother might stumble erratically for several long minutes before falling to the ground, to tremble and die and eventually become absorbed skin-and-bone into the land he loved so deeply. But the wolves had an appetite now. Kieran searched for his flint – he'd dropped it when opening Louise's rib cage – but couldn't find it in the long grass. Instead, he pulled a larger, blunter rock from the soil, too heavy to swing with accuracy. Nathan lurched toward him, his arms held out, a wild sound rising from his throat. Kieran lifted the rock to shoulder height and brought it down in a tired, awkward arc. It connected with Nathan's chest. He swayed for a second or two, took another step forward, then the wolves intervened.

They attacked simultaneously, their pointed muzzles diving in, each grabbing some part of Nathan and pulling in a different direction. He came apart in four ragged pieces, and so effortlessly; the tearing sounds were short and brutal.

"Make way for salvation," Kieran whispered. His brother was as big a man as Kieran had ever known, in size and character, but to the wolves he was no more than a field mouse.

They chewed and swallowed and sniffed at the scraps.

*   *   *

Kieran fell to his knees and bowed his head. He offered a rambling verse of service and devotion. The wolves acknowledged him silently and returned to their posts. They watched.

At some point he realised his headache had faded, not completely, but it wasn't a needle anymore, or a blunt wooden stake, more like a crack of daylight from a door recently opened. It motivated him to move. He stood wearily and faced the patchwork of streets and buildings he called home. Lights shone from the direction of Bane Woods, where his friends and family were gathered, waiting for the rock-placing ceremony to begin. They were all unaware that they would soon follow Kieran along a different path, with new beliefs and sacrifices. It would not always be easy. They would fear the wolves, yes, and there would be judgement, but the rewards were immeasurable.

First Green. His people.

They would be loved.

BEST SAFE LIFE FOR YOU

Muriel Gray

Tess had biscuits ready. The last two times the cops had come she felt bad she had nothing to offer them. Now she had biscuits. She'd asked Andy not to lose it, but here he was, already red in the face and pointing.

"You. Are. Shitting me!"

Tess stroked his arm. Then squeezed.

"Language, pet. No need."

He shrugged her off. Still pointing in the cop's face.

"It was bloody you! Well, not actually you, but one of your guys, yeah? Said, 'Oh, these fake CCTV cameras are mince'." Andy affected a high-pitched mimicking voice. It was not going down well, but he carried on. "Didn't you? Said thugs could spot them a mile off. Your words."

The big cop's radio crackled on his shoulder and he turned it down. He said nothing but leant back, recrossing his arms over his stab vest. Andy went on, pacing now in front of the laptop on the desk.

"So, okay, we get a real one. Not cheap. Here it is. And look...voila! All-you-can-eat footage of the pair of little shits actually in the act."

He jabbed a finger at the screen. It was frozen on a clear picture of two hooded figures climbing over the fence, heaving James's birthday bike over the top like Marines wrestling a log round an obstacle course.

The cops both nodded sagely.

Andy stared at them.

"So?"

The smaller cop shifted his weight.

"Yeah, that doesn't give us anything to go on. We'll give you the crime number. To pass to the insurance company."

"It's not bloody well insured."

Both cops made disapproving noises.

"Would you like some tea? Biscuit?" said Tess, noting the rising colour in her husband's face.

Andy clenched his fists by his side.

"Let's be clear. We're looking at a four and a half minute high-resolution video of a couple of robbing little bastards climbing over the back fence, breaking the lock on the shed, taking our son's bike, pushing it back over the fence and riding off up the street on it. On three different cameras. Three!"

He held up the requisite number of fingers.

"With the date and time code!"

He tapped the screen for emphasis.

"And you say there's nothing to go on? Nothing?"

Big cop sighed. Little cop had taken a biscuit with a grateful nod. Tess smiled.

"Could be anyone," said big cop.

"And that's it?"

That was it.

The cameras in question dutifully recorded the two policemen leaving the front door, walking down the small driveway, opening the gate and driving off. The clarity of the images was outstanding, proving that at least the £875 for equipment and installation reflected the quality of the purchase.

Tess watched the screen as Andy walked down the path after them, hands on hips watching them go, then turned to stare back up and into the lens.

He picked up a stone and threw it. Straight at the camera. It missed.

*   *   *

"We're not getting a dog."

Tess wiped the pot and put it away without comment. Andy wasn't finished.

"Know how much these big ones cost?"

"Just a thought," she shouted back from the kitchen.

"Thousands. Not even kidding. For a puppy. Never mind pet insurance. And you're going to walk it, are you? Every sodding day?"

He was lying on the couch idly flicking through loud sports channels, which was lucky. Andy didn't hear the gang of boys kick over their bins in the street. As she watched them through the kitchen window, she thought she recognised the tall one. From that family at the edge of the estate by the bus stop. One of about five or six brothers, and a mother who shouted in the street when she was drunk. Tess worried that one day Andy would get out there in time to confront them. And then who knew what would happen? You read about knife crime every day. Some have-a-go homeowner being stabbed.

So Tess watched the rubbish tumble out over their tidy square of grass and neat monoblock driveway and waited until the gang had moved on, laughing and kicking idly at fences and tins in the gutter as they went. She fished out a black binbag from the kitchen drawer, pulled on rubber gloves and went outside. It was better this way, that she tidied it up without telling him. Andy would chase after them. Then they'd only come back.

Outside she discovered her bird table had been broken. The sweet shell-shingled roof was lying on the grass, one side smashed and splintered. She picked it up tenderly, then put the pieces into the binbag. Tess really wished this would stop.

★   ★   ★

"What d'you make of this?"

Andy called his wife over through to his computer desk in the front room.

She left Kieran eating cereal at the kitchen table, looking at his phone and ready for school.

"Guaranteed. It says so. One hundred per cent guaranteed or you pay nothing."

Tess wiped her hands on her jeans and bent forward.

"But what is it?"

The website was a colourful affair, festive reds, yellows and greens like Chinese supermarket graphics. In the centre of a circle was a painting of a pantomime robber, hands up, screaming in fear as his sack of loot fell to the ground.

"Home security company."

"It doesn't look as if it means this country."

Andy pointed to it again.

"No, it does. Look at the reviews. All UK. All five stars."

Tess read the page.

AOYIN Security. UK number one in stop crime.

Free instalment. 100% satisfaction guarantee. Monthly payments. All money back if not happy. No argue.

AOYIN. Best Safe Life for You.

Tess stood straight and looked incredulously at her husband.

"Why would you trust that? It's ridiculous. Not even properly translated."

Andy tapped the side of his nose.

"Searched the tiny name at the bottom there. See? Then I found this on a map."

"A lock-up down the back of the railway line?"

Andy smiled. That satisfied smile when he'd researched something to its limit and was the new expert. He clicked a few times and zoomed into a satellite picture. The greens and browns started to focus into a picture of an idyllic mountain setting, in the middle of which were the ancient walls of a solitary building perched on a rock. From this aerial vantage point, red tiled outbuildings and a walled garden full of blossom trees was clearly visible.

"There you go. See? It's a monastery."

"A monastery's address being used for a scam security firm?"

"No. They must make the device."

Tess stared at her husband.

"You being serious?"

"Straight up. Why not trust them? It's monks make that Buckfast wine, isn't it? Would trust monks more any day of the week than that bloody shower at AllYouTech."

"How much is it?"

"Five pounds a month. Direct Debit."

"Oh, come on. That's just stupidly cheap. You wouldn't even notice it."

Andy flitted around the page, clicking on reviews.

After the simplest of installations, we have enjoyed complete peace of mind and security. S. Henderson. Middlesbrough.

AOYIN security is so good we've stopped locking the doors. So lovely to have the children, friends and family come and go as they please. Can't recommend highly enough. Mrs. Sahid. Largo.

Tess shook her head.

"I don't know, Andy. It doesn't even say what they're installing. Has to be a scam."

He clicked on the menu.

"Here. Look."

Full instructions by AOYIN person installer.

Andy pulled down another page. He wore that smile again. The researcher smile.

"You know me. Amateur keyboard detective. Found this bit of blurb about it. Monastery's called Gi Kumpa in Tibet. Nearly a thousand years old. Read this bit."

He tapped the screen.

"Says that because of its remote location, political unrest and local depopulation, the monks now 'rely on a variety of commercial ventures to fund their order'. Order members are all over the world now, it says."

Tess knelt, pointing. Her other hand went to her throat.

"Oh, it's beautiful. Look at the carvings on the walls. Zoom into that bit."

The single grainy black and white picture enhanced to show intricate carvings above an ornate door that stood at the top of a seemingly endless flight of vertiginous steps. Figures merged with snakes, tigers and monkeys, and writhing around them were dragons and winged, sharp-toothed creatures twisted into terrifying shapes. In the background the massive peaks of mountains rose into clouds.

"I'd love to go there. See that," sighed Tess. "Stuff like that," she said, turning to her husband and putting her hand on his arm. They never went anywhere. Andy was a stay-at-home person. His home was everything.

"Fat chance. Strictly closed order, it says. That photo's from the fifties. The last time anyone was allowed to approach it."

She harumphed. Removed her arm.

"Not surprised they need money then."

Kieran's kitchen chair scraped back as he got up to leave for school. Tess would have to drive him now. Until they could afford to get him a new bike.

She left Andy scrolling through, humming quietly.

★ ★ ★

Tess looked through the spyhole before she opened the door. The camera had shown a small man holding a box walk up the driveway. He wore a thick, fur-hooded anorak with a light blue robe hanging below it to his ankles, like a surgeon's scrubs.

He knocked on the door, ignoring the bell. She opened it.

The man bowed.

"Sykes?"

"Yes. I'm Mrs. Sykes."

"Aoyin."

Tess was confused.

"Yes. Yes, I'm in at the moment."

He squinted at her.

"Aoyin." He held up the box. A small, aged wooden crate. On the side a paper label reading 'AOYIN Home Security' was peeling at the corners.

Tess took a small step back.

"Ah. Right. Of course. We were expecting a call first. About installation?"

The man bowed again.

"Here now. Install."

She looked beyond him onto the street to see if there was a van. The street was empty.

"I'll just get my husband." She cleared her throat. "He's more technical than me."

There was quite a gap while Andy spoke in quiet tones to the man. After a while he came into the kitchen to fetch her. He seemed pleased.

"You have to come and do this too."

"Do what?"

"Don't know. Part of the installation."

For the next twenty minutes Andy and Tess followed the small man around their garden. Tess tried conversation.

"So have you come all the way from China? Tibet? Is that part of China? I'm so sorry I don't really know my geography," she asked the man tentatively.

He looked at her as though it were a child who had spoken.

"Huddersfield," he replied.

"Oh well. Quite far enough, I suppose." She threw a weak smile his way, embarrassed.

He didn't return the smile, continued his task and she made no further attempt to engage him, blowing her nose with a tissue to hide the flush on her cheeks.

Every so often he would stop, open the box, take out a small scrap of paper and ask them to say the words on it. They were meaningless. Jumbles of consonants and vowels.

Several times he had to correct them, making them say it again until he was satisfied it had been correctly pronounced. Then he would kneel and bury the paper in the ground.

Tess whispered to Andy.

"This is ridiculous."

He shushed her. "Don't offend him."

Tess raised an eyebrow. Her husband wasn't usually this reverential about tradesmen.

"What is this? Where's his equipment?"

Again he raised his finger to his lips.

Tess did as she was bid and after half a dozen more stops, in unlikely places such as behind the shed and under a broken flagstone, the man finally turned to them and bowed very low indeed.

"Install. Good."

He stood up and spread out his arms, offering the box to Andy.

"Om Vajrapani Hayagriva Garuda Hum Phat."

Andy took the box.

"Right. Thanks. Instructions inside?"

The man waved his arm at the garden.

"Installed."

"Would you like some tea? Biscuit, perhaps?" asked Tess.

He shook his head, bowed once more, then turned and left.

Tess and Andy looked at each other and the corners of Tess's mouth twitched in mirth, but the look in Andy's eyes stopped her from laughing. His look was hope. Trust. He wanted to protect her. He wanted to protect his family. Somehow any merry mockery had died in her. She slipped her arm through his and they went back inside.

★　　★　　★

Tess knew what she should do with the video. Relieved that Andy was still at work, she picked up her glass of wine with a hand that trembled, and sipped as she rewound it again.

There they were. Five of them this time. They'd been sitting on the Hussains' low wall across the road, smoking and mucking about. Lobbing their rubbish, cans, bottles and cigarette packets into the garden behind them. She watched as Kieran opened the gate and walked up the drive. You could see from his backward glances and swiftness of step he was scared of the boys. Though there was no sound, it was clear they were shouting and jeering. Kieran entered the house quickly and the camera framed their empty garden once more, the gate swinging open as her son had left it.

She switched cameras. The one at the side of the house was only partially able to pick up the boys crossing the road.

Privacy laws insisted they could only film their own property, but a gap in the hedge meant this camera sneakily could see a portion of the street. Over went the wheelie bins. Rubbish was picked up and thrown after the departed Kieran. One of the boys pushed at the half open gate. He seemed to hesitate, then stepped onto their path.

She stopped the recording, freezing the frame on the picture she'd now looked at a dozen or more times.

The boy's body was making a star shape, arms flung wide. His feet seemed to be inches off the ground, as if he'd jumped but without having first bent his legs to make the movement. And grainy as it was, she could make out the shape of his mouth beneath his hooded top. It was open in a wide black scream.

She tapped the keyboard. The next frame showed he was higher still in the air, back arched like a high jumper taking a pole backflip.

Tess took another mouthful of wine, because despite having seen the next picture so many times it got worse instead of better.

She switched to the camera feed that looked onto the small fragment of pavement. The hooded figure's body was partially visible, its splayed limbs arranged at hideously unnatural angles on the ground like a dropped doll.

Her hand paused over the keyboard and then tapped. It was gone. Erased. That day, and the day before. The day with the cat incident.

Though she had waited, nobody had come to the door when the ambulance arrived. It had been high drama in the street, flashing lights and panic, and neighbours with their arms crossed holding mobile phones. She'd told Kieran to stay in his room and she watched from behind the bathroom blinds upstairs with the lights off. But Tess feared the cops might come. Blinding the cameras was for the best. She finished her wine in one gulp and switched off the computer.

⋆　　⋆　　⋆

They did come. Just the one. A policewoman. Doing door to door. They could see other cops at other neighbours'. She didn't even ask to come in.

"Na. We've never had a dog," she heard Andy say.

He called Tess to the door.

"You know anything about this? Kid got mauled or stabbed or something. Just here in front of the house."

Tess shook her head, shrugged.

"God. No. Was this the other night?"

The policewoman looked at her.

"Thursday evening. Did you see anything? Hear anything? Any kind of commotion?"

She shook her head, looked at Andy, her eyes wide in surprise.

"Nothing. Nothing at all. Well, I mean, of course, not until that ambulance came. There was lots of shouting and so on then. But before? No. How horrible."

The policewoman nodded, took their names, thanked them and left.

Andy closed the door gently and looked at his wife.

"You okay with lasagne again tonight?" she said.

He nodded. Tess went back to the kitchen.

They sat in silence as they ate their dinner, broken only when Andy told Kieran for the hundredth time to put away his phone when he was at the table.

The teenager sighed and did as he was told.

"That's three now," he said sulkily into his plate.

"Three what?" asked Tess.

"Cats missing. There's posters on lampposts."

"They should take more care of their pets." Andy stirred his food around, then gestured widely with his fork. "Used to be a good neighbourhood this. You let things run wild, well then…" His voice trailed off.

Kieran looked glum.

"There's still blood on the pavement, Mum."

Tess patted her son on the arm.

"That was that accident. With the boy? It's fine now."

They finished their dinner, Tess cleared away the dishes and Kieran retreated to his bedroom.

Tess glanced at Andy. They both knew they'd done what was right. Everyone wanted a safe life.

★ ★ ★

The young couple seemed nice. She worked for the NHS and he was something in IT. The difference in the street in the last five years had raised house prices to a new level. The fact that people like these, professional people, were looking to buy proved it. Tess had made quite the effort to spruce up the place. Scatter cushions and throws. Nice-smelling wooden sticks in jars in every room.

Outside on the estate gardens were attractive and well-tended. Litter was gone and children played happily in the street. Not many played around the Sykes's house, but then they were on the corner nearest the busy road, so that seemed like a reasonable explanation. Theirs was one of the quietest houses in the neighbourhood. All the Sykes's CCTV cameras had been taken down, though one or two in the houses opposite had been recently installed.

Sometimes Tess had noticed glances from neighbours as she left to go shopping, and she would smile and say hello, but mostly they would look away. Nobody ever parked in front of their house and having that space for the car was an unexpected bonus.

Today Tess had put out the little solar water feature on the front lawn. There wasn't much sun, but the limp trickle of water was pleasant. More importantly it hid the mess on the grass where those magpies had been killed.

"So how long have you lived here?" asked the nice woman as she opened a cupboard in the hall.

"Nearly ten years. We don't really want to move, but our son's at university now and Andy's promotion means we have to relocate."

The woman nodded. "We're hoping to start a family ourselves. This neighbourhood seems very quiet. Good place to raise children."

Tess nodded vigorously.

"Oh, it's ideal. Safe. Very, very safe."

She and Andy watched through the window as the departing couple took another look up at the house from their car and hugged each other. Andy thought he should have put the price higher.

★   ★   ★

Amara picked up the pile of mail from the doormat and shouted to her husband. "That's me off, Jack. Can you get this mail? My milk's in the fridge. Text me if you need anything on the way home. I'm doing Nadja's shift, so Tesco'll still be open."

Her husband wandered through and kissed her, picking up the pile of letters and closing the door behind her.

Nothing exciting. Electricity bill. A thank you card from Amara's niece. Some spam about a pizza takeaway. And then the usual. At least six business envelopes with the same logo, the same postmark and the same bloody demand.

He walked back into the kitchen and sat down. He picked up a piece of toast and chewed on it as he looked at them. He opened one.

'Sorry for inconvenience,' the letter started as usual. 'Please note that payment is needed now for last chance to keep install AOYIN Security Best Safe Life for You. Please tell bank. We thank you.'

He smiled at the ridiculousness of it. The guy they'd bought the house from had mentioned this. Told them how to keep paying some standing order or something to this firm for security. In fact, he'd been pretty insistent on it, giving Jack the Direct Debit bank account number and writing it down on a pad in case he forgot.

Of course, they hadn't bothered. What did it even mean? Subsequent demands for payment, a paltry sum it had to be said, were ignored and binned. But this was becoming a nuisance. Worse than a private car parking firm. At least there hadn't been any fake bailiff letters.

There was no address on these irritating missives. No email or phone number. Otherwise, he'd have enjoyed giving them a piece of his mind.

Upstairs the baby started to cry. He opened the pedal bin, dropped the letters in and went to attend to her.

*　　*　　*

Spring was stunning this year.

Jack was working at the window on a spreadsheet but kept being distracted by the sweeping and whirling finches and titmice that flocked over the neighbour's garden across the road. They swooped in and out of a beautiful Kanzan cherry, paying little attention to a squirrel happily stripping the tree of its buds. It occurred to him as he watched how little wildlife their garden enjoyed. Maybe a bird table and feeder would help. Amara would like that. Now she was nearly six months old, Nala would love it too. She was already sitting up, and he imagined her squeal of delight and chubby hand reaching out for hopping and chirping robins. He logged out of his work and started searching online for garden products.

Movement made him look up from his guilty diversion.

It was the postman. He was waving at him from the street, from the other side of the hedge. Jack stood up and looked. The postman saw him and waved again.

He opened the front door and walked down the path to the gate.

"You okay, mate?"

The postman looked sheepish.

"Just wanted to let you know there's post. I just left it here at the gate."

Jack looked down to the small pile of mail on the pavement, then back up to the postie.

"We've got a letterbox."

"Yeah. I know. I just didn't want to…I thought I saw. Anyway, there it is."

He strode quickly away.

"Thanks a bunch," called Jack sarcastically to his back. He picked up the letters, sighed and walked back into the house.

"Well, well," he thought as he sat back down at his desk. "Haven't had one of these for a while."

He opened the familiar letter; familiar except that this time it was accommodated in a blue envelope.

Sighing, he leant back and read it.

'Please be knowing and warned that AOYIN security is now not installed. NOT INSTALLED. Please make plans to be safe.'

Jack read it again, and something about its tone, the repetition, the capitals, and not just the clumsy translation, made him uneasy. But that, he reasoned, was the intention. It was incredible how people could be scammed these days. But part of him admired it. If the guy who'd sold the house had been paying this fiver every month for years, along with all the other mugs this shower had conned…well, it all adds up. Somebody somewhere was doing very nicely indeed.

Jack shook his head at the letter's audacity, laughed, crumpled it up and binned it.

"I think we'll struggle by," he said out loud to himself, and carried on with his work.

One bird table and squirrel-proof wire feeder added to his cart and he was back on the accounts of a law firm, tidying up their quarterly report.

On the crackling baby monitor Nala started to cry. He waited. Sometimes at this time in the afternoon she'd get restless and settle back down. The crying stopped. He carried on scrolling.

She screamed. A piercing, shrill screech, the real thing doubled in intensity by the electronic version of the monitor.

Jack stood and arched his back. He walked to the kitchen to get her feed, and fussed around getting the bottle ready.

Nala screamed again.

He stepped out the room and looked up the stairs.

"Daddy's coming!" he called.

He went back into the kitchen to attend to the ping of the microwave, unaware of the tiny spot of blood that had dripped from the upstairs banister and landed softly on the back of his shirt.

"Somebody's very, very hungry, aren't they?" he said to the nicely warmed bottle.

SOUVENIRS

Sharon Gosling

The rain had been tilting at them all day. Above the motorway the wide sky was a slick bruise of cloud, dark in the middle and a sick grey-green at its distant edges. It reminded Reg of the weeks he'd spent on Kamchatka, so many moons ago, although those skies had spread wider still, and when it had rained it had felt as if it were the end of the world, probably because it very nearly was.

Donna was behind the wheel, peering through the slashing wipers of the Transit at the spray sent up from the tarmac by the surrounding traffic.

"I'll drive, if you like," he told her, not for the first time.

"It's all right, Dad," she said, voice somewhere between distraction and anxiety, not looking at him. "You just relax."

Reg leaned back in his seat and studied his daughter's profile. It seemed like only yesterday that he was scooping her off pavements and teaching her to ride a bike. Now here they were, on his last journey. Not that she'd appreciate hearing him call it that.

"It's not the end of your adventures," she'd said, as they'd pulled the door shut on the house that had kept him still for the past twenty years. "It's just the start of a new one, that's all."

He turned his head toward the wet window and went back to Kamchatka. Wild green pastures full of vivid bursts of meadow flowers that stretched towards the climbing crags of snow-capped mountains, bears roaming the forests, beluga sinuous in the waters. He hadn't been prepared for East Russia to be so beautiful, and all told, he'd ended up staying six weeks. Six weeks at the end of the world. He could have stayed longer. Perhaps he should have, but there was always a reason to move on.

A face floated to him, dark hair beneath a white headscarf, khaki shirt, sturdy boots, firm thighs, a figure lying back amid that lush pasture grass. He searched the years for a name and came up with Elise. He'd met her in Osaka, Reg remembered now, an American nurse with dark eyes and a beautiful smile, perfect white teeth. It had been a while since he'd had a companion and she'd declared herself open to adventure, but as usual it had turned out that Reg's understanding of the word exceeded that of others.

He'd travelled on alone, at twenty-five the years stretching ahead of him like an endless road, the ones behind having already woven through a dozen countries. He'd boarded a cargo ship in Petropavlovsk and lumbered across the Bering Sea towards Alaska with winter closing in. Cold enough to freeze the proverbials off a mythical metal ape, but there wasn't a single day he hadn't gone up on deck. *Now though,* he thought, *now I quake at the slightest drop in temperature, a weak old man perpetually wrapped in a blanket.* Reg shifted in his seat, dispelling the bitterness. There was no sense in it, after all. Life was what it was and his had been a good one, no doubt about that.

He'd enjoyed that first time in Alaska, even in ice. The hugeness of it, the clear white cold, the secrets it must hold. He'd worked his way along the fishing routes, heading for Canada, restless and uncontained. Somewhere in the midst of it he'd met Natasha. The clarity of the name after all these years surprised him, but then he supposed their dalliance had lasted longer than others. Two years they had travelled together, criss-crossing the barest expanses of Canada and then down beneath the big skies of the American mid-West, traversing both Dakotas and on. They'd both been heading for Colorado until her eye had been caught by a cowboy somewhere just south of Broken Bow, Nebraska, and that had been the end of that. He'd found himself alone again, pausing to walk the central vertebrae of the Rockies before spending the next ten years moving ever further south until he eventually dropped off the end of the continent.

After Natasha there had been many other faces, attached to less memorable names: beautiful, all of them, in their own ways, he was sure. Reg spent a few minutes trying to recall each, but faltered after the first two or three and wasn't convinced that he'd remembered even those correctly. Some had barely lasted a night a handful of decades ago, so it was inevitable that the strength of his memories would wane, he supposed. Besides, it had never been about the company but about the journey. So much to see, so many places to visit. Why else would he have spent so long moving on, always moving on?

Reg glanced at Donna, wondering what she'd make of her father's early exploits. Not that he felt guilty, exactly. That had been a different life, long before she'd been even the merest twinkle in her mother's eye – long before, in fact, he'd had any notion that Agnes even existed. Donna had been a late addition to a late marriage, neither advent something he'd anticipated but had found himself welcoming nonetheless, a journey into a different type of country.

"I think I could do with a cup of tea," Donna announced now, as through the wet afternoon gloom shone a sign that indicated civilisation in the form of Harrogate. "Perhaps a bite to eat, too. What does the clock say? It must be past time for lunch, anyway."

They were barely an hour from Doncaster, but Reg wasn't going to argue. Anything to postpone the inevitable. He hadn't been in this neck of the woods for years, but Donna had insisted that the best thing he could do now was move closer to her and Michael. 'It's time you came home, Dad,' is how she'd actually termed it, although she'd only grown up in Doncaster because her mother had been born there. Reg hadn't had the heart to point out that it wasn't home for him, aware that such a statement would probably hurt his daughter's feelings. He didn't want to rock the boat. Reg didn't want to cause a bother at all – he would have been quite happy to fade away in his own small house, the one he'd bought in the Borders after Agnes had shuffled off. Donna had put that move down to grief, perhaps unwilling to acknowledge that her father was merely attempting some small return to a pattern of life that had pre-dated her appearance, and that she only knew through half-told stories that must have seemed more like legend than history. The house had been miles up a dirt track in a forest so dense that he could be cut off for weeks over winter if the snows were bad. It reminded Reg of those weeks in Colorado and then New Mexico and, much later still, the Andes. If Britain had been that kind of country, it was where the bears would have been, and that suited Reg just fine. But of course, the reason he'd bought the place became the reason he was forced to leave it. What was manageable when one was knocking sixty became lethal when fast approaching eighty.

Donna pulled off the motorway. Reg expected her to head for the service station but instead she made for Harrogate itself.

"I've read about a great place a little further on," she told him. "I've been meaning to visit it for ages. A salvage warehouse with a café and all sorts of interesting independent stalls. It sounds like just your sort of place, Dad. Let's go there."

Reg said nothing, but nodded. Behind them his accumulated possessions of years, many of them brought back from his overseas trips, sat in boxes along with the last of his furniture. Donna had nagged and nagged him to 'minimise' on the basis that his room in the residential home would be too small for the majority of it. What he had saved had been by way of argument, cajoling and outright stubbornness, and was still deemed to be too much. Why she thought a warehouse housing bric-a-brac of the sort he would habitually gladly take home would be a good place to stop he had no idea.

The rain eased as they approached the town, a shaft of sunlight illuminating the Yorkshire sandstone of its oldest buildings. They did not head for the centre, but instead pulled down what seemed like a residential street.

"It's hidden behind here somewhere," Donna said, leaning over the steering wheel as the van crawled forward over speed humps. "There, look."

A break in the houses heralded a narrow road that ran between two large rusty open gates. Donna turned in and through them. Beyond, the road widened into a yard with parking space at the near end, closed off at the other by a substantial old barn. The arched entrance, which would once have featured solid wooden doors, had been replaced by glass panels, through which Reg could see laden pitches stretching back into the dimly lit interior. A sign proclaimed that the café was somewhere to the rear.

"Come on," Donna said, killing the engine and unbuckling her belt. "Let's get inside before the rain starts again." She opened her door and hopped from the driver's seat, rounding the bonnet to help him as he clambered out of the passenger side. His hip protested as his feet hit the pocked tarmac and Reg cursed, just a little, under his breath.

"I'm sorry, Dad," Donna said, one arm under his, as if to hold him up. "We should have stopped sooner."

He extricated himself from her grip, trying not to show his annoyance at his own frailty. There was a time when he'd been the strongest man she knew.

They headed for the bathrooms first, situated just inside those big glass doors. As he left the Men's, Reg looked out into the grim grey daylight and saw Donna back out beside the Transit. She was talking to a large man in weathered black overalls, gesticulating as she explained something. Reg blinked, slowly, assimilating this new information. His daughter's decision to bring him here suddenly made a lot more sense.

They saw him coming. Donna took a hurried step back, as if she'd been caught in a compromising position, which Reg supposed she had been, in a way. The man greeted Reg's approach with an encouraging smile.

"Dad," said Donna. "This is Adrian, he owns this place."

Reg nodded at this new acquaintance. "I gather I've been the victim of a ruse, Adrian. I'll have a word with my daughter alone, please, if I may."

Adrian smiled again. "Of course. I'll let you two come and find me in a bit. No rush."

Reg watched him walk across the wet tarmac.

"Dad—" Donna began.

"Poor show, love," Reg said, mildly. "Poor show."

Donna sighed, half in sadness, half in exasperation. "Dad, you can't keep everything. You just can't. Your room at Wisteria Lodge—"

"Wisteria Lodge," Reg repeated, bitterly. "Why don't they just call it what it is? The Death Wagon."

"Don't," Donna said. "I'm doing the best I can, Dad. There was no way you could carry on living on your own up there at the house. Look at you, you can barely walk ten paces. You know Mike and I would have you at ours if we could, but we can't, there's barely room for the two of us as it is. Wisteria Lodge is the best option close by, and we've got you the biggest room there that we could. Try to understand, why can't you?"

"Understanding," Reg said, "is not the problem. Acceptance, my dear, is the issue."

They stood facing one another, and he realised, perhaps for the first time, that his daughter stood head and shoulders over him. The thought imbued Reg with a sense of hopelessness he'd hitherto held at bay.

"Adrian will take everything you don't want," she said.

"Fine. Get him out here. Let's get this show on the road. Can't keep Wisteria Lodge waiting."

"Dad," Donna said, softly, but he turned away.

When Adrian returned, he had a couple of younger men with him, also dressed in black overalls. As they rolled up the back of the Transit, Reg said, "You can take it all."

There was a pause.

"Dad, that's not necessary. You don't have to get rid of everything. You just have to be a bit more selective."

Reg, who thought he'd already been pretty damn selective back at the house, shook his head. "There's only one thing I want to keep. Burn the rest, for all I care."

He watched as the men went about their work, lifting down tables, chairs, curiosities from far and wide, pieces of art, even an old wooden globe set on its own legs.

"Don't you want to keep the globe?" Donna asked, probably because she remembered it from her childhood. "There's room for that, at least, I'm sure."

"You have it, if you want it," Reg told her, trying and failing not to let his voice slide into sullenness.

The single remaining object of his desire had been jammed unceremoniously between the carved oak legs of a large armchair. One of Adrian's lads pulled it out, coughing slightly as a faint plume of dust flickered from the chair's upholstery.

"There," Reg said. "That's it. Give it here, would you, son?"

"Oh, Dad," Donna said. "You can't be serious."

Reg held the old rucksack up before him. He'd bought it from one of the American army boys he'd met in the Philippines when his first such companion had finally given out. He'd lost count of the years they'd passed through together since, this old pack and him. The straps were frayed and in places worn through entirely. There were patches of oil on the base where he'd set it down to crawl beneath that waste-of-money truck he'd rented in Namibia. A black pillow of duct tape signalled the spot where a good old-fashioned cutpurse had tried to slash through its base that time in Mozambique. There were the holes the families of mice had nibbled in it over the twenty-five years it had stood on the metal utility shelves in their garage in Doncaster, not fifty miles from this very spot.

"It's falling apart, Dad," Donna tried, again. "It's full of dust and god knows what else. That can't be the thing you want to take with you, not to your beautiful new room."

"This is what I want," Reg told her, stolidly, "so you'll have to make a decision. Let me take it or leave me here with it and the rest of Adrian's relics, because I'm not leaving without it."

They didn't stop for lunch in the end. Reg wandered around inside the barn while Adrian and his boys finished unloading the truck into the intermittent rain. Donna hovered nearby, apparently too uncomfortable to accompany him indoors. Reg didn't feel the need to set her at ease. He was the one being asked to give everything up, after all.

He kept hold of the bag, just in case. When he put it over his shoulder, Reg found that it fitted there just the same as it always had. It struck him that he should have taken better care of it in those years after he'd abandoned his travels. It seemed now that it had always been the best home he'd never had.

Back on the motorway, he kept it between his feet, a familiar weight he'd all but forgotten.

"What's so important about it?" Donna asked. "I can understand it went a lot of places with you, but surely all your photographs – they must be better memory keepers than that disgusting old thing."

Reg looked out of the window at the looming bulk of Doncaster. He tried to remember the last strange city he'd arrived in and couldn't. He knew the pack would have been with him, though, its bulk settled firmly against his back.

"It was there," he said. "It was always there."

Wisteria Lodge was a large Victorian building of red brick, standing in an adequate amount of greenery that had reached the end of its season. A gravel driveway led up to the large arched front porch. It might once have been impressive, but its wide steps had been augmented by a ramp with a handrail on one side and a wheelchair lift on the other, both of which had been installed with practicality in mind rather than any sense of aesthetics.

"Mr. Sanderson!" squeaked the nurse who came out to greet them, in that tone caring types reserve for the very old or the very young. "I'm Nancy. How lovely to meet you. Your daughter's told us all about you – we're all excited to hear your stories about travelling. I hear you've been all over the world, not just once but many times! Can I call you Reg? I can, can't I? Oh, good."

Reg regarded her, close-lipped. Nancy was short and dumpy and looked as if wiping elderly arses was about as much exercise as she ever got. Not unattractive, though, at a push, especially if one only looked at her face.

"We've had a long journey," Donna confided, as an apology for her father's silence. "It's been rather fraught."

The nurse maintained her bright mask, still smiling as she ushered them inside. "Of course. We'll get you settled, then you'll feel much better. We've got the boxes you brought down earlier, Donna, with your father's clothes and whatnot, they're all unpacked and waiting for Reg in his room. It's this way…"

She led them down a corridor carpeted in a thick, loud pile that might have been considered stylish for a week or so sometime in the late Seventies. It smelled of old boiled food that had been liberally sprayed with air freshener. There were more handrails, this time on both walls. Reg felt the passageway closing in, threatening to squash him between its patchy papered walls. His hand tightened on the strap of his pack, wondering if together they could make a bolt for it – one final trip for two empty old sacks.

"There, you see," Nancy gushed, as she pushed open the door to number 23, the siding into which the long train of Reg's life had now been shunted once and for all. "It's a lovely room, this one – looks right out over the rose garden. They're not in bloom now, obviously, but in summer it's beautiful. You'll like that."

Donna let him go ahead of her. Reg walked in and looked around. It was bright and airy, but there wasn't much to take in. Single bed, chest of drawers, wardrobe, bookcase and a small desk, which was bare apart from a tray bearing a kettle, a couple of mugs and a bowl of PG Tips sachets alongside mini long-life milk cartons.

"It might feel a bit sparse at the moment," Nancy agreed, to Reg's silent assessment, "but we'll get more of your own things around you and it'll feel like home in no time, mark my words."

Reg looked at Donna, whose cheeks coloured a little. Then he swung the pack from his back and dumped it on the bed. Flakes of dust hit the pristine white coverlet.

"I'd like to be alone now, please," he said. "If that's not too much to ask."

He felt rather than saw the two women exchange glances.

"Supper is at six, Reg," said Nancy. "I'll pop back and get you then. It'll be a good chance for you to meet the other residents."

"I'll leave you to it then, Dad," said Donna. "Mike and I will come in and see you tomorrow. All right?"

Reg didn't answer either of them. They made a quiet exit and he could hear them murmuring to each other beyond the blank white of the fire door that closed him off from the rest of the world. He hobbled to the window to look out over the garden. It was barely five o'clock but the light was already beginning to disintegrate. The faded roses, dead but with their heads still waving aimlessly on their stalks, seemed to him to be a particularly malicious joke. He turned away and pulled the curtains, returning to the bed.

"Just you and me now, kid," he muttered, perching beside his old pack. "Just like the old days."

Reg unzipped one of the small outside pockets, the one where he knew his trusty old Leatherman was waiting. It had saved his life many times, this piece of kit – literally as well as metaphorically. He pulled open the blade, which had stiffened during its long period of disuse. Then he turned the pack over and went to work on the duct tape. He took his time, worrying at the edges, pulling a little here, peeling a little there. He didn't want to just rip it off. That might cause more damage. The pack was plenty threadbare in places already.

Reg worked carefully, the time slipping away as the light faded still further. He left Wisteria Lodge and Doncaster far behind, passing down the narrow lanes of time and memory as he worked. He'd just about freed enough of the tape to reach what was stored beneath it when there was a knock at the door.

"Reg? It's Nancy again," said the familiar voice. "It's five to six. Are you ready for something to eat? Your daughter said you hadn't stopped for lunch, so you must be starving."

Reg didn't answer. He was too busy coaxing out the string. It made him smile to see it after all these years. He'd just succeeded in freeing it completely when Nancy opened the door, knocking softly, as if doing so precluded the need for guilt at the intrusion.

"Reg, is everything all right? Are you—"

She stopped in the doorway. The light from the hall behind her spilled into number 23.

Reg slipped from the bed, still holding the string as he looked around for somewhere to hang it. He settled on the mirror of the dressing table, which had round wooden handles on either side so that it could be adjusted. He shuffled across the floor and hooked the old string over one of these knobs. The long line of yellowing molars clacked gently against the wood and each other as they settled themselves. As he looked at them Reg was satisfied to realise that more names were coming back to him. A little *aide-mémoire*, that's all he needed, and he was right back amid the brightest of his days. He'd give them each a good clean later, he decided, treat himself to a real trip down memory lane.

Reg turned towards the nurse. She was still standing at the door. The expression on her face was uncertain. As he watched, she looked at the pack on the bed, then back towards his little souvenirs, then at the open knife still in his hand.

"You're right," Reg said, offering a pleasant smile. "It does feel better. Now – time for dinner, is it?"

Nancy backed away as he moved towards her, the uncertainty taking on a thin edge of fear. Reg moved past her with a lighter step than he'd managed in years, the smile still on his face. Beneath his feet, the turgid carpet seemed somehow less offensive, the smell receding to the periphery of his awareness. He could hear the hubbub of voices somewhere ahead of him. Behind him, Nancy's feet began to move, albeit with a somewhat hesitant step.

Perhaps, he thought, life at Wisteria Lodge had the potential to be more fun than he'd anticipated. After all, life was what you made it, wasn't it?

THE OPERATED

Ramsey Campbell

Long before they finished hauling the tube out of him, Beal was as close to prayer as he had ever ventured. When he was able to use his mouth at last, he had to swallow more than once before he could ask "What's the verdict?"

"Doctor will tell you," the assistant said and kept her face neutral while she saw him to a scrawny plastic seat in the waiting area. A receptionist illuminated with tattoos was saying "All right there?" to anyone who strayed near her counter, and Beal glanced at every newcomer in the hope if not the dread that they were coming for him. At first he didn't look again at the man who sidled into his row, but when the seated fellow turned towards him Beal met his eyes. "You're..." the man said.

"Jack Beal." More out of resentment than interest Beal said "And you're."

"Benny Fender." As if he shouldn't need to add the information Fender said "The Apothecary."

It was a pub, not his profession. Beal would have recognised him sooner if an untypical toothy grin hadn't done its best to broaden Fender's cramped face. Some new experience had pinkened its skin, as if Fender had touched up a monochrome sketch of himself. "What are you in for?" he said.

"Nothing I'd care to talk about in public." As Fender loosed a laugh like an indulgence of a tasteless joke Beal said "And you, what's brought you here?"

"Megameta did."

"I don't believe I know them."

"It's time people did." Fender had more words and more enthusiasm to offer than his habitual complaints about the world. "They'd never have to come to hospital again once they had the chip," he said. "Notill, it's called. The name tells you all you need to know."

"Are you saying you've got one?"

"I've had mine all right. You could too." He stopped short of fingering the back of his head. "Don't do that," he muttered before raising his voice. "Just a habit, that. You won't even know where you've been done."

"What's involved?"

"In and out in half an hour or less," Fender said and stretched his grin wider. "You, not the chip. You won't feel them do it, but you can wave goodbye to every illness."

"Then why have I never heard of them? I mean, why aren't they better known?"

"They just want word of mouth till they get bigger. We're only meant to tell people we know."

Beal thought this overstated their acquaintance, but had to ask "How much did the procedure set you back?"

"It doesn't cost a penny. They operate inside the system."

"So where can I read up on them? They're online, I suppose."

"They're not. I told you, you get recommended, and then you have to be referred by your doctor."

As Beal reflected that the facility was bound to be discussed online a nurse called "Jack Beal."

"I've got him here." Not much less loudly Fender told Beal "Remember, Megameta. Notill."

The nurse stared after him as he headed for the exit, and then she murmured "Trying to do us out of a job?"

"I'd never want to do that to anyone."

"Better know what you do want," she said and turned her back to make him follow.

Her code on a wall pad let them into a corridor where every door displayed a name. Halfway down, a Megameta logo caught Beal's eye. Though the letters were almost as white as the door, they stood out somehow. The nurse scowled at them on her way to ushering him into the next room. "Jack Beal, doctor," she said and left them.

"Have yourself a seat, Jack. I'm Don Spall."

Beal thought him too young to be so bald, without even eyebrows to compensate. Face and pate looked scrubbed hygienically smooth.

Perhaps his manner was designed to deny his age if his watchful grey eyes weren't persuasive enough. "I have to tell you," he said, "the news isn't altogether positive."

Until that moment Beal had managed to avoid acknowledging how fervently he'd hoped the opposite. "What is it, then?"

"There's some cancer. To be clear, a few. I've every reason to suppose they should respond."

"To chemo, you're saying."

"At this stage I favour surgery, Jack. A procedure like the one you've just had, with instruments, of course."

Having swallowed, Beal found the breath to ask "What's the alternative?"

"None I'd recommend, and my colleagues wouldn't either."

Beal's desperation found a voice. "What about Megameta?"

The doctor's gaze grew so keen it blotted out any expression. "What do you know about them?"

"One of their patients was saying they cure you of everything."

"Are you thinking of putting yourself forward?"

"He said my doctor has to do that." The encouragement Spall's question seemed to offer let Beal add "If you don't mind, I'd like to ask her."

"I can refer you if you're certain that's your choice."

"Then it is."

"Wait here for me." The doctor shut the door behind him, so that Beal barely heard his voice in the next room. The words and the higher ones were indistinguishable, but they sent Spall quickly back. "Go through," he said. "She'll be with you once she's changed."

The Megameta room resembled a sketch of an office. A pair of chairs, plump expensive leather relatives of the seats next door, faced each other across a rudimentary white desk on which a computer screen kept its back to Beal. Certificates and tributes decorated the walls, and he was quitting his chair to examine them when a woman bustled into the room. "Jack," she enthused, delivering a large handshake. "Paula Sandown."

Her voice was deeper than he'd heard through the wall. If her shoulder-length blonde hair didn't guarantee her gender, lipstick and eye makeup did the job. "So who told you about us?" she seemed eager to learn.

"Just someone I see at the pub."

"I hope you know their name."

"Benny Fender."

"That jolly chap. Well, we should thank him. You're as eligible as he was."

"You know what I've been diagnosed with."

"We know you inside out, Jack. You won't be like that much longer. Our implant fixes everything it finds, and then it keeps you in condition."

"Can I ask where you put it in?" Beal touched the back of his head. "Round here?"

"That's a trade secret, I'm afraid. Don't worry, you'll never know where."

A fierce flare of pain in his guts persuaded Beal the information didn't matter. "When could you book me in?"

"Let me see what we have for you." She laid a finger on her lips as if silencing herself while she consulted the screen. "We can fit you in," she eventually said, "early next year."

This felt like a threat of intensified pain. "That long," Beal said.

"Recommendations have been on the increase. Let me have one more look," she said, then offered him a laugh. "Well, aren't you glad you asked. I can tell you we've just had a cancellation."

"How soon would that be?"

"Now," she said, only to qualify it with a chortle. "Not quite this very moment. As soon as the theatre's ready for you if you're happy to proceed."

"More than."

"Let me print out your consent and you can sign it while you're waiting." Seconds later she handed him the sheet on a clipboard. "We'll find you where your friend did," she said.

"Not too bad at all," Beal felt happy to tell the receptionist. He was expecting to fill in his details, but the form already held them all. *I hereby authorise Megameta LLC to furnish me with a Notill implant.* He'd scarcely signed when a nurse escorted him back into the corridor, where she stowed his belongings in a tall tin locker. "Jack Beal for the procedure," she announced as they reached the far end of the corridor.

Beyond the door was mostly white: the walls and ceiling, the caps and gowns and masks of the three figures waiting by the table laid with a sheet for him. He couldn't tell which blank mask said "Lie down whenever you're ready, Jack."

As soon as the back of his head touched the table a bunch of lights on a stem stooped towards his face. Someone slid his left sleeve to his elbow, and another figure with an erased face loomed above him. The clustered light was so relentless that he had to squint to see the surgeon's eyes, which were intensely grey. Had he seen them before? For that matter, what had the Megameta representative's eyes looked like if you ignored the distractions of her makeup? "Hang on," Beal blurted, "could I just—"

His mouth stayed uselessly ajar while he searched for words. He only knew he felt rushed into a decision he should have had more time to consider. "What are you trying to say, Jack?" said the nurse who had released his arm.

"Can I have a think before you start?"

"You're already fitted. You're all done."

Beal sat up, which felt like folding himself on a hinge newly oiled. There was no sign of the surgeon. "How long have I been in here?"

"You were under half an hour."

"I don't even remember getting the anaesthetic."

"The chip will have reset you when Dr Poulsown put it in," said the nurse who might not just have been holding his arm. "You won't have lost anything you'll miss."

"Careful stepping down," her colleague said, "but you should be fine. Just in case you need to call, we'll give you a number."

"Call about what?"

"Everybody's different. I'm not saying you will." As he followed her along the corridor she dodged into the Megameta office, reappearing too swiftly for Beal to see anyone beyond the door she shut. "There you are," she said as she might have rewarded a child for braving an operation, and handed him a card.

"If you could give me some idea what to expect—"

"I've said why I can't." Having seen Beal out of the corridor, she called "Mary Marsden."

The young woman made a visible though apparently not painful effort to correct her stoop so as to look Beal in the eye. "Have they done you?"

"Can you tell?" When she shook her head he felt bound to say "No need to be anxious. You won't even know where they've put your chip."

"Do I look anxious?" As the door closed behind the women she said with an amalgam of shame and triumph "I'm going to be fixed."

The rush hour was stuffing all the buses. Beal thought standing in the aisle so soon after surgery might be a task, but he was able to join in the sluggish dance the careless driver choreographed. Along Beal's suburban street leafless trees were feeling for the February wind. His three rooms kept out most of it, though the window crammed between the shower stall and the toilet let draughts seize him by the neck. He bought fish and chips from Cod Be With You up the road, but his appetite fell short halfway through dinner. Should he make another sortie into *War and Peace*? The concave spine of the obese paperback on the shelf resembled a reproachful vertical frown. Instead he gave the boxed set of a television crime serial another chance, but two hours of it left him as confused as ever. Everything felt indefinably delayed in reaching him. He returned the disc to its tattered sleeve, then crossed the room to bed.

A sense of wrongness wakened him. The tone of Mary Marsden's parting remark had caught up with him, and the darkness felt like his perplexity rendered visible. The dark wouldn't be so total if his eyes weren't shut, and why should he hesitate to open them? He widened them and felt them swell up from the sockets before floating like miniature balloons out of his head.

As he sucked in a breath like a gasp in reverse it seemed to suck his eyes back in. He dug his fingers into the mattress while he lay on his back, staring at the dimness until it convinced him he was seeing as he should. Surely the illusion had been the tail end of a dream. All the same, he was afraid to sleep in case the nightmare was waiting for him, and when he found he'd drifted off he had to force himself to open his eyes. If they trembled in their sockets before settling down, that had to be nervousness, and soon he was on his way to work.

The local branch of Frugish occupied a unit in the Buybuy retail park. When Beal left the staffroom, having shed a third of his girth in the shape of his padded coat, a supermarket supervisor accosted him. "Did they find out what your trouble was?"

"They did and it's dealt with."

"Nothing too serious, then."

"Cancer."

As if he'd tricked her Delia objected "What do you mean, it's been dealt with?"

"They give you an implant that cures everything you've got."

"It sounds too good to be true." Before he could react she said "I'm glad for you. Management were saying if you had to take much time off you might need to find another job."

"But they were saying just the other week nobody knows my section better. What sort of job?"

"Up to you to find out. Not one here." As Beal felt his lips part in search of words she said "Anyway, you've told me there's no need to worry. Better start tagging your shelves. You've a new offer starting tomorrow."

The wine section already swarmed with yellow tags. Three for two, buy three and get the cheapest free, three selected bottles for the price of two – none of these should be confused, although quite a few customers were, some blaming Beal. Now there would be discount throughout the Frugitipple range: Share a Shiraz, Yay Cabernet, Not Merely Merlot... Beal was slipping the shiraz discount tag into the transparent slot on the edge of the shelf when his fingers began to squirm.

They hardly felt like fingers. He could have thought his hands had sprouted worms. As they recoiled he had a sense of flinching from himself. His eyes bulged ominously as he gazed at the fingers, struggling to let the sight quell his panic. Although he could feel them swelling and rippling, the way worms burrowed into earth, they appeared just to be shaking with the effort to fend off the sensation. "Not happening," he muttered and covered his mouth with the squirming objects, clamping them together to hold them still as a customer stared at him.

He couldn't afford to be caught having difficulties. He glared at his hands until his eyes stung to convince himself his fingers were functioning as they should, however much he felt them imitating grubs. While he was able to insert all the tags that way, he didn't trust it to help him replenish the shelves. Desperation suggested a ruse. He was transferring wine from a trolleyful of cases, pinning one bottle at a time between his palms, when Delia came over. "Why are you doing it like that?"

"It's easier for me just now."

"And a lot slower. Is it to do with your operation?"

"Maybe temporarily. Honestly, not worth mentioning."

"I do hope not," Delia said and left him a dissatisfied look.

The warning lingered when he took his break. Alone in the staffroom, he took out the Megameta card. Had it faded overnight, or had he lost the angle that made the details legible? The only pen in the room was a fractured ballpoint bandaged with parcel tape, and he tried to blame it for hindering his fingers while he inked the details on the card – the Megameta logo and a mobile number, but no address. His unaccustomed clumsiness left him afraid of mistyping digits until the number appeared on the phone screen.

"Press one to recommend a client. Press two for finance. Press three for follow-ups…" Jabbing that digit with a fingertip that felt gelatinous brought him the same bright brisk female voice. "We are experiencing a high volume of calls at present. You may prefer to call back later." He didn't, and five minutes of a Mozart concerto for synthesiser or at least a few reiterated bars of it rewarded him with a voice unnecessarily like the one he'd already heard. "Megameta, how can we help?"

"Can I speak to someone about a condition?"

"Which of our conditions will that be?"

"No, it's one I've got. I'm a patient of yours."

"We don't have those. We only have successes." The response sounded as automatic as the recorded messages had. "You're not from the media," she said, having dimmed her brightness.

"I've told you what I am. You gave me the treatment yesterday."

"And what was the concern?"

"If you must know, it was cancer."

"You won't have that any more." Just as briskly she said "I was asking why you felt you had to call this number."

"My body…" His mind seemed reluctant to grasp his state. "It feels wrong," he succeeded in saying.

"You'll have to be specific if I'm to help."

"My hands." More of an effort was required to add "My eyes. It feels as if they're, they're getting away from me."

"That's quite common."

If this was meant as reassurance, it only enraged him. "Why didn't someone say?"

"We wouldn't have wanted to bias you."

His anger let out just one word. "Bias."

"If you're expecting something to happen you may think it has. I'm hearing you say your body feels different."

"That's putting it politely."

"It'll be adjusting while your implant beds in. What you say you feel isn't really happening, is it?"

"I hope to God not."

"See if you can live with it till it goes away. Or ask your friends to confirm it isn't happening. They should be able to tell you what's real and what isn't. But if all that fails, you know where we are."

"Now you mention it, I don't. Where are you exactly?"

"Where you just found us. At the other end of your phone."

He could always find them at the hospital, and so he said only "Had I better give you my details?"

"We have them all, Jack." Her voice regained more enthusiasm as she said "We'll know if you call again."

He couldn't risk betraying his state to any of his colleagues, but perhaps there was a solution out there in the shop – the security mirror that reflected the wine aisle, demonstrating that his fingers were behaving as they should. Its objectivity helped him fend off the sense that they'd grown boneless, so that he managed to pick up bottles one-handed. When Delia loitered to watch him he was able to hope her silence denoted approval.

That night's dinner came from Nothing Bizza Pizza. Half the contents of the steaming carton would do for tomorrow. His mind fell short not just of Tolstoy but the year's bestselling comic novel. Another bid to grasp the first hours of the crime serial felt like straining to retrieve a memory, as if depending on the supermarket mirror had detached his perceptions. He went to bed in case that solved whatever problem he had.

When he woke in the depths of the dark he knew something was amiss. If it was outside, let it go away without involving him. Or was part of him outside him? While lying on his back he couldn't tell, and he made himself raise his head. He didn't need to recapture his eyes after all – that wasn't why he clutched at the mattress so hard his arms shook. He'd left the back of his head on the pillow.

Had it fallen loose or sagged like dough? He let go of the mattress, having realised his fingers were working as they should, but it took a good deal more effort and determination to reach behind his head. His scalp was where it ought to be, but he couldn't judge how soft his skull had grown. Whichever section of his head he laid on the pillow felt capable of staying there if he turned over, and there was no more sleep for him.

Earlier than dawn he strove to rouse himself with the coldest shower he could bear. At the supermarket Delia was waiting to scrutinise him. "Better today?" she hoped or warned him.

"I will be." In case she found his intention too remote he declared "I am."

He did his best to concentrate on finding space for a Frugitipple consignment – Really Pouilly, Not Too Shabby Chablis, Shine On Chenin… Since his fingers had returned to normal, he didn't need the mirror. Whenever he had to climb his stumpy ladder he avoided glancing at the bulbous image, where the sight of his head swelling under glass made him feel his skull was being tugged bigger on its elongated neck. "Not happening," he muttered until he saw customers peering at him, and then he knew he had to make a call.

The unrelenting trills had counted off at least five minutes of his break by the time a voice he thought he recognised said "Megameta."

"You told me yesterday to call if there were any complications. My name—"

"I'm seeing all about you, Jack. You'll want finance, will you?"

"I just want to be put right. I'm not looking for compensation."

"I should think not." With no lessening of briskness she said "I'll pass you over now."

Mozart was back, though the trapped scrap of a tune resembled a ringtone that had lifted some of his notes. Having given Beal more than ample time to appreciate the performance, a man said "Plans."

Beal had none beyond repeating "My name—"

"I've got you here in front of me, Jack. Just confirm your details for me." Once the protracted process was done the man said "What were you looking to obtain today?"

"Whatever you need to do for me. Your operation's made it so I can't work properly. If it carries on like this I could lose my job."

"We'll have to see that doesn't happen, won't we?" Quite as much like a doctor projecting his bedside manner at a distance the man said "We can offer you corrective treatment and any follow-up you need."

"That sounds right. What's involved?"

"It depends which plan you go for. Up front is the most inexpensive, but may I assume you'd rather pay in instalments?"

"Pay what?"

"Outright would be one hundred thousand, if you're able to raise the amount. Instalments add up to more, depending how far you spread them."

Beal's lips were testing a variety of grimaces. "Nobody mentioned any of this," they managed to pronounce.

"Maybe they were hoping your surgery would be satisfactory for you."

"I should have figured out they didn't mean free is free, should I?"

"Don't despair yet, Jack. You haven't heard our alternative."

"To what?" Beal demanded through an aching grin.

"If you successfully refer a client to us we'll waive all your payments."

Beal's words felt jagged in his mouth. "So that's why he sent me to you."

"You'll appreciate we can't discuss our other clients, Jack. Do you want to have a think about your options?"

"I'll be thinking all right," Beal retorted, though his mind was fixed on Fender. His eagerness to confront the fellow made his skin feel impatient to squirm off the flesh.

When he tramped clammy-footed to the Apothecary that evening he found his drinking acquaintances at a table by the bar, beyond which a vintage chemist's jars had gathered among the downturned bottles of spirits. Just now the reference to bygone medication felt like a mirthless joke about the modernity of Megameta. The beery trio were competing at ailments, a contest Ricko might have meant to win with a cough he'd brought in, having stepped out the back for a cigarette. "Get your round while you're up, Jack," he spluttered. "I'll have my usual."

Once Beal had set down the quartet of tankards and himself he said "Has anyone seen the character who's always complaining?"

Ger took so large a gulp of dull dun ale that Beal would have been unsurprised to see him bulge. "There's a few of those."

"The one who never has a smile for anything," Beal said and was enraged to realise why that had changed. "He calls himself Benny Fender."

Wilf took a drink that rivalled Ger's, and a suffusion climbed his neck as if he was visibly filling up. "Then I expect that's his name."

"Can you all keep an eye out for him?"

Beal was regretting his choice of words and resisting an urge to secure his own eyes in the sockets when Ricko doused his cough with ale to say "There he is now."

"You mean he was," Ger said. "Looked in and buggered off."

Beal's ale slopped across the table as he struggled out of the chair, which had embedded the tips of its legs in the carpet. By the time he reached the door Fender was halfway across the car park. "Mr Fender," Beal shouted. "Benny Fender."

The glare of the towering security lights seemed to sear all expression from Fender's face. "All better now, Jack?"

"No more than you were."

"You've called them, have you?" Yet more like an accusation Fender said "That didn't take you long."

"And just how long did you take?"

"Longer than that. Maybe I'm made of stronger stuff."

Beal clenched his fists before he could judge whether it was rage that set his fingers writhing. "Your lies got me into this and you can get me out."

"Nobody's lied to you. You hear what you want to hear."

"More like I should have seen what I saw, you having trouble with your head."

"You've had that too." With equal carelessness Fender said "What are you expecting me to do? I'm no better off moneywise than I should think you are."

"It's up to you to make things right, and by—"

"Like you said, you're no worse off than I was." As Fender made at speed for the road alongside the car park he called back "You've spoken to them, so you know what to do."

"Wait," Beal shouted and tried to hurry after him. "You can't walk away from what you've done."

"You watch me. No point in coming after me now I'm fixed. You need to find someone like we were and I'm telling you, it took me weeks."

Beal floundered in pursuit, but not far. His moist feet felt swollen to the limit of his shoes, and so softened he thought they might slither out to flop larger on the tarmac. He supported himself on the icy roofs of two parked cars until the sensation shrank. He couldn't face Ricko and the others after that, and it took him far too long to trudge home when every step felt like a threat of squelchy flabbiness.

Apprehension kept him away from the bed. He sat in his chair with a quilt draped over him. When it persisted in slipping down he grasped it with a fist beneath his chin. He couldn't judge the hour at which the light he'd left on wakened him. He might have fancied he was in a thinker's pose if he hadn't sensed how his fist was propping up his face, which had oozed off the bone to heap itself on his knuckles. In a panic he staggered across the room, nearly sprawling over the quilt, to peer at himself in his bathroom mirror. When at last it persuaded him his face had stayed solid or at least reverted to that state he stumbled back to the chair, but not to sleep.

He was up well before he meant to leave. A shower went some way towards persuading him he was awake. As he lolled in the aisle of a rush-hour bus he felt like a side of meat in a freezer. The tattooed receptionist gave no sign of recognising him. "All right there?" she said.

"I'll be making sure it is. Can I see somebody from Megameta?"

"Not here, sir." Without varying the smile she'd raised for him she added "Sorry."

"I know where they are, and I need a word with them."

"Not here."

"Don't try and tell me that. I've seen them. I've rung the number they fob you off with, and now I'm going to deal with them face to face."

"Not here." The phrase had begun to sound like a reprimand. "If you'd like—"

"I've told you what I'd like. What are you, a recording?" Beal's fingers squirmed deep in his pocket until they succeeded in snagging the Megameta card. "I know you know them," he said. "They gave me this last time I was here."

With the barest glance at it she said "You wrote that yourself."

"That's another of their tricks, is it?" Beal grew aware of somebody behind him – an excuse to move him on? He twisted around to see a nurse not yet in uniform. "You'll remember me, won't you?" he said before he had quite enough breath.

"I don't believe I do."

"You said we were putting you out of a job, me and another of your patients."

"I hope I'd never say any such thing."

"Not us personally. You meant Megameta."

Her gaze strayed past him to the receptionist before she said "I'm afraid I've no idea what you're talking about."

"Megameta. They're hid in there." Beal struggled to point at the secretive corridor. "You took me to see Dr Spall," he insisted while his fingers worked like grubs, crumpling the card, "and he sent me to them."

"Then you'll need to speak to him."

"Now we're getting somewhere. Let me at him."

Should Beal have been less forceful? The nurse strode to the corridor without another word. He was tempted to slip into it while the door was unlocked, but retreated to a seat instead. The receptionist's phrase had greeted several patients by the time somebody loomed at Beal's shoulder. If security had come to throw him out he would cling to the plastic seat and make all the row they deserved – but no, the man was Spall. "I understand you were asking for me," he said.

"You saw me a couple of days ago. Jack Beal."

"We see quite an amount of people, Jack." With no increase in recognition the doctor said "What can we do for you today?"

"You referred me to Megameta, so you can take me to them."

"There must be some mistake. We don't deal with anyone like that."

"Why, because you've found out what they're like? Bit late for me and whoever else you sent. You've still got to follow up what you were responsible for."

"What are you saying that is, Jack?"

"This kind of thing." Beal seized his face in both hands while his fingers were under control and set about yanking his doughy cheeks lower than his chin. "That's just some of it," he said as distinctly as his distorted mouth would let him.

He watched the doctor manage not to recoil. "Would you like to make an appointment to see someone?" Spall said.

"I'm seeing you, and I'm telling you you're liable."

"Your condition isn't my field," the doctor said and backed away to the reception counter. "This lady will make your arrangements for you."

Why hadn't he interviewed Beal in his office? Was he hoping his victim would discredit himself in public? Beal kept his seat until the doctor made for the Megameta corridor. As Spall typed the admission code Beal headed for the desk, only to lurch aside. Despite the encumbrance of his bloated soggy feet, he was just in time to sidle swiftly past Spall into the corridor. The doctor grabbed his shoulder, which was so far from solid that Beal was able to squirm free. "Where do you think you're going?" Spall demanded.

"We both know, don't we? Make that all of us, Dr Spall and Dr Poulsown and Paula Sandown while you're at it." By now Beal was at the Megameta door, where confusion halted him. Instead of the logo the door displayed the solitary word EXAMINATION, and the room contained a sheeted table watched over by a bank of lights. There was still the theatre where they'd operated on him, and he dashed to that end of the corridor. The door was marked X-RAY, and the room beyond confirmed it. As Beal stumbled away – his entire body felt like confusion rendered palpable – the doctor met him. "Please leave immediately," Spall said, "or I'll have you shown the door."

"That's still here, is it? Where have you hidden it now?"

When the doctor only stared at him Beal stalked unsteadily out of the corridor. Might Megameta be lurking in another one? He couldn't use the same trick to search it – not today, at any rate. On his way out of the hospital he phoned the Megameta number. "Are you recommending someone to us, Jack?" the relentlessly bright voice said.

"No," Beal began and was instantly cut off. The next time he phoned he was unable to get through, and that was how he used the day up, all the way to the pub. As he opened the door of the Apothecary he was rewarded by a painful development of Ricko's hacking cough. Ger looked puffier than ever, and Wilf's neck had grown more suffused. Beal was buying his round at the bar when Wilf called "What the Christ have you done to yourself?"

He was pointing at the back of Beal's head. Beal felt his scalp begin to slither backwards off the bone. As he clutched at his skull the mirror showed him his eyes sidling forth on their way to examining the problem, and he grabbed his face with his free hand to squeeze them back in. If he couldn't feign calm he was done for. "Nothing I can't get fixed," he managed to declare.

By the time the barman brought the drinks Beal had regained enough temporary control to carry them to the table. "At least you've found something to grin about," Ger observed as Beal sank onto a chair. "Like your friend."

Beal knew Fender had been grinning not with mirth or optimism but with determination if not panic. He strove to maintain the expression as Ricko frowned at him. "How are you going to get yourself sorted?"

"It's the latest treatment. It changes your whole life. They've given me the option to nominate a friend as well." As Ricko coughed while Ger contemplated his bulging stomach and Wilf gave his neck a tender massage, Beal started his prepared speech. "Everyone who's had it says there's nothing to it," he said. "Nothing except good."

IN THE WABE

Alison Littlewood

My daughter vanished three years ago. I'm no closer to finding her. Every time I think I've found a new clue, it only puts me further away. The more knowledge I gain, the less I can believe in any of it.

She disappeared on May 13th from Central Park, a little to the north of the East 72nd Street and Fifth Avenue entrance. Anyone familiar with the Park will tell you that's close to Conservatory Water, where you can rent remote-controlled sailboats any day as long as it's not raining. My daughter wasn't interested in sailboats. She preferred to sit at the north end of the lake, on a giant bronze mushroom: Alice at her back, the White Rabbit on one side, the Mad Hatter on the other, patches of their heads and arms and shoulders rubbed shiny by generations of New York children. I always thought that was fitting somehow, since Alice too had left her home in England and eventually found herself here.

One side will make you grow taller, and the other side will make you grow shorter. I think it was the Caterpillar in *Alice's Adventures in Wonderland* who said that. I picture my little girl, Vivian, reaching around and breaking off a piece of mushroom, nibbling it with her front teeth, just like the time I got her to try broccoli. And I picture her shrinking, shrinking, shrinking, until she's as small as Alice in the story, smaller even, just the right size to captain a remote-controlled sailboat and sail away, then smaller, smaller still, until no one can even see her any longer.

That day, I turned around and she'd gone. Every mother's nightmare. There's a rabbit hole that opens inside you, one that never seems to end, blacker and blacker, deeper and deeper. Falling, falling. There was no answer when I shouted her name. No one had seen her. There was no sign my daughter had ever even existed; she'd gone, and I hadn't a clue where to find her.

It was a cop who spotted the bag lady a couple of streets away from the park, wearing – or trying to wear – my five-year-old daughter's clothes. A tiny pink T-shirt with glittery stars, ripped from under the sleeve to the hem, was pulled across her shoulders, a gauzy purple skirt twisted around her leg. The clothes were dirty, half hidden by a ratty old blanket. The woman claimed she'd found the blanket by a dumpster and I always thought that was odd. She could have said she'd found my daughter's clothes, not the blanket that no one cared about, but she didn't.

No: those shiny pink and purple things, she said they were hers.

* * *

My husband was a cop too. I met him when he took an extended vacation in England and I moved out here for him, thrilled by the sudden new potential in my life. We separated a few years after Vivian was born; he was killed on duty not long afterwards. And I'd begun to dream of home again, little green lanes, quiet roads, all so familiar, *safe*; then my girl disappeared and I was forced to stay.

* * *

It's someone from my husband's old precinct who shares the audio with me. "Picture it," he says. "A grown woman, sitting right there on the Alice statue."

I don't comment, since I've done that same thing plenty of times myself. It's not illegal. Children – and kids at heart – are welcome to climb, crawl, sit on, touch the statue. It belongs to them, after all. It's their story.

Each time I go there, I'm surprised by the size of the thing. It looks friendly, moulded to a human scale, but that sculpture is eleven feet tall. When you get up close, the mushroom is above your waist. You have to use the smaller mushrooms as steps to get up there, the bronze Dormouse on one of them always getting in your way. When you reach her, you realise that Alice is not life-sized. Even adults are like children when they're next to her: that huge face, big eyes, wrong somehow. Central Park's Alice is a giant. She must have been nibbling at the wrong side of the mushroom.

Picture it.

A mom – she says her name is Sandie Gordon – sits down next to Alice. She's watching her daughter play. Her daughter is called Bree-Anne, a stupid name I always thought, but don't say. It wouldn't be right, under the circumstances.

Now imagine Sandie with the squeaky, whiny voice of a little kid. Listen.

I WAS WATCHING HER. SHE'S MY GIRL, OF COURSE I WAS WATCHING HER. I DIDN'T EVEN NOTICE THE KID SITTING NEXT TO ME. I TURN AROUND, DON'T KNOW WHY, AND THERE SHE IS. SURE I WAS SURPRISED. SHE'S RIGHT THERE, A LITTLE GIRL ABOUT THE SAME AGE AS MY BREE-ANNE, SO I SAYS, 'HEY! WHERE'D YOU COME FROM?'

SHE SAYS, "HERE, SILLY." AND SHE GIVES THIS LITTLE SMILE, LIKE SHE'S GOT A SECRET, YOU KNOW THE ONE? SO I ASK HER WHERE SHE LIVES AND SHE GIVES ANOTHER SMILE, A WEIRD SMILE, AND SAYS, 'UNDER THE MUSHROOM.'

I WOULDA LAUGHED, BUT RIGHT THEN, BREE – SHE'S RUNNING WITH SOME OTHER KIDS AT THE EDGE OF THE LAKE, AND SHE TRIPS. SO I'M LOOKING AT BREE-ANNE AND THIS KID NEXT TO ME, SHE SAYS, "SHE WON'T FALL." I JUST MENTION IT BECAUSE BREE-ANNE DIDN'T, EVEN THOUGH I WAS SURE WE'D HAVE SCABBED KNEES AND TEARS AND WAILING FOR EXTRA ICE CREAM, BUT THE KID WAS RIGHT, BREE JUST CAUGHT HER BALANCE AND KEPT ON RUNNING.

On the tape, there's a sniff. It kind of sounds like she's being snotty about this kid, knowing better than she did about the girl not falling. But I wonder if she's trying not to cry. I wonder if it's really because she's talking about Bree-Anne and wanting her and missing her and needing her and she can't have her.

SO I SAYS TO THE KID, "THAT'S A FUNNY PLACE TO LIVE, IN A MUSHROOM. WHADDYA EAT UNDER THERE?" A DUMB QUESTION, I MEAN SHE COULD EAT MUSHROOM, BUT ANYWAYS. AND SHE SAYS, "YEARS." JUST LIKE THAT.

YEARS. LIKE SHE SITS DOWN WITH A KNIFE AND FORK AND DIGS RIGHT IN.

SO I ASKS HER HOW THEY TASTE.

SHE SAYS, "THEY TASTE JUST LIKE MILK. CAN I KISS YOU?" JUST LIKE THAT, JUMPING FROM ONE THING TO THE NEXT, LIKE KIDS DO. BREE-ANNE DOES THAT ALL THE TIME.

She sighs. I hear that quite plainly, and I don't think anyone needs to try and explain what it means.

SO I SAYS, "I GUESS SO," AND I PAT MY CHEEK TO SHOW HER WHERE, JUST LIKE MY GRAMMA USED TO DO. AND THE KID—

A pause. When she speaks again, her voice falters.

—I GUESS SHE DID KISS MY CHEEK. I THINK SO. ONLY, THERE'S A WORD I CAN'T GET RID OF, THAT GOES ROUND AND ROUND IN MY MIND. LATCHED. THAT'S WHAT IT MADE ME THINK OF – SHE LATCHED ON. LIKE BREE-ANNE USED TO DO WHEN SHE WAS BREAST FEEDING, SOMETHING LIKE THAT, AND THEN I SORT OF WOKE UP.

Another pause, a longer one.

NOW, I WANT TO SEE MY DAUGHTER. I HAVE TO SEE BREE-ANNE. YOU PROMISED ME.

A cop's voice responds. He says she can't, not just now. What he means is, not ever. What he's not saying is, she'll never see Bree-Anne again. She won't even get near her, because she isn't Sandie Gordon; she's not Bree-Anne's mother. That's who she claims she is, who she seems to think she is, even who she believes she is, but it's not her. It can't be.

On the tape, there's shrieking. Screaming. It all gets a bit incoherent, but it's plain enough when she starts yelling at the cops to let her the fuck out of there, she wants her daughter, she has rights, and why don't they just open the fucking door?

They still don't know her real name. But I've seen the photographs, and it's clear that the person claiming to be Sandie Gordon, mom to Bree-Anne, is about six years old.

It's incongruous, even grotesque, hearing her speak, knowing what she looks like. Talking about breast feeding her daughter in that squeaky little-girl voice. Shouting. Swearing. OPEN THE FUCKING DOOR.

I picture this little girl in the park, sitting on the mushroom, watching the other kids play. Witnesses said she grabbed Bree-Anne and tried to drag her off, but Bree-Anne wouldn't go. A passing tourist intervened. The unidentified child told him where and how to fuck himself. She said she was Bree-Anne's mommy, and everyone could get out of her damn way. Bree-Anne was crying. It didn't help the situation when no one could find her real mom, nor that this kid – this strange kid – appeared to be wearing her mommy's clothes.

The cops were called, but Sandie Gordon has never been found. Bree-Anne has been sent to live with her father, who was divorced from Sandie last year. The little kid who tried to grab her is with Social Services. They've confirmed she was wearing clothes way too big for her – a T-shirt more like a dress, an adult's miniskirt down past her knees. I wonder where they are now, those clothes. It hasn't been proved that they were Sandie's. Bree-Anne wasn't considered a reliable witness.

I try to find out if there were DNA tests, on the clothes or the kid. They can't or won't tell me, but I think I know what those tests would say. I just don't know how, or how to begin to explain. I don't suppose anyone could.

*　　*　　*

I've seen some freaky stuff in New York. I know about the weirdos of this city. People who follow you, put their faces up close to yours. Kids with too much in their eyes. Adults with too little. A vagrant clutching a toy car like it might save him, or maybe a doll. Someone showing a photograph. *Have you seen her?* A bag lady in a gauzy princess skirt, way too small. Little boys with shaved heads, smoking, drinking, shooting up. Teenagers kicking a tramp to steal a paper cup full of change. Maybe they want to buy drugs. Maybe they're dealing drugs. Thirteen-year-olds living alone, forging parents' signatures, making rent. A geriatric woman in make-up that could have been applied by an infant. A pretty woman who, close up, has skin stretched taut and unnatural over her bones. Who's to say how old anyone is anymore? You can't judge any longer. You can't even guess.

*　　*　　*

The bag lady wearing my daughter's clothes had grey hair and ugly creases running down her face, her jowls sagging.

Like the kid in the audio, I screamed and swore.

"How did you get Vivian's clothes? How the fuck did you—"

Fear froze her. Her eyes were blank with shock, her mouth hanging open. She seemed unused to being screamed at, but how could she not be, living on the streets? There was something missing in her, I could see that. It wasn't just her expression; it was in the way she kept saying, *I am Vivian, I am, I am*. It was in the way she called me *Mommy, Mommy*, and all the time staring at me, not laughing, not smirking, not even blinking. Not looking away from me for a second.

I told her, "I'll kill you. You say that again, I fucking will."

That time they did run DNA tests, but they must have mixed up the results somehow. They took samples from the clothes and from the old woman – under her nails, in her hair, a cheek swab. Every single one of them was an exact match for my daughter.

They admitted they must have contaminated the samples. It was all messed up anyhow, and they had to let her go. Apart from the clothes – which she could have found, same as the blanket – they didn't have much to go on. If she'd snatched Vivian, what had she done with her? There was nowhere she could have kept her or hidden her. And after all, the woman was mad. Mad as a hatter, but harmless as a little child.

*　　*　　*

These days, I often go to the sculpture. I climb up onto the mushroom – past that damned Dormouse – and sit and wonder where my daughter went. Is she lost in the rabbit hole? Sitting by the side of the Red Queen? Playing croquet with flamingos on a smooth lawn under a strange sun? Deep down, I know there are worse things, real things, but I try not to think about those.

Sometimes, when the sculpture is busy with kids crawling over it, mommies and daddies taking their pictures, I sit at the edge of Conservatory Water and simply stare at the bronze figures.

There is Alice, frozen forever in the act of reaching for the White Rabbit's pocket watch, the Mad Hatter standing by. The design is based on Tenniel's original illustrations for *Alice's Adventures in Wonderland*, but it never seemed quite right to me, and now I know why. I looked it up. The Mad Hatter is a caricature of George Delacorte, the man who commissioned the sculpture. Alice is actually the image of a girl named Donna, the daughter of José de Creeft, the sculptor.

That seems strange to me, almost sad. What must it have been like for Creeft, knowing that his daughter was always here, yet unreachable? He created this thing in 1959. No matter how she changed or grew, where she went or what she did, even after she died, she would always be here, always caught in the act of reaching for that pocket watch. Always the same, but no matter how many people look at her, they'll see someone else; never who she truly is. Not Donna, but Alice.

But kids – maybe they do see something else.

One day, there's a little boy. He's pulling on his mom's arm, pointing towards the base of the sculpture, showing her something.

"That's funny," I hear her say. "I didn't notice her till you said she was there." She shrugs before pulling her child away, suddenly keen to be gone.

I look at where he pointed. My first thought is of a missing child, but then, I'm always thinking of missing children. And I can't see anything, only the granite base of the sculpture with the words inscribed there: *'Twas brillig, and the slithy toves did gyre and gimble in the wabe*. Lines from 'Jabberwocky', Lewis Carroll's poem, but in that second they almost seem to mean something different. Is that where Vivian has gone – into the wabe? It makes as much sense as anything else.

The next time I'm there, a dad is holding up his phone, telling his son, who's sitting almost in Alice's lap, to smile. When the boy clambers down, Dad shows him the screen. His son frowns.

"Where's the girl gone?" he asks. "Where's the girl who was sitting next to me?"

They walk off, both as confused as each other, perhaps to find the statue of Hans Christian Andersen instead: besuited, benign, civilised. Sane. Or so they probably imagine.

That boy really looked like he was chatting to someone when he was sitting on the mushroom, though. I'd told myself it was the Cheshire Cat, peeking over Alice's shoulder – but was it?

I begin to look at photographs online. Pictures of other people's holidays, their kids sitting in Alice's shadow, posing, grinning. After a while, I begin to notice.

Sometimes there's a little girl lying full stretch under the Alice statue. Sometimes it's a woman. I stare at her face, always obscured by shadow, and feel the intensity of her gaze as she watches the world. She rarely seems to bother anyone else. Their smiles are all the same.

I picture a hazy form materialising at Alice's side, not the Cheshire Cat, but *someone*. First her grin: there's always a grin. White teeth, sharp. *Can I kiss you?*

What do you eat under there?

Years. They taste just like milk.

★   ★   ★

There are billboards on the streets. The latest moisturiser. A miracle diet. Cosmetics. Surgeons. Everyone wants to look younger. Even the oldest of stories knew all about that. The youngest princess, the littlest mermaid. No one cares what happens to the others. Why should they?

Women's voices on the subway.

"Youth: it's wasted on the young."

"If I could be that age again, knowing what I know now…"

The women never see the little girl who steps off behind them, her hair in ribbons, and skips off towards the park entrance. A little girl who's the exact same age she wishes to be.

But perhaps she isn't a little girl, the youngest, a princess. Perhaps she's really a crone, a hag, a wicked witch: a witch who drinks years.

Maybe, for some, that's a good thing. She gives them another go-round at their lives, knowing what they know now, and still remembering their names, even if no one else can recognise them any longer. She puts things right. She puts things wrong too, but shit happens, and anyway, who can say she doesn't enjoy that just as much, or more?

But sometimes, she might meet with a little child. She can't drink their years. They don't have enough to satisfy her. Instead, she feeds them: she gives them everything all in one go, year after year after year, until they shrivel and the skin droops from their bones.

I wonder how she chooses. Is she punishing the kids who notice her, who see her for what she truly is? Or does she actually think she's making their wishes come true? Kids are different, after all. They always dream of being older. Vivian was always three and a bit, four and a half, five and three quarters, always looking ahead to the next birthday, always longing to grow up.

No one is ever happy with the age they are.

I can see why she chose the statue for her home. She's as nonsensical as the story, as capricious as a child. Or perhaps it's that the Alice sculpture makes people show the age they are, inside. It makes them show her their hearts.

One side will make you grow taller, and the other side will make you grow shorter.

*   *   *

At last, I find her. It's easy, in the end: impossible and easy. I always knew where she lived, after all. I'd searched for her there before, many times. Watched for her. I just hadn't looked for her the right way.

One side to make you taller, the other to make you shorter. I had begun to wonder if, in some way, that applied to her too. I'd often circled the statue, running my hand along the brim of the Mad Hatter's hat, glancing down to read the words *in the wabe*, edging around the back of the mushroom and past the White Rabbit's shoulder to the beginning again, and never arriving anywhere.

This time it's different. I look for her in one direction and she isn't there. Then I turn and move gyre-wards, gimble-wards, this time reading the words as they were meant to be read. I look the other way – contrariwise – and there she is.

Or perhaps the witch wanted to be found. Maybe she wanted to find me. She's been here a long time, after all; I can see that in her face. I wonder if she was always here, even though her eyes are shiny and round and blue as a child's. They are also as endless and deep as the rabbit hole. She might be older than the city. Maybe she came on the *Mayflower*, or maybe she was here before that, just a little girl in a Wonderland, waiting for someone to play with.

After all those years, maybe she needed to talk. Wouldn't you?

She peeks up at me and slowly she grins. Her teeth are white and very sharp. She pulls herself from under the sculpture and gets to her feet, then walks past me, no taller than my waist. She steps up onto the smallest mushroom, then the next, wrinkling her nose at that inconvenient Dormouse, and sits down next to Alice. She smiles at me and indicates the place next to her. After a moment, I haul myself up and sit beside her. Together we look out over Conservatory Water, where miniature sailboats leave long white triangles reflected in the lake.

The witch lets out a long sigh. She's wearing a blue pinafore dress, matching ribbons in her yellow hair, shiny black Mary Jane shoes. She looks about six years old.

"I get tired," she says. "Some days, my back hurts. Some days it's my hip. My eyesight comes and it goes. I think I might have cataracts." She sighs again. "I really need a fucking drink."

I feel, rather than see, her glance. She says, "That's not why you're here."

I shake my head. "You know why."

"You want her back. You want it all to be the same, but it won't be. There's a price."

I nod. I already know what I might have to do. I picture the cops coming for me, but not my friends, not any longer. I won't even recognise them. I'll be on the ground, looking at concrete, my hands spread wide while they point their guns at my back.

"I'll kill you anyway," I hear myself say. "If you don't give her back to me, I'll kill you right here."

I wonder if I've gone as mad as the Hatter to be sitting here, in the Park, saying these words. The day is cloudy but warm. Families wander the paths around me, eating ice cream, exploring little bridges and tunnels, peering at the skyscrapers reflected like ghosts in the pools. I swallow. She's still a child. She's always a child and here I am considering bashing out her brains on a bronze mushroom, a sculpture that belongs to children, to stories, to fairy tales.

My hands twitch. It's obscene, but I'll do it anyway. I will. I have to.

Then she says, brightly, "Okay."

She flashes me a smile so white it seems to hang in the air as she shuffles to her knees and turns to stare up into Alice's giant face. She twists to sight along Alice's right arm, the one reaching for the White Rabbit's pocket watch, then turns her head to look at the other.

I'd never thought much about the other, but I do now. What was it that Alice is reaching for with her left hand? Nothing but air? Is she trying to take the hand of a child, to lead them – where?

The witch reaches out as if she'll be the one to take that huge bronze hand. But when she turns back to me, she's holding another pocket watch. This isn't like the other. It's smaller. This one is life-sized, on a human scale. When I glance away it turns insubstantial, nothing but a haze, but when I look at it directly it has a sharp, bright clarity; it's almost too bright. It glows.

She holds it out to me and I take it. The watch is as cold as ice and impossibly heavy.

Then the witch leans back, crosses her arms over her chest and slides off the mushroom. Her Mary Janes grit on the floor as she ducks under its gills and I know I won't find her again, no matter how I search. She's gone, nothing left of her but the memory of her grin.

But I don't search for her. I do jump down after her, though. I'm still holding the pocket watch and I can sense all the years it holds, the hours, the minutes, captured within its smooth, cold, curved weight. I heft it higher into the air, then I flip it over and bring it down on the bronze Dormouse's ears.

I feel more than hear it shatter, although I hear it too: a bass *clang* that starts low then begins to grow, louder, until it resounds in my bones, until the whole bronze sculpture chimes in sympathetic resonance. There comes a higher sound, like sproinging springs, like cogs de-cogging, and then there is silence.

I open my fingers, half expecting to see delicate golden watch parts falling to the floor, but it's gone. My hand is empty.

★   ★   ★

For days, I wander the streets. My clothes and skin and hair become soiled with dust and disapproval and hostile glances. My skin grows dry, the lines digging in deeper around my eyes and lips. I don't care. I don't want to be younger. I want to be just the age I am, for how else will my daughter recognise me when she sees me again?

Then one day I'm walking along yet another city block, staring at the concrete, and an alleyway opens at my side and I turn and see her.

A little girl about eight years old, just the age she would have been if she'd never gone into the wabe, never passed beyond my reach. Vivian's hair is the same dark brown it always was, although it's ragged and tangled now. Her cheeks still possess the smooth curve of a child's, but her eyes are different. There are things in them and I wonder what my child has seen in the time she's lived alone, out here, fending for herself.

I wonder what words rung in her ears as she scavenged for food, hungry and cold and afraid.

Mommy, mommy, she had said. *It's me, I'm Vivian.*

She'd sounded so scared. And I had only been repulsed by that child's cry emerging from such a worn throat; the pink sparkles wrapped around that aging body; the little girl's tears springing from her wrinkled eyes.

And I hear again the words I said to her in return, my daughter, my baby.

I'll kill you. You say that again, I fucking will.

I walk towards her. She doesn't run away from me. I don't suppose she has anywhere to run to. Her expression doesn't change as I put my arms around her. She doesn't even move, not to hug me back or hold me or push me away. I rest my chin on her shoulder, ignoring the smell of her, taking in the familiar-strange feel of her. And I tell my daughter I'm sorry. I have nothing else, there isn't anything else, so I keep on saying it, like a spell or an incantation: *I'm sorry, I'm sorry, I'm sorry.* I say it over and over and I don't stop, because how could it ever be enough?

You want it all to be the same, but it won't be, the witch had said. And she hadn't lied to me. I'm not certain she knew how.

There's a price.

And I know that there always will be.

I PROMISE

Conrad Williams

Alex came out of sleep and his first thoughts were for his father, dead a year now. He felt he had yet to fully come to terms with his death, to properly grieve for him. It had been a strange death. Unexpected. Expected. In any case, still raw.

It was 4:00 a.m.; cold in the room, an hour too early for him to feel justified in rising. Alex knew from bitter experience that trying to burrow back into sleep would result in him moving further away from it. He switched on the light, and then switched it off. His next breath was difficult to take. He felt his heart lurch. The remnants of sleep, catching in his thoughts. A bruise in the air. A stray memory.

He sat up in bed and switched on the light again. It was still there, hanging in the room like a half-deflated helium balloon, angled in a way so that Alex could see the jawline's familiar sweep. He stared at the face, or what was visible of the face. It was like something half-buried. It was like something emerging.

"Dad?" The name felt foreign to his lips, he had not uttered it for so long. The...what was it? – Visage? Mask? Dream projection? – showed no sign of recognition. His father looked much as he had in the days leading up to his death. Gaunt. Pale. Defeated. "Dad...what are you doing here?"

Alex swung his legs out of bed and placed his feet on the floor. Cold air swirled around them. *I'm dreaming*, he thought to himself. *I'm having a nightmare.* He stood up, keeping his eyes on his father. He looked as if he was trying to hatch himself out of the air. Was he trapped? Was he lost?

What am I thinking? He realised his entire body was tensed, and forced himself to relax. Something gave way in his head, a dull ache just above the back of his neck. He felt dizzy, and put out a hand as his balance shifted.

No, he thought. *No.*

He left his bed unmade, the lights on, and went downstairs. He dug through the laundry basket and put on some clothes, then he left the house.

Alex walked the streets until dawn edged the rooftops with colour. His stomach was churning at the knowledge that he would have to go back. He was worried his dad would still be there. He was worried his dad would be gone.

As soon as the coffee shop was open, he bought two flat whites and headed round to Sarah's house. Sarah was his girlfriend, but he didn't see much of her. She was always busy with work, or with fitness – when she wasn't doing yoga, she was doing Pilates. And when she wasn't doing Pilates, she was running. He wondered why they were even in a relationship, given the lack of time they spent together. Often, he wondered if he was the only person who thought he *was* in a relationship.

She answered the door in her yoga gear, hair damp from the shower.

"I'm not drinking that," she said. "Just put it down there and I'll heat it up later. Jesus, Alex, do you not know me by now?"

No, he wanted to say. *I hardly know you at all.*

"I'm sorry. I didn't realise you were starting so early."

"It's Tuesday. I have to start early otherwise I don't get any exercise in before work. I have one coffee, after lunch. Are you okay?"

He wondered if she meant was he okay in the head for bringing her a crack-of-dawn coffee. But then he saw how she was looking at him, and how he might look to her after his shock that morning. He was never any good at concealing his feelings.

"I didn't sleep too well," he said.

"Don't start that again," she warned him. "We agreed, separate houses, separate beds. We need our own space."

"I walked in on my mum and dad once, in their bedroom, when I was a teenager. And they were getting on in years. And they were sitting up in bed together, in their pyjamas, holding hands. Not talking or watching TV or anything. Just holding hands."

"And your point is?"

"There is no point," he said, hating how crushed he sounded.

"What's going on?" she asked him.

He told her what had happened in his room. The face hanging in the air like some impossible exhibition in a gallery. To her credit, she didn't accuse him of drinking too much, or eating cheese. She nodded sadly, and held his hand. "You never got over it," she said. "You haven't properly grieved for him yet."

"I don't know how I'm supposed to feel," he said. He meant it. His father dying was the first major bereavement in his life.

"You still haven't told me what happened," she said.

He held his cold cup of coffee and looked around the room. The fruit bowl with its bounty of items destined for her blender. The homemade sourdough cooling on a wire rack (when the hell did she make that?). The three jars lined up by the kettle for her favourite tea infusions: peppermint, turmeric and fennel.

"He was mobile, in his old age," he said. "He loved to get a bus into town and potter about the bookshop, buy a newspaper, read the headlines over coffee. He'd walk back. But then Mum went into the care home."

Sarah knew as much, but she didn't hurry him along. Alex appreciated that.

"She wasn't aware, really, of what was happening. I don't think she recognises me anymore when I go to visit. But anyway, when she was admitted, so was my dad. It was meant to be on a residential basis, of course. He didn't want to go. He hated the place. But he went. And the first night he was there, he had a bad fall. He'd got out of bed to go to the loo, became disoriented, and tripped. Broke his hip and his shoulder. He needed an operation. I went to hospital to see him. But I couldn't find him. There was just this tiny old figure in one of the beds. I wouldn't accept it was him. He wasn't my dad. But it was. Of course it was.

"I sat by him and he reached out his hand for mine and I held it and he said he loved me. Straight off the bat. I didn't know that was in him. He was always very reserved. We sat like that for an hour and then I left. I saw him the next day and the next. And each time he was...I don't know...withdrawing. He wouldn't eat. I think he just...because he wasn't able to walk anymore, because he didn't want to go back to that place...he just...he just..."

"He gave up."

"Yes. He basically starved himself to death. He knew he wasn't going to be coming back from that. It took two months. From browsing the non-fiction bookshelves and doing the crossword over a latte... to oblivion."

He felt a tug inside him then, as if something had become unanchored. Perhaps it was an understanding. An acceptance. But it felt like something forgotten, a tip-of-the-tongue frustration. He concentrated on the feeling, trying to unpick it, but it wouldn't lay itself bare for him.

Sarah said: "I'll cancel my class. I'll come home with you."

He didn't protest. He knew her mind.

She changed out of her yoga gear and walked back to his house with him, holding his hand. He knew she meant to show him that the face in the air was an illusion, but he already knew that it was meant only for his eyes. His father would not reveal himself to anyone else.

In the bedroom she seemed more interested in the state of his sheets than the area he was fanning his hands at. "He was just here. His face, tilted, as if he was rising from bed. You know, getting up."

She was making the bed for him. She had lost interest. "You need to establish a sleeping regime. Go to bed at a certain time. You need to factor in some winding down time, so your body knows that sleep is coming. Bath, herbal tea, ten minutes reading a book... A routine."

He made all the placatory gestures and sounds. She kissed him. "Come on," she said. "I'll buy you breakfast."

*   *   *

A bath. Some tea. A book.

He took off his glasses and folded them. He switched off the light.

There was a roughness building in his skin that he had not noticed until Sarah mentioned it over their breakfast (pancakes and bacon for him; fruit and yoghurt for her). He thought she was having a dig at him over his dietary choices, but now, in the dark, as he ran his fingers over his face, he saw she was right. He felt papery, dry. There were little edges and crevices that he could feel, as if his face was developing cracks. Panic rose in him like water, filling him up. He hurried to the bathroom and turned on the light. Staring back at him in the mirror was the face he knew so well, but which was suddenly that of a stranger. He looked grey and spent, like a bag intended for a cheap sandwich at a roadside café. He rubbed some moisturiser into the worst places. Sarah would have been to the GP by now. He always prevaricated. He could get a job as a prevaricator.

Dad was there when he returned to the room. There seemed to be no rhyme nor reason for his appearances. But maybe they occurred when Alex was active, or disturbed in his dreams. He liked the idea of his dad appearing when he was under stress. As he used to as a child in the night, afraid of the dark, or the thing slumped and hungry in his wardrobe, mustering the strength to push its doors open before devouring him in his bed.

Another teasing glimpse of a moment shared that wasn't quite remembered. He imagined his father's face as he sat on the edge of the mattress, looking down at him, the soft smile, the crinkles at the corner of his eyes. His father's warm fingers smoothing his hair, and assuring him that everything was all right. He checked under his bed. He checked in the wardrobe. He said something. You said something.

"You said something," he whispered now, as his father's face waxed and waned in the air. He wanted to touch him, but he was afraid that doing so would cause him to vanish, like a balloon under a pin. "Back then. You said something to me. What did you say?"

His father's face creased, as if he was in thought. The edges of it moved against the borders in the air, and there was a strange glimmer there, like the rim of ice at the edge of a pond at the start of its freezing.

"Open your eyes, Dad," Alex said. His father's eyelids twitched. He looked like someone struggling out of a sleep that was too deep to be beneficial. "Dad, can you hear me?"

The glimmering seam which collared his father's face sagged a little, allowing more of it to be revealed. There was the mole on his left cheek. The suggestion of five o'clock shadow. How much of that breach needed to be loosened before he would slither out of it, as if newly born? Could he do anything to hasten the process?

Alex watched for an hour as his father twitched and frowned, his eyelids fluttering under the weight of some fantastical dream. He remembered sitting by the hospital bed scrutinising him in the same way, as he sank towards death, his eyelids smarting. *What do you see, Dad? Where do you go?*

He glanced at his watch and there was a shiver around him; he knew when he looked back his father would be gone. So it was. There was time yet for Alex to catch up on his sleep. His was dreamless, or of dreams unrecalled. When he woke again, just before nine, there was a contour of blood on his pillow, where his jawline had been resting.

★   ★   ★

"It's non-negotiable," Sarah said. "You're going."

She was a confident driver, but tended to speed. Alex realised he was gripping the seat tightly only when she lightly slapped his hand. "I'm fine," he said.

"Fine…right. Because bleeding from the face in your sleep is no cause for concern. We all do it, don't we?"

"It's just dry skin. Maybe I've got eczema. It's just a stress thing."

"I'm suffering from a stress thing too. The Latin name for it is Alexii Irritatum. I'd pay a lot of money to have that surgically removed."

"Very funny."

She parked near the GP's surgery and shooed him out of the car. "I'll wait for you," she said. "Go."

He hurried through a mist of rain to the entrance and stepped inside. The smell of lemon bleach. Tulips past their best in a vase on the windowsill by reception. He was just in time to hear the voice of Dr. Ferguson over the intercom calling for a Mrs. Watkin. He gave his name and his date of birth to a woman wearing a surgical face mask who couldn't sit still on her office chair. She gestured with her eyes and he went to sit in the waiting room where he had once sat with his father, thirty years previously. Some tummy bug. Some cold. The clock on the wall ticked off the minutes. Ten. Fifteen. He watched Mrs. Watkin leave, her long fingers plucking at her flimsy green blouse, pulling it back into shape. A lump under the breast. A swollen gland.

"Alex Barlow." A deep voice. Sonorous. Wet.

He traipsed through and Dr. Ferguson – Fergie, as Alex's dad had called him – was standing by the window. All those years ago he'd had the cold stethoscope to his chest while Fergie asked Dad about his holidays. The same desk. Dr. Ferguson was old now, way past retirement age. He loved the job. His hair was white, but still styled the same way as it was when it had been deep chestnut. Long and wavy, swept back off the forehead.

"You look like something you'd find in the shitter on a gastroenteritis ward," he said. "I was sorry to hear about your father."

Suddenly close to tears, Alex could only nod. He liked Fergie. He liked the lack of propriety. You didn't find that in people anymore. Everyone was careful of what they said, lest it offend, as if offence was the most harmful thing there was now.

"What's going on with your boat race?" Fergie asked. "I assume that's why you're here. Unless your knob has dropped off."

Alex shrugged. "Dry skin? I don't know."

"Let's have a look."

He prodded the tender edges of Alex's face with a tongue depressor. Through the thick lenses of his glasses (probably the same frames he wore in the 1970s), Alex saw a pale blue corona around the iris similar to those his father had developed.

"Bugger me," Fergie said. "I've never seen anything like that in my puff."

"Dry skin?"

"It's not dry skin. It looks…it looks as if your skin is aging rapidly. It's coming away from the younger flesh surrounding it." He said this in such a matter-of-fact way that the shock of it was delayed. Alex's heart lurched.

"It's cancer?"

"I don't know. I'd refer you to a specialist but they'd tell you they've never seen anything like it either, I'd bet a pony on it. How long has this been going on?"

Since my father appeared out of thin air.

"Three…four days?"

"You're kidding me." Fergie took off his glasses and sucked one of the ear rests, tapped his teeth with it. "Right. I'll take a swab and I'll send it to the lab with a rocket under its arse. I'll prescribe you something topical to ease the discomfort and hopefully soften the skin, make it want to seal itself back up again. You never know. And some bastard-strength antibiotics. Let's nuke the sod and see what happens."

*　　★　　★

The following day Sarah visited him first thing. She gestured at the large yellow pills he'd picked up from the chemist. "Are you going to take those?"

He shrugged. He nodded.

She came to his bedroom but would neither look at him nor at the area where his father was struggling to be...

To be what? *Birthed* was the word he kept circling around.

"I don't want to know," she said. Her gaze flitted from one place to another, but couldn't settle, as if everything she saw triggered a memory too painful to consider.

"I think he might speak soon," Alex said. "He looks ready to talk. He looks as if he's trying to say something. Trying to tell me something."

Now her gaze crystallised. What was she looking at? It seemed suddenly very important. The staircase? The picture on the wall of a child playing cricket on a beach?

"I'm sorry...what did you say?"

She closed her eyes. Breathed deeply. He knew that look. Her exasperated look. He realised with bitter clarity that it didn't matter what she was trying to tell him.

"You are falling apart, Alex," she said. "You have...there's this smell on you...coming off you. It's sweet. Rotten. You need to go to the doctor."

"I went," he said, seizing on the one thing he could understand. "You took me!"

"You need to go back," she said. "It could be fatal, this thing you've got. Like a flesh-eating bug or something. I'm not going to watch you die."

"I feel...fantastic," he said.

Her lips disappeared to a flat line. It was a look he knew better than he would have liked. It meant she was close to tears. She was struggling to say something; she kept opening her mouth to speak and then either thinking better of it, or hitting a wall. It scared him. She was always so effortlessly articulate.

"What?" he said, and he said it with such vehemence her head snapped up. Her eyes were red-rimmed. Reluctant. He felt something give in his jaw, and a wet release across his throat. He put his fingers there and they came away wet with a thin wash of blood and lymph.

"Jesus fuck. Jesus, Alex. What will it take? Your entire face sliding off your skull?"

"That's not what you were going to say. That was easy. That was too easy. Tell me what you meant to say."

"Stop trying to divert me. The issue here is your health. You will not acknow—"

"Tell me."

She held up her hands. A gesture of surrender; a barrier against his aggression. He couldn't tell. But then she said: "Your father."

Those initial words uttered, her voice grew tremulous and high-pitched. She rushed the rest of it, as if she needed to get it out of her before she could stop herself.

"Your father is dead, Alex. End of. Whatever's going on, you have to leave it. Let go. It's eating you up. Whatever this is. Grief? Let go. Let him go. Christ. Christ." She was walking away now. He didn't know what to say. He felt whatever control he had over the situation slipping away. He thought she'd have been thrilled to know his dad was coming back. That he was trying to speak. But she was treating him like someone suffering a kind of breakdown. He could see it in her eyes. That mix of pity and concern and fear.

At the door, she seemed to dither, and then she forced herself over the threshold and into the street. "This is what happens," she said, "when you deny yourself the process. Bereavement. You blocked it out. You refused it. It's not healthy. And now look at you... What did the doctor say?"

"Well, he gave me some antibiotics. Told me to eat an apple and call him in the morning."

She was crying, but she wouldn't allow him to hold her. She walked to her car. "You know what to do," she said. "Christ, Alex. Find balance."

He stood there long after the sound of the engine had dissipated. He might have stayed there till dark if it wasn't for the voice he heard coming from his room.

"What, Dad? What is it? Can you hear me?"

His dad was slowly turning in the air, and Alex was put in mind of something cocooned, rotating on a thread. He thought his dad was somehow distraught, that he had in some way overheard his conversation with Sarah, or was able to feel in him his disquiet. He leaned in close to him. Could he detect those Dad smells? The Old Spice. The tang of copper from the loose change he collected in a large whisky bottle.

"Dad?"

There was a movement of air. A twitch in the throat. Then sound shifting there, deep in his chest. Alex wanted to get hold of…whatever it was – the rent, the fracture – and tear it wide, but he worried his father might slip away into whatever existed beyond. And in any case, he wasn't ready to see what was beyond.

But he felt he should do something to try to *induce* his dad's reappearance. Cook the food he liked? What was that, anyway? He closed his eyes to think. Dense, meaty stews. Chinese takeaways. Fried breakfasts. He liked instant coffee made with hot milk. Tinned fruit in syrup with evaporated milk.

He played the music he had grown up listening to. The album titles as known to him as the street names around the house of his childhood. *Catch Bull at Four. Blood on the Tracks. Diamonds and Rust.* He watched his father while he did this. He seemed more animated. Alex remembered him encouraging him to sing along to the lyrics printed on the album sleeve. Sitting in their living room, the record spinning on a turntable, reflecting light in strange, waxing patterns across the ceiling.

When the record ended, his dad would look at his watch and say: "Apples and pears."

Alex would go up to his room and change into his pyjamas. Brush his teeth. When he turned the light off in his bedroom, the glow-in-the-dark King Kong on his desk was the colour of lemon, so bright initially that he could have used it to read by.

Now, going to sleep was hard. It felt as if he was mining for it, perhaps in a way similar to his father's travails. Everything hurt. He thought he could feel his bones, spongy and damp within their aching parcels of meat. If he opened his mouth to yawn, his face shifted alarmingly, and he felt pain lancing like sutures along its circumference. Shifting on the pillow alerted him to damp areas where his skin had leaked onto the cotton. He was aware of the smell of himself, decayed and cloying. He could taste it, perhaps via some kind of osmosis through the tissue of his jaw. It hung, claggy and bitter at the back of his throat, like the aftershock of a dismal meal. *What have I become?* The languor of pre-sleep moved through him, and he settled despite his disquiet. His eyes fluttered, and he saw, through his narrowing lids, his father appear in the air, nested in eternity's socket, the edges of the aperture encrusted with ice. Frost blued the hollows of his father's cheeks. He seemed agitated. His face lifted and fell. Alex was convinced something other than his own need was causing it.

"Dad? It's okay. Don't force it. You'll be here soon. And we'll do all the things we should have done when…when, well, you know. All those times when you were too busy, or I was doing something else. When I said: later, maybe. When you said: not right now. The time we thought we had. We had no time at all."

His dad's eyes opened and Alex fell into deep sleep. But the image of him remained. The skin on his father's neck red raw where the ice collar was irritating him. The eyes distant and confused, questioning. For the first time he wondered if his dad was in pain. It was a birth of some kind, after all. A rebirth. A deliverance from death. How traumatic must it be? It occurred to him too that his dad might not want to be there. That he had earned his rest, that he had died, after all, tired of life, of the constant pain and the exhaustion. He felt a lurch of panic as he considered this, and in the dream his father twitched and shuddered. The collar loosened somewhat; he heard the crackle of ice as the aperture shifted. Alex imagined his dad trapped at the neck, suspended above countless miles of screaming nothingness. What had he done to get to where he now was? How hard would it have been to try to reverse what ought to be irreversible?

Fingers poked up through a slender gap between his father's throat and the aperture's edge.

Dad?

He wanted to believe they were his father's own. But they were long and slender, tipped with horribly curved, ragged purple nails. How could they be his father's? Especially as they were now lightly scoring the white flesh of Dad's neck, causing him to wince.

Leave him alone. Dad? Dad?

The fingers withdrew, but not before they'd made shapes in the air, as if essaying a wave, or a beckoning.

Alex jerked out of sleep to find his pillow wet with blood. His neck was criss-crossed with deep scratches. His fingers came away slick when he touched them. *Oh God. Oh Jesus.*

His face in the bathroom mirror looked ready to cantilever away from the fascia of his skull. He felt all it needed was a little tug at the break of his chin and it would lift up like the faceplate on a welder's mask. Some of the scratches on his neck were welling with blood, deeper than he'd reckoned. What had he done to himself? Had he tried to kill himself in his sleep?

His mind turned to the fingers he'd seen slipping out of the aperture. He hurried back to his bedroom, but his father was not there. Only a rumour of cold where he had been hanging.

★   ★   ★

He tried calling Sarah throughout the day but she was either busy, or ignoring his calls. As darkness sifted through the streets once more, he found himself dreading his father's return. He tried Sarah one last time. She answered.

"I'm sorry," he said.

"I'm sorry too," she said.

"I don't know what to do. What did you mean when you said 'find balance'?"

"You know what I mean. You're hot or cold. Either, or. You can't compartmentalise. You can't shelve things for a later date. You wallow. You can't...you don't know how to forget."

"I don't...I've never had to deal with anything like this before."

"It's a club and we're all members, Alex. Like it or not. No option. Everyone deals with it, or they don't."

"I'll change," he said. "Give me time. I'm trying to learn. I'll change. I promise."

"I'm here," she said. "But I won't shoulder your burden."

She was saying something else but he had gone cold, turned deaf.

I promise.

He put his phone down and went upstairs to find his dad lying on his bed. He looked no different to the reduced figure who had died in hospital. He was staring at Alex. "I'm scared," his father said.

"I'm scared too," Alex said. He could feel something spreading inside him. A monumental coldness too big for him to contain. He thought it might be death, and that this was what balance meant. A man who had escaped from death left a vacuum that could not be sustained. Someone needed to fill it. "I miss you, Dad."

"I miss you too. But I'm tired. I just want to go to sleep."

"The fingers, Dad. The hands."

"They carry me down. They lull me to sleep. Don't worry. Don't worry about me. Live your life. Just like how I taught you, right?"

"Right, Dad. I'm tired too."

"Then let's have a nap. You and me. In the morning you can go and visit your mum. Tell her I love her."

Okay. Okay. Night, Dad.

Night, Alex. Sweet dreams.

★　　★　　★

The boy woke up in the semi-darkness and he was instantly afraid. The landing light was on; his parents always left it on for him. He was minded to get out of bed to turn it off, to show that he was a big boy, but it was cold and the darkness surrounding his bed was close and seemed full of movement; he was certain that if he moved it would touch him. Smother him. He felt his heart leap to meet the thickening of his fear, gelid there in his chest, like a cold chunk of something difficult to digest. He tried to call out around the lump of fear lodged in his throat. He could barely muster the breath to do so.

When he was able to call out, his voice was filled with misery. He wished he could be a little more like his dad. To be grown up and unafraid of anything. It must be such a relief to be a big boy, to not let anything bother you.

He heard his father's footsteps on the stairs, the reassuring squeak of the sixth and eighth risers. His shadow in the doorway.

"All right, Alex?" The whisper. His dad's weight on the mattress, tipping Alex towards him. His smell. His thereness. "What is it? What's wrong? Can't you sleep?"

"No," Alex said, and his voice and his eyes were heavy with tears.

"Why not?"

And the reason was there in him, a fear he had never really considered before, let alone given voice to.

"You're going to die one day."

His father held him while he sobbed.

He said: "One day. Yes. But not for a long time. You mustn't worry. I won't leave you. I'll never leave you. I promise."

FLAT 19

Jenn Ashworth

Someone made a speech about her unique vision and incomparable talent. They weren't going to name who they were describing until they called the winner up to the stage but Eve sat through it with her hands twisting in her lap and the dread closing over her head in dark waves. And yes, it was her – she'd won, and it was thousands of pounds.

She went up to the stage and her lips stuck to her teeth and her eyelids dragged on the suddenly sticky surface of her contact lenses. She should have been pleased and certainly tried her best to appear so. She smiled as people clinked their cutlery against their wine glasses. She'd made a proper effort, wearing a good dress and uncomfortable shoes. The little award and the big cheque were handed over and afterwards there was champagne, and she mingled among the white tablecloths, nodding and making sure her face was appropriately arranged for photographs that would, they assured her, appear in their trade journal the very next month.

★   ★   ★

When the issue arrived at the office Eve stared at her own face on its cover. Who was this person, who had worked tirelessly on a project, enhanced her company's reputation and won a significant and unexpected amount of money? Were those really her own eyes? How was it possible? What had possessed her? She rolled the magazine up and put it in the bottom drawer of her desk. Steven would want to frame it in the downstairs toilet. Guests would ask about it. She'd have to make a joke or enjoy being the subject of someone else's joke. She stared at the carpet underneath her desk. One of the senior partners had asked to meet with her that afternoon to have a conversation about what came next.

It had been the same with the bread-baking. She'd tried it once, as a mindful activity that might relax her on the weekends, and something educational for the younger children to help out with. The weighing and measuring would be good for their maths. It would kill a rainy morning. The dough was sticky and grey in the first few attempts and refused to rise. She persevered. It was a good thing to do. Eventually she got the knack of mindful kneading and the little loaves swelled and browned in the oven. She became so competent a baker that a return to shop-bought bread had felt like a drop in standards and was experienced by her family as akin to an insult.

"What, no loaf?" Steven asked once. "Have you fallen out with us?"

Now she rose at five to put the dough in the oven for forty minutes before everyone else rose at seven to eat it. She'd have to pull things like this – prizes and magazine covers – out of the bag all the time from now on.

Eve kicked off her shoes and crawled under the desk. She lay down, her cheek against the expensive, regularly cleaned wool loop pile. She'd chosen the carpet from a thick album of samples that she'd been presented with last year. That had been work too. Creating the right impression. She turned onto her back and stared at the underside of her desk. Her email and instant message alerts and calendar reminders pinged first on her desktop computer, then a half second later on her mobile phone. She preferred not to answer these electronic demands for her attention. And as she lay motionless, she noticed that taped to the underside of her desk was a business card. She quickly peeled back the tape and retrieved the card, got up and sat in her office chair to inspect it.

It was a tasteful card made of creamy, thick paper with deckled edges. A navy blue 'W' in an understated font. Underneath, a phone number, and the phrase 'professional assistance'. Someone had spent time and effort on designing and producing this card. Someone – a whole team of someones, perhaps – had been keen to give the right impression. The impression she got was of a company that was expensive and had good reasons to be discreet. That name! She crawled out from under her desk and rang the number. It was as she'd hoped, only better.

★　　★　　★

When she got home that night, Steven was beating eggs while watching a video of a man in a chef's outfit talk him through the procedure on his tablet. Omelettes were his new obsession. An organic, protein-heavy diet was good for the health, he'd said. And though anyone could knock up an omelette it didn't cost anyone anything to learn how to do it properly. The French way. Sometimes, when he wasn't looking, she did it herself, using a folding plastic contraption that went in the microwave that she'd bought from a pound-shop and was not French at all.

"What will you do with the money?" he asked her. He really was only curious. He had plenty of his own, after all. The prize itself was enough for him: evidence, Eve thought meanly, that his careful nurturing of her potential through the years of their marriage had finally come to fruition.

"I haven't thought about it much," she lied. He carried on beating. In about two minutes he was going to say, 'It's all in the wrist' and wink at her and she might scream or break a window. She might lie down under the kitchen table and pretend to be deaf. She might begin undressing and walk out onto the street without a stitch on and start singing the National Anthem on the village green. But all this would take effort, and the little lie didn't.

"I'd like to reinvest some of it. I have an idea for another project," she said, and sketched out the idea – using lots of jargon so he'd be impressed and stop listening.

Steven left the eggs to settle and started grating cheese. There were two plates warming under the grill. Steven didn't like eating from cold plates, or from plates that were only hot because they'd just come out of the dishwasher.

"And I also thought I could set up some kind of fellowship. A paid internship. For people who want to get into the business but don't have any connections. From disadvantaged backgrounds."

Steven smiled and poured the eggs into the hot pan.

"What a nice idea," he said. He liked helping people from disadvantaged backgrounds become more like himself. Isn't that what he'd done to her? *For* her, she corrected herself. "Here, eat up. You don't look well. Did you skip lunch?"

He pushed the plate over to her and she picked up her fork gratefully.

It was a very good omelette. Later, she sat in her car and called W to set the whole thing up.

* * *

W messaged her the address of an out-of-town hotel. There she would meet with one of their agents and he would 'take her particulars'. A small conference room had been hired. She'd wondered, as she'd parked in the hotel car park, if this would feel like having an affair. To have your particulars taken sounded wonderfully mid-century and could be a euphemism for almost anything. She marvelled at the energy some people had for taking each other's particulars in the backs of cars and empty boardrooms and in hotels like this one, during the day. It was happening all over the place, according to Steven.

The hotel was cheap-looking and drab, and the lobby smelled like old frying pans. The conference room contained a vase of artificial flowers with dusty petals and bulbous orange plastic stamens that did not attempt to convince. A man stood by the window, waiting for her.

"Take a seat," he said. She'd have to tell Steven she was sleeping with this man if he somehow discovered she'd been out of work that afternoon. He would be big about it – perhaps even indulgent. Wasn't being mature about things like this what people like them did? Eve saw immediately this man was not the type you'd start something clandestine with. He was mild, neat-haired and wore a suit that looked bespoke. He gestured towards a chair.

"It can feel awkward," he said gently, "to start. But I find this works better if I just," he produced a tablet from a briefcase, "work through the preliminary questions, and we can save some time at the end if you want to ask me anything. Water?"

There was a jug and glass. The water in the jug had dust swirling on its surface and Eve did not touch it. But she sat, and he used the tablet to record her answers to a dizzying variety of questions, from her waist measurement to her morning routine to the various tasks she performed for her children and husband each morning and evening.

"I'm not sure that you need to know..." Eve protested, as the questions progressed into the third hour and into the darker chambers of her marriage.

"Everything," the man said with a reassuring smile. "Even if you don't think it an important detail, you just don't know what would turn out to be important."

It was as if he was a policeman and she a witness to a crime. The crime of her own life. Eve risked a smile. Now someone would surely see why she was so tired – why the whole business of her existence was so unbearably relentless she'd rather just be rid of it entirely for a while. Eventually, they got to the end of his list. He'd never introduced himself. She thought of him as 'W' – a name like a spy, or if he and his company were the same thing.

"I think that's all we need now." He flipped the cover down over the tablet's screen and tucked it away. "Now if you could just roll up your sleeve."

"My sleeve?"

His hands were still in the briefcase, putting the tablet back, then he retrieved a pair of latex gloves, and a kit for taking blood.

"You're okay with needles, are you?"

She wanted to ask the man if he were a nurse, or in some other way qualified. Did you need special training to handle a syringe? Even hairdressers would give you Botox these days. The man's fingernails were absolutely flawless and disappeared inside the latex gloves. She complied.

"Sharp scratch," he said, and filled one vial after another. Her blood was dark, and she turned away as she heard it squirting into the bottles. She thought of Steven, pressing organic oranges through the juicer on Sunday mornings, listening to the radio and humming. Doll-like, she stared out of the window and blinked slowly, keeping her face free from any expression of pain or disgust.

★   ★   ★

That night she lay beside her husband in her long-sleeved nightdress even though it was a warm night, because she didn't want him to see the little round plaster on her inner elbow. He'd made some kind of almond and clementine cake from a recipe book, and they'd had it after dinner, and because he'd baked, Eve had felt obligated to make proper coffee in the pot with the matching cups, and now she was awake, ruminating. There'd been something not quite right about the man from W's bedside manner. She began to wonder – in a paranoid manner that seemed very reasonable (in fact, the worst of the paranoia was in not being able to entirely trust her own sense of disquiet) if this man was altogether there. If he was, well, *real*. She stared into the dark, listening to the tick of Steven's alarm clock. He hadn't dispensed any of the usual niceties. No congratulations on her being able to answer all the questions so fully, no response to her answers. It would have been nice, she thought, if he'd commented on how impossible and exhausting the maintenance of all her various lives had become – to tell her he quite understood her predicament. Once he'd taken her blood – such a lot of it – he'd plucked two strands of her hair from the nape of her neck and tucked them into a little plastic bag. Then he'd rubbed a cotton swab around the inside of her mouth, declining eye contact while he did so. Eventually, he'd turned his back to her while packing his things away. It was as if he was giving her privacy to recompose herself into a person after the detailed autopsy he'd just performed was complete.

"All done. We'll contact you. Couple of weeks."

"I see." She'd stood, reached for her handbag. Her feet were numb after so long sitting in the chair and hurt once she put her weight on them.

"And where will I go, while it all…happens?"

The man had smiled again. He seemed to have no other setting. She may as well tell him she was planning to use the time she was in the process of buying to perform an axe murder or a terrorist attack and all he'd do is dispense that tight, precise little smile of his.

"Well, that's up to you, Mrs. Smith. We'll give you a telephone so we can contact you privately in case there's some problem or emergency but," (he must have caught her look of disappointment) "we've been operating for nine years now and never had to disturb a client."

"No, that's not what I mean. I know I need to stay out of the way. But where will I live?"

"We give you a flat. Nothing luxurious, I'm afraid, on your current scheme." He glanced at his watch and handed her a brochure and she looked through pictures while he listed the options for upgrades and instalment plans, apologising for the flat's tiny size and dated furnishings, which he repeatedly referred to as 'simple' and 'uncluttered'.

"No, this one is perfect," she'd said. And it was. She'd felt the way actresses in films always seem to feel when they fall in love. A recognition, a coming home. *So there you are*, she'd thought, gazing at the brochure.

And now, lying with Steven, she tried to think of it again – to enjoy the feelings of desire she had for it – her own flat for three whole months. But the man himself kept intruding into her fantasy. The not-quite-rightness of him.

Of course. He was one of those. The thought came to her suddenly, and once it arrived it felt like someone had thrown a rock in her face. He was one of those *things* the company made. It would make sense – they probably didn't get paid in the usual way, so it would be economical to have the assistants administering the scheme. And perhaps it would work as advertising too. Give the client a good old look at the product before asking for the first instalment. She shuddered and closed her eyes, making up her mind to dream of the flat and not of the man from W, if 'man' was the right word for what he was.

★ ★ ★

Two weeks later, she was summoned back to the hotel. She braced herself and managed not to scream or vomit at the sight of what waited for her. W had done an excellent job; exactly as promised. The agent – the same one as last time, or another one, waited discreetly while she inspected it.

"Will he be able to tell?" she asked eventually.

The woman – the thing – was standing quite still, staring unblinking into the middle distance. She breathed, and when Eve drew close and put a hand on her arm, her skin was warm. She had an urge – an almost unbearable one she would certainly have given in to if she had been alone with it – to slap it, to push it over, to pull its hair. But she contented herself with tugging its bottom lip down gently and inspecting a minute chip on the front bottom tooth, caused by her falling from her bike and hitting her face on the kerb when she was eleven years old. She touched her own tooth with her tongue, as if to reassure herself she was still there.

"Your husband?"

Eve nodded.

"Oh no, I shouldn't think so," he said. "It's never happened before. Not in…"

"Nine years," Eve finished. This one had definitely been programmed with the sales patter.

"Yes," he said. "Isn't she beautiful? The lab were very pleased with how she turned out." The man clasped his hands in front of him, like a well-trained butler. "You must think of this period – this next three months – as a kind of alibi."

"What a word."

"Yes. A watertight alibi allowing you to be absent from your own life. You can do what you want with the time. One of our clients wrote a novel. Another went trekking in Nepal. It's a once in a lifetime opportunity for a once in a lifetime experience. The time doesn't count. You're still there, for all intents and purposes."

That was sales talk if ever she heard it, and she'd already paid the first two instalments.

"And what happens afterwards? To the…" she gestured uncomfortably. Was it rude to talk about these things while their backs were turned? Before they were activated? Was it – *she* – on standby, or was she somehow aware, hearing but not responding, like a patient in a coma?

"Hello?" Eve whispered. The assistant did not respond. Its breathing continued, soft and even and regular. Eve was standing close enough to smell its hair, and it smelled of her own shampoo – which of course had been one of the questions.

"Once the commission ends the assistants remain the property of the agency, I'm afraid. Your image and your data belong to you, of course. But the component parts, the raw materials. We decommission them safely. There's a decreation process and a recycling programme." He was being deliberately vague and smiled apologetically. "It is humane, though not especially pretty. Your data is kept on our system for five years, in case you'd like to book again."

Eve sat down heavily and he pressed a glass of water into her hand.

"Some people want a closer look. Would you like me to activate? I have the others in hotel rooms upstairs. I can ask them to come down?"

Eve shook her head quickly, her mind full of operating theatres and butchers' shops and the lairs of serial killers – imagining and trying not to imagine the decreation process. The recycling of parts. She supposed everyone was recycled, once you came down to it. She'd read that the water in her body was a thunderstorm last week and would be part of a fancy soufflé served in a Parisian café in a month's time. Her suitcase was at her feet. Seeing one of the things was enough – having the whole team in front of her would only be like naming the pigs that were destined to become bacon.

"No need," she said, picked up the suitcase and asked the man at reception to call her a taxi to Flat 19.

★   ★   ★

The name of the flat was some kind of joke. It was three rooms above an empty workshop – the type that would have belonged to a mechanic or a joiner but was now blissfully empty – in a decrepit coastal town less than twenty miles from her home. There was no flat 18 or 20, and no flat number 1, either. She wondered what the postman thought, delivering letters, then supposed that if W regularly stashed its clients here, like cadavers in cold storage, there would never be any need for letters.

If she had wondered how it would be to have this time, unfettered and untethered, Eve would have supposed she'd have spent it eating chocolate in front of the telly, catching up on some box sets, reading trashy thrillers, ordering takeaway and sleeping. The team of deputy Eves, overseen by the man from W who assigned them their tasks, and he himself overseen by a team of shadowy others, all connected with some vital technology somewhere, would keep things ticking over. They were all at least as competent as she was, and more so. So there would be literally nothing for her to do. Eve might have imagined long baths in the afternoon, getting squiffy on fizzy wine before 6:00 p.m. and not bothering to wash her hair or shave her legs. But as she had not allowed herself to imagine what she might do with the time – she hadn't dared to – when it finally arrived, she locked the door of the little sea-view flat behind her, and found herself unable to do anything except sink into the little armchair in front of the window and stare, unseeing, out at the water.

At the southern end of the little bay was a nuclear power station. She had no idea how they worked, and did not wonder, only regarded its blocky shape on the horizon, sometimes obscured by mist. Once every three days there would be a test alarm that echoed out from the station, over the wide bay and the cold flat water and into the flat. At first that was how she measured the time, emerging from her inner drifting only to note the siren, wailing out over the featureless bay, the sound bouncing around sea and rock and beach, and disturbing her only for a moment before she sank blissfully inwards again.

Of course, there were memories that drifted in and out like the clouds that drifted across the sky. Andrew would need new football boots, and there was a presentation to prepare for the Lessing account, and someone ought to come and look at the bifold doors in the kitchen, which leaked a little in rainy weather, and Jenny was going to need a dress for the end of term prom and someone needed to write a cheque for Esme's swimming lessons. There were Gantt charts to organise for the team, and a mole on Steven's back that needed looking at. She should visit her mother and get her to do something about the fence in her back garden, which was sagging.

Each of these thoughts she dispatched, as if they were misdirected letters, mentally redirecting them to the appropriate assistant. The man from W had explained the natural human flexibility to ricochet a self between a legion of roles and functions in life – the way we were never quite ourselves, but always somebody's wife, somebody's mother, someone else's friend or lover or daughter – was beyond the current capabilities of the company to replicate. They resolved this by creating a team of assistants, all different versions of Eve, and dispatched each to their individual work from a hotel, where they waited until they were required. The administration of the scheme sounded incredible, but W's man had shrugged off questions. "We have our own team co-ordinating things," he'd said.

Eve sometimes imagined the assistants sitting, as she was, inert and staring unseeing into the dark of an unheated hotel room until they were requested. But eventually the inner roar of thought fell silent for longer and longer periods, and she sank into the blankness. She'd heard stories of Zen masters sitting in caves for years on end, staring at nothing while the snow fell around them and their feet rotted into gangrene. It was not waiting, what she was doing, because she was not expecting or anticipating anything. Apart from the siren coming and going every three days and reminding her to eat something, she let go of time entirely.

★   ★   ★

The agency had issued her with a phone for emergencies and promised to contact her on it to arrange her debriefing and return interview. She'd left it in a drawer in the kitchenette of Flat 19 and it had run out of charge. On one of the siren days, disturbed from her unselfed nothing by the gentle wailing, she retrieved this phone, plugged it into the wall and looked at the date and time on her screen. Four more days. That was all.

W had been sending her updates, little videos and pictures of the Eves about their business: dropping the kids at school, presenting to her colleagues, sitting on the train with a travel cup of coffee on the table in front of her. Eve swiped through the pictures hungrily and felt a great and powerful love for them, these little parts of herself, granted agency to do their work without her interference. How diligent and careful they were. How relentlessly efficient. These Eves, she realised, were precisely what Steven had in mind when he'd picked up the girl from the wrong side of the tracks at university and ended up marrying her while she was still grateful and pliable.

What would the agency do, she wondered, if she failed to turn up to her re-orientation appointment, where detailed reports, video montages and online records of her various selves would be shared to bring her up to speed and assist her in making a seamless, if reluctant, re-entry to her own life? Maybe she could message Steven and ask to meet him somewhere private. She'd take him out to the beach. Buy him a bag of chips which he'd sneer at, complaining about the cholesterol and the carbs. She'd explain the situation to him. Point out what a wonderful job her understudies were doing. Perhaps he'd prefer, she'd suggest, to keep things the way they were. Perhaps he'd like that better? Was there a way of suggesting it that would make him feel it was his idea in the first place? Would he agree to remortgage the house and pay W whatever they asked so she could come back to the flat? Or if not the flat – she looked around desperately at the drab little walls she'd barely noticed, the cloudy sand-scoured glass of the kitchen window, the grease spots on the tiles behind the cooker – then somewhere else. Nowhere else. She'd walk into the sea if she had to.

Eve clutched at the phone, swiping and scrolling. It was hopeless. Steven would never agree to it – her having her cake and eating it. Or having fewer cakes or eating none of them. Or hiring someone else to eat her share of the cake. He was always going on about *authentic* this and *artisanal* that. Spoke cuttingly about his sister, who sometimes brought counterfeit handbags home from trips abroad and bestowed them on her nieces. He'd never let the girls keep them. *People can tell*, he'd say. *People who matter can always tell*.

She knew without trying that not being able to tell would be so humiliating for him he'd simply refuse to believe it. The agency wouldn't back her up. Would vanish discreetly into the ether along with the assistants, leaving her trapped again in the competent prison of her life with a husband who'd commit her to a rehab or a rest home or a sanitorium somewhere. Wherever he put her away, it would be no Flat 19. There'd be wholesome group craft activities. Batik and macramé before lunch, brisk walks in the grounds among some council-planted daffodils, then a group encounter session for the inmates to talk about their mothers in the afternoon.

Eve used the phone to write a text message. She sent it to herself, to the mobile phone she'd handed over to W so they could clone it for the Eves to use while she was away. It was forbidden. There were many clauses in the contract on this matter. But they were her assistants, Eve reasoned. Who else was she supposed to call on? W would not help. Steven would not help. She'd ask the Eves.

★   ★   ★

The Eves came at the time and place she'd asked them to. This was a surprise: she imagined that they'd been assigned or programmed or instructed not to know of the existence of the original mother. But there they were: she saw them on the beach from a long way off. They were gathered, huddled, almost, as if sharing a secret or gossiping about an absent colleague. She wondered what they were speaking to each other about. Or if they even needed to speak at all. Perhaps they could communicate some other way, some signal or impression passed between their dark heads like messages carried in radio waves.

Shh, they were saying. *Look sharp, she's coming.*

A passer-by might have noted the general similarity between this group of women, but Eve was not striking in her looks and a group of averagely sized brown-haired white women on a beach in winter was hardly a remarkable sight apt to draw attention. The Eve that went to the office was wearing a good wool jacket and sensible leather shoes. The Eve that existed for the children seemed softer, somehow, in her jogging bottoms and with her shiny, scrubbed clean of make-up face. There was an Eve designed just for visits to her mother: not too successful, not too downtrodden, always wearing the god-awful purple cardigan her mother had presented to her the Christmas just gone and ready to smilingly absorb another instance of artless passive aggression. There were another couple of Eves she didn't recognise; one in impractical shoes, a too-tight silk blouse and a pencil skirt, the other one faded somehow, less defined than the others and seeming to exist only to display a long camel-coloured coat and some expensive looking choker sparkling around its neck. These two had been brought into being to answer some desire of Steven's the algorithm had detected, no doubt. Eve approached them all, walking carefully over the wet rocks and sand. She'd chosen the beach as a peaceful, private place, out in the open. But the waves crashed noisily and gulls screeched overhead, tossed around by the wind.

Eve had explained the decreation process to them in the message she sent. She'd done it brutally and cruelly, assuming that their end was forbidden knowledge they did not know. She'd told them about the deleting of data, the dismantling and recycling of parts. She'd made it sound worse than it probably was, but it had got them here, hadn't it? They'd gathered, and they waited. It was clearly the first time they'd met each other. Eve smiled to see her internal conflicts made flesh: Work Eve could not stand to be too near the Eve meant for the task of relating to her mother – they looked like two different women, thrust together by circumstance, and it was clear these two would never be friends. But seeing them like this felt the way it sometimes felt to see the children playing together nicely, unaware of her presence. Being able to witness their private conversation and rituals – how they were when mother was not in the room – invoked a rush of tenderness in her.

"Hello," she called, still some way away now, but hurrying closer. The wind whipped away her voice and she slipped on a seaweed covered rock, hurt her wrist breaking her own fall, then righted herself and carried on. "Hello," she said, "hello, all you lot. It's me. I'm here."

Would they all also feel the rush of love she was feeling now? That gratitude, and understanding of their sometimes difficult and unattractive ways? They all only wanted the best for her, after all – and deserved much better than they were destined for. She'd planned to try to explain the situation. To soften the gruesome brutality of her earlier messages. To help them understand what they were and where the responsibility for living and directing a shared life as complex as theirs most appropriately lay. Finally, she'd propose a compromise, and ask each of them to work together on hammering out the details of it. They would have to take some kind of vote.

Let's be democratic about this, she'd planned to say. *Let's put our heads together.*

There would be some solution. Some rota system. Perhaps she could go back to the agency and give them more money. Take out a loan. Get each of the Eves to take out their own loan. They'd need to be more: the multiplicity of her could expand infinitely, Eve thought, giddily – populate a city with deputies and create one dark nothing at its centre where Eve herself could wait. They could (this last thought came reluctantly, and even as it flickered through her mind, she knew she didn't mean it, would never do it, would never ever give it up) even share the flat and take turns with the drudgery that took place outside of it.

★   ★   ★

Eve remained curious about what was left of herself until the very end. Curious at her own surprise that these women who were the best, most efficient and well adapted parts of herself would be as reluctant to release their grip on her life as she was to take it up again. Curious at the relief and – yes – even gratitude she felt as she finally reached them and saw, as they turned one by one to face her, they were all quite prepared and organised, each of them holding a large and jagged rock from the shore's edge.

Of course. Of course! They're going to stone me, Eve thought joyfully, and laughed.

The first rock struck her – hard – on the side of the head. There was no pain, only the sudden heat of her own blood swiping down the side of her face and neck like the stroke of an unseen hand across her skin. A blessing, really. Eve turned to watch the grey rocking surface of the sea as the beach rose up to meet her and the women, who continued to hurl their rocks, screamed to each other like gulls.

THE FORBIDDEN SANDWICH
Carl Tait

Dr. Melgar was crying again.

Gilbert heard the quiet sobs as he entered the room. The doctor was bent forward in his angular desk chair; a cheap and uncomfortable piece of furniture that matched the low-rent ethos of the nursing home. Dr. Melgar's elbow was perched precariously on the narrow arm of the chair, his hand covering his eyes. A few stray tears had leaked through his fingers and dripped onto the leg of his threadbare pyjamas.

Gilbert had been working at Slender Pines for several years and knew what to do. He placed a comforting hand on the doctor's back.

"I'm here with you, Dr. Melgar. My name is Gilbert. Is there anything I can do to help?"

Dr. Melgar lifted his head. His crying abruptly ceased. "Is it time for lunch yet?" he asked.

Gilbert was taken aback by the mundane nature of the question, but he answered calmly.

"Almost, sir. It's coming up on noon now."

The doctor nodded. "I was famous once, you know."

Gilbert knew. He also knew that Dr. Melgar suffered from early-onset dementia, so his random wanderings from one subject to another were to be expected.

"Yes, Dr. Melgar. You are a physicist, correct?" Gilbert was careful to use the present tense.

"A very great physicist, if I may be immodest. You have heard of the Melgar singularity, yes? That is mine. My discovery. My very great discovery. Like the space shuttle."

"The space shuttle?"

Dr. Melgar made an irritated clicking sound with his tongue.

"The Discovery is a space shuttle. Didn't they teach you that in school?"

"Yes, sir. So the Melgar singularity had to do with the Discovery space shuttle?"

"No, no. I was mentioning the shuttle because you young people find that sort of thing interesting. Where did you hear of the Melgar singularity? I discovered that, you know."

"I believe you may have mentioned it, sir."

Dr. Melgar nodded. "Perhaps. My mind is not what it was. The loss pains me greatly. Most of the time now, I just cry and wait for lunch."

"Is lunch important to you?"

"I keep worrying they will serve the Forbidden Sandwich."

"What is that?"

"It's a tomato sandwich with…ah, you nearly caught me. You NSA types are all alike. Trying to get me to reveal the secret ingredient."

Gilbert wasn't sure whether to nudge the doctor away from this odd subject or to humour him. He chose an intermediate option.

"I love tomato sandwiches," he replied.

"Aren't they delicious?" said Dr. Melgar, with simple happiness. "Blood-red tomatoes. White bread. The best mayonnaise. Salt and pepper. But if you add…my God, young man, you're good. You almost got me to tell you the secret part of the recipe."

Dr. Melgar's eyes were bulging. Gilbert tried to return the conversation to normalcy, or at least to its usual disjointed rambling.

"I'm not here to extract any secret recipe from you, doctor. Why don't you tell me about the Melgar singularity instead?"

"You can read the journal papers yourself. I wrote three of them. Three complex, groundbreaking papers in three months. Unheard of, they said. Impossible, said the research team. Time to punt, said the football team. That last part might be wrong. I don't understand football very well. When is lunch?"

"Soon, soon." Gilbert was more uncomfortable than he wanted to admit.

"I hope they picked the logarithms right at daybreak," the doctor said. "Otherwise, they'll be too sour."

He smacked his lips.

★ ★ ★

Gilbert glared at his painting and threw down his paintbrush in disgust.

Why couldn't he get it right? The man in his picture was supposed to be screaming in unhinged horror. Instead, he looked like a drunk at a bar struggling to hit a high note while singing karaoke.

Gilbert was an artist. That was his real job. His work at Slender Pines was intermittently rewarding, but its main purpose was to pay the bills while he established himself as a painter.

He had a natural talent for art. His mother had always said so, from the time of his earliest vague smears of paint on paper in elementary school. *Beautiful colour choices*, she had told him. *You're going to be an artist.*

Gilbert sighed. He had tried not to doubt himself, but years and years of polite, half-hearted compliments on his work had made this increasingly difficult. No one really liked his paintings. Sometimes he had trouble admiring them himself. The images in his mind proved to be disappointing when they materialised on his canvases.

He glanced at his watch. His girlfriend Kat would be arriving soon. She made an effort to say nice things about his paintings.

Gilbert went to his tiny kitchen and poured himself a glass of apple juice. He would have preferred bourbon but he didn't want Kat to think he was an alcoholic. He drank the juice slowly while staring at his failed painting with anger and shame.

The doorbell emitted a tinny buzz. *Even my doorbell stinks*, thought Gilbert as he went to answer it.

Kat's cheerful face refreshed him, as it always did. She gave him a quick peck on the cheek as she entered the cramped apartment. She caught sight of Gilbert's painting and stopped.

"Oh. That's nice," Kat said. "Really nice. I think it's one of your better pieces." She smiled.

Gilbert was encouraged. Kat's compliment was hardly a rave, but it sounded sincere. Maybe he had underestimated his work.

"Do you think Rand might be interested in taking a look?" he asked.

Kat's smile faltered and Gilbert realised it had probably been artificial to begin with.

"Not yet," she answered. "We've already talked about this. You'll need to have several outstanding paintings before Rand would consider showing them in his gallery."

Rand Putney ran an art gallery with a modest cachet. He and Kat had known each other since they were children. Gilbert reminded himself that this had nothing to do with his reasons for dating Kat.

"Well, do you think this might count as one of those outstanding paintings?"

Kat's smile was in tatters. "I suppose it might, once it's finished. But let's not talk about that now. We're going to be late for the movie."

They were going to see one of those dreary British period pieces. Gilbert found them tedious, but he wanted to make Kat happy. Solicitude and kindness were all he had to offer. His questionable artistic talent was not a significant asset.

Gilbert smiled faintly. "Let's go," he said.

★　★　★

An unfamiliar woman sporting a severe bun of grey hair extended her hand.

"I'm told your name is Gilbert," she said. "I'm Judith Melgar, Harold's wife."

"Pleased to meet you," answered Gilbert. "Your husband and I have had some interesting conversations."

Dr. Melgar was seated in his usual chair. He looked up and Gilbert was pleased to see a focused look in his eyes.

"I'm having one of my good days," the doctor said. "Judith sometimes brings that out in me. I'm not going to make any spectacular discoveries, but I might be able to hold a normal conversation. Given the circumstances, I count that as a notable accomplishment."

Judith's eyes were less focused than her husband's.

"Please forgive me for not visiting you more often. The last time I was here, you thought I was a Slender Pines nurse who was spying on you for the CIA. It was very troubling."

There was an awkward silence.

"I do what I can," said Dr. Melgar quietly. "I'm sorry I can't always follow what's going on, and I sometimes forget who people are. If you want me to apologise, I will. I'm sorry I ate the Forbidden Sandwich."

Mrs. Melgar let out an exasperated sigh.

"Harry, we've been over this more times than you've mistaken your caregivers for spies. There is no Forbidden Sandwich. That was just a silly legend that caught the attention of your otherwise brilliant mind."

"It sounded like a legend, but it turned out to be true."

"No. You had your breakthrough and you shot off fireworks like a Roman candle for a few months. Then something went wrong and your brain burned out. I'm sorry for putting it so bluntly, but you've got to stop thinking the stupid sandwich had anything to do with it."

"Excuse me," interjected Gilbert. "I'll give the two of you some privacy."

"No, no," said Dr. Melgar. "I want you to hear this, young man. I may never again be able to explain it this clearly." He smacked his lips and looked up at his wife.

"Judith, I am an extraordinarily rational person. I found the sandwich story entertaining but entirely implausible when the tour guide told us about it."

"I wish we'd never taken that trip." She glanced at Gilbert. "He wanted to visit the land of his ancestors in Appalachia."

"Beautiful country out there in western North Carolina," said Dr. Melgar. "Very old. Lots of secrets."

"Lots of superstitious drivel," Judith answered. "You insisted we visit a place called Mystery Towne."

"Towne with an E. I remember. Tourist-trap nonsense, but fun. Except for the sandwich."

"Except for your fixation on the sandwich. The guide was a dolt who was trying to impress the out-of-towners."

"I liked him, Judith. Poor fat kid without much of a future if he stayed in that little town, but he had theatrical flair."

"That's it exactly: hillbilly dinner theatre. Yet somehow you swallowed every morsel."

"The story was simple but compelling. A tomato sandwich, when laced with a certain secret ingredient, stimulates the mind in an inexplicable way, leading to uncanny brilliance. But the brilliance fades into darkness after a short time. Thus the sandwich is forbidden and has a carefully guarded recipe. The guide said the secret ingredient was something very common."

"Why did that fascinate you so much, Harry?"

"It was a good story. I love stories. And I'd sometimes wondered about the effect of certain foods on the brain."

"You're a physicist, not a biologist."

"Well, I still wondered. Oh, there was that final touch: once you've eaten the sandwich, you can never get the taste and feel of it out of your mouth. You'll certainly never want to eat another one."

"I thought the guide made that up on the spot because people were getting bored."

"Perhaps. Nonetheless, it was effective." He smacked his lips.

Judith shifted uneasily. "Then you started eating tomato sandwiches constantly when we got home. I didn't like that."

"I love tomato sandwiches. And it seemed harmless to experiment with different ingredients as a lark. Most of them were terrible. I can assure you the secret ingredient was neither peanut butter nor marshmallow whip. It also wasn't dirt, and it certainly wasn't logarithms. They're way too sour."

Judith looked at Gilbert in alarm. He shook his head sadly.

Dr. Melgar's eyes had lost their focus and were filling with tears.

"I finally found it," he said quietly. "It should have been obvious to me, of all people."

He rose from his chair.

"I found it!" he screamed. "And it was wonderful! And awful! Awful! AWFUL!"

He continued to scream the word until a pair of orderlies rushed in and poked a hypodermic needle into his arm.

*   *   *

Gilbert stared deep into his miserable painting, lost in the unfathomable problem of how to replicate Dr. Melgar's scream on the canvas. The howl still echoed in his mind, but the artistic equivalent remained as elusive as ever.

Growling, he put down his paintbrush. Maybe it would help if he learned more about Dr. Melgar and his work. *Do your own research*, he thought. The unofficial motto of self-important dilettantes everywhere.

The information he needed was easy to find on the internet. Harold C. Melgar, PhD, had been a solid but unexceptional physicist for most of his career. His breakthrough on the Melgar singularity had been both breathtaking and unexpected. Colleagues agreed he had a nimble mind, but several anonymous sources commented that Melgar lacked imagination and vision.

Could the Forbidden Sandwich have been responsible for the discovery? The question, which had been simmering in the back of Gilbert's mind all day, now came to a sudden boil. No, he thought; that's ridiculous.

Could he discover the secret recipe for the Forbidden Sandwich? He reassured himself there was no such recipe. The whole idea had been fabricated by a bored guide at a tawdry North Carolina tourist attraction.

Could it hurt to try? Gilbert had no ready answer. He loved tomato sandwiches. Why couldn't he try adding some odd ingredients, just for fun?

Dr. Melgar hadn't found that fun at all. Dr. Melgar wound up with a ruined mind, crying and screaming and chattering about sour logarithms.

Gilbert knew there was no connection with the sandwich. The doctor had physical deterioration in his brain; Gilbert had seen his chart. That was tragic but not mysterious.

But the uncharacteristic brilliant insights that had made him famous? Was it possible that a bizarre combination of flavours in a sandwich had given his thinking a productive sideways jangle? Unlikely, of course.

Gilbert took another look at his amateurish painting and made his decision. Unlikely or not, he was going to try.

He went into his micro-kitchen. His conversations with Dr. Melgar had brought back fond memories of tomato sandwiches and he already had the requisite ingredients on hand. The guide had said the secret ingredient was something very common, so Gilbert hoped he had that as well.

The experiments began. Gilbert might have claimed he was treating the enterprise with the lightness it deserved, but his intense, methodical approach belied any claims of frivolity. Sandwiches were prepared and quartered to maximise the number of ingredients that could be tested.

Oregano: no, though the sandwich was tasty. Garlic: no. Baking soda: absolutely not. Chocolate pudding: not even close.

As he prepared the next sandwich, Gilbert brushed his hair back from his face. A detached strand found its way into his mouth. Gilbert sawed his tongue against his upper teeth in desperation, smacking his lips as his tongue darted in and out. He couldn't get rid of the hair.

It hit him all at once. A feel you can't get out of your mouth. Dr. Melgar's lip smacking. The doctor's insistence that the secret ingredient should have been obvious to him, of all people.

Harold Melgar. Harry.

Hairy.

Could the secret ingredient be hair?

Gilbert had never before had an intellectual epiphany and he enjoyed the exhilarating sensation. He grabbed a pair of scissors from the counter and snipped off a generous chunk of hair from each side of his head. *I needed a haircut anyway*, he thought wildly. He took a full, unquartered sandwich and sprinkled his hair all over the tomatoes, slathering on some extra mayonnaise in an effort to lessen the revolting appearance. Gilbert put the top piece of bread in place and took an enormous bite of the sandwich before he could change his mind. He chewed vigorously.

The sensation was appalling. A mouthful of slimy hair mixed with partially masticated tomatoes. Gilbert thought he might vomit. The prickly hairs infuriated his tongue and poked angrily at the roof of his mouth.

Poke, poke. Tickle, tickle. Sour tomatoes. Creamy mayonnaise. Spongy bread as a substrate.

Something was happening. Something wonderful. Something wonderful and awful.

Gilbert saw it.

He saw his painting as it should be, still fuzzy through a shimmering haze.

He took another bite of the dreadful sandwich. And another. With each bite, the vision of his painting grew sharper.

Gilbert finished the sandwich, swallowing the last bite with a mixture of nausea and wonder.

He saw.

★   ★   ★

The bright shaft of light cutting across his sofa pulled Gilbert's attention away from his painting. He turned with annoyance to inspect the distraction.

A sunbeam. Sunlight was leaking through his blinds. It was morning and he had been painting all night. He briefly worried about being late for work before remembering it was Saturday.

Gilbert turned back to his painting and shuddered anew at what he had created. A snarling, agonised mouth. Scorched flesh. Mutilated digits of some kind. A vast caliginous abyss he would have been utterly incapable of painting a day earlier.

Gilbert smacked his lips. The sandwich was still with him, as he suspected it always would be. The sensations were maddening, but Gilbert would willingly have suffered far more grievous discomfort to acquire the dark visions that now filled his mind.

The painting was complete. His pathetic earlier version had served as a useful first draft, letting him slash his finished masterwork onto the same canvas in a single frenzied overnight session.

Masterwork. He had used the word without thinking. In the past, he had applied the term to his own paintings only with rueful sarcasm. This time, he believed the expression might be accurate.

Gilbert needed a new canvas for his next painting, which was already clawing at his brain in its hunger to be realised. More mundane matters had to come first. He began by standing up, against the protest of muscles that had been tensely focused for too many hours. Then showering. Eating breakfast. He half-hoped that conventional food would cleanse the crawly feeling from his mouth, though he was not surprised when the sensation failed to dissipate.

Gilbert walked briskly to the small art supply store down the block. He had planned to purchase additional paint and one more canvas, but he now felt that a single canvas would be only one brick in the long road he envisioned.

"You want six of the twenty-by-twenty-four-inch canvases all at once?" the young clerk asked, raising his bushy eyebrows. "Man, you usually don't go through that many in a year."

"I need six," Gilbert repeated.

The clerk shrugged and wandered into the back room. He returned balancing a stack of plastic-wrapped canvases and laid them gently on the counter next to Gilbert's assortment of oil paints and brushes.

"You need a glass of water?" the clerk asked. "Sounds like your mouth is dry."

"No, thanks," said Gilbert, gathering his purchases. He tried to keep his mouth closed as he flicked his tongue across his teeth.

Back at home, Gilbert set his art supplies on the floor near his easel and was immediately overcome with fatigue. Sleep, he told himself. The sandwich says it's okay to sleep for a while. He retreated to his bedroom and fell into the unmade bed.

The pattern continued all weekend. Long, manic sessions of painting. A bit of food and drink. A few hours of sleep, tortured by relentless nightmares. Repeat.

When his doorbell rang on Sunday evening, Gilbert cried out with surprise.

"Gilbert? Are you all right?" called a voice from the hall.

Kat. He had completely forgotten. They had planned to have Thai food before seeing a crushingly dull movie on animal migration.

He manoeuvred his way to the door, carefully skirting his first painting, which he had propped on a shelf to dry. He opened the door and tried to meet Kat's smile with one of his own.

"Gilbert, what's wrong? You look like you've hardly slept."

"I'm fine," he said. "Come and see."

He stepped aside and Kat saw.

She stood motionless, frozen. Gilbert wanted to paint her in exactly that attitude, perhaps with the ragged claws of an unnameable creature reaching out from the darkness towards her face.

"My God," she said. "My God."

"Do you like it?"

She was silent for a moment before answering. "'Like' isn't the right word. I am overwhelmed by it. This is a brutal, eviscerating painting. And it is quite wonderful."

Gilbert walked over to his easel and turned it around to face Kat.

"This is my second one. It's not done yet, but the heart of it is here."

Kat's head swivelled. Her hand went to her mouth. Gilbert heard her shuddering gasp.

"That one is even worse. By which I mean better. I don't know if I can look at it for very long, but I do know it is a stunning work. Let me call Rand." She pulled out her phone.

"Wait, wait," Gilbert said. "Didn't you say I had to have several outstanding paintings before he would look at my art?"

"Yes, I did say that. I didn't want you to embarrass yourself. But now...it's different. Something has happened. Rand would very much want to see these."

"Not yet."

"Why? I thought you were desperate to have him look at your paintings."

Gilbert took time to cringe at the word 'desperate' before he answered.

"There's more," he said simply. "I have a few more images in my mind, but I need time to paint them. I have a lot of unused vacation time at Slender Pines and I'm going to lock myself in here and do nothing but work on my art."

"How long do you need?"

Gilbert considered. "Three weeks."

"I guess we're not going out tonight."

"No. I'm sorry."

"You're not sorry, but that's all right. You're full of fire and you need to spew it out."

Gilbert nodded gravely as he closed the door.

*　　*　　*

The ecstasy of the following three weeks restored the colour to Gilbert's faded worldview. No more monotonous drudgery of working and sleeping, with an occasional lackadaisical session of painting thrown in. Instead, Gilbert was able to turn himself inward to meditate on his ideas and realise them in vivid and disturbing ways in his art.

His style was changing. He could sense the condensation, the distillation to essentials. He was restricting the number of elements in each painting, relying on his increasingly refined eye to build subtle distinctions within a narrower range. Every completed painting was better than the last, in his view.

As the end of his artistic marathon approached, Gilbert found himself slowing down. He had completed six paintings – his original one-night wonder and five more – and decided that was enough. Kat and Rand would be coming to see the collection the following afternoon and Gilbert gave himself an evening of rest.

He slept for sixteen hours, awakening only an hour before his guests' arrival. He showered and dressed hurriedly, then worked on setting up his six paintings to present the strongest possible effect. He decided to arrange them in the order of their creation, ending with the nightmarish piece of minimalism he considered his finest work.

His doorbell buzzed its annoying buzz and he went to answer it. Kat's smile glowed. By her side stood a man whom Gilbert had met only once, at a cocktail party.

"Gilbert, you remember Rand Putney, my old friend. Rand, I've told you about the paintings that…" She trailed off. Rand was staring fixedly over Gilbert's shoulder and had stopped paying attention to everything else. Gilbert moved aside to give him a better view.

Rand's focus shifted from one painting to the next, down the row and back again. Kat stepped inside and gently pulled Rand along with her. Gilbert closed the door behind them.

Rand finished his survey and spoke.

"You have some extraordinary pieces here. I rarely see work that is simultaneously so visceral and so beautifully executed. Congratulations."

Gilbert grinned. "Thank you. I thought you would like to see the full progression of my work."

"I understand," Rand said. "But one needs to be selective."

"In what way?"

"Assuming these end up in my gallery, I believe it is best to leave the three weaker pieces behind. They are much less successful."

Gilbert felt that his moment of triumph had been tarnished. He spoke carefully.

"The first three paintings are my earlier works. I agree they are lesser accomplishments, but I still believe they are strong pieces. Kat was quite taken with the first two when she saw them a few weeks ago."

He glanced at Kat for confirmation but she looked confused.

"Of course the first three paintings are strong," said Rand. "I assumed that's why you put them first. It's the last three that are, frankly, rather poor. I thought you simply wanted to show me some of the work that led up to the brilliance of those first three."

Gilbert felt defensive, as if a stranger had insulted his children. He tried to tamp down his anger, but it refused to be contained.

"'Rather poor'?" said Gilbert in quiet fury. "I'm sorry, but you're wrong. They are my most recent work and are easily the best of the set. Especially the last one, which is an immensely powerful minimalist statement. I don't believe you have looked closely enough."

Rand squinted his eyes. "I have seen a great deal of art and I can assure you that the last painting in particular is an inferior work. If that's the way you're painting now, I question my decision in coming to see your art."

"You can leave any time you like." Gilbert smacked his lips defiantly.

Rand's mouth twisted.

"Gilbert, your first three paintings are enormously good. I do not say that lightly. If you can produce more work like that, I will be happy to talk about showing your paintings. For the moment, though, we're done. Kat, we'll talk soon."

Rand turned and left.

Kat's expression was full of pain.

"Gilbert, what happened? Is this a twisted joke? That last piece is dreadful. Even the paintings you used to do were better than that."

Gilbert was more successful in controlling his anger with Kat than he had been with Rand.

"Kat, I need to think for a bit. Why don't you go get us some Thai food? We were going to have that on our date."

Kat tried to steady herself. "Okay. You like the massaman curry with chicken, right?"

"Yeah. Just come on in when you get back. I'll leave the door unlocked."

Kat left without saying another word.

★   ★   ★

The last painting. Gilbert stood in front of it, admiring its blackened twists and curves. He shook his head and turned to walk towards the kitchen. He glanced back for one more look.

No. Impossible.

For a moment, he saw the painting exactly as Rand and Kat had seen it. The shapeless black scribbles of an angry child. Haphazard writhing swirls. *Terrible colour choices*, his mother said in his mind.

He closed his eyes and looked again. His monochromatic masterpiece was back. Wasn't it? He blinked slowly and the childish scrawl reappeared.

Gilbert experienced his second intellectual epiphany. This one was excruciating.

He finally understood the Forbidden Sandwich. It condensed and enhanced a person's greatest strength. Melgar's mind. His own artistic vision. But the turbocharged condensation was short-lived, and it permanently damaged the cherished ability. Melgar ended up with dementia; Gilbert had lost his artistic sense. What could he do?

Eat another Forbidden Sandwich.

Dr. Melgar was terrified he might accidentally eat another sandwich because it would destroy the remnants of his rational thought. In Gilbert's case, there was no barrier. He had already lost his artistic vision except in brief flashes that were more painful than not seeing artistically at all. He didn't care if he lost those flashes.

Gilbert went into his kitchen and prepared the sandwich. The bread had a few spots of mould and the tomatoes were getting mushy, but Gilbert didn't care. He scissored off a tuft of hair from above each of his ears and pressed the hair into the tomatoes. He didn't bother with extra mayonnaise.

Gilbert picked up the sandwich and devoured it.

After a moment, he began to scream.

*   *   *

Kat was coming down the hallway when she heard the screams. She rushed to Gilbert's door and threw it open. She dropped the take-out bag on the floor and ran to the kitchen, where the screaming continued.

Gilbert was lying on the floor. His hands were over his face and one of his feet was bare. He had kicked off a shoe in his agony.

"Gilbert! What is it?"

He removed his hands from his face.

Clumps of coarse black hair were growing out of his eyes. Kat saw a flash of white at the base of each thicket and realised the hair must have grown through his eyeballs.

"Kat! Help me!"

Kat knelt beside him, struggling to control her nausea.

"I'm here with you, Gilbert."

He screamed again. Kat leaned in more closely and saw why.

The hair was still growing. It swayed gently, as if blown by an impalpable breeze from an eldritch place.

AUTUMN SUGAR

Philip Fracassi

The boy's name is Sam. The missing dog – the family dog – is named Tucker, a Springer Spaniel with shaggy, chocolate-patched fur often tangled with bits of leaves and snapped twigs after a spirited run around the Jones's wild acreage, a domain of half-tamed grass and thin woodland that partially encircles the cream-sided two-storey Garrison Colonial, the only home Sam and Tucker have ever known. But now Tucker is nowhere to be found and Sam, only six years old, grows tired of searching. Of calling: *Tucker! Tuuu – cker! Come here, come here boy!* He's hot inside his blue jeans and wool sweater, annoyed how the coarse collar itches and irritates the sweaty skin at the back of his neck.

Fatigued, he sits heavily beneath the naked, wiry branches of a sugar maple, breathing hard through doll-like lips, his cherubic face dappled with crawling shadow. Around him stands the hemline of an urban forest filled with fat old maples and gnarled oaks, the dark canvas occasionally broken by a spattering of white-barked birch. Only a few weeks prior these trees were alive and vibrant, bursting with hair the colours of fire – bright orange and deep crimson, flares of mustard yellow. Now the hard-barked pillars that surround him shoot from the earth crowned only with a tangle of bare limbs, wretched bent arms reaching toward a flaccid sky in futile agony, desperate to touch the aquamarine pate, demanding their colour be returned.

But that silent, distant sun droops listlessly toward earth, weary as an old man reaching the end of a long walk. The deepening red an alarm signalling the dying of the day.

Sam lets his hands rest on the grass between splayed legs – small fingers toying with the star-patterned points of a crisp maple leaf – and stares up into the thickening blue. The hazy cycloptic eye of the interloper moon glares down, out of place in the late afternoon, boldly sharing the sky with its sallow counterpart. The sight of it confuses Sam. He knows – has been told – that the moon only shines in the *night-time*, and its appearance throws him off balance, disturbs his way of thinking, pricks holes in his self-assurance of knowing the truth of things.

He will ask his father about this new burden, about the day-moon, and about the whereabouts of Tucker. All in a moment, after he cools off a bit, when his racing heart no longer thunders in his ears.

★   ★   ★

"Why did you have to yell at him?"

Charles rests his rear end against the countertop's edge, arms folded defensively tight against his chest. His gaze pierces the old hardwood kitchen floor, searching for rationale in age-darkened cracks, hoping to find answers among the punctured black eyes of ancient nail heads.

I didn't really yell.

I've been working too hard.

He surprised me, that's all.

"I don't know," he says, settling for honesty. He shakes his head, lifts his eyes to meet the stern, beautiful face of his wife. "I don't know," he repeats, feeling stupid, but grateful for this feeling of humiliation, mistaking it for conscience.

Margaret and Charles have been together nearly a decade. What was seeded in Southern California, amid her failed acting career and his night-time profession as an uninspired bartender, eventually took root in the Northeast, at the house his father left them, where their child was born, where their respective, hard-earned professions as a public relations director for a local television station (her) and the manager of a semi-exclusive dining club (him) pumped oxygen into the shrunken lungs of their lives, and together – all of them, together – breathed deeply, as if for the first time.

"He's just a little boy, a funny little boy who wants to run and yell and spin and dance…" She stops, wanting to go on, to describe all the things her boy does. "And sometimes he makes a mistake."

Charles nods and nods. "I know. I'm sorry. I'm gonna… Look, baby, I need to go finish the leaves. When I do…" He rubs at his face, the scratch of growth on his cheeks and chin, feels older than his thirty-some years.

"I thought you finished the leaves yesterday."

"I...yeah, I raked 'em, honey, and I dragged them to the clearing. But I gotta burn the pile today. Too damn windy yesterday, that smoke..."

"You men and your fires, I swear. Just throw them out with the trash. It's what the neighbours do."

Charles debates explaining how long and arduous a task it would be to bag their autumn refuse every season. But he lets it alone, something he's grown quite good at: leaving arguments alone. Letting them dissolve and flow away like a rotten smell, a wisp of hot smoke. Charles can't tell his wife that, when he was a kid, he'd watch his dad rake a burn for hours, and how, when it was good and controlled, the two of them would sit at a distance and watch the pile smoke and whisper and spark. He can't tell her how close he felt to his father in those times, or how the smell of burning leaves – what his dad called autumn sugar, because there was a sweetness underneath the sharp stench of soot – brought an *aliveness* to the thick autumn air, a physical pulse to the heavy column of black smoke; how that smoke swarmed with hot dancing sparks that made him think of his boys' encyclopaedia of outer space, filled with pictures of stars born deep within a galactic cloud within a faraway, chaotic nebula. The fire didn't smell of life – not exactly – but the boy Charles once was thought it carried the heady aroma of creation, as if he and his father were sitting together, shoulder-to-shoulder in the grass, at the start of all things, watching the universe burn into being.

"Anyway, I'm gonna finish," he says, feeling sullen, distant from all things that mattered. From his father, from that inspired little boy. "Then I'll find Sam and we'll have a talk. I'm sure he's playing by the creek." He turns away from her, focuses his stare out the thin glass of the windows – *the original glass, the original frames*, he thinks proudly, without reason. "I'll go find him. We'll have a chat about, hell, about..."

"Not breaking your shit?" his wife says.

But he knows, without turning, that she's smiling, one eyebrow playfully arched. Happy that her husband is soft, that he's pliable. That he's the kind of father who *talks* to his son after a fight, after a misunderstanding. A modern father who believes in hugs rather than the belt. To make him feel...

"Yeah," he says, and reaches his hand behind him where she can clasp it with her own, her fingers safe and warm. "About not breaking my shit."

*   *   *

I'm sorry, Daddy.

The thought floats out of his head and up, up into the leafless branches high above, where it tangles like drifting spider silk, wraps and sticks.

Sam is unsure of himself. Unsure of what to do. Find Tucker? Go back inside the house? Find his dad and...

Sorry. Say you're sorry.

He shakes his head. He's afraid. Confused. He hated the yelling, how mad his father was. But what he hated most was the look in his daddy's eyes.

Loveless. Empty. Hateful.

Sam cried when he saw that look – had screamed at the pain of it as if burned – hardly hearing the words his father bellowed as he stood, lifting the wet computer, pushing Sam away, pushing him *hard*...and then...

It was the *look* that undid him, that brought the tears, made him run run run from the room, screaming and crying and then pushing through the screen door and bursting outside, into the massive backyard. Tucker had followed at a sprint, excited, barking, not understanding. Thinking it was a game, maybe. A game of running. Of chasing. Of hiding.

And Sam, being a boy with a young boy's elastic mind and volatile emotions, soon forgot about the laptop, about his dad's angry words, that hateful glare, and instead began to run after Tucker. Laughing. Screaming with joy as the young spaniel turned and lunged at his feet, snarling playfully, the dog's body shivering with the excitement of play. Of freedom. Love unfiltered.

But then Tucker had stopped, cocked his head, as if he'd heard something Sam could not. Then the dog had run away, run into the trees, toward the little creek that passed through the woods, where Sam and his mom once built a dam, like beavers. Afterward they'd knocked it down, laughing while ankle-deep, and Sam remembered how very cold the water was on his bare feet and the feeling of *life* the river gave him as the water flowed past, and he imagined it was also laughing; rippling reflections dancing in the dazzling sunlight. He'd become lightheaded and then they released the stacked wood and watched it leap into the stream's eager flow…rolling, spinning, flying away, away.

And now, beneath the tall trees, their limbs gold-tinged by a warped halo of dying sun – and with the sly one-eyed moon peeking through overhead – Sam weighs his options, surrounded by the scatter, the leftover remnants of shattered leaves.

★   ★   ★

Charles steps into the cool dusk. He wears a Carhartt jacket the colour of old canvas, stained and roughened from a decade of service, and a pair of broken, bone-white leather gloves, the webbed grooves between each finger bruised black by use. A blue ballcap is pulled low over his forehead, work boots laced over denim cuffs. He walks doggedly toward the shed, which won't last three more winters, already sagging and rotted at the wide-planked seams (last summer's whitewash doing little to improve its position as a long-term resident of their homestead).

As Charles trudges toward the old shed, he replays the events of that morning in his mind.

Having already wasted a good portion of his day working up a budget for the owners of Mackenzie Hall, the spreadsheet filled with best guesses for the upcoming quarter, he'd been mentally buried in numbers when Sam appeared from nowhere, yelling an incoherent cry of joyous ferocity and jumping into his lap, in doing so bumping the legs of the table (and scaring the shit out of his father). Charles's hand had jerked, knocking over a glass and spilling a pint of light beer over the keys of his MacBook, where the suds fizzled between letters and numbers like acid on flesh.

"Sam! Goddammit!" he'd screamed, leaping to his feet, grabbing the laptop from the table and turning it over, shaking the beer out of whatever circuitry lay buried beneath the plastic surface, away from whatever made the thing *work*. The beer pooled on the smooth wood of the mahogany table before gently pointing its way – like a budding stream – toward the edge, where it dribbled over onto Margaret's antique Oriental rug (the Great Splurge from a farmer's market auction three years prior – the edges a floral border encased in beige, the rectangular middle red and ripe as a human heart centred by an ornate mandala, which the seller told them represented universal consciousness).

What his wife doesn't know – what she can *never* know – is that Charles (instinctively and without malice or forethought) had struck out at his son with the back of one beer-drenched hand. His knuckles smacked the child's soft temple, connected with enough force to send the boy face-down to the ground. Sam flipped over and looked up at his father, his only father, one palm pressed to the point of attack, blue eyes wide with horror, pain. Betrayal.

Charles, stupidly holding the dripping laptop, went pale. "Sam," he said.

But then Sam had jumped to his feet and ran, ran howling through the hollow-roomed old Colonial like a banshee through the corridors of a Gothic castle, a spectre made of stomping feet and cries of pain, chest-tearing bellows of impossible, unforgivable loss.

Now, after the passing of a few healing hours, he must mend the broken fence, the link of trust between him and his boy. But first he must finish the day's work. He must…

The shed's loose-hinged door creaks open as he steps inside and up onto the duckboard floor, distractedly brushing away a cobweb tickling his cheek as he reaches for the sturdy garden rake, hung on rusted hooks against the tool wall, then plucks a yellow metal can from a worm-eaten shelf, the liquid inside sloshing to-and-fro, as if awakening.

★ ★ ★

Sam hears the screen door open and slap shut, the squeaking hinges a bird call, as welcoming and familiar as hearing his own name. From behind a jagged line of trees he watches his father step into the dusky light and walk brusquely toward the teetering shed, away from the house, away from him.

He waits for his dad to stop and look around, cup a hand to his mouth and yell: *SAM!*

Anticipating this call, Sam nervously grips the coarse bark of the tree he hides behind, waiting…waiting…

But then his father is gone, slipping into nothingness beyond the shed.

He's going to the leaf pile. Sam steps away from the tree to better see the distant clearing, ignores the icy teeth of the wind nibbling at his cheeks, its slim cold fingers curling around the back of his neck where the skin is chafed, but now dry. His heart has calmed down, doesn't bounce against his ribs like a thing caged, a swollen and heavy THUMP THUMP THUMP in his chest. Now that he's cooled off, it's as if his heart has disappeared completely – comfortably vanished, leaving him clean and empty. The feeling carries to his mind, dulling the memory of his father's rebuke, of striking him in the face, knocking him down. With the passage of time, Sam is able to think clearly of his daddy's heated, hateful eyes, as if from a great distance, with an adult's understanding that it had only been a *moment*, not a life.

Because life is not a single moment but all the other things – the love, the warmth, the eternity of goodnights and good mornings, the small kisses and the long hugs. The protection. The always being there.

Sam has a mad, painful rush of affection for his parents; a burst of such strong, raw emotion that he feels like soaring, flying across the earth to them, shouting out that *he's home!* That he's ready to be forgiven. That he's ready to be loved.

Then, as if whispered to him by the fat, full moon, an idea springs into Sam's head. A funny, wonderful idea of how he can win back his father's affection, make things right again. Like they used to be – not in one lost moment, but in life. In *his* life.

Grinning, Sam scampers through the trees, careful to be quiet, to stay behind the tree line so his father will not see where he's going, where he will hide. And then, when his dad comes close, comes to do the work, Sam will leap out, and maybe he will *ROAR,* bare finger-claws; or maybe he will run and jump into his kneeling father's chest who will catch him and hold him and lift him, and together – *together* – they will go home and it will all be okay.

It will be perfect.

*   *   *

Margaret calls for Sam from the back door. Charles turns from his work, sweat beading his temples, and leans his weight on the worn handle of the rake. From a distance, Margaret appears to him as a doll, a living doll inside a child's toy playhouse. So idyllic do they appear, this petite woman in her green sweater and dark blue jeans, a bright red scarf in her raven hair, the house seemingly unblemished by time, without rot, without decay. A flawlessness made true by the soft haze of burgeoning twilight.

He squints and his gaze leaves his wife, wanders the giant yard, the scattered beginnings of the woods that stretch back acres, some of it their land, most of it owned by the state, but left alone. A reserve.

Charles frowns at the darkening sky, the trees now rife with an army of shadows. *Sam knows not to go past the creek,* he assures himself. The creek is the boy's boundary when playing outside alone, one he never crossed. Not to Charles's knowledge, anyway. He'd been raised well, after all. He'd been...

"Sam!" he bellows, not from fear, or anxiety. Only wanting to help. To parent. To be a *good* father, a *good* husband.

Margaret stands across the breadth of the yard as if pacing an opposing shoreline, the sea a blanket of thick Kentucky bluegrass; the expanse a rising swell of blue-green between their two bodies, a rolling wave of stretched hillock that protrudes along the rear of the property. Charles once joked that it must have been an old burial mound...

"Charles! It's getting dark!"

He lifts a weary, gloved hand and nods, showing that he understands the newfound severity of the situation. His wife turns and goes abruptly into the house.

Annoyed with me. With my damned temper. With her adventurous son.

He sighs, looks around the yard once more, watches the reddening sun cut through its middle, clinging to the horizon as if struggling against the oncoming night, the cunning moon, lengthening the already long shadows stretched like taffy from the trees. "Sam!" he yells, and in the distance hears barking.

"Tucker?" An unwelcome flutter fills his chest. A jingling bell of worry, the early pangs of panic. "Shit," he says, surprised to see the white mist of his breath. He sets the rake against the low cinderblock wall surrounding the burn patch and heads for the sound.

As he walks toward the woods, he calls for the dog. The barking comes and goes but doesn't appear to be moving, and Charles can't help but wonder what the dog is going on about. Maybe he's chased a raccoon up a tree, or a woodchuck into its winter burrow.

Or maybe he found Sam. Maybe the boy is hurt. Or face-down in the creek, head bloodied, cracked open by a wet rock when he'd slipped, slipped and fallen, and was even now breathing in the rough cold water.

"Sam! Tucker!" Charles quickens his pace toward the trees.

★   ★   ★

As Sam watched his father rake leaves into a giant pile, he once more debated going home. Forgetting the game.

He'd remained quiet when his mom called for him, felt bad ignoring her, for pretending not to hear. Instead, he stayed hunched behind the little wall next to the clearing while his dad worked the rake, piling the leaves he'd brought over the day before.

Now Sam waits, quiet and unmoving – not even daring to breathe – as his father walks off toward the woods, calling for him, calling for Tucker. That's when he knows it's time.

He climbs up and over the low wall of scratchy cinderblocks, crawls across the dirt and ploughs head-first into the massive pile, as broad and tall as any he's ever seen.

Upon entering the dark pyre, the leaves whisper crossly in his ears, as if angered, or disturbed. But he ignores their complaints and crawls deeper, the sickly-sweet aroma filling his senses as leaves crumble to mush and powder beneath his pudgy, dirty palms and hard knees; cling to the rough fabric of his sweater, fill his hair.

Finally he stops, deep enough to not be seen when his father returns.

It's dark beneath the pile and his eyes sting so he closes them tight. His breathing is heavy. There's a sick feeling in his stomach from inhaling the cloying, syrupy taste of the air, thick with the aroma of ripe decay. But his dad will be back soon, and then he will spring from the pile and surprise him. They'll laugh like madmen, best friends once more, then go inside for dinner. Later, they'll read another chapter of their night-time book, a story Sam adores, filled with pirates and magic and great adventure. They'll lie together in his bedroom, the room his mother painted the colour of a summer sky, decorated with fluffy white clouds high up along the walls; always floating, floating…

A few minutes pass and Sam allows himself to sink sideways into the densely-packed leaves, which catch his weight easily, happily. They are barely whispering now, no longer upset. Just tired.

Relax, Sam, they say as they absorb him, cushion his small body like a pillow, like the soft, perfumed hand of God. *Relax now.*

★   ★   ★

Margaret is chopping potatoes when Charles comes into the kitchen. His face is rugged with exertion, darkened by a shadow of beard he will shave clean in the morning before he goes to the club. His eyes are dark, as if brooding, or lost.

"Did you find him?" she asks, focusing on her task, feigning apathy. Margaret doesn't want to be one of those young mothers. The ones who over-worry. The ones with only one child who carry around a fraught disposition like a cheap purse.

"No," he says. "But I did rescue a jackrabbit Tucker trapped inside a Maple hollow. I had to chase the dog across half the damn yard before catching him. Tied him up by the shed, gave him a few of the biscuits."

"Jesus, Charles, what about Sam?"

"Relax, I'll find him. You worry too much."

Margaret says nothing to this. The sound of the knife hitting the wooden cutting board – THUMP THUMP THUMP – fills the small room like a dying heart.

Outside, by the shed, Tucker is barking to raise hell.

"Anyway, just came in for a beer. Gonna go watch the burn. I used a little fluid…" He smiles sadly. "My father would have hated that."

Margaret nods, not liking the currents of despair beneath his words. "Dinner will be ready in a half-hour. Please find Sam while you're out there, you know…" she waves the knife through the air pointedly, "watching your manly inferno."

As she goes back to cutting, she says: "And for what it's worth, I think your father would be proud."

Charles smiles, kisses his wife softly behind the ear, enjoying the way her neck reddens in pleasure. "You know, sometimes I think he's still here. Lingering. Watching me. Us. A lonely old man…"

"Please don't be morbid," Margaret says.

He puts his arms around her waist, squeezes her tight. "You should grab a beer and join me. It's a beautiful night."

"Maybe I will," she says. "I just want to get the meat in the oven and then we'll see. Now go on, before you torch the whole forest."

But Charles is already halfway out the door.

Margaret turns, face strained, and watches him through the wavy glass of the old window, walking away across the humped mound of green grass, through the twilight, toward a rising pillar of black smoke that she knows, from experience, reeks of death.

In the window's reflection she sees a small shadow standing behind her, hovering at the kitchen door. "You better get cleaned up," she says.

But the shadow does not move, and does not answer.

"Sam?" she says, and frowns, the air sour, thick with the stench of burnt leaves.

COLLAGEN

Seanan McGuire

The vertebrate body is a miracle. Cells self-organising into organs and tissues, specialising themselves according to the needs of the body at each specific stage of its development, growing from a single zygote into a fully functional, independent organism. While there may or may not have been a divine spark behind the origins of evolution, the body itself is a miraculous thing, and deserves to be appreciated as such.

The miraculous is also present in the invertebrate world, in every cellular organism, from the simplest algae to the most complex mammal. It binds them together, tissue to tissue, membrane to membrane, connecting the animal world. Present in all things.

Miraculous.

★　★　★

Maybe it started with a virus, although if it did, it was something subtle enough to be overlooked, some minor infection that everyone passed around like the broccoli at a church supper before they even realised they'd gotten sick. A little tickle in the back of the throat, a little softness in the stool, and then you're feeling fine and hearty and completely unaware of what's brewing deep down in your guts, masked by a hundred layers of immune response and biological process.

Or maybe the conspiracy theorists are right, and it started as a weapon somebody slapped together in a lab somewhere, thinking they'd finally figured out the way to win the next war, and the one after that for good measure. If that's the case, I hope the architects are still around to be proud of themselves, because they did it. They won the next war. They won all the wars, forever and ever, all the way to the end of history.

Which, if my guesses are correct, is about seventy-two hours from now.

I think the most likely answer is somewhere in the middle. I don't think it was a weapon. I think it was the consequences of our choices coming back to bite us on our aging asses.

See, what I think happened – and it matters because I'm still here to write this down, when almost nobody else is, when I probably shouldn't be wasting the time or taking the risk of the small impact of my fingers on the keys – what I think happened is that we spent decades telling people they were only as valuable as their youth. Women, especially, but everyone when you really stopped and looked at the messages we were sending. And they were global. Beauty standards might change by country and culture, but the idea that youth was wasted on the young, that a person's value was measured in the smoothness of their skin, that grew and grew and grew.

If you did something early enough, you were a genius, a prodigy, and the world would shower you in riches for the chance to hear the next pearl of impossible brilliance that dropped from your lips. If you didn't, if you wrote a perfect novel or painted a perfect painting, but didn't do it until you were thirty-one, you were a has-been before you even got the chance to be.

It was worst for the women. Women were expected to be effortlessly thin and beautiful, even if their professions had nothing to do with thinness or beauty, their faces unlined and their hands unwrinkled, and oh, didn't we build an industry around making that possible? Didn't we build a dozen? Diet industries to sell you skinny in food made from designer molecules the body couldn't figure out digesting, fitness industries to make you feel like any amount of skinny wasn't quite skinny enough, and endless cosmetic industries to make sure you knew exactly how hideous and *wrong* your skin was. We sold creams to reverse the effects of aging, and serums to rebuild collagen in the skin, trying to convince people that every seventy-year-old could have the complexion of a dewy-eyed seventeen-year-old if they'd only try hard enough.

We sold and we sold and we sold, and people bought and bought and bought. They bought by the gallon, by the tanker, by the ton. They slathered themselves in liquid youth, chasing the impossible, and when it didn't work, they washed it off, right down the drain, on to the next miracle.

Which miracle was it? Fucked if I know. But it must have been one of the more successful ones, the ones that made enough of a splash that they were sold globally, and to a whole lot of people. Probably something with a celebrity spokesperson or high-profile influencer at the helm, standing there and smiling with all their porcelain teeth as they swore that one little jar would make you look just like them. Promising to change the world.

Guess they did that much.

So yeah, logically, I'm going to call it a skin serum gone wrong, something that sold enough that when people washed it off their hands, it built up in the water. It went from the sewers to the seas, and from the seas to…well.

You know where it went from there.

★   ★   ★

A lot of people have wasted a lot of time arguing about where it started, as if we can see that far back. But where it started to become *visible* was in the aquariums.

It was the jellyfish.

Jellyfish are both surprisingly sturdy and surprisingly easy to kill. The wrong salinity in the tank and they're done for. The wrong level of filtration and you're dealing with dead jellyfish everywhere. But for all that they're animate plastic bags possessed by the malevolent spirit of an elemental force of pain, they still exist. What kid with access to a coastal beach hasn't seen a jellyfish washed up, looking like a clump of snot on the sand? When they die, they leave bodies behind. They don't get to opt out of the mortal coil.

Until they did. Marine biologists and hobbyists with home aquariums alike began waking up and finding that their jellyfish were just…gone. Not in their tanks. Nowhere to be found. Oh, there might be a thin protean slurry at the bottom of the enclosure, depending on how strong the filters were, but the jellyfish themselves had basically dissipated, like bubbles in the water.

Jellyfish protein consists almost entirely of collagen. Collagen and water, that's a jellyfish, and not much else. An undifferentiated protein slurry. Nothing to get excited about.

Except that we *should* have been getting excited about it. Maybe if we'd gotten excited when it was just a few disappearing jellyfish, we would have been able to isolate the problem and resolve it before it could become a global catastrophe. I don't think so, however. Jellyfish play a major role in the global food chain. Everything eats jellies. Fish, sea turtles, dolphins, if it's in the ocean, it eats jellyfish, and then – because humans are apex predators who own giant fishing boats – we take those things out of the ocean, and we eat *them*. So long before whatever this is had built up in complex tissues enough to make itself known, every piece of sushi and fish stick in the world was helping us to saturate ourselves with it.

After the jellyfish came…well, after the jellyfish came a lot of things, all at the same time, but apparently unconnected, so no one drew the lines that needed drawing. Caterpillars spinning cocoons and turning into goo, the way they always had, the way nature designed them to… but instead of turning into butterflies, they stopped at goo. Little tubes of goo, inert, not metamorphosising, not changing. Just goo.

Fishermen pulling up nets where half the fish were dead or deformed, scales melting into an undifferentiated sludge or bodies dripping off their bones. Some of them looked almost like jellyfish themselves, little bundles of meat and scales with no bones at all.

The empty shells of sea turtles washing up on the beach in Honolulu, not a scrap of flesh or sinew left inside, only a few bones with a soft, gelatinous quality to them. And then, whales, beached in much the same way, their bodies dissolving even before they hit the sand.

We had so many warnings. Warning after warning, and we ignored them all, because that's what people do. That's what works for us. We ignore. We let it build up, until we can't ignore it anymore.

★   ★   ★

This became something we couldn't ignore on August 8th, during the two o'clock BBC news broadcast, when the latest chirpy blonde talking head settled behind her desk and smiled her perfect, expensive smile at the camera, and started to explain the horrors of the day. Her smile didn't waver as she described horror after horror, except in the few cases where she had clearly been instructed to seem solemn – people found a smile reassuring, but not when it was attached to reports of children dying in apartment block fires or cancerous chemicals in the water.

Her smile returned as she moved on to more pleasant matters, and perhaps people found it reassuring again, for the few minutes it remained before it began to run down her face. As her skin softened and dripped like heated wax, exposing raw tissue and ligaments beneath. Incredibly, she kept speaking, muscles untouched by this spreading dissolution, at least until her nerves realised they had lost their protection from the stinging outside air. Sensing something was wrong, she paused, raising her hand to touch her cheek, and saw the skin dripping from her own fingers.

She screamed for ninety-seven seconds before someone thought to cut the feed, and by then, it was infinitely too late. The footage was uploaded to every file-sharing site in the world, and aired on every news broadcast, and still people thought – foolishly, incorrectly – that this was an isolated incident. Until it kept on happening, over and over again. Until we figured out that we were wrong.

★   ★   ★

Maybe we would have put the pieces together faster if it had looked the same in everyone, but I honestly don't think so. There were too many manifestations, too many ways for the dissolution to begin. There's a lot of collagen in the human body.

Because, of course, that's what this does. We didn't have time to finish the analysis, though – once your scientists start melting, research into 'why' goes on the back burner, and the focus tends to shift to 'can we make it stop?' To which the answer was, tragically, 'no, because we don't know how.' Collagen is present in the entire animal kingdom, in greater or larger proportions. It makes up muscles and mantles and connective tissue and the exoskeletons of insects. It's in snails and squid and jellyfish…and people, of course. People are just chock full of collagen. It protects our organs, it cradles our brains, it makes up our skin and our muscles and our bones. Collagen for everybody.

And thanks to whatever was going on, the collagen was breaking down. Not at the same rate for everybody. Vegans living in Ohio who had never been exposed to the ocean were falling apart more slowly than people who lived on the coast and ate a lot of sushi, but they were still falling apart, because it was in the water, which meant it was in the rain, and in the plants. Not eating the primary concentration just bought them a little more time, and I'm honestly not sure it was worth it. Would you want to be the last person standing as the world melted around you?

People started to come apart. The lucky ones were like that reporter, skin first, melting off their own tissues before going into massive systemic shock or picking up an infection. None of them lived more than a day. The world's best burn wards couldn't save them. No one could.

But they died fast, and since they went into shock so quickly, they died relatively painlessly, compared to the ones whose muscles began to turn to goo inside their bodies. On the outside, they looked perfectly normal. On the inside, they were collapsing. That form of dissolution tended to begin with the extremities, the arms and legs breaking down, then the muscles of the face and neck, moving inward to the torso and finally dissolving the heart. It was a slower process. It could take weeks from the moment when someone's legs buckled for the first time to the moment when their heart gave out and they stopped breathing, but once the process began, there was no stopping it.

Then there were the ones whose skeletons dissolved inside their bodies, collagen breaking down and leaving the rest of the bone too eroded to hold up against the clenching pressure of muscles and the heavy weight of organs. Those people died faster, and in agony to the very end, most making it all the way to the moment when their skulls collapsed inward like rotting pumpkins. It was a horrifying process to watch. People watched it anyway, of course. People will watch anything, and in the beginning, we still thought these things were unconnected, that we might have a chance.

The last, and least common, form of the syndrome began with the brain, the collagen of the dura dissolving and leaving the tissue to swell and smooth and surrender its crenulations. It looked like dementia to the outside eye, but appearing in all ages, and coming on over the course of hours, rather than taking years. Those people died as well, of course, but they died unaware of their own names, crying in corners for mothers they wouldn't have recognised even if those mothers had still been alive.

Bit by bit, we were being taken apart.

Not just us – anything with collagen, meaning anything belonging to the animal kingdom. It started in the fish, which reinforces my belief that it was something in the water, and then it took out the insects, and then it moved on to everything else. The reptiles and the birds and the mammals, all of them, from the smallest mouse to the greatest elephant, went through the same horrifying decline as we did, coming to pieces in the hands of the people who loved them.

We couldn't be content with damning ourselves. We had to take the rest of the world with us.

Life will go on. There are still plants, and bacteria, and potentialities. If anything in the Cambrian Period was intelligent enough to be self-aware, they probably thought the end of their kind was the end of the world, that without them in all their strange, innovative glory, life was coming to an end. But life found a way to come back again, transformed into something they would never have recognised, and life went on.

Earth will go on. Whatever we've made will work its way out of the water, and animal life will rise again, slowly but steadily. It may take a long, long time. That's fine. The planet can wait.

I, however, can't.

My wheelchair has been my constant companion since I was a child. I realised the process had started only when I noticed the unnatural sponginess of my thighs, the looseness of my hips. There may be no one left in the world to read this, but I wanted to get it down while I still could.

The softening has spread to my shoulders. If I don't go now, I won't have the strength to transfer myself into the bed, and there is no one left. I know how I'm going to die. I've made my peace with it. But I'd rather not die sitting up.

Maybe someday, when life has formed again, some new intelligence will rise, and find our writings, and decode them. When they do, may they find this, and may they take my warning:

Do not fear your own biology so much you would destroy the world to change it. Be what you were made to be. The world can be good. Treat it more gently than we did.

When it calls on you to age, allow it.

REMAINS

Charlie Hughes

Travel south by train from central London, via Blackfriars or St. Pancras, perhaps on your way home from work or on a daytrip to the seaside, and you will pass me by.

I wait at Crofton Station.

Imagine an in-between place, a link in the metropolitan chain – south London, forgotten London, swallowed London.

The station sits on concrete stilts above the tangle of streets, surrounded by Victorian terraces and stumpy 1950s council blocks. There are two platforms, two routes for escape: back into the madness of the city or away to the commuter belt and the sea.

My body rests on a patch of land beyond the furthest end of the platform, trapped between tracks and boxed off by concrete walls. The construct around my corpse suggests some essential piece of railway engineering. Instead, the cavity is filled with thick twists of overgrown brambles and mountains of rubbish – my grave goods, my shroud.

I am almost hidden, but not quite. To have any chance of spotting me, a Crofton commuter must do something unnecessary, counterintuitive: walk up the platform, beyond the benches and the information screens, away from the place where the trains come to a stop. If they peer down into the opening, focusing on the gaps between the overgrown shrubbery, in the right light, they might see white bone and the remains of a pastel-green kitten-heel shoe, poking out from beneath black polythene.

There was a teenage graffitist in '01. He climbed the end of the platform to tag the barrier, looked down, and saw my femur in the dawn light. He knew what he was seeing. He pondered the news for a moment, then went back to spraying.

He's a father now, working in a warehouse in Colchester. He still thinks of me, sometimes.

⋆   ⋆   ⋆

I had a flat and a job and a life.

Crofton was an easy route to work, an affordable place to buy. Back then, it didn't seem strange to be single, on a low income and purchasing a home in Zone 2. In 1995 and '96, I worked long hours, ate badly and went to gigs in Camden, Kings Cross and Brixton whenever I could afford to.

I wasn't stuck. I had forward motion. Three years at university, four years working at the museum in Derby. Eventually, I got the job I really wanted, at the British Library, and so arrived in the capital. My parents were proud. They told their friends how I worked with rare manuscripts, mended them, catalogued them. It's a precious thing to love your work, more precious still to be admired by your family for doing it. I treasured their admiration, kept it close when things were tough.

I had Olly too, with our half serious, half not-so-serious relationship. It wouldn't have lasted, but I didn't know that then. We'd met through work, kissed at the Christmas party and traded night-time trysts three times a week thereafter. By the spring of '96, just before my transformation, we talked teasingly of moving in together.

After, when I was gone, Olly left his job at the library. He couldn't stand the looks from our workmates, even the sympathetic ones. He lives in Edinburgh now. He drinks too much.

⋆   ⋆   ⋆

It isn't how you think. I don't rise from the brambles and float around the station, spooking commuters.

No, I receive the world in strange, uneven layers – images and smells and sounds that come in and out of focus. Time washes over me, through me. I am never tired, never hungry, never lonely. The rhythm of the trains leaving and arriving, the shifting moods of the passengers give me structure and meaning. You would be surprised how comforting it can be to see a regular leap onto a rush-hour train just as the doors shut behind them.

Jadon is my favourite. If I re-dressed him, took him out of those hipster dungarees, gave him a '90s Gallagher-haircut, and a Shed Seven

T-shirt, he could be Olly. A younger version. He listens to terrible dance music on headphones and draws pictures in his notebook while waiting for the train. I think he wants to be an engineer or an inventor or a designer for a theatre. I try to guess from the pictures he draws. Outlandish steampunk contraptions that defy imagination.

One of my favourite things is to sit next to him on the bench as he draws, watch them morph and grow.

There is a 'me', a location for my consciousness, but different to when I was alive. Inside the station, I am nowhere and everywhere at once – on the steps, inside the ticket office, on the platforms. When something happens, anything which heightens the nerve endings of my visitors, I am instantly present, in the thick of it.

Place is important too, but it's hard to know how or why. This is where my bones are, so this is where I am. The station is my universe, my cage. I can go anywhere I want, as long as I never leave.

Last week, three teenagers accosted a boy on the platform, deep into the small hours of the morning. He was from the wrong postcode, the wrong school. He shouldn't have been in Crofton, they said.

They held him down, placed a kitchen knife at his throat and made him beg for his life. He pissed himself and cried for his father and they laughed at him. In moments like this, I see and feel everything in vivid emotional detail.

I reached out for the boy with the knife. There was no hand for me to see, nothing visible resting on his shoulder, only his reaction, the knowledge on his face. The price I pay for breaking the veil is always heavy. In an instant, I knew more about the young man than any human should know of another. All his traumas, all his humiliations, the inside-out of his pain, the full force of his hatred for the world. A terrible thing.

To his friends, to the kid on the ground, it appeared the distant sound of a siren made him turn and run.

I know different, and so does he.

★   ★   ★

I am aware of the Railwayman immediately, the very moment he enters the station. A chemical odour surrounds me. A cloying memory, an alarm.

He has thick, dark brown hair, swept back, sculpted with a product which makes it glisten in the winter sunshine. There are wisps of grey at his temples, a counterweight to a smooth, featureless face. Medium height, average looking, no need to notice him at all except for the forced muscularity of his shoulders, which bulge beneath a blue office shirt.

I call him the Railwayman because that is how he thinks of himself. Come into this station and there is a good chance I can guess your name, your home address and whatever gripes or joyous victories are dancing across your mind.

But the Railwayman is harder. All I see is his name, and the red spots of anger that pulse around his head like midges in summertime. I want him to go away, now.

It is midday and the station is quiet. A smattering of college kids, toddler parents and the elderly wait on the platform. He walks casually between them, looking at his phone screen, circling back and then turning again, pretending he has no specific destination in mind. A train for Blackfriars arrives. All the people get on. He does not.

When the train pulls away, he moves more quickly towards the end of the platform. I do not want him to come nearer to my bones. They are sacred, a binding with the physical universe. Whatever he has in mind, his nearness is sacrilege, a desecration.

When he spots my leg, my shoe, he tilts his head to one side, as if puzzling out a difficult maths problem.

From his perspective, he is looking down on me. From mine, I'm stood beside him. I want to know what he is thinking, but I don't want him to know I am here. I brush my finger gently against his arm, and instantly wish I had not.

*   *   *

You might think the manner of my passing has trapped me here. 'Taken before her time…damned to purgatory etcetera, etcetera.' Nonsense. Before it happened, there were twenty-five years of highs and lows, choices, mistakes. A whole life for me to form bonds, break them and mend them again. During that time, I learned some things about myself, faculties distinctive to me, things you don't know yet. Some you never will.

But I'll tell you about one. Something that made little sense when I was alive, but has taken on new meaning since 17th October 1996. I possessed, I believe, an ability to connect with the dead. There were times when I could feel and imagine the presence of people who had passed.

Touching objects helped. The more personal, the more emotive, the better. Letters worked the best.

I first realised this at the age of sixteen, long before I ever worked at a museum or library.

Shortly before my grandmother's funeral, when we were clearing her house, I found correspondence written by her, hidden in a false drawer in her dressing table. These love letters were addressed to a man fighting his way towards Berlin in 1944. They were returned, unopened. As I read, certain names and unknowable understandings came to me: images of my grandmother as a teenager sat at her desk writing the notes, her heart yearning for the young man. These pictures came with vivid clarity, alongside her emotions at the time, transported, undiluted across the decades. My grandmother never stopped loving him, not even on the day of her marriage to my grandfather, and she thought of him constantly throughout the following forty-seven years of her life, never once mentioning his name aloud again.

It was no coincidence that I eventually landed in a job where contact with personal correspondence was commonplace, and intuitive knowledge could prove useful. At the British Library, I quickly gained a reputation for my ability to spot forgeries. Eventually, it would have made me a rich woman.

So, I ask you, am I here now, stranded at Crofton Station because this is the fate awaiting all victims of murderous assault? Are the graveyards of the world crowded with the spectral presences of the buried? Or is it more likely that we only get to hang around if, in life, we're comfortable in the blurred spaces between death and the ever after?

★　　★　　★

He's back with his chemical stink and tight-fitting shirt, visiting my station again and again. Never taking a train, just wandering around looking to the place he left me twenty-six years ago.

The Railwayman wants my remains. He thinks endlessly about how he can recover them without setting off alarms or being seen by the station CCTV. Having left me here for decades, the idea of my clothes and bones being found by the authorities fills him with dread. Something has happened, recently, to make this a matter of great urgency to him.

I must stop him, of course. If he takes what remains of me away, hides me in his home or destroys my bones somehow, two things are certain: he will never pay for what he did and I will no longer have my station and my people.

He stands at the end of the platform and casts his eyes over the cavity between the tracks, his nose twitching as if he can smell me.

He's taken life many times and left us all next to places like this. Stations are his thing. Trains are his thing.

"Bitch. Bitch." He mumbles this under his breath, over and over. I can't tell if he's referring to me or someone else.

After an hour of wandering the platform, he turns and rushes out of the station. As he exits, he passes Jadon who is on the way in, one of my regulars. Jadon follows him with his gaze. There is a momentary crackling in the air, static feedback.

I wonder. I wonder.

Jadon continues into the station, sits in his normal spot on the bench and takes out a notebook.

I've never done it before. Never tried to communicate with them. My passengers come and go as they please, and I enjoy their company, but there has never been a need to ask anything of the living. I don't even know how.

He puts in earphones and heavy bass overwhelms his senses. Jadon takes out his notebook and begins to draw.

I place a hand on his back. Jadon's pen hovers over the page.

Before anything can happen, before I can form the image in my own mind, I remove my hand.

The Railwayman is walking back up the platform. I don't want him to see anything. I don't want him to know Jadon exists.

⋆　　⋆　　⋆

How could I have been so stupid, so slow to react? I hesitated, and now he is back in the dead of night.

The Railwayman is dressed all in black, an Action Man Paramilitary. He moves fast, sprints down the platform and climbs the safety barrier. No alarm sounds. No siren calls from the street. The only sound is the low, anonymous hum of the city moving around the station, turning away from me, turning away from him.

He bounds through the stones which bed the ground between the tracks, crunching the gravel beneath rubber-soled boots. At the wall of my grave, he unclips something from his bag, extends it and places it on the ground. Steps, to help him over. He sets them down, gets on top and grips the apex of the wall, shifts his weight up and hauls himself over to the other side, my side. The chemical smell is overpowering now. Details of what he first did to me come pouring back, memories I tried to banish forever come flooding in.

The cloth over my mouth, the van, him over me.

I rage against his presence, but I'm impotent. I may as well be a soulless bundle of bones and rags wrapped in polythene.

With a large knife he hacks at the brambles. He only needs to move in a few metres when his head-torch catches my feet and the polythene. He bends down and pulls at me. I stay in place. The thicker brambles are locked around my neck and upper arms. He pulls again and my body separates, ribs dislodge, my hips come away from the backbone. He pulls me out, but only half of me.

Quickly, he stuffs bones and rags into a bag. Once full, he slings it over the wall. It makes a loud crashing sound on the other side. He breathes, unevenly, heavily.

He starts to grab the rest of me, but then he hears it and I hear it too. Metal wheels on rail. The unmistakeable sound of a train approaching. It gets louder and louder as it nears. He'd planned around this. He'd checked the schedules. There are no trains due at this hour, not even through trains, travelling fast to major stations. Panicking, knowing the bin bag is exposed on the other side, the Railwayman jumps onto the ledge, and hauls himself back over. He scoops up the steps and the bag and sprints across the tracks to the other side of the junction.

What he doesn't see as he flees into the hedgerows is that the slowing train has no illumination inside the carriages. The out of service train will wait here until morning, then proceed to the coast.

I feel myself waning as he moves away, and I start to understand how this works now. The world seems to shrink from me, the lights on the platform lose their sparkle. I want to be on the platform, watching him run through the trees, but I move slowly, heavily from my place. By the time I get there, he is long gone.

He will be back for the rest of me soon.

*   *   *

Jadon sits on a different bench, further down the platform. I need to be close to him, but the distance between us feels impossible.

I am fading, disappearing. For a while last night, after he'd gone, I went blank. Not sleep or unconsciousness, I mean complete oblivion. The absence of existence. When I came back, it was worse than ever. The colour has drained out of the world and suddenly movement requires effort and concentration.

Thankfully, Jadon is still in place when I arrive at his bench. I raise myself up and stand behind him, like a country baron posing for a family portrait. Tentatively, I reach out and place a hand on his shoulder. There it is again, just like before, a crackling, a change in the air pressure. I feel him tense, then take in a long, deep breath, but he continues sketching.

There is no trauma in my contact with him, not like the Railwayman or even the boy with the knife. We are aligned, attuned to each other. His life is rich and complex and even painful, but his soul has not been twisted out of shape, nor deformed into something ghastly and unnatural. Games. That is his thing, he wants to design video games. He loves to make dozens of moving parts fit together, creating something that flows perfectly from one element to another. Jadon works for minimum wage at a development company in north London. He is more talented than all the people he works with, but struggles for opportunities to demonstrate this skill.

I place my other hand on his opposite shoulder and squeeze a little, willing a stronger connection. Again, the crackle in the air, stronger this time. His pen starts to move more quickly over the page, abandoning the contraption which had held his attention, and now beginning something new. I cannot see Jadon's face, but his body is shaking, juddering under the pressure of our connection. For my part, I concentrate on one image, one idea. The pen flashes this way and that, creating new shapes and shading on the page at an unlikely speed. I squeeze again, and the pace increases. Jadon is in a frenzy now, a fugue of possession, as he reproduces the image in my mind, in his.

A man passing on the platform stops and stares at Jadon. "Are you all right, mate?" he says. I want to swat him away, but I can already feel the connection loosening, Jadon's pen slowing.

"Fella?"

And it's gone. I rock back, falling away, towards the platform, and I may have gone too far now, dug too deeply into my reserves, because this time the descent feels final. The world goes blank.

★   ★   ★

When I come to, I am looking up from my resting place, through the brambles, thorns, beer cans and crisp packets. I feel weak, tenuous.

Jadon is there on the platform, looking down at me. I would smile and wave if I could. I realise he cannot see me. Not yet. Jadon keeps looking at the notebook and then back down here.

I want to scream, "I am here! Come and find me, Jadon."

But then another figure appears alongside him. Medium height, bulging shoulders, the faint smell of formaldehyde accompanying his arrival. To me, they are silhouettes against the grey sky. He stands too close to Jadon.

"What are you doing?" he asks. In my head, the Railwayman's voice is booming and distorted, louder than it can possibly be.

"I think there's something down there," Jadon says. "Something that shouldn't be there."

"Oh yes? What makes you think that?"

He proffers the notebook.

"Who drew this?"

"I did," Jadon says.

"I don't think there's anything down there. Just a load of old rubbish."

"I can feel her," Jadon says, quietly.

"What was that?"

"Nothing," he says and walks away.

★   ★   ★

It is night-time, freezing cold. Wisps of white breath appear above the wall. The Railwayman is scrabbling over, desperate to get the last of me, to wipe me out forever. He hacks away until he can reach my torso, my skull.

He lets out a scoff, a half-chuckle. His hand takes hold of my cranium, his thumb pushes deep inside my eye socket. "There you are," he says. "Caused me enough trouble, haven't you?"

Proximity brings me one final insight: the reason behind this mad-cap retrieval of my bones. His younger brother – a man on a downward spiral, divorced, no access to his kids – was recently arrested after a bar fight. The Railwayman spoke to him on the phone, feigned brotherly concern and casually asked if he'd had to give a DNA sample. He had.

He hasn't forgotten my scratching, fighting, grasping hands, nor the hair I pulled from his head. He was right to be worried. Tiny strands still adhere in my closed fist.

The Railwayman wants perfection, to never get caught. He fantasises about confessing on his deathbed, telling them that he beat them all. The brazen location of my body has always brought him amusement, but suddenly I've become a dangerous loose end, a vulnerability.

"What are you doing?" The voice is high, scared.

The Railwayman spins around, almost falling. "Wha...who's that?" He looks up to the platform.

Jadon repeats the question. "What are you doing?"

The killer gathers himself with unlikely speed. "I could ask you the same question. What are you doing here in the dead of night? No trains now, son."

"I can't sleep. I can't stop thinking about it, about what's down there. It's a body, isn't it? A woman?"

"No," the Railwayman says. "But I wondered about what you said, so I came to look. I'm a policeman, see. There's no body, but there is one thing. You might be interested."

Jadon recognises him now. The man who spoke to him about why he was looking. "You're police?"

"Yep. CID. I thought to myself, 'If that young lad thinks there's something down here, I should come and check it out.'"

"Where are the others? The police dogs?"

"No need for all that just yet. I needed to check. And I found one thing. Stay there, I'll come up and show you."

In one smooth movement, he leans over to his bag, takes out a knife and slips it into his pocket.

Why isn't Jadon running? Can't he see what is happening?

"Just a minute," the Railwayman says cheerily before swinging back over the wall.

"You've got ID, right. Police ID?" Jadon asks.

The Railwayman shouts over his shoulder as he lands on the stones. "Wise boy. Yes, got that too."

Run! But Jadon just stands there, waiting for him.

I feel it boiling in me. A rage beyond description, a hatred for this man bound up tightly with all that he took from me and the thought that he will do it again. I feel it all, exquisite in its purity. It lifts me up high, so that I am suddenly looking down on the station, down on the Railwayman walking towards Jadon.

The pain he caused my family, my poor mum and dad, Olly and his emptied heart. All the beautiful moments he stole from me. And now he will do it again, smother this bright light of intelligence and insight and beauty just because he can, just because he needs the power of it coursing through him. The arrogance, the idea that he can just kill, kill, kill, taking the young to sate his evil, his inadequacy.

Dogs in the back gardens around the station begin to bark. First one, then another, then a chorus of canine alarm fills the air.

He is below Jadon, clambering up to the platform. Jadon still waits, but his head has turned to wonder at the noise made by the dogs.

I see it again, so clear. *The cloth over my mouth. The van. Him.*

Whatever essence of me remains now glows white hot with outrage. I can feel it snapping through the air. Connecting, conducting along unknown pathways of energy.

The lights on the station platform flicker.

Jadon takes one step back as the Railwayman pulls himself up on the barrier and clambers over.

It grows exponentially: a certain knowledge that I must protect Jadon, must stop this killer from enacting the slashing, stabbing, slicing, which has formed into a fantasy in his mind's eye.

Wind bends the trees inwards towards Crofton Station.

"Where's your ID?" Jadon is moving back now, still facing him, but is aware of a wider turbulence, a warning.

"Don't go away. I want to show you what I found." He steps forward.

The lights on the platform flash on and off and the air is pierced by the sound of the station alarm. The Railwayman is shocked rigid by the piercing din.

The wind grows stronger. One of the benches bolted to the platform strains against its brackets.

With the alarm and the dogs and the wind, people are starting to come out into their back gardens and look up to the station. One voice calls up, "What's going on up there?"

Jadon looks down towards the station exit and sees the information boards have lit up. Instead of train times and details, a single word is repeated over and over:

run run run run run run run run

The Railwayman draws the knife. "Look what I found. Is this yours?"

Jadon looks back and sees the grey metal of the blade.

"Stop now. Police. Stop there."

But Jadon is gone, darting away, flying down the platform towards the exit. The Railwayman follows, but pulls up short when he sees the glow of flashing blue lights beyond the station entrance.

I am expired now, fading fast into oblivion again, knowing I won't return, but also knowing Jadon is safe.

The Railwayman looks up and sees the new message on the information screen:

caught caught caught caught caught caught

And I depart.

THE FLOOR IS LAVA

Brian Keene

Mark was bleeding again. He knew that if he wiped and then checked it, the white tissue paper would be red with blood. But he didn't need to do that. He could feel the wetness on the back of his balls and the inside of his thighs. He was pretty sure it was from his haemorrhoids, but Marsha thought he had an ulcer. Every time it happened – and he bled when he pooped about three times a week – he'd hop in the shower immediately afterward, spread his ass cheeks, and watch the red-brown water swirl down the drain until it turned clear again. Then he'd apply some ointment and wince until the burning and swelling subsided. The problem was, Marsha knew what those impromptu showers meant, and then she'd get after him to have a doctor check him out.

"You're not a young man, anymore," she'd say. "You're almost sixty! You should be getting colonoscopies and prostate exams on a regular basis."

And she was right, of course. Mark knew that. His father and his paternal grandfather had both had prostate cancer, and his maternal grandfather had died of colon cancer. But the latter had also had diabetes and the other two had suffered from early onset dementia, and there was no sign of either of those things in him. Every time Marsha brought it up, Mark complained to her that he hated the doctor, but promised that if it kept happening, he'd make an appointment. Then they went back to their lives, both enjoying their first full year of retirement, and Marsha would let it drop until it happened again.

Mark wasn't lying when he said that he hated going to the doctor. He did. But he wasn't being entirely truthful, either. Since turning fifty, he'd developed an all-encompassing fear of the doctor. He knew it wasn't reasonable, but the emotion persisted just the same. He was afraid of what the doctor might tell him. Afraid that those genetic ailments might be present in his own body. Afraid of his own mortality.

But that fear was nothing compared to the terror and panic he'd been experiencing for the last half hour.

Ever since the bathroom floor had become lava.

Mark hadn't pondered an explanation, because there was none — at least, not anything that followed logic or reason or science. Marsha had left the house for tea with her friends, and he'd finished his coffee, then come upstairs to use the second-floor bathroom. He preferred this one because they'd recently remodelled it, and the new brown tile was soothing beneath his bare feet. But at some point, after he'd sat down on the toilet and opened his *TIME* magazine, that new tile had turned red and orange and molten.

The first thing he'd noticed was the heat. Suddenly, he found himself sweating profusely, and felt his eyes and nose drying out. When he looked up from the magazine to check the baseboard radiator to his right, he'd discovered the change. Mark's first reaction had been to let out a shrill, strangled sort of squawk, and yank his feet up off the floor. His pulse quickened and then began to hammer in his throat and chest, and for a moment, he thought he might die right there – a heart attack on the crapper. But he didn't die, and so his panic had increased.

The floor churned and flowed, bubbling and smoking and letting out little burbles of sound. It ringed the sink, the vanity, the shower, and the toilet, leaving about ten inches of tile between each of them and the molten pool. The bathroom door was closed tight, so he couldn't tell if the flow extended out into the hallway or not.

His next thought had been to call Marsha and then 911, but he'd left his cell phone downstairs.

And so he'd sat here for the last half hour, cowering on the toilet, knees drawn up and feet resting on the porcelain rim. Strangely, his initial terror had turned into a persistent but low-grade dread. His bottom half had long since fallen asleep, his toes and legs going well past the tingling stage, and now simply consumed by numbness. His lower back ached. And the worst part of all was that he'd continued shitting throughout the ordeal, shivering in the heat as each cramp wracked his body.

"I've got to do something," he said aloud. His tongue felt thick and swollen, and his mouth was dry. "If I don't, I'm going to die here."

And he would. His head already ached from dehydration. If he spent another half hour sitting here, he'd pass out and topple over into the lava. The heat and the fumes were oppressive.

Mark eyed the window, just out of reach. He wondered if he could reach it. Not from where he was sitting, obviously, but if he stood up and balanced on that sliver of tile that the lava edged, maybe he could stretch out and slide it open. It was autumn, but he still had the screen windows in place. If Norton was outside, then maybe he could call for help. And Norton was usually outside. The neighbour seemed to be spending every day of his own retirement caring for his lawn.

Mark took a deep breath of stifling air and then eased his feet off the rim. Immediately, a jolt of pain ran up both of his legs, slicing through the numbness. Gritting his teeth, he tried to move and found that he couldn't. He grabbed his left ankle with both hands and worked his foot and toes, twisting and flexing, trying to get his circulation flowing again. Eventually, sensations returned to the appendages. Pain came first, followed by tingling. He repeated the process with his other foot, and when he felt confident enough, Mark slowly stood up, holding his breath and steadying himself against the toilet tank with one hand.

The tile was surprisingly warm. He'd braced himself, assuming it would be scorching hot, but the remaining floor was no more unpleasant than walking barefoot on a sidewalk in the summertime. Carefully, he tiptoed forward and reached for the window. Another cramp seized his calf muscles. Mark cried out and stumbled forward, his feet leaving the safety of the tiled floor and landing on…

…more tiles.

Gasping, Mark glanced around at the bathroom. The lava was gone, and the floor had returned to normal. Even the heat, so present and overpowering just a moment before, had vanished.

His gasp turned into a sob. Trembling, Mark sank down to his knees and cried. He couldn't explain what had just happened, but there was one thing he knew for certain – he didn't want to die. He didn't want cancer or diabetes or early onset dementia. He wanted to live. Wiping his eyes with a piece of toilet paper, he struggled to stand up again and resolved to make an appointment with the doctor for a full check-up. He'd even get the colonoscopy.

Mark was halfway across the bathroom when he felt the floor move again. It wasn't a flowing or bubbling sensation this time. It was more like a slithering and coiling type of movement. Mark looked down and screamed as what felt like a dozen tiny needles jabbed his feet and ankles.

The floor was snakes.

THE TRUE COLOUR OF BLOOD
Stephen Laws

It was a hotter than hell day in July when we pulled up outside the MacInlay State Penitentiary. We'd used the pickup that day 'cause the family car was still in the garage getting her brake cable fixed. No air conditioning then, and even with the windows down the kids complained all the way there.

I parked the pickup on a vacant lot just opposite the main gate and sat there for a while just looking.

Big steel door, with a little steel door down at the left. No one came out and no one went in, and the heat seemed to be beating off that big door right at us, like there was a blast furnace on the other side or something.

Renee hadn't said much since we set out. Just kept popping soda cans from the Koolbox on the back seat for the kids because of their complaining about the heat and such, and for the first time I could remember not saying anything about what it might do to their teeth.

I wish I could come with you, she'd said. In the back, Torry and Pete started squalling about how hot it was again. Both nine. Twins, see? But they don't look alike. Like they should be in different families, almost.

Mail man and grocery delivery boy, Renee would say, and we'd laugh.

No laughs today, though.

Renee bawled at the kids, told them to play games or get out and walk around, stretch their legs, look for rocks or something – and the way her voice sounded made me realise how strung out she was. Strung out for me, that is. And even though it made me love her even more, right at that minute I couldn't take my hands off the wheel or keep from staring at the big prison door.

The kids got out of the pickup, kicked up some dust looking for something, anything interesting. After a while, I realised that Renee was looking hard at me; not knowing what to say or do.

You don't have to stay here, I said.

I know, said Renee.

Why don't you take the kids into town, find a diner or something? Get outta the heat.

No, said Renee. *I want to stay here and wait for you. Plenty soda in the Koolbox.*

Okay. Maybe a half hour.

Half hour, okay.

Or an hour. You know, by the time I get in there and everything.

An hour, okay.

Okay, I said again and found myself getting out of the pickup, like someone else had made the decision and my body was just doing what it was told.

I'm gonna go straight in, Renee.

Okay.

You sure you don't want to…?

No, baby. You go in now and we'll be waiting here for you when you're done.

An hour.

As long as it takes.

All right, honey.

Not sure why, but I couldn't bring myself to look back at her. Like the sight of her might change my mind. The beautiful, long black hair. Those big eyes. Dark skin, damp with sweat. Powder blue shirt, tied round her tight waist. Loved her when we met fifteen years ago. Love her more now. But just looking at her and maybe thinking too much about what I was going to do and why, might make me climb back into the pickup and take us back home.

I set straight off, wiped the sweat from my face, took off my hat, ran my fingers through my hair and set that hat tight back on top with the brim low. For a while it was like I was walking on the spot, not moving forward at all. When I looked up, those steel doors just seemed to be as big as they were when we first saw them. That seemed to mean something, but I didn't know what. I didn't look back, but I could hear the kids squabbling with each other again. Renee didn't say anything to quiet them.

And then I was at the door – the little one.

Only it didn't seem so little now.

The heat seemed to get worse. Part of me wanted to stop right then; another part wanted to go on. Now I was aware that Renee would be watching me as I walked and there was some kind of knot inside me about that. Was she waiting for me to stop? Waiting for me to go on? I didn't know what that meant, but I knew that it was something about what I felt as a man and as a father, particularly because of the man I was going to see behind those walls.

The request had come out of the blue.

I'd not heard a word from him in twenty years.

Not since he'd finally been caught, tried and put behind bars for the rest of his life.

But now – this handwritten message on prison-headed notepaper. Apparently, he'd refused to have an email or other message sent to me, preferring the 'personal touch' – said the formal typed letter from the Governor that arrived in our mail. The prison people had my home and email address and all my other details. But I'd had no contact with them or from them. Why should there be? I wanted nothing to do with him and even if he had reached out to me, I would have denied him. I wanted no contamination. Even the thought of him was contaminating.

But now, the handwritten 'letter'.

And in that formal typed letter from the prison the Governor also told me that my father was dying.

It was leukaemia, and he had been receiving treatment for some time. In a matter of months, perhaps weeks, he would be bed-bound until the end.

Now or never seemed to be the top and bottom of it.

This was his letter.

I no you hate me.

Thats OK.

Lots of people do.

But they tell me Ill be dead in a little wile.

Thats OK, to. The thing is thers somthing you shud no about me and you. Somethin that is important and cud change the way you think. Not about me. Im gessin that aint changed much since Im gessing you will all ways love yor

Mama and hate me for what I done. But somethin I lerned may change yor
thinkin and if you com Ill tell you. If you dont well thats on you.
   But this thing is about you, me and everbody it seems.
   Cum see me, youll lern.
   If not well lyk I say thats on you.
   Lyk it or not Im yor father.

So that's the note or the letter or whatever that I got, and without getting into the whys and wherefores of whether a letter (or whatever) should be sent from a prison by a man like that, even to his son – not to mention the official covering letter – well, let's just say that I talked with Renee long and hard about whether I should reply or not, never mind whether I should go and see him – or not. Renee knew about him, of course. This had all happened when I was a boy and he'd been long locked up and forgotten when she and me got together. If I'd wanted to, I needn't have mentioned a thing about him. But there had always been the possibility that she'd come across the story eventually. I mean, it's not like I changed my surname nor nothing. Meeting Renee was the best thing that ever happened to me, and being honest with each other was just about the most important thing we shared; that, and our love for each other and for the kids, of course. But I guess this is all tied up together. So – she knew about everything. Not all of the details at the beginning, I guess; but enough about how my father was a killer and he'd come home one night when I was a kid, covered in blood, and my mother had scooped me up and fled the house. We'd been on the run for three weeks when he found us in a motel. She made me run out the back into the desert. A police patrol car found me a day and a half later, out of my mind with thirst and bad memories.

He'd killed my mother, of course.

Telling Renee – well, telling her the other details – came out when some television people came around saying they wanted an interview for a documentary they were doing. Turns out he'd been killing people for years. Twenty-seven of them. Or at least the killings he admitted to eventually, although they reckon there were more. I never gave an interview and I never watched their television documentary.

Renee and me discussed whether I should go see the monster that was my dad.

A lot.

Sometimes I felt no, sometimes yes.

Sometimes Renee felt yes, sometimes no.

Leukaemia was going to finish him soon.

Seemed like what they call 'poetic justice', doesn't it?

A killer like him, with so much blood on his hands, being killed by his own blood.

And so here I was, standing in front of that big old-fashioned iron door. My legs had done the walking on their own, like they hadn't been told what to do, and damn it if that door – still bleaching its heat at me – was just like the big front prison door you see in those old black and white gangster movies on TV.

Now what was I supposed to do?

Knock?

There was a blast of noise from behind me and I spun around to see Renee with her hands up to her mouth, and in the next second a truck seemed to appear out of nowhere, trundling straight towards me in a red dust cloud. I skipped the hell out of the way as the driver, hidden by the dust but now his face an orange blur through the windshield, flicked on the windshield wipers. There was more noise now as the big steel door seemed to split down the middle and began opening up. That first blast of noise that had scared the hell out of me I now knew to be the truck's horn, and it seemed to have been the signal to whoever was behind that door to open up and let it in. Had I got the wrong damn public entrance to this place? Did prisons have tradesman's entrances?

The big door opened up wide down the centre to let the truck into some kind of forecourt area, amid the billowing of more dust as uniformed guards seemed to appear on all sides, one of them waving at the truck to slow down, be inspected and escorted. Maybe a whole bunch of cons in a truck were trying to break *in*? And then the smaller door was suddenly opened and as the dust cleared I could see that this was the main security entrance for members of the public. Two other uniformed guards were standing there as if they had been expecting me. This whole...*thing* seemed wrong and unsettling.

I walked on ahead, into the security entrance, taking out my paperwork, my ID and the 'special' pass that had also been included in my envelope from the prison Governor.

Inside, the heat was instantly gone and I walked into a kind of grey coldness on all sides. The first guard checked my ID, took my hat, belt, watch and keys in a plastic tray, like I was passing through customs on my way to an airport lounge. I was told I'd get them back when I left. And then the full 'check-in' began. I soon lost track of the gates, the manned plexiglass booths, the electronic barriers, the scanner checks and the grey faces of the guards who checked my ID, patted me down, waved me through or walked me on. It seemed to go on for a hell of a long time. Sometimes I seemed to be walking straight ahead; other times, it felt like I was on an incline headed down. At some point, I don't know when, I was aware there were other 'visitors' like me, also being 'processed' but I can't tell you anything about them. I know that sounds weird. But it was like I'd walked into a different world, concentrating hard on what was ahead.

A voice called my name.

"Yes?" It was a tall guy with a round face and close-cropped hair. Uniformed again, but he looked more 'military police' than prison guard.

"Follow me."

Now it was just me, following him down a stone corridor. There was no one else around. He stopped at a door marked 'Utility – Waiting', and held it open for me. I walked in.

"Make yourself comfortable. Someone will be here for you soon."

The room inside had a plastic table and a chair. There were no windows and nothing on the bare plaster walls. One single strip light buzzed from the ceiling.

The door shut behind me, and I was alone.

I'm not sure, but I think my escort locked it.

I sat.

After a while, I wondered if I was ever going to get out of this place again. Crazy, I know; but a part of me wondered if some new law had been passed – a law that meant anyone related to a serial killer would now be automatically locked up forever if they turned up at a prison for any reason whatever, even as a visitor.

With no wristwatch or clock on the wall I had no way of knowing how long I waited in that room.

When the door opened again, it seemed like a *long* time.

A different uniformed guy walked in.

This guy was big, black, smiling and confident as hell. I can't say why, but he seemed somehow superior in rank to the other guy who had brought me here. His uniform was certainly different. He checked my ID again, asked me politely but firmly about the reasons for my visit (like he'd asked many times before, and making me also feel like I was being read my rights). When I seemed to have given the right answers, he smiled again and asked me to follow him.

The breeze-block corridor made me think of Death Row, our footsteps ringing loud and bouncing back from that high ceiling. All the way, I still couldn't shake the feeling that the deeper I went into this concrete maze, the more likely it was that I'd never be coming out again. Like I said before, crazy.

More security cages and checks.

More bars.

And yet more pat downs and body searches. What were they expecting to find on me that the scanners couldn't pick up? Every time, I felt that *this* time someone would find something on me that would have klaxons blaring, guns drawn and a heavy cell door clanging behind me as I was thrown into solitary confinement for the rest of my life, never seeing my wife and children again.

The big black guy stayed by my side all the way this time, while other security people checked me over. On another long stretch walking down yet another concrete corridor, I jumped a little when he spoke, like he'd been reading my mind or something.

"We're taking you in through a different route."

We?

There were two of us in the corridor, but clearly eyes following us all the way.

"He's in solitary," he said, striding ahead. "But you'll see him in a separate visiting room."

When he suddenly stopped, I almost ran into the back of him.

He turned to face me, sidestepped and reached to the wall, tapping out numbers on a small keyboard that I hadn't until that moment seen, set head-height into a door that I'd also missed, being the same colour as the wall. Red LED lights flickered on the keyboard and the guy with me gave his name and ID. When a tinny voice said something I couldn't make out, my escort stiff-fingered more digits into the keyboard and the door opened.

We walked into a small room not unlike the one that I'd previously been in, except that this one had a single glass window in the wall facing the door and a white plastic chair in front of it. I could see some kind of microphone monitor set into the window. My escort closed the door behind us.

"Did anyone tell you that you'd have to have an officer present for the duration of the meeting?" asked my escort, with a smile that was so polite it was chilling.

"Yeah. In the Governor's letter."

"Okay, well that officer is me, and I'll be over there." He pointed to the closed door. There was no chair, so I guess he'd be standing to attention. "Your father will also have a guard. On the other side of the glass."

I nodded my understanding and he moved to a keyboard intercom in the wall by the door, stabbing at it with a forefinger.

"Prepared for visitor," he said into the intercom, flat and business-like – now waving a polite hand to the chair in front of the window.

I crossed the room and sat as my escort took up a straight-backed stance in front of the door, hands behind his back, looking into space.

The room on the other side of the glass looked identical to the one I was in, with the same chair facing me and with grey and featureless walls. As I watched, a door opened and a guard with the same uniform as my own escort stepped briskly into the room, and then aside as a man in red overalls entered. The guard stood with his head down as the man shuffled forward a few steps, enough for the guard to close the door, point at the chair and window on their side before taking up the same pose as my own escort. Head still down, the man in red shuffled to his seat, and now I could see that he was manacled and chained at the wrists and ankles.

He sat, but kept his head down.

I cleared my throat and looked back at my escort.

He just looked straight ahead.

What the hell was supposed to happen now?

I looked back at the prisoner.

Just before I could say something, he looked up.

I did not recognise him.

This guy was almost bald with a thin haze of hair behind his ears. His face and pate were very white and heavily lined. The small eyes were deep set and barely visible but with a mean, beady glint in them. The moustache was ragged and the heavy, dark stubble on his cheeks and neck made a startling contrast with his paper-white features.

"Hello, son," said the stranger.

As a boy, I remembered the imposing physical size of my father; the thick and darkly curled hair, the even white teeth and the muscled frame. It had been twenty-five years, and I'd known there would be changes. Of *course* there would be changes. I'd expected that. But there must have been some mistake, because this man in front of me bore no resemblance to the man I remembered.

"What? Not even a hello-how-are-you for your old man?"

Even his voice was unrecognisable.

"I'm not surprised. Been a lot of water under this old bridge."

I couldn't find anything to say.

"So – what? You want us to take a blood test or something? Think there's time for that? Maybe hook me up to a lie detector? Something like that?"

I searched his face again and recognised nothing.

"Hey – this is *good*."

"Good?"

"Don't you get it? Maybe all the time I've been in here, they got the wrong man. Sure. Tell that to the Governor. Miscarriage of justice. Mistaken identity. Make me a claim against the state. Get a shitload of money. Spend the rest of my days in style."

He laughed then.

And I knew.

I recognised that laugh. God help me, I did.

"Give me a million dollars and I still wouldn't have time to enjoy it. Hey, I might leave it all to you when I croak. Which won't be long from what they tell me."

"I recognise you."

He leaned forwards, toward the glass.

"Really? I don't recognise you. Last time I saw my boy he was a skinny runt clinging to his momma. Now what I see is a full-grown man."

"Right, that's it," I said. "Visit over."

I began to rise.

"Hey! No, don't. Hey, man. I'm just messing with you. Don't go."

"You don't get to talk about my mother. Not after what you did."

"All right, all right! I'm sorry. I won't say nothing else about your mom. But please, sit down, son. I know it's you. And I am your pa, dad – father, whatever."

I sat again.

"Just tell me what you want."

"That's it. That's it, son."

"Don't call me 'son'."

"Okay…okay… I won't. But please, just sit down and let me say why I asked you here."

I looked past him, at the guard in his room. He hadn't moved an inch. I didn't have to turn to know that my own 'guard' hadn't moved either. Not knowing how this was going to play out, but knowing I could end this any time, I sat back and stared at this guy who was my father and waited for him to play his cards.

He took a deep breath, looked up at the ceiling.

Exhaling, he looked down and at me again.

"You're looking good," he said, at last.

"Thank you," I said.

"Don't mention it. I got some information over the years. You know, your wife and family and things. Nothing detailed. Just – like – basic stuff."

"Right."

"How's…?"

He struggled to remember my wife's name.

"Renee? Fine. She's fine."

"Good. That's good. I heard you got…"

"Yeah, we've got two kids."

"Two, yeah. That's right. That's what I heard. Boy and a girl, right. That would be…"

He waited for me to give their names. I said nothing.

"Good, good. But a boy and a girl, eh? So that makes me – what? Grandpa? Grandad?"

"That makes you a grandfather."

"They know about me?"

"No."

He nodded then, as if he was being reasonable.

"That figures."

Silence.

"Didn't expect to hear from you. Didn't expect no..." He made a sign with his fingers that I think was supposed to be speech marks. "No family 'updates'. Not after..."

"Not after what you did, no."

"Right. But, just shows you. First time we've spoken in more'n twenty plus years, but I know you're married and you got a son and a daughter. Me in solitary. No guards 'palling-up' to me. But I still get to find out stuff. Neat, eh?"

"Very neat. What do you want?"

He laughed then. I didn't like it. It felt like he thought he was taking control of the situation.

"You got nothing I want, son. What the hell you got that I'm gonna want? You gonna get me out? I'm not getting out of here breathing, that's for sure. When the time comes they're gonna put me in a pine box, burn me and scatter what's left in the dirt outside."

He paused, waiting for some kind of response that didn't come.

"Unless you want to ship me out," he continued. "In a fancy coffin. Put me in some nice see-ma-tery with flowers and a stone cross and shit. Think that might save my soul if you did that?"

"You haven't got a soul."

"Now *that's* the truth."

"So what do you want?"

"Like I said, nothing."

"So why send me a letter after all these years?"

"Ah, there you are! Sent the letter but don't mean I want something from you. Maybe it's the other way round. Maybe I *got* something for you."

"What could you possibly have that I might want from you?"

He started to make a noise that was something like a laugh, but quickly stopped himself when he saw my reaction and knew it was hair trigger whether I walked out on him. He took a deep breath again, closed his eyes and calmed something inside him.

"Your granddaddy was a special man. You never knew him. Killed by the cancer 'fore you were born. But he showed me lots of stuff. Showed me lots of truths. Secret truths. Now, don't get...riled, when I tell you this. There were some killings off the interstate close to Byersville when I was a boy. That was your granddaddy."

Behind him, I saw the guard raise his head. Even though nothing had been said in the Governor's letter, I wondered if someone was recording this conversation.

"He used to take me up in the hills there, overlooking the highway. He had a high-powered rifle with a scope. He'd ask me to pick the cars, and then he'd pop them. *Pop, pop, pop!* Then we'd hightail it. He'd make sure to take the empty cartridges. They never caught us. Later – there was other stuff, but I don't need to go into that here. He was a much better father to me than I was to you. Know why? 'Cause he never got *caught*. My trouble is, I was stupid and kept getting caught. Not for the important stuff, not for the *big* stuff. Not for the kind of stuff I'd want to share with you in the same way my daddy shared stuff with me. But for the pissy little stuff that used to keep me away from home. Either locked up like this or on the run."

"Or Mom on the run from you, with me. She did a good job, keeping me away from you."

"By God, she did. A real good job. But that's why I wasn't able to share what I wanted with you. That's why you've got big holes in your education. Your granddaddy told me about the Great Mystery. Told me what he'd been searching for all his life."

"Is that it? Because I'm going now."

"Don't you want to know what he was looking for? What I've been looking for?"

"No."

"You know I'm dying. If I could turn myself inside out I'd show you what's going on inside me. It's the blood, boy. It's all about the blood."

"All about the blood. That I believe. Goodbye."

"Please! Please…if you give me just two more minutes I'll be done. And then you can be done." He held his hands wide in a plea. "Please?"

"Two minutes."

"Okay, okay." He took a breath to catch and put together his thoughts and then he launched right in. "One of the things I have in here – *have* had in here – is plenty of time. Time to think. But more important, time to read. There's one hell of a prison library in here. And

I can read pretty much anything I want. Not fiction. No, sir. Not any of that made-up stuff. Textbooks with facts. Facts!"

Those small, beady eyes were wide back there in the white slits of his face.

"Medical textbooks. Full of facts. So I started looking. Reading everything I could get my mitts on. But I still couldn't find the answer that I was looking for, that your granddaddy had been looking for. I kept reading, though. Kept searching. Lotsa big words I didn't understand, so I used that dictionary a lot."

He was filled with some kind of energy now. He wasn't looking at me anymore. He was looking up and to the side, as if he'd started giving a lecture or a speech in a preacher's tent somewhere.

"Here's some facts."

He cleared his thoughts and pulled something out of his mind, something he'd committed to memory.

"Why are veins blue when blood is red? It's a wonderment, it truly is. Con...sul...sultant...cardy..." This wasn't coming easy to him so he started again. "Consultant cardiologists at the...Tayburn Cardo... Cardovascular Society..." He smiled then, because he'd got it right. "They say that red blood cells travel from the heart out to the body's extreme-ittys." Another smile. "Where they give up their oxy-gen. The dee...de-oxygenated...deoxygenated blue blood cells then travel back to the heart. So why, I say *why* do we only see the blue veins? That's because the arteries pumping the red blood cells out at a higher pressure have thicker walls than the veins that carry the blue blood back. Veins have thinner walls, see? And they're closer to the surface of the skin."

He stopped then and looked back at me, eyebrows raised as if he'd made some incredibly important point. He continued.

"So why don't we bleed blue blood?"

I just looked at him.

"We do if we cut a vein," he went on. "But it doesn't stay blue. It's *blue-red* when it comes out. The deeper you cut the darker blue it gets. But when it comes out − the air gets to it, and it turns red. See?"

Something turned inside me. My stomach rolled.

"I said two minutes..."

"Sure, that's what we agreed. And this has been one minute. Another minute left. Ever heard what people call 'Blue Blood'? Came from

Spain years ago. Spicks used it to explain the difference between…"
He struggled again to remember the exact phrasing he'd committed
to memory. "The diff'rence between 'pale-skinned Yooro-peings
and darker-skinned North Africans'. Did you know, back in those
olden times, them meddy-evil times, those Royal Family types, those
Kings and Queens and Princes and Princesses – they suffered from this
disease called…"

He paused again, intent on getting the word right.

"Argy-rosis. That's it – argyrosis."

A smile. He was pleased with himself. When he looked at me dead
straight again and no smile came back, he cleared his throat, looked
around and went back to lecturing again.

"They used lots of silver in their medicines and stuff back then. Can
you believe that? Silver! Lots of silver in them Royal Family medicines
– and it turned their skin blue. *Blue!* And you heard about them Royal
Families having 'blue blood', right? Gotta be a connection, right? Then
there's what those others say in the books, about 'Blue Bloods' – Royal
Families, I mean. They were so damned rich, they could afford to have
them peasants working for them all day long while they stayed indoors
and got waited on and stuff. Never got no sunlight, see? So 'cause they
never got no sunlight, their skins got real pale and them there peasants,
when they come begging and scraping, they could see that pale white
skin and underneath that skin – *underneath* – they could see those blue
veins running deep and bluer than blue. That's why they called 'em
'Blue Bloods'. Still do in foreign places like England."

There were drops of sweat on his forehead and he wasn't looking at
me anymore. Deep down in his face those eyes were somehow inside-
out and looking at a place deep inside him that was completely mad.

"That's your two minutes now," I said. "For definite." I stood up.

It refocused his inward-looking eyes.

"Sorry." His smile was thin and sickly. It reminded me of the
expression I'd once seen on a wild dog that had been lying dead in the
underbrush back of our garden lot years ago. "Thing is…" he said, and
I turned to look back at the guard by the door. "It's a family thing. My
daddy knew – just *knew* – that the real colour of blood is blue, not red.
Blue. He knew it. But he also knew that it's got a magic to it. And it can
hide that magic and its secret even from them scientist guys and those

doctors and those so-called experts. It hides the secret that it's blue. And when things are — *opened up* — it turns red. That's why he did what he did, trying to catch it out. Find out *why* it keeps that secret. Maybe the biggest secret ever. He passed that on to me, and after he passed away I kept looking. Kept searching and a-hunting. Kept on opening them up and digging deeper, trying to catch it out. But it hangs on to that secret hard, son. Turns red in the first openings, but then — later — just when you think you're getting somewhere, it turns brown and black in the drying. Like it's laughing at you."

"Get me out of here," I said to the guard, who was now looking at me. I couldn't make out what was in his eyes, but I knew that he didn't want to be in that room anymore either.

I stood up and turned my back on the man behind the glass.

He said: "Heard the saying, 'It's in the blood'?"

I didn't look back at him as the guard turned and began finger-stabbing numbers into the wall-set keyboard next to the door.

"Well," my father continued. "That need to know the secret about the colour of blood — what it all means — that was in your granddaddy. And he gave it to me, that need in our blood, see? Needing to know. In our family. In our blood. And it's in your blood too, boy! Blood will out. Blood is blue, not red. Pretty soon, you're going to want to know why that is. Maybe not now, maybe not tomorrow. But soon. And when your blood sends you out to follow in *my* footsteps — in your *family* footsteps — you're going to want to know why it hides that secret from us all, more than anything else in the world. It'll come, boy."

Why the hell was it taking longer to get out of this room than it took to get in?

"When I'm gone, you'll carry on what Granddaddy started and I continued. You won't be able to stop from looking for it. And if you don't find out and they get you? Well, your boy will just take over from you, and maybe the boy that comes after him. Thing is, you just got a heads-up from me."

When the door to my interview room finally opened and the guard stood to one side to let me pass through, I did look back at him.

"Blood's blue, boy. Not red. When you find out why, it'll be the most important discovery in the world. You'll be a big man."

"Your own blood hates you, Dad. What you have in those veins of yours is going to kill you."

"It got me beat, that's for sure. But you'll carry on what we started. You'll find out. It's in our bloodline."

I turned and walked out.

I don't remember much about my walk back out of that prison block, but it seemed like a weird reverse of the way they walked me in. I remember the clashing of gates and doors, the high echoes of voices far away – some of them jeering, but not at me as far as I could tell. The flat sound of my footsteps on cold concrete floors. More security questions that didn't seem to make much sense, but my answers seemed good enough to not have me slapped inside a cell. The beeping of security lights. I just seemed to let it all happen. Somebody asked me to raise my hands once, which I did. Don't know why. But I did.

When I was properly aware again, I was standing outside the prison and I was suddenly aware that all the stuff I'd handed in for security when I went in – my belt, my wallet, the stuff in my pockets – was all back with me again, although I couldn't remember being given it. That great steel door was behind me and the sun was still high in the sky. Only now, that big door seemed to be giving off a wall of coldness – the complete opposite of that blast furnace heat when I'd first arrived. That just didn't make any sense at all.

I walked away from that big door towards our pickup, seeing the driving door open as Renee saw me coming and began to climb out.

I waved and kept walking towards her, feeling that cold on my shoulders and back.

The last image of the man who called himself my father was still burned in my mind.

The true colour of blood is blue, not red.

Now I could see the look of real concern etched on Renee's face, waiting to see how I'd react and what I might say.

It's in the blood, boy. Sooner or later, it'll come out in you. You won't be able to help yourself. You'll have to take it on, keep looking for the answer.

Both of the pickup's back doors opened, making little swirls of dust in the dirt around the wheels. Pete and Torry tumbled out and ran toward me. Torry was running just like the time she'd won the sprint race on school sports day. Elbows tight into her side, forearms like little bronze pistons. Pete was running his gangly scarecrow way, arms all over the place. Renee called to them, but suddenly the kids were on me and I managed to sweep them both up in the crooks of my arms. The kids laughed and wriggled, but there were shadows in Renee's smile when I reached her. When I leaned down to kiss her, both kids still wriggling in my arms, she kissed me back hard with both arms around my neck.

When she stood back to look at me and I lowered the kids carefully down, I could see the unasked questions in her eyes.

"It's okay," I said.

But the questions were still in her eyes.

"Later, okay?"

"Okay," she replied, and her eyes were that startling blue.

The kids were pulling me to the car and making noises about previous promises of a new ice-cream parlour visit in the middle of town somewhere, ten miles away.

Their eyes were the same startling blue as their mother's.

I laughed, and when I wiped sweat from my brow and looked up at the sky above – it was cloudless.

And beautiful.

A beautiful, beautiful blue.

THE NINE OF DIAMONDS

Carole Johnstone

It's a strange building. A commercial high-rise in the city centre with mean-sized, green glass panels and neon-orange metal uprights. I've seen it before, of course; passed it every day on the way to the job I no longer have, and wondered often what company in their right mind would choose to have offices inside it. Now I know who chose the first floor at least.

The doorman is skinny and young. I mistake him for a smoker until he sidesteps in front of me as I reach for the door.

"Who you here to see then?"

He has a skewed badge close to his collar; gold and dull with fingerprints, a big hole where the pin has been shoved through his shirt too many times.

Jim Easton
Temple Buildings

"The Nine of Diamonds. I've got a job interview at ten. Annie Paisley."

Jim Easton looks down at his phone and shakes his head. "Don't have you on the list."

"Well. It must be a mistake." I take out my own phone. "I can call them—" But he's still shaking his head. "What?"

"If you're not on the list you're not coming in."

I snort. "Did you *really* just say that?" But when he only goes on looking at me like I'm a fencepost, I narrow my eyes. "Is this a joke?"

He blinks. He has a dilated pupil, I notice. The left one, like Bowie.

"Okay." And under the impatience – I was running late before I even encountered this entirely pointless person; who posts a bouncer outside an office block? – jitters something close to becoming panic. I *need* this job. "Guess one joke deserves another. Three fish are in a tank. One asks, 'How do you drive this thing?'"

He gives me another blank look that makes me want to scream. I smile instead, throw in a quick wink. Tony always used to say he'd jump off a cliff if I asked him with a wink.

"What's the difference between a hippo and a Zippo? One is really heavy, and the other is a little lighter. No? What do you call cheese that isn't yours? Nacho Cheese."

This last earns me a chuckle that rattles as if he might be a smoker after all. "That's a good one."

"My best one."

He studies me for a bit, and so I go on smiling the way girls are supposed to smile at boys who are in their way and happy about it.

"All right then," he grins, displaying very straight teeth. "Guess I can make an exception just this once."

★ ★ ★

"So. Do you know what it is that we do?"

Now that I'm sitting in the very ugly and very maroon office of the man who could be the deciding factor in whether or not I become homeless in the next couple of weeks, my something close to panic is now just panic. I don't know how to answer that question without admitting that I found the job advert on the floor below my neighbour's mail-dookit – a PhD lecturer whose hobbies are screwing his students and ignoring his junk mail long enough that gravity eventually scatters it to the four corners of the communal lobby. Until someone – usually me – picks it up.

"I don't. Sorry." My chair creaks every time I move, an unpleasant squeal that makes me wince.

"Good," Mr. Campbell, *call me Billy*, says. The name doesn't suit him at all; he reminds me of the guy who played Dougal MacKenzie in *Outlander*. He has a very impressive moustache.

"Good?"

"Well, let me put it this way." He leans back in his chair, steeples his fingers. "We don't *want* people to know what we do."

"Right." I suddenly wonder if this is going to be legal, and my panic gets a little sharper when I realise I don't care.

"Do you know what the nickname for the nine of diamonds is, Ms. Paisley?"

"Annie. No." And this time I manage to squash the *Sorry*.

"The Curse of Scotland. There are lots of theories why – pretty much all of them tied up in one bloody Scottish defeat or another. There are plenty to choose from."

He looks at me expectantly as if that's explanation enough, but I bite my tongue and endure the silence, the better not to screw up this interview any more than I suspect I already have.

Billy stands up and then sits down on the desk opposite me and my creaky chair. He's incredibly tall; his boots almost touch the toes of mine.

"Have you ever been tailgated or cut up on the motorway? Of course you have," he says putting up a hand. "What about cheated on or swindled? Dumped? Treated like shit on someone's shoe? Ignored? Fired? There's an awful lot that can go wrong in a person's life because of other people. So much that is unjust and unfair."

He has this way of looking at you that is both comforting and incredibly unnerving – it's very *undivided*. Perhaps it's his equivalent of a wink.

I think of that big client that complained about the order I stuffed up – even though I know I didn't; all the times Frank the Wank said yes to me coming in late and then snitched on me to HR; all that unpaid leave before Tony was convicted and sentenced. How Frank didn't just fire me, but did it at a staff meeting for the Christmas party. And then I get hot with shame when I think of Tony, who doesn't even have the luxury of wondering if he'll be homeless in a couple of weeks.

"And have you ever wanted those other people just to see it?" Billy says. His big hands are gripping the desk either side of his thighs. "To see you? To visit it back on them ten-fold? Have you ever just wanted to walk up to someone and say *I curse you*?" He leans more than just a little too close and my chair squeals. "And have them *be* cursed?"

I think of the nine of diamonds. And then about a dozen bad horror movies. And then that last day in court when Tony had been sentenced. Héloïse Dupont in the same black trouser suit she'd worn every day of the trial, hands folded in her lap, staring always at me. "You *curse* people?"

He leans back and I see the flash of very white teeth through his beard and moustache. "Indeed we do."

"*How?*"

"Every case is different. We might hack their email, their social media. Cancel subscriptions, redirect their mail. Write letters of complaint. Sabotage their job, leave bad reviews. Sabotage their relationships. On occasion, we defraud them out of money, but we always return it." He shrugs. "One client wanted us to leave bags of dog poo everywhere the subject went, that was it."

My relief is tinged with almost disappointment. "It's not real."

"Oh, but it is." He gives me a wolfish grin. "The subject will always at some point wonder – *is* it them? *Is* it their curse?"

"It's about power."

"Yes! The point is less to ruin the subject's life than to give back control to the client. To have someone believe that you actually have the power to curse them is very…therapeutic."

"But it's still not real."

"The subject's perception is real. And the client's power is very real. They have the authority to stop it at any time, after all. The world turns, Annie, on people's sense of fairness, of justice." He shrugs. "Even if, deep down, it's always about revenge."

I swallow. "How bad can it get? I'm not going to hurt anyone."

He grins again. "There's a sliding scale of…punishments, for want of a better word. Various packages are available. Like I said, it's mostly just inconveniencing people, unsettling them, freaking them out. Every once in a blue moon we'll get a doozy – big client, big pay-out – but the rest of the time it's disgruntled ex-lovers, victims of road rage, con men, and so on." He stands up and goes back around his desk, opens a drawer and brings out a clear wallet. "Our latest subject, for example, is this guy. Ricky Crawford, age thirty-two. Serial cheater; his fiancée found him in bed with her cousin two months ago."

"Ouch." The chair shrieks as I lean forward. The photo of Ricky Crawford is smugly handsome in a suit and striped tie.

"Since the fiancée hired us, he's been on multiple dates with women, via a few very exclusive…" he pauses, smiles, "dating services. But poor

Ricky hasn't had much luck. In fact, if he hasn't developed some kind of complex about the number of rejections he's been on the receiving end of, then there's a lot more wrong with him than an inability to be faithful." He sits down, raises his eyebrows. "So. Would you do that?"

"What?"

"Go on bad dates with bad guys. To make them feel bad."

A flash of Tony's smile and the way my skin always prickles when he touches me. "Sure."

Billy nods, pushes the wallet back into his drawer. "There are many things you can choose to do working for us – as much or as little as you like, depending on what money you want to make."

"How do they end? The curses."

"Usually they just end. Most often, all that's needed to trigger some kind of remorse is being faced with direct consequences, karma, however they choose to see it. Of course, the real success stories are when the subject begs for the forgiveness of the client. It affords closure to them both. And, with a bit of luck, peace."

"But what about violence? Surely a subject has gone after a client if they think they're responsible for what's happening to them?" A kernel of anger pops inside my belly – small, far smaller than the rage, hot and white, that wakes me up at 3:00 a.m. most nights. "That's what I'd want to do. Take care of it myself."

"There are risks. And there have been…incidents." He gives me what I think is supposed to be a reassuring smile. "But we take every precaution. We provide surveillance for our clients and for our employees, and, if needs be, protection. We have no moral compass about what we do, Annie. We're hired to do a thing and we do it. But we take absolutely no unnecessary risks either, be sure of that."

"Okay." Even though I care as much about that as whether what he's doing is legal. "So, is that what my role would be then? Ghosting cheats?"

"Perhaps." He smiles. "Every employee is considered on an individual basis, just as every client is. What are your talents, Annie?"

"My talents?"

"Are you any good with computers?"

"No, not really. I mean, I know I said in my application that I—"

"No matter. Besides, I would say that your biggest asset is that you're unobtrusive."

I blink. "You mean invisible."

He cocks his head. "You're also charming. When Mr. Easton refused to let you in, you didn't get angry or loud, you charmed him. That is a talent."

"That was a test?"

"You'd be surprised by how many folk actually give up and go away." He shrugs. "You didn't."

I jump when the phone on his desk starts ringing.

"That will be a gentleman wanting to confirm a dinner booking at *Le Gavroche*. Tell him there's no record of him having made it."

"*Le Gavroche* in London?"

He doesn't reply, only looks at me from under raised eyebrows. I reach over and pick up the phone.

"Uh...hello?" I look at Billy and he raises his eyebrows a little more. "*Le...Gavroche*. How can I help you?"

Billy reaches over to press the loudspeaker, and an English voice, fast and impatient, bursts into the space between us.

"Yes, hi. Look, I got an email saying I had to confirm a dinner booking I made months ago. Harrison, next Friday at seven."

I look down at the desk. "I'm sorry, sir, but we have no booking under that name for that date."

A pause. "What?"

"We have no booking for Harrison next Friday evening."

"*What?* Are you serious?"

"I'm afraid—"

"Do you have any idea how important this meeting is for me? D'you have – wait, why the fuck would I have been sent an email today asking me to confirm a booking you're saying you don't have?"

My pulse quickens a little at that, and this time when I look across at Billy, there's a small smile at the corners of his mouth.

"You must have been double-booked in error, sir. We've recently switched our software systems, and unfortunately—"

"Well, you can just un-double-fucking-book me then." Panic has turned his impatience ugly; his voice vibrates. "In fact, let me speak to your fucking manager right now."

"I am the manager, sir," I say, sitting up a little straighter. "And *Le Gavroche* has a zero tolerance policy towards the abuse of our staff, so I'm afraid this conversation is now over." I pause as his curses echo around the maroon room. "Good afternoon, Mr. Harrison." My hand is shaking as I set down the handset.

"Bravo, Annie, that was not bad at all," Billy says, his smile bigger.

"How did you *do* that?"

He shrugs. "No idea. Many of our employees are, in fact, good with computers."

"Oh." I look down at the phone, and then back at him. "So, am I an employee now too?"

Billy stands, and then nods, holding out a large hand for me to shake. "You are, Ms. Paisley. Welcome to the Nine of Diamonds."

★   ★   ★

When I hear the footsteps behind me as I exit the tube and turn towards home – short-heeled and quick, always so quick – my good mood is only slightly dampened. This has been the first great day in weeks. Months. And I refuse to let her ruin it.

I cross over the road, take my keys out of my pocket. Even though it's barely four in the afternoon, it's dark, and the white LED streetlights do little more than blacken the shadows between them. She only ever follows me in the dark – at first, I thought because she wanted not to be seen, but it's just the opposite. She always wants me to know she's there. And she does it in the dark because she thinks it will frighten me more. And – at first – it did.

I pick up speed as I turn onto the path up to the flat, and I have the keys in the lock before I hear the gate reopen behind me. I rush in and slam the door without looking at its wire-grid window. Spin around instead to look at the flickering overhead fluorescent, the bank of rust-coloured mail-dookits next to the communal stairs. The already overflowing junk mail. I can hear her fingernails tapping at the window and the big handle of the door rattles – there's a loose screw at its top. One of these days – nights – I'm sure she's going to wrench it right off.

I don't confront her anymore because it serves no purpose. She *wants* me to confront her. Instead, I pretend I don't see her; I pretend I can't hear her. I pretend that on the few occasions she manages to get close enough, that I can't feel her warm breath against my skin. I pretend, as

I run up the stairs and fight to hold on to that first great thing to happen to me in months, that she isn't there at all.

*   *   *

Nothing happens for days. Almost two weeks. No one answers the number I called to arrange that interview with Billy Campbell. And I start to panic. I'm three months in arrears on paying for the ludicrously expensive lawyer I hired for Tony. I'm already being threatened with the prospect of a debt collection agency and bailiffs for utility bills. Next month's rent is due. I applied for a loan before I got fired, but haven't heard anything about that either, and now don't expect to. I speak to Tony most days, but I can't tell him about my money troubles or my weird maybe-job because every time he sounds a little worse, a little more subdued, and no matter how bad it gets for me, I'm not the one serving eight years for killing someone while driving drunk.

And then, finally, a big brown envelope. Inside it, a letter addressed to me with the Nine of Diamonds stamped in its top-right corner, and several more envelopes that are completely blank.

Post these letters to the addresses that will be emailed to you in the next hour. Post BY HAND only within the next 24 hours. Reply to the email once job is completed.

All the letters look the same as each other: white, A4 business envelopes with what feels like only one page of paper inside them. I think about steaming one open, but chicken out. This is my first task; I can't risk fucking it up. I think about Jim the skinny bouncer. Besides, it might be another test.

I wait until it's light, and then I go out on foot. I take buses to each location, having already mapped out my exact route in forensic detail. Although all the houses are in south London like my Lewisham flat, they range as far west as Kingston and as far east as Bexley. It takes an alarmingly long time; eventually my adrenaline runs out of steam even if my panic doesn't. I keep my hood up and my head down; avoiding faces and the buses' CCTV. By the time I get home, I'm so cold and exhausted that I collapse on the sofa and don't wake up until the next morning. And when I remember to email that I've done it, two hundred and fifty pounds appears in my bank account less than ten minutes later.

★　★　★

She knows when I go to see Tony. Every second and fourth Friday between 13:45 and 14:30. It's the only time she follows me during the day. It's harder to ignore her then, too, those quick sharp clicks in sensible shoes, but I do it. I keep walking and I don't look back. I think instead of turning into a pillar of salt. I think of a lover left in hell for all eternity. And the whole way to the prison, I don't look back once.

Tony smiles when he sees me, and hugs me just as hard and long as ever, but there are bigger and darker shadows under his eyes, and he's lost even more weight.

"Did she follow you again?" is the first thing he says.

"It's fine. Don't worry."

He starts to ball his big hands into fists until he remembers that he's holding mine. I squeeze his back.

"How are you doing, honey? You don't look like you're taking care of yourself."

He winces and closes his eyes. When he opens them again I see how bloodshot they are. "I'm all right, Annie. I'm more worried about you. What about the overdue payments? How are—"

"I got the loan!" I lie, with as big a smile as I can muster. "And a new job. It's not much, leafleting mostly, but they pay well, better than I expected."

"That's good," he says. "The sooner you get that law firm off your back, the better."

"But what about the appeal? I mean, that's why we're doing it, right? That's why we need to pay the—"

"I'm not appealing."

"What?" I look at the crown of his bowed head, and panic starts to tighten my chest. "But we...you promised that you—"

He looks at me. "I'm not appealing. There's no point."

"Of course there is!" But I can see in his eyes that he's decided, that nothing I say will change his mind. And worse than that, I can see something else, something far more terrible.

"Annie," he says, reaching across the table to take hold of my hands again. "Baby."

I realise that I'm shaking my head and trying to stand up.

"Stop," he says, and I stop. Whenever he uses that voice, sharp but so warm, so full of all the things he's always been to me – love and want and family, but most of all, safety – I never think of saying no.

"You have to get on with your life, Annie," he says. "You need to find someone else."

"I don't want anyone else, you know I don't. *You* don't want anyone else." My face is hot, my eyes blurring and stinging, and the last is a question, a plea, because he promised. He promised that we'd be together forever.

"Listen to me," he says, and his hold on my fingers tightens. "I don't want you coming here anymore."

"She'll follow me anyway," I say in desperation.

"It's not just that. This doesn't have to poison both of our lives." He lets go of me, taking back his hands even as I try to grab hold of them again. "If you love me, you'll do what I'm asking you to do. I want you to go. And I don't want you to come back."

★   ★   ★

Sometimes I dream about the boy. I wake up to darkness, red and white blurry lights, and then the sound – the terrible thud that I feel even in my toes. The scream of brakes and splash of water and the fear in Tony's curse. The crash against the windscreen, the squeal of a wiper. The circles like a jagged bullseye flashing red and white in the dark. The boy.

And then I wake up for real.

★   ★   ★

Life goes on. I start to get regular big brown envelopes, and spend most days pushing those white business letters into letterboxes and mailboxes, even PO boxes all over south London. Many times to the same addresses, again and again, but I force myself not to wonder about what's inside those letters. Or what might happen to me if I get caught posting them.

Less often, I'm asked to stay in and answer phone calls like the one in Billy Campbell's office: booking confirmations for restaurants, hotels, and holidays. Or I'm sent a list of places to phone and bookings to cancel myself. Those days I don't like; I have an irrational terror of being recognised, and the shouting, worse, the upset or panic is too real, too close. Too immediate. It's the hardest thing of all. That I'm contributing to the suffering of other people – no matter what they've done to deserve their *curse* – when so many things are going wrong in my own life. When I know what it feels like to suffer, to sit in the dark all alone, but seeing no point in getting up, in switching on a light.

Tony hasn't called, and he's taken me off his visitor list. And it feels like my bad luck has truly peaked when, on the afternoon of what would have been my next visit to the prison, the first debt collection agency letter arrives. And in the next post, a 30-day eviction notice for outstanding rent. I drink two shots of vodka, think of Billy's *There are many things you can choose to do working for us – as much or as little as you like, depending on what money you want to make*, and then I email the Nine of Diamonds.

★   ★   ★

The multi-storey car park is mostly empty, even though the shopping mall next door is still open. The top floor is emptier still, and I find the car easily: a silver Audi with the right reg. There's no one in it.

I'm as dismayed by the bright light in here as I was by the dark late-afternoon outside. I don't think she followed me; it's not like she ever tries to hide. And, although there are plenty of CCTV cameras in here, I'm wearing gloves, two hoods, and a scarf pulled up to my nose. I still jump when tyres squeal on a ramp a few floors down, and my heart starts to stutter and flutter.

Come on. Get it done.

I hurry towards the Audi, check again that it's empty before I swing my rucksack onto the concrete floor. It makes a loud *clunk* and I cringe, squatting down to peer through the Audi's windows until I'm certain no one has heard. My hand closes around the screwdriver, and I stay on my haunches as I push it into the first rear tyre. It's surprisingly difficult. Inside the gloves, my fingers slip and grow quickly sweaty as I push and push, until finally the tyre gives and I hear the whistle of air, feel it cool and quick against my wrists. I shuffle slowly round the car, until every tyre is done, and then I shove the screwdriver back inside the rucksack and bring out the hammer instead. I close the rucksack and put it on; I've no intention of stopping to do anything but run once I've done this.

There's a tartan tree air-freshener hanging from the rearview mirror. We had two cherries on stalks. I can see my reflection in the Audi's front passenger window: a faceless black hood. I think of waking up in my dream, those blurry red and white lights, a jagged bullseye. I draw back the hammer, and at the last minute, close my eyes – so that I feel rather than see the window smash into pieces. I brace for an alarm, but it doesn't come; the email assured me the Audi was fitted with an immobiliser and nothing else. I glance left and right as I move around to the front windscreen, and when I draw back the hammer to hit it too, I've time to fiercely wish that they'd sent me on a bad date with a bad man instead before someone rushes me from behind.

I know it's her before I spin round. She flies at me again as I try to ward her off, her hair wild and wet, eyes wide – nothing at all like the woman who'd come to court every day in expensive suits; cool and impervious like a waxwork. Most unsettling of all, she doesn't say anything, makes no kind of sound. Whereas I'm grunting and shouting and breathing too hard, my panic unwieldy. She grabs hold of my arms – I can feel her nails through my shirt and coat as they dig in and twist – and my scream is more than alarm or shame or anger, it's horror, instinctive and real – I *need* to get away. As soon as I remember the hammer I'm already bringing it down towards her, towards that face, that silence.

I miss, and the loud sob that comes out of my chest frightens me more than anything else – a terrified sense of relief that doesn't come close to registering in her eyes at all. I wrench myself away, and then I'm running back towards the big number 5 on the wall next to the staircase, the hammer clutched to my chest and the rucksack thumping against my back.

★   ★   ★

"You're lucky, Ms. Paisley," Billy Campbell says. "I don't usually meet with employees in person. But I'm assured your message was very *emphatic*."

I think of the email I sent once I'd got back from the multi-storey and cringe a little. Today his office seems suffocatingly maroon. As ugly and unsettling as those green glass panels and neon-orange metal uprights outside. Thankfully, there had been no Jim Easton.

"I just..." I look down at my bitten fingernails. "I just wanted to be clear – in person – that I don't want to do anything illegal. Not again. I want to make more money than I have been, but I don't want to do anything illegal."

"I see. And is someone forcing you to do—"

"No, but I'm not being offered anything *else*. I just get sent lists of names and phone numbers and those bloody envelopes, and I can't survive on that. I asked if I could do what you said, the whole dating cheats thing, and they said..." I make myself look at him, and my chair gives a very pained creak. "They said I wasn't suitable."

"Ah."

That kernel of anger pops inside my belly again. "I mean, don't you *know* what they said? Aren't you in charge?"

"Of recruitment, yes." His smile is brief. "And I suppose I'm an HR of sorts, hence this meeting. But no, I have no involvement in the day-to-day, so to speak." He leans forward and his eyes narrow. "Ms. Paisley, pardon my saying so, but you do not look well. Is there something else?"

I blow out a breath, close my eyes. "There's a woman. Héloïse Dupont." It feels strangely good to say her name aloud, as if it might diminish her power. "My boyfriend – fiancé – and I...last year we were in a car accident. She and her ten-year-old son were crossing the road. It was dark, wet, and we didn't see the zebra crossing, and the boy..." The memory of that terrible thud shakes through me; the squeal of a wiper. "It was an accident. The boy died. But it was an accident."

Billy's lips press together, but his eyes are sympathetic.

"Tony had been sure he was under the limit. He'd barely had anything at all. But it... She blames both of us. She follows me because she can't follow him, I guess. I...I can't imagine what it's like to lose your son, so I don't go to the police, it isn't fair. But she won't leave me alone. I can't sleep, I have nightmares, and Tony... Tony—"

Billy stands up and comes round the desk. He leans down to pat my arm before folding his own. "Perhaps, then, we could be of some help?"

I look up at him. "You? How?"

He gives me the benefit of that *undivided* look again. "You could curse her."

"What?" And my head shake is furious enough to crack something inside my neck, because instantly a big part of me wants to say yes. Even wonders if that's why I've told him at all. Instead, I think of that rage, hot and white, that always comes back from the nightmare with me. I think of Tony's face, its dark shadows and concave cheekbones; *Did she follow you again?* I think of her wild eyes, her never-ending silence; her fingernails against the flat's wire-grid window, against my skin. I think of sitting in this very office months ago and telling Billy Campbell exactly what I'd want to do if someone ever persecuted me.

"No." I stand up. "I'll take care of it myself."

★   ★   ★

She works at a school. She's a history teacher. I remember thinking at the trial that it was strange; she didn't look like a history teacher. Or any kind of teacher. And then I remember thinking that perhaps she used to. Before her son died.

The foyer is shiny-floored and bright with light. Empty in the way a place otherwise full of people always feels – a silence that is liminal and fleeting.

"I need to speak to Héloïse Dupont," I say to the young receptionist.

"She's teaching at the moment."

"It's important. My name's Annie Paisley."

The receptionist eyes me with suspicion, not that I blame her. I know I look a mess because I feel one. Frazzled and hollowed out. Down to my last nerve. And it's raw, thin, about ready to snap.

"It's an emergency."

Finally, she nods, picks up the phone, and as soon as she says my name, I hear the dial tone, abrupt and loud.

When Héloïse Dupont appears, I'm startled that she looks like the Héloïse Dupont from the trial again, and not the wild-eyed wraith that has tortured me in the dark for months. She's wearing another trouser suit, navy rather than black, and her hair is shiny and straight, pulled back into a ponytail.

I walk away from the receptionist, who isn't even trying to feign disinterest. Héloïse follows me. When I turn around, she looks at me, says nothing at all. And that last nerve frays a little more, all the hot, white rage a rolling boil beneath.

"I came here because I want it to stop."

She raises just one eyebrow and folds her arms. I jolt, as I belatedly see the traces of a black eye beneath her make-up. Did I do that in the multi-storey? I'm appalled to realise that I don't know.

"I want all this to stop."

I fiddle with the strap of the rucksack, its weight heavy against my back. Héloïse recognises it from the multi-storey then, and steps suddenly back, her eyes widening, fear animating her face. When I swing the rucksack around onto the floor to open it, she steps back even more – quick, always quick – her gaze darting to the fire escape.

I think of how much I've prided myself in never looking back. In just walking and walking, and only looking ahead. But it's a lie. My lover is already in hell for all eternity. And worse than a pillar of salt, I'm a statue of stone – carved into a shape that can't be dissolved or remade. Only shattered.

I reach into the bag, and Héloïse finally makes a sound. The same small sound she made when they found Tony guilty. And when I try to give her the photo, she only looks at it wordlessly and backs a little further away.

I set it down on the foyer floor. Its wooden frame makes a loud clack as I look at Tony and me grinning and holding half-full champagne glasses out towards the camera.

"We got engaged that night. At Carluccio's. I was so happy."

I stand up. And hot, white rage bites and burns as I look down at the photo one more time. At my grinning bright-eyed face. *Stop*, Tony says in that voice, sharp but always warm.

"I wouldn't let Tony drive. I thought I was okay. Halfway home, he fell asleep, and then…" I swallow. "I must have too."

I force myself to look up, to look at her. Héloïse Dupont's face is so white, her eyes look black. She's trembling all over like an animal.

"I didn't see you. I didn't see your son, I didn't see...Christof... until—" The tears that are running down my cheeks are cool against my too-hot skin. "And I'm so sorry. I'm so sorry that we said you were lying. I'm so sorry I let Tony take the blame; he thought...we thought he'd be okay, that he'd be under the limit. And I let him lie. *I* lied. And I'm sorry. I'm so, so sorry."

★   ★   ★

The police arrest me a couple of days later, and I'm only surprised that it takes that long. I decline a solicitor. I can tell they think that I'm going to deny my confession because they don't even ask me if I did it. If I killed Christof Dupont and then lied about it. Instead, they sit me down, make a big production out of reading me my rights again, offering me legal aid, a coffee, a glass of water. And after all that they start talking about Héloïse instead.

"A complaint of harassment has been made against you following an incident on Wednesday the twenty-fifth of November when you confronted Ms. Dupont at her place of work, Claremont High School. Do you deny being there?"

I look at the man who introduced himself as PC Derek Munroe, and wonder how old he is. He's trying to grow a beard and the tops of his cheekbones are very pink; I wonder if this is his first interview. Beside him, the older and not at all nervous police sergeant whose name I've forgotten, leans closer with a glower.

"Answer the question, please."

"No," I say. "I was there. I just wanted to talk to her."

The sergeant spins around a laptop so that its screen is facing me and presses Return. The footage is grainy, from a phone. The angle makes me think it must have been the receptionist. I look even worse than I remember: angry and unkempt, gesticulating wildly, my hair swinging around my face as Héloïse keeps backing further and further away from me, her face pale and distressed as she glances towards the fire exit.

"Looks to us like you're threatening her," PC Munroe says.

"I wasn't. I just wanted to—"

"Seems she might already have had plenty to be threatened about. We have CCTV evidence of someone assaulting her in the East Oak Mall's multi-storey car park on Thursday the nineteenth of November – that she alleges is also you."

"No. That was an accident. *She* attacked me. I wasn't—"

"*You* were slashing the tyres and smashing the windows of her car," PC Munroe says.

"*What?*" My chest gets suddenly tight.

"You've been following her for weeks," he says, no longer nervous at all. His eyes are bright. "Stalking her. Terrorising her."

"No." I try to stand up but my legs feel hot and heavy as if I've just downed a shot. "She's been stalking me! For *months*." A brittle kind of dread skates between my shoulder blades like an itch, an almost-knowing that I don't want to acknowledge.

The police sergeant takes a piece of paper out of an evidence bag and unfolds it. Places it in front of me. Cut up letters from a magazine glued to A4 like something out of a bad film.

You've destroyed my life. Yours will be next.

Have you ever just wanted to walk up to someone and say I curse you? *And have them be cursed?*

"Again, unfortunately for you, Ms. Dupont has just had cameras installed above her front door and window. You've been delivering notes like these to her house for weeks."

We take every precaution. We provide surveillance for our clients and for our employees, and, if needs be, protection.

I wonder what was in the letters that I posted to all those other houses, mailboxes, PO boxes. Perhaps nothing at all, just weeks of blank empty pages.

I think of that big client order that I didn't stuff up but which got me fired anyway. The failed loan application. The debt collection letters. The eviction notice. Maybe even Tony. *There's an awful lot that can go wrong in a person's life because of other people. So much that is unjust and unfair.* I think of finding that Nine of Diamonds flyer on the floor of the communal lobby, below the PhD lecturer's mail-dookit.

"I'm the doozy," I say, and when I laugh, both policemen visibly jump. I'm not surprised; it's a high jangling thing, that last tortured nerve finally snapped. "I'm the big pay-out. The every once in a blue moon."

And at once the dread drains out of me – the heat, the panic, that endless keep walking away, don't stop, don't look back.

The subject's perception is real. I think of Billy's grin. That undivided look that was never his version of a wink. *And the client's power is very real. The world turns, Annie, on people's sense of fairness, of justice. Even if, deep down, it's always about revenge.*

And I find that I don't care. I find that I'm glad. I let out the breath I've been holding for so long I forgot that I was drowning. I put my hands on the table and breathe in a new one. I look PC Derek Munroe straight in the eye, and I even manage to smile.

"I'd like to make a confession."

ROOM FOR THE NIGHT

Jonathan Janz

Mr. Nelson looks at me and says, "I almost fucked a cat once."

I start toward the door.

"Now don't get all high-and-mighty on me," he calls. "I never *did* it. I said I thought about it is all."

"This isn't worth it."

"Isn't worth...boy, do you know how long I had to work when I was your age to scrape up twenty bucks?"

I frown. "How old are you anyways?"

"Fifty-six."

I note how the living room curtains turn his pale skin a drab dill-pickle hue. See the sparse, downy hairs clinging to the liver-spotted wasteland of his scalp. The pouchy eye sockets and the overlarge nose. Mr. Nelson looks closer to ninety-six than fifty-six, but whatever. His money will fill up my gas tank as well as anyone's.

I sigh. "I'll give you a few more minutes, but you gotta pay me thirty."

"Done."

"And no more cat-fucking stories."

"I never did!"

I exhale heavily and wander back to the ratty calico couch.

Mr. Nelson eases into his duct-taped recliner. "She was a big white cat. Had this silky coat—"

I start to rise again.

"Wait!" he pleads. "Simmer down. For this to work, I gotta tell you some stuff."

"For *what* to work?"

"I'll get to that," he says. "Just please...sit."

I do. Reluctantly.

"I was drunk that night," he says, eyes glittery. "I was alone, like usual. And Laura, she was sittin' beside me, purring."

"Your cat was named Laura?"

"What's wrong with that?"

"Laura's not something you name a cat. It's something you name a daughter."

"Well this one was named Laura, and she was the best damned cat I've ever had."

He watches me to see if I'll argue, but I don't. The quicker I get this over with, the quicker I can get to Catherine's. But to do that I have to gas up my car, and my parents aren't helping. I get one B-plus and they act like the world's ending and deprive me of my allowance until I prove I'm 'applying myself'. Hence the reason I'm sitting here with the cat-fucker.

"I'd been drinking quite a bit," he says and shoots me a quick, crafty look. "More than usual anyway. And I was watchin' this movie about a guy who falls in love with a mannequin. I forget the name…"

"*Mannequin?*"

He snaps his fingers. "That's it! It had the lady from *Porky's*, what's her name…"

I make a speeding-up gesture.

"Anyhow, the movie had a happy ending, and I got choked up. There was this song, I think it was Jefferson Airplane. And I started in thinking…goddammit, it's *good* that people find each other sometimes. In this case it was a dude finding a mannequin, but that's not the point. They *found* each other."

His eyes take on a bleary look. He has a six-pack of Natural Light beside him, five cans empty, but I don't think it's the alcohol misting him up.

"I know how pitiful this sounds," he goes on, "but some people, they never find somebody. I remember back when I was your age, staying home on Friday nights and askin' my mom why no girl was interested in me." A lost look seeps into his eyes. "Mom said 'They will be, Buster. They will be. One of these days, when you come into your own'…"

I listen, a little disconcerted. I didn't know his name was Buster. To me, he's always been Mr. Nelson, the weird old drunk from down the

street. But now, knowing his first name, picturing him as a teenager...
alone...

I don't like knowing that.

He shakes his head, gazing into the past. "Even then I remember
thinking, 'What if I *don't* come into my own?' What if I stay like this?
The type of guy no one wants to hang out with?"

He looks at me with those pleading wet eyes and I think, *Christ. No
amount of money's worth this.*

"So I'm on the couch," he goes on. "And there's Laura. Just gazing
up at me and purring. Looking at me the way that mannequin lady
looked at Rob Lowe in the movie."

Please stop, I think, bile percolating in the back of my throat.

"So I start to pet Laura, and she pushes into my hand the way
she always did. And it was...a *moment*, you know? That song playin'
on the TV, that cat, my best friend in the world, lookin' at me
the way no one ever had. And I thought, 'Why not? Just why the
fuck not?'"

Holy shit.

"Mr. Nelson—"

"Buster," he corrects, and leans forward to clap a hand on my knee.
When he sees how I tense, he shows me his palms. "Now don't freak
out. I'm not Jeffrey Dahmer."

I'm not entirely convinced, but whatever. The clock is ticking,
and every moment brings me closer to milkshakes and burgers for
me and Catherine.

"What then?" I ask.

He shrugs. "Went upstairs and tried to sleep it off. That's when the
trouble began." He glugs some beer and stares into the can. "That's
when the trouble always begins."

I can tell he's building up to something, and for reasons I can't
explain, I'm dreading this more than some feline sex confession.

In a scarcely audible voice, he asks, "You ever get scared at night?"

"Sure."

He doesn't smile. Doesn't look up. "I don't mean normal scared. I
don't mean scared of the dark or the wind."

I peer out the window, where the sun is tumbling fast. If I don't get out
of here soon, Catherine's folks won't let her leave the house, and my Friday

night will be shot. Sure, there's always Saturday, but my heart is set on seeing her tonight. She's been showing signs lately...gradually wearing down...

"It started when I was a kid," Buster says, "after I looked up a girl's skirt and didn't get caught."

For some reason, this grabs my attention.

A wistful chuckle. "Suzette Barr. Ninth grade. Sat behind me in Bio. Used to watch the doorway for her to come in, hopin' she'd have a skirt on."

"What's your point?"

"After I peeped her, I couldn't sleep. I laid there, not a sound in the world, not a light in my bedroom. But I felt like something was wrong." He pauses. "You ever have the feeling of being watched, Stu?"

I don't like him calling me by name. But he's staring at me, not to be put off.

"Of course. Everyone feels that way sometimes."

"Not like this," he answers. "Not in your own bedroom. Not in the middle of the night." He traces a thumb over the sweating can. "I started to feel...I don't know, exposed? Like I was vulnerable, lying there. I always slept shirtless, and my shoulders, my arm...I felt like anything could touch them."

"So wear a shirt."

"I did. It didn't do any good. There was still my neck, my face. My fingers. Clothes don't cover everything."

The living room's growing dimmer and dimmer. If I don't get out of here soon...

"You felt like you were being watched," I prompt.

He nods. "Felt guilty for what I'd done. For peeping that girl."

I try on a grin. "Most guys try to catch a glimpse at some point."

"I did it a lot," he says. "To a bunch of girls. You do it enough, it consumes you. Can't think of anything else. There's no *room* for anything else."

His tone makes it impossible to hold my grin.

"What if..." he says, "...what if there's something that stores up all our bad things, our lust...and waits."

I shift on the couch. "We talking religion here?"

"Not exactly. At least, not traditional religion. I'm talking ancient stuff. Something elemental. Something that was there at the beginning."

"You need to take it easy on yourself. Stop beating yourself up."

In his haunted gaze I see the desire to believe me. I realise all but the meekest glow has bled from the evening, the curtains admitting just enough light I can still make out Buster in his dinged-up chair.

"Look, Mr. Nelson," I begin, sitting forward. "I really need to get going. If I could have the money now, maybe Catherine and I could still go out."

Though I don't really believe that. Catherine is home for the night, probably pissed at me. Or relieved she doesn't have to climb into my backseat. She let me go further than ever last time, but her body had been as taut as baling wire. Like she was pinching her nose and knocking back some nasty medicine.

Buster nods. "I suppose I should tell you now."

"Tell me what?" I murmur, my mind still on Catherine's firm body.

"Tell you the real reason I need you."

"I knew this was bullshit."

"Please," he says. "I swear I won't hurt you."

"No? Then give me my money."

"I'll pay you a hundred dollars."

"Fine. Pay me a hundred."

His voice quavers. "I don't want anything from you. I just need you to spend the night in my bed."

This time I'm off the couch and to the door in a few lunging strides. I was a moron to enter this weirdo's house, was foolish to ask if he needed his overgrown grass cut. No amount of money is worth doing whatever perverted things he wants me to do. What the hell was I thinking?

I'm wrestling open the door when he seizes my arm, and instinctively I spin and shove him away. He's on his back then, gaping up at me, his bottom lip quivering.

"I won't be in the bed!" he shouts. He nods at the recliner. "I'll be out here."

I face him, hands on hips. "You want to pay me a hundred bucks to sleep in your bed?"

"How much will it take?"

I grunt. "I don't know, a thousand?"

His shoulders slump. "I don't have that kind of money. Not on me, at least."

I consider him, slouching there on his heels. I'd cast him off so easily. We probably weigh roughly the same, but I'm a good deal stronger than he is.

"How much *do* you have here?" I ask.

"Three hundred or so?"

Don't do it, I think. *This is the worst idea ever.*

But an image of Catherine flits through my head, Catherine in my backseat, sliding her bra straps down. We could get dinner tomorrow night – a nice dinner, not McDonald's – and I could drive her to the lake. Hell, with that kind of money I could book us a hotel…

"You promise you're not gonna chain me up in my sleep?"

"Swear to God."

"Three hundred tonight, another seven hundred tomorrow?"

He nods vigorously. "I'll go to the ATM in the morning, drop the money by your house."

I grimace. "Don't come to my *house*. I'll pick it up tomorrow afternoon."

A hurt look passes over his face, but it's gone quickly.

I scratch the back of my neck and mull it over. I know it's a mistake, but I say, "Fine."

Because all I can think about is Catherine.

Catherine and the hotel room.

★   ★   ★

The deal is simple. Buster wants me to sleep in his bed from 10:00 that night until 6:00 a.m. On the way to his bedroom, he asks, "Won't your folks worry about you?"

"I'll text them I'm at a friend's," I say. I pause and glower at him. "But they can track my cell. If anything happens to me, there'll be records of my whereabouts. It's been pinging right from this house, so even if you chop me up and bury me somewhere, they'll know it was you."

I have no idea if this is true, but it sounds good.

"Fine, fine," he murmurs absently. "I won't hurt you. I won't even go in there."

He opens the door and goes in there.

I follow. "You haven't even explained why you need me."

He flips on the ceiling light and moves to the queen-sized bed. The brown blankets are rumpled, his sheets the yellow of overripe onions. The closet door is open just a crack.

I eye the bed. "I'm not gonna get crabs, am I?"

A *pfft*. "I haven't had a woman in here in so long, the crabs woulda died by now."

I arch an eyebrow at him.

He says, "All I need is for you to be here in the dark. I need to find out…" He rubs his scruffy chin. "I need to know if you feel the same thing I do."

I squint at him.

He massages his brow. "Look, this is gonna sound batshit, but bear with me, all right?"

I wait.

Buster says, "I believe certain…desires can become physical. Or can summon something physical."

"That ancient, elemental thing?"

He won't meet my eyes. "Yeah."

"And you're worried it's, what? Living in here?"

He nods.

"Why don't you just sleep somewhere else?"

A pained face. "I've tried that. I've tried everything."

"And?"

"I can't *tell*," he moans. "I've slept in my chair. My car. Even hotels."

"Did the boogeyman follow you?"

"*Don't joke about it!*"

I gape at him. It's the harshest he's spoken all evening.

"Look, kid," he says, "I'm sorry. It ain't your fault. And I probably shouldn't be involving you in this."

But you are, I think.

"It's just," he flails his hands, "I don't know what else to do. When I sleep somewhere else, it's not as bad. But I can't tell if that's because I'm safe or because I'm tellin' myself I am."

I study him. His scraggly facial hair. His mottled scalp. Most of all those watery, egg-yolk eyes. "The feeling is strongest in here?"

He nods.

I move past him. "So what will set your mind at ease?"

"Don't you *see*? If you feel it, that means the *room* is haunted, not just me. I'll sell the house."

I begin to shake my head, but he interrupts.

"You don't understand, Stu. I'm losing my fuckin' *mind*. Can't sleep. Can barely function. You try makin' friends looking like I do. You go out there and try to meet a nice gal."

I bite my lip, look around. It doesn't feel much like a haunted room. Just rundown. And smelly.

"You'll do it?" he asks.

"What happened when you stayed in a hotel?"

His eagerness fades, something haggard and doomed taking its place. "I dunno. I felt like someone was there. Sitting in the corner, in the dark. Staring at me."

He slides open the dresser door, moves some stuff around, and comes out with some crinkled bills. "There's three-oh-eight here. I'll get the rest tomorrow."

I take the money, which feels slightly greasy.

"It's 9:53," he says. "Guess I better leave you to it."

"You'll be out there?"

"Right in the next room."

He's nearly to the door when I call, "Hey, Buster."

"Yeah?"

"What do I do if the thing shows up?"

His expression goes solemn. "I don't know, Stu. If that thing does come…get out of here. If you can."

I try to smile. "If I can?"

He looks at me. "When I feel it drifting toward me, I find it hard to move. Impossible, in fact."

And with that, he goes out and closes the door behind him.

★   ★   ★

I lie there staring at the gloom-painted ceiling for a while. My mind keeps churning from Buster and his strange beliefs, to Catherine, and back to Buster again. I can't see how this little experiment will prove anything. I know nothing will happen, know I'll experience, at worst, a sleepless night. But

I'm already three hundred dollars richer, and unless he's lying, I'll be a lot richer tomorrow.

I close my eyes and roll onto my side.

Catherine.

Man, she's gorgeous. We're both eighteen, but she somehow seems older. Where I'm eager to have fun, take chances, she's always ready with a responsible answer.

If we lie to our parents about where we are, they could find out.

If I get caught drinking, I'll miss half the tennis season.

We can't do that, Stu. I could get pregnant.

God. That terrible word.

I hate the way she says it, like it's inevitable. I explain how effective condoms are, how I'll stop before I get there if that eases her mind. Though I doubt, in the moment, I'll be able to stop.

But man, it would feel good. I think of Catherine's neck, the scent of her perfume. I don't know what it's called, but it drives me crazy, reminds me of lazy summer days and swimming in the lake and her fingers around my neck, her nails teasing my hair…

I open my eyes. Peer into the darkness of Buster's bedroom.

I have to piss.

I reach toward the nightstand and thumb on my phone. Only 11:25. The night feels endless already.

I sit up. The nearest bathroom is off the foyer, so I creep out of bed and get halfway across the living room before a bovine snort freezes me where I stand. I glance over and spy Buster with his mouth open, a silvery filament of drool still deciding whether it wants to make contact with his hairy shoulder.

He snorts again, and I scurry into the bathroom. I don't trust the guy, but a thousand bucks is a thousand bucks, and if spending the night in a farty-smelling bed is the cost, I'm willing to pay. I relieve my bladder, tiptoe past Buster, and re-enter the bedroom.

And the smell hits me.

I tell myself it's the same odour, but it isn't. Not quite. There's a depth to it that wasn't there before. Like something has stirred while I was in the bathroom and kicked up this withering stench. Lakebottom mud tinged with sulphur. My hand trembling, I reach out and paw at the light switch. Yellow floods the room.

Empty.

Sure, the sheet and blanket are bunched in a not-pleasing way. And I don't appreciate how Buster has arranged his nightstand just far enough from the wall to create a murky moat of shadow. Or the fact that the closet door is slightly ajar, even though I'm pretty sure I closed it.

I rush over there, barge it shut, but the *click* doesn't come, something shouldering against it from the inside. Teeth bared, I rip open the door and spot the impediment. Only a belt. I swat it out of the way and jam the door until it clicks.

There. I back away, heart jitterbugging.

Now...

I pivot to face the room.

...about that smell.

Could it be that I'm more aware of it because it's approaching midnight? Buster's tale of a malignant presence is absurd, but it must have done a number on me because there's no denying the sweat sheening my forehead or the persistent throb in my temples. I need water, but I don't want to leave the room again. What if the sulphurous dead-fish smell is worse when I return? What if the closet door is open?

I switch off the light and the darkness enshrouds me.

It's hot in the room, so I shed my shoes, socks, and jeans. I peel off my T-shirt and add it to the mound on the floor. I rush to the bed and jerk the covers up to my chest. I lay back and tell myself to relax. It takes a while. But at some point I nod off.

★   ★   ★

I awake in two stages. In the first I'm with Catherine and we're making out in a hotel room and it's so good I suspect it can't be real. And *because* it's so good, because it's so perfect, I know it's a dream and then I'm awake and I realise where I am.

And the fear floods in.

I scrabble for those mental sluice gates, the ones that keep you from becoming a toddler sobbing in the darkness and begging for the monsters to go away, but it's useless. My body is taut, a tingle running from forehead to toes. The covers feel leaden, oppressive. My breathing is laboured. I'm on my back, and I don't usually sleep that way, and with my chest uncovered I feel totally exposed. I haven't opened my eyes because if I do I'll see whatever it is that haunts Buster, whatever terrible fiend dwells in this room. And lying there, paralysed, I realise what this is, what I've really agreed to. I'm bait, dammit. A sacrifice. Buster is hoping it'll take me before it takes him. He'll placate it the way the ancients appeased the gods by burning a goat or a lamb. I can almost hear the tortured bleats and smell the scorched flesh, and fearing the terrible presence will seize me, my paralysis breaks, and I roll onto my side.

Cool air whispers over my shoulder, and I open my eyes, sure some monstrous face is hovering over me.

The room seems empty, but the surge of relief doesn't come. Instead, an icy breeze sweeps over me, chilling my bare shoulder, so I jerk up the covers to shield myself, but only the sheet comes up. I wriggle down and grasp a handful of blanket and stretch it all the way to my underjaw. I'm not quite to the point of burying my face, but that level of infantile panic isn't far off. My hackles thrum, so I squirm lower to conceal the nape of my neck.

I still feel exposed. While my left arm is tucked safely under the blanket, my right arm, the side I'm lying on, juts out parallel with my pillow, and now I'm certain the presence is here with me, drifting closer, its pitiless shadow crawling over my shins, my knees, as surely as a thunderhead darkens a wheatfield on a sombre summer's day.

Jesus God, what a mistake this was. The air's so cold my flesh gathers into nodes and I've never felt smaller, never wanted my mother more. I think of her and Dad, just down the street, oblivious to my plight, sleeping the sleep of the unmarked.

I suck in breath. I've been so transfixed by my terror that I've neglected to listen for the presence, for the elemental being that's shifted its gaze from Buster to me, but now I hear the slightest creak of a floorboard, the subtlest whisper, a hungry sound, the presence so eager for me that it mutters to itself, its foul lips writhing in anticipation. I'm powerless to stop it. My arm is exposed, my crabbed fingers offered up as surely as plump earthworms squirming on baited hooks.

I whimper, not giving a damn how weak I sound. I want to bolt from the room, want to escape, but it's too late. My eyes have adjusted enough to discern the length of my body under the blanket, the freighted darkness beyond. And...

...I close my eyes, scourging them of the illusion. That's what it had to be. But over my body, flowing out of the darkness like a slender funnel birthed from a rampart of nimbus clouds, a shape is gliding toward me.

That's not possible! a voice inside me screams, but the voice is faint, the evidence of my eyes infinitely more compelling. The sound of the presence squeezes my eyes closed again, the low, throaty exhalation, a horrifying orgasmic sigh that sets my skin to crawl. I grind my teeth and realise I'm weeping, my sobs silent, my chest shuddering, and I pray for it to stop, plead for forgiveness even though I haven't thought of God in years. But my pleas are a breathy stew, just gibberish, and tears leak and the freezing chill grips me and...

...I realise there's a change in the room. An electricity surrounding me, a psychic *leaning*. The odour of sulphurous lake mud clogs my nostrils and I clamp my lips to keep it out. I tell myself it's a panic attack brought on by Buster's hideous paranoia. I wait, wait, and I'm about to open my eyes when moist fingers slither through my own, the flesh slimy, fever-hot, grasping my hand, and I open my eyes and see it leering at me, eager hungry eyes, vast and ivory and purple-irised with hateful ebony voids in their centres and I gag and push away and beyond it I discern movement.

"*Oh my God, kid,*" Buster gasps and the light floods on. He rushes toward me and I slap at the covers and crowd against the headboard and Buster's voice is frantic, and I recoil from him and scramble out of bed.

"Kid!" he's saying. "Hold up, Stu!" But his words reach me from a distance. I snatch up my clothes, fumble a shoe, and scurry to the doorway. I've got to get out, got to breathe the outside air.

"You can't leave, kid," he's saying, but his words elicit no pity in me, all emotion seared away by the terror of what I saw, what I felt. I'm shaking so badly by the time I reach the front door that I can't even turn the knob, much less operate whatever locks are there.

"You can't leave me, Stu!" he moans. "We had a bargain. You said you'd stay till morning."

I shake my head, slap the light switch, and finally locate the deadbolt. Buster asks, "Was it maybe a nightmare?"

"Nightmare," I repeat. Anything to get the hell out of there. I twist the deadbolt and the door jumps. I yank it open, my other shoe clunking to the floor. Screw it. I still have my T-shirt and jeans. I'll go naked if I have to. Anything to escape this house.

But something makes me pause, one foot on the porch, the other on the threshold. I glance back at Buster and see him standing slump-shouldered in the doorway of his bedroom. Defeated. Not even looking at me.

I shrug off a pang of guilt and rush to my car.

But it's locked. I rummage through my jean pockets, but though the wad of cash is there, the keys aren't.

I turn back to the house. *Ah, fuck.*

I stand there, chest heaving. The foyer light is on, the interior door open. Nothing in there but Buster.

I think of the torrid, mucous-slick fingers snaking around mine. The purple irises crop-dusting me with loathing.

To hell with that. My house is right down the street.

I can get my keys tomorrow.

*   *   *

Safe in my bedroom. Under my own blankets. Not Buster's foul-smelling ones.

Not in his accursed bedroom.

Lying in my bed, I think of the slimy fingers threading with mine and devise an ingenious safeguard. By positioning my hand next to the opening of the pillowcase, I can sheathe my fingers inside it.

Drowsy but not sleeping, I check my phone. Four in the morning.

I think of the arguments I've been having with my dad, how pissed he's been at me. He's an early riser. By six he'll be at the kitchen table crunching his burnt toast and nursing his coffee and scrolling through his phone for stuff to bitch about. And he'll notice my car isn't outside. And no matter how I come at it, I can't invent a plausible reason for my car being at Buster Nelson's house. I can't say it broke down. That'll kibosh my night with Catherine. Can't tell him the truth. Hell, I can't tell *myself* the truth. I can't spin some ridiculous lie—*Yeah, Dad, I felt nostalgic last night. I parked down the road and took a stroll around the neighbourhood to reconnect with my childhood.*

Horseshit.

I have to retrieve those keys, and I have to do it soon. Else my dream night with Catherine at a hotel – a *fancy* hotel – will never come to pass.

Before the superstitious terror can creep back in, I push out of bed and drag on some clothes. I pad through the house, taking care not to step on the creakiest floorboards. Outside, I marvel at how bright the sky is, the moon a swollen pearl that floods everything with its lustrous glow.

It doesn't take long to troop to Buster's. I stand on the lawn a moment, studying the darkened windows and the lightless rectangle of the foyer. I don't like the darkness, and I hate the notion of sneaking back in to find my keys. But they can only be in one of two places. They either fell out of my pocket as I sat on the living room couch, or they tumbled out in my mad flurry to escape the bedroom.

Hell. I have to go in there.

But what if Buster owns a gun? What if he blasts a hole in the middle of my chest because he mistakes me for a burglar? I stand there debating it, fingers twitching. I could just knock on the door and wake his ass up. It's not like I've done anything wrong.

We had a bargain, he'd pleaded. *You said you'd stay until morning.*

No, I tell myself. *The bargain wasn't fair.*

I trudge up the porch and listen at the screen door.

Nothing. No wind, no floorboards, no anything.

Just go in and grab the keys. Get some sleep and call Catherine before she makes some bullshit plans. Watching TV with her grandma or something.

I open the door, grimacing at the *screek* it makes, then step inside. I slide my phone out, finger-sweep the light. Creep to the couch, flick the light over the cruddy fabric, knowing I won't find the keys.

I regard the bedroom door, which is closed. I blow out a trembling breath.

I edge forward, and I'm maybe three steps from the door when I hear it: a croupy chuffing sound. Like a seriously ill dog. One of those huge ones, a St. Bernard or a mastiff.

I creep closer, lean toward the door, and the chuffing grows louder. Phlegmy, but not sick. No.

Effortful. Rhythmic.

Squishy.

My flesh crawling, I twist the knob and draw open the door and the sounds amplify. I take a step and the toe of my sneaker nudges something, and I splash the floor with light and discover my keys. I snatch them up, and the chuffs intensify.

Oh Christ, I think. *That's not Buster.*

My whole body numb, I raise my phone light and behold what's on top of him. Nose-to-nose, a hideous alabaster face leers at him, its thick black eyebrows arched, its tongue sliming over Buster's lips. The putrid stench rolls over me, acrid, exultant. I sway on my feet and try to look away, but the sight of its nude body, sinewed and glistening, rivets me where I stand. The creature's worm-wet fingers fondle Buster's chest, blistering his skin, a trail of crimson boils bursting and spilling over his torso like rancid wine. Buster's eyes implore me, his mouth open in a voiceless scream. I hear a squelch as its midsection grinds into his. The creature's legs writhe languidly against Buster's. His skin bubbles, pops, the pus drooling down his thighs like bacon grease. The creature swivels its head toward me, the purple irises aglow, hateful, and I back away. The creature laughs deep in its gullet, and I don't know how but I make it outside and manage to drive home.

★   ★   ★

I don't sleep again that night.

Buried under a snowdrift of covers, sweating, yearning to lock my bedroom door but unwilling to leave the sanctuary of my blankets, I think of the creature atop Buster. Its maggot-white body. Its satyr's leer. I thrash my head to rid myself of the memory, but it only crystallises, fixing me with its violating gaze.

I whimper and shudder and perspire within my nest and pray I don't feel the weight of it press down on me.

I remain that way until six that morning, when I hear Dad puttering around the kitchen, burning his toast and slurping his coffee. I shower with the door open and mess around on my phone until seven, when Catherine usually wakes up. But before I call her, I search up the nicest hotel in the area, which turns out to be the Marriott two towns over.

I slouch on the foot of my bed and give them my info. I see my reflection in the door mirror, my bare chest, the arms I've been working so hard to bulk up. Soon Catherine will be squeezing these arms and clawing these shoulders. I'm thinking of Catherine's fresh, unblemished body when the lady on the other end asks me a question.

"I'm sorry," I say. "Could you repeat that?"

She asks her question again.

"That's right," I answer. "One room. King-sized bed."

She asks another question. I close my eyes and smile.

"Yes," I begin to tell her. "We'll only be staying..."

But I can't finish. Because the smell has returned, and my gorge clenches and I know when I open my eyes I'll see the creature hovering over my shoulder.

When I look there's nothing behind me, but I'm not me anymore. My eyebrows are furry and arched and my mouth has widened to a harlequin's leer. My irises glow purple, my skin is bleached and slime-glistened. I want to cry out, to bellow in horror, but I've lost all volition. I slide my fingers over my chest and watch the flesh bubble. The aroma of seared ham merges with the lakebottom stench, and the boils redden to bulging domes. Tears leak down my cheeks, and as my fingers slide over my thighs and the boils overrun my skin, I hear myself breathe, the chuff of mindless craving.

WELCOME TO THE LODGE

Alison Moore

Helena stepped carefully over the threshold into a high-ceilinged entrance hall. She had been expecting something much more mundane, more like the ear clinic. A woman in a white doctor's coat was waiting for her. The doctor, if that's what she was, welcomed Helena, who thanked her and shook her cool hand, though at the same time she was distracted by the hunting trophies – deer, mainly – which decorated the wood-panelled walls. The doctor, seeing her looking, said, "This was established as a hunting lodge, a long time ago now. We've retained this aspect of the building's history." Helena nodded, sorry to see these beautiful creatures preserved in this sad state.

"If you come with me," said the doctor, "we can get you registered."

There was a comfortable chair in the entrance hall, in which Helena sat with her paperwork, inking her personal details into the relevant boxes, skimming small print, ticking permissions, accepting terms and conditions, signing and dating on the dotted lines.

"Very good," said the doctor, taking back her clipboard, along with Helena's personal effects, which would be kept behind the reception desk – like on holiday, said Helena, thinking of summers in Europe where the hotels held on to your passport until you checked out.

"I'll show you to your suite," said the doctor, taking hold of Helena's weekend bag and leading her from the entrance hall into a corridor, past a series of closed doors – private suites, she said, occupied by other guests – to an identical closed door at the far end. "This is where you'll be staying." The doctor opened the door and escorted Helena into a small room dominated by a comfortable-looking bed.

"Lovely, thank you," said Helena. It looked like a hotel room, if you ignored the medical equipment. She smiled at the doctor. "You'll be able to keep a good eye on me with all this."

"Oh yes," replied the doctor, putting Helena's weekend bag down at the foot of the bed.

"I've not brought much with me," said Helena.

"You won't need much," said the doctor. "I'll leave you to get settled in. Supper in an hour."

"Lovely," said Helena, "thank you." The doctor closed the door behind her, and Helena stood for a moment taking in the neutral décor, appreciating the peace and quiet. She felt like ringing someone to say she had arrived safely, to say it seemed nice, but her mobile phone was among the things that had been taken from her on arrival, in accordance with the policy here. Electronic devices were not allowed in the bedrooms because they caused interference – with signals or sensors or whatnot – and, more generally, technology at bedtime could disrupt sleep. Helena had become something of an expert on clean sleeping, on the importance of a pleasant environment, a relaxed state, a lack of disturbance. At least, she was an expert in theory; in practice, she still had so many bad nights, which was why she was here.

She would get her phone back when she left. Anyway, she thought, as she unpacked her weekend bag, she did not really have anyone to ring.

After putting her few belongings away in the chest of drawers, she stood at the window and admired the view of the garden, a long lawn divided by paths and dotted with shrubs, bleeding into extensive woodland at the far end. At the edge of the woods, she could see movement. From this distance it was just a gingery blur but she thought it might be a fox, a young one. She watched with delight as it came further into the garden, trotting through the grass, getting surprisingly close to the lodge before she saw that it was just a cat.

She wished she had a patio door so that she could sit out there. It was a nice afternoon, quite mild. But there was at least a chair by the window, so she sat there and waited for suppertime.

★   ★   ★

Helena had not been expecting a dining room – she had imagined being given something on a tray in her bedroom – but not only did the lodge have a dining room, it was rather a grand one. She could imagine it housing a banquet table back in the day, though now the diners – *Are we residents*, she wondered, *or patients, or something else?* – sat alone at little tables. They all looked rather dazed; she supposed that was normal in a sleep clinic.

It was like being back in the classroom, seated at desks, in rows and columns, waiting for break or lunch or home time, except that instead of exercise books and sharpened pencils they had spoons. And none of them were young: the youngest looked to be in their sixties. The gentleman to her left might have been in his nineties, and had come for his evening meal in striped pyjamas and chequered slippers. The lady to her right was closer to her own age, and Helena leaned towards her and said, "How do you do?" The lady slowly turned her head until she saw Helena. She opened her mouth and then closed it again, and Helena thought of fish, that opening and closing of the mouth which could apparently signal stress, a lack of oxygen. The lady looked away again and Helena turned to the gentleman, who was already watching her, and said, "This is my first night."

The man had a twitch in his eye, and touched his fingers to the spasm. "Oh, it's bad," he murmured.

"Are you being treated?" asked Helena.

She supposed it was a silly question – what else would he be here for? – and he seemed lost for a response. He only repeated himself, as his fingers fluttered from his spasm to her sleeve: "It's bad."

Helena arranged her features sympathetically and said, "I'm sure they'll put us right, with all their gizmos." She asked if the meals were good here, and at that moment a trolley was steered into the dining room, laden with bowls of soup and plates of sandwiches, and she added, "It *looks* good." The girl – perhaps a carer or just a helper – drew the trolley between them, and the gentleman said, "The meals here are very good. I have no complaints." The soup and sandwiches were handed out, and the meal was eaten in peace. The soup was quite nice, very filling, but Helena was disturbed throughout by the heads, the hunting trophies, a continuation of the horror show she had seen in the entrance hall.

She spent the hours after supper in the communal lounge, where the seats were arranged around a television that showed repeat after repeat, old game shows and reality shows and programmes about fishing. She saw the ginger cat in the doorway and tried to coax it nearer. It looked like a cat she'd once had, which was buried in a vegetable patch. It slinked its way towards her and jumped up onto her lap. It settled down so nicely that Helena was reluctant to move even when her legs went to sleep.

She enquired about coffee, but was told she was not to have caffeine, not even tea, and not even cocoa. She accepted the Ovaltine that was brought round, and decided she could bear it for a night or two. When the Ovaltine was finished, the lounge began to empty, even though it was still quite early, only just nine o'clock. The gentleman in striped pyjamas ambled past, and Helena said to him, "What's happening?"

"It's time for bed," he replied.

"That's right," said a carer, or an orderly or whatever he was, who was coming for Helena. Quite a few of the residents or patients – or perhaps they were *clients*, she thought – were unsteady on their legs or else confused and in need of help.

"It's only nine o'clock," said Helena, as the television went off. "I like to watch the news."

"It's bedtime," said the carer, helping Helena to her feet.

"It's still quite early," said Helena as she was escorted from the lounge.

"It's important to have a fixed routine."

The dead-eyed stares of the creatures in the entrance hall were unnerving. Helena did not like to say so; she did not wish to offend the people who were responsible for her care. She tried not to look at them.

"It's still quite light," she said as they entered her room. Although dusk was falling, there was enough light left to tempt her into the garden. The gentleman in striped pyjamas was out there, skirting the lawn, making his way, in his slippers, towards a rather impressive rhododendron whose scent Helena could just imagine hanging in the evening air. "May I go for a walk in the garden?" she asked.

"It's bedtime," insisted the carer.

"That gentleman's out there," said Helena.

The carer turned to the window, where the pale gleam of pyjamas could still be seen in between the shrubs. "He'll be coming back soon." He closed the curtains and went to the door. "You can put your nightclothes on now," he said. "Someone will be in to see to you."

Helena fetched her nightie from the chest of drawers, and then peeped through the curtains. She could no longer see the gentleman, who had perhaps already completed a circuit of the garden and returned to the lodge. She was about to turn away when she saw the guards – not guards, she thought, orderlies, if that's what they were – hurrying over the lawn, searching the grounds and then heading, with torches, into the woods. She wondered if they were out looking for that poor man, who had, after all, seemed somewhat confused at suppertime. She told herself it was just as well she had seen him and alerted the staff.

She used her private bathroom and then changed awkwardly next to the bed, conscious of the camera fixed to the ceiling, not knowing if she was already being watched. Her nightie had peaches on it. Graham used to say, when she wore it, that she looked peachy. Helena missed him, all the time. Often, when she was stuck in a bad dream, she was trying to find him. This peachy nightie was not the same one she'd had back then, it was just an identical one.

She was not sure whether to be reassured or alarmed by the medical equipment. She didn't really understand what was going to happen here, only that they intended to cure her. During the decades of her marriage, Helena had got used to having Graham beside her at night; when she had a nightmare, he was there to hear her whimpering in her sleep, and he would wake her up. Now she was alone at night. She had been trying yoga and meditation and cognitive behavioural therapy, but nothing helped with the nightmares. She had been training herself to know she was just dreaming, and teaching herself methods to wake herself up: you could count to ten, and when you reached ten you were supposed to wake up, or you could go to sleep in the dream, and that was supposed to wake you up. She was still trying to get that to work. This was the first sleep clinic she had been to, but she did not expect it would be the last.

While she was here, her environment and her routine would be controlled to provide uninterrupted sleep, which sounded wonderful. The bed really was marvellously comfortable, and the room was so quiet. The heavy soup and the Ovaltine had left her feeling sedated.

Helena was just fiddling with the buttons on her nightie when the door opened.

"All ready?" asked the doctor.

"Just about," said Helena, pushing the last button through its hole.

The doctor sat her down and set about attaching electrodes to various places on Helena's body – to her chest to monitor her heart rate, to her shins to detect her leg movements, around her eyes to track her eye movements, and on her scalp to measure her brain activity, "so we'll know when you're sleeping, and what stage of sleep you're in, and when you're dreaming." Everything was connected by wires to a bedside device which would record her data. All hooked up, Helena felt as if they were going to try to read her mind, or as if – like something from a science fiction story – they were about to shock her into life. The doctor helped her to settle down. "You go to sleep now," she said, going to the door. "I'll be watching you from the control room."

"Doctor," said Helena, "did they manage to find that gentleman?"

"They'll find him," she said, turning in the doorway. "I'm not a doctor, by the way. I'm a technologist. My name's Gail. Sleep well," she added, as she shut the door.

Helena, left alone, thought about this. A technologist. She tried to remember what it meant: *ologist*. A studier of something, like a psychologist studying the mind or an ornithologist studying birds; an expert in something. She thought the technologist ought to be called a sleepologist, and, in fact, she had a feeling there *was* another word, something to do with insomnia, although, in Helena's case, what was required was a *dream*ologist, or more specifically a *nightmare*ologist, since that's why Helena was here, because she could not stop having these bad dreams, getting stuck in these dreadful nightmares.

*　　*　　*

The subject had been asleep for nearly thirty minutes and was in stage two of her first sleep cycle. Gail watched the computer screen, monitoring brain waves and breathing, muscle tone and movement, heart rate and oxygen levels. Everything looked normal. Another screen showed a television image of the subject sleeping: she slept on her back, and stayed very still. Gail could never fall asleep on her back, or stay still in her sleep. She fell asleep on her front and might wake on her back or at ninety degrees with the bedding kicked off. As a child, she'd had night terrors, which she did not recall but which she had been told about. Twenty years later, it had been her son's turn to experience the night terrors. Gail, woken by screaming, would hurry to his room to find him sitting bolt upright, beside himself. *It's all right*, she would say, *it's all right*, wanting to soothe the little boy, who cringed from her with fear in his eyes. She wondered what he was seeing, but he could not tell her, and when he woke in the morning he did not remember the night terror, the night-time, at all.

She used to think night terrors were like nightmares, but nightmares occurred during REM sleep, while night terrors were experienced by sleepers moving between stages of non-REM sleep. She had been desperate for her little boy's night terrors to end, but, she thought, it was not as if you could stop someone moving from one stage of sleep to another, or so she had thought until she came to The Lodge. Anyway, her son had eventually grown out of that phase; the only problem, now that he was a teenager, was getting him up in the mornings.

Gail, watching the monitors carefully, saw that the subject had entered REM sleep, and, based on the eye movements, and now the audio, a nightmare had begun.

She had come to this job fresh from qualifying. Conducting a polysomnography was quite a responsibility, not least ensuring that the subject's vital signs remained normal, or, if they did not, taking the right course of action. Gail had always tended to avoid responsibility, which, her dad had reminded her, meant that taking on this level of responsibility would be good for her. By nature, Gail had always avoided things she did not like, while her dad, seeing that she was afraid of water, threw her in at the deep end of the pool. After she disclosed her fear of spiders, she came home from school to find dozens of them crawling around her bedroom; her dad locked her in there overnight. It might have seemed cruel to some – it had seemed unbearably cruel to her at the time – but it had worked: she had learnt to swim, and in due course had taught her son the same way, and she no longer feared spiders, because she had spent not just one night but many nights trapped in her bedroom with those creepy-crawlies and nothing bad had happened to her.

When asked in her interview about challenges she had overcome, she had related this experience. The director of the clinic had been impressed by her testimony, her positive attitude. He was himself, he later explained, exploring the potential of exposure therapy, which was a highly effective anxiety treatment. Through prolonged exposure to the stimulus within a safe setting, subjects were enabled to confront their fears without engaging in the escape response; distress had to be tolerated until it faded. It was systematic desensitisation.

The director had developed an innovative technique that involved manipulating the subject's brain waves and eye movements and so on, to hold them in the REM stage for the duration of their sleep. He trained Gail in this experimental approach, and while he acknowledged that it was early days and that the early cohorts might not feel the benefits, he believed that over time, as the approach was refined, his technique would become a valuable intervention for those suffering from persistent anxiety dreams and nightmares.

Although Gail could see that the subject was dreaming – and having a bad dream – she could not, of course, see the dream itself. She had, however, been briefed by the psychologist responsible for the initial consultation, and knew that the subject's nightmares tended to occupy urban structures such as multi-storey car parks and university campuses and hospitals, whose uncanny sprawl she tried to navigate while her legs grew heavier and heavier. The subject, Gail noted, had taught herself to notice when she was dreaming, and had attempted to use techniques such as counting to ten to wake herself up. This could be overridden, however, by keeping the subject sedated and keeping the subject's brain in the REM state. It took some concentration – Gail had to be constantly alert to the subject's brain attempting to progress to non-REM sleep, or to the subject attempting to wake up, and it was a real skill to ensure that this was not allowed to happen.

By the end of the night shift, Gail was exhausted. Before going home to sleep, she roused her subject, who looked pale and drawn, which was entirely normal. Gail detached the electrodes and gave her something for the shaking.

"I understand how you're feeling," said Gail, taking a seat on the edge of the bed. She patted the subject's trembling hand and told her all about the first night she had spent with the spiders, how she couldn't bring herself to go to sleep or to switch off the light, and how in the morning she had felt utterly ragged, "Just like you look now," she said. "And it was just as horrible the second night, except I did sleep, with the light on. And eventually, *eventually*, it just becomes normal." Her report, which would accompany the polysomnographic record, would have to mention this fluttery hand, this glazed look, the difficulty in making eye contact. "I expect you'll feel better after some breakfast," she said. "Someone will be in soon to take you to the dining room." She was looking forward to her own breakfast, which her husband would have ready for her when she arrived home: toast in the toast rack, marmalade, a boiled egg. Breakfast before she went to bed – it felt wrong, as did going to sleep when everyone else was getting up, being asleep while everyone else was going about their business, but, like anything else, you got used to it.

"All right?" she said, standing up. "I'll see you when I come back this evening." In the meantime, the daytime staff would keep things ticking over.

★   ★   ★

Helena did not like to be rude but she could not manage her breakfast. It had been hard enough just getting to the dining room, crossing the entrance hall beneath the glassy and reproachful gaze of the heads in the hallway.

After breakfast, or after her non-breakfast, they sat her in the lounge, next to a window; they gave her some gardening magazines but she did not open them, or did not remember doing so. She barely noticed the morning passing. By lunchtime, she had some appetite, though, and managed most of her spaghetti bolognese. She tried to speak to the lady seated at the table to her right, but she looked fearful and unfocused and in the end Helena left her alone. Evidently, everyone in here had terrible trouble with sleep, with nightmares, which was this clinic's speciality. The table to her left was empty.

She even had dessert, and felt up to trying those magazines. On her way from the dining room to the lounge, she paused at the reception desk to ask for her phone, worrying about unread texts, unheard messages, not that she was expecting any, but still.

The receptionist, regarding Helena through cat-eye glasses, reminded her of the policy at The Lodge.

"I understand about not using it at bedtime," said Helena, "or in the evening, but it's only lunchtime."

The receptionist reminded Helena of the paperwork she had willingly signed. There was a correlation, she said, between addictive

phone behaviour and high anxiety levels. Helena said, "I'm hardly—"
but the receptionist interrupted to say that her device would be returned
to her when she left, and Helena agreed to wait until then.

The orderlies, or whatever they were, were coming in through the
front door, saying to the receptionist, "We nearly lost him that time!"
They were bringing in the gentleman in striped pyjamas, who looked
exhausted; he looked how Helena felt. His slippers, she noticed, were
very muddy.

While one of the orderlies was taking the gentleman to his room,
the other took Helena into the lounge, to her seat by the window. She
accepted the same gardening magazines and turned a page or two of
the top one, but found herself looking through the window into the
garden, looking at something colourful whose name she did not know,
and those woods at the end. There was the ginger cat, stalking through
the grass. Helena was about to tap on the window to draw the cat's
attention when she saw the bird – a soft little thing – in its mouth. She
knew it was natural – her own cat had killed birds – but she hated to see
it. She turned her head away, though she could not get the image of it
out of her mind.

She did not see the gentleman, even at suppertime. When the carer
came with the trolley of soup and sandwiches, Helena asked after him
and was told he was probably sleeping. "I think he must have been out
all night," said Helena, "poor thing."

The soup was the same as before. Helena ate most of it before she
gave up. There was bread and butter too, which was just as well because
the lady to her right could barely hold her spoon.

Helena sympathised; she was feeling strangely tired herself, and had
been somewhat out of it all day, even though she must have had a good
night's sleep – she did not remember waking up at all. She'd had the
most appalling nightmares though. Well, she thought, that's precisely
what she was here for.

Before bed, there were the hours in the lounge, the repeats on the
television. The ginger cat wanted to sit on her but she did not want it
now; she could not get the thought of its jaws around the limp bird out
of her head. It jumped up anyway, purring, and she did not push it off
but did not pet it either, and did not move until they had been round
with the Ovaltine.

She found herself, as she passed through the entrance hall, afraid of going down the corridor to her room. She supposed she was overtired, like children who got overwrought, and in the end she had to be escorted.

★   ★   ★

"Welcome to The Lodge."

The new arrival, looking around as he was brought to the reception desk, asked, "Is she all right?"

"Is who all right?"

"That lady," he said, pointing – she was standing at the end of the corridor that led off the entrance hall, neither coming nor going. She was wearing a polka-dot nightie. "She looks a bit lost."

"She's one of our long-term patients. We're helping her with her nightmares."

"Does everyone here suffer from nightmares?" he asked.

"Everyone. It's what we do."

"I just want them to stop," he said. "They say I'm disturbing everyone else in the home."

"Everyone here is in the same boat. Let's get you registered."

The new arrival was taken to the comfortable chair, where he put on his glasses and, in his careful handwriting, filled in his paperwork.

"Very good," he was told as the clipboard was taken away, along with his personal effects. Left alone for a moment, he got to his feet and took a look at the hunting trophies that hung at intervals on every wall. He moved along, nearing the lady in the nightie who still stood in the mouth of the corridor. "Are you all right?" he asked.

She was counting. "Six, seven, eight…"

Up close, he could see that the pattern on her nightie was not polka dots but fruit – faded oranges, or peaches or apricots, something like that.

"Nine, ten," she said, looking hopeful, pained.

A voice beside him said, "I'll show you to your suite," and he allowed himself to be led away, down the corridor, while the lady in the nightie started counting again, from one.

GOING HOME

Evelyn Teng

Water ran from Isla's shoes. Pondweed tangled with his hair. He did his best to wring out his shirt, the new one his mother had sewn for him last birthday, but it remained a sodden layer on his torso.

"Mother, I fell in the pond," he shouted as he neared his parents' house, a little two-room shack at the edge of a hazel thicket. "Mother?"

There was a gasp from the charcoal ovens behind the shack, and a flurry of heated whispers.

That was odd. His parents seldom fought. Not even when their dog had gotten caught in a hunter's wolf snare when they moved from the previous thicket. Not even when his father fell asleep at the makeshift oven and ruined an entire stack of charcoal, which meant less money to tide them over between winters.

Isla, ten years old, walked towards the ovens. He could hear his father's deep voice, punctuated by odd, dry sobs.

"Mother? Father?"

His father emerged from behind the shack. When he saw Isla, his mouth fell open.

"I'm sorry," Isla blurted out. "I didn't mean to, but the fish dragged me in and I ruined the shirt, but if we dry it over the oven it should be good as new and – and – why is Mother crying?"

"I'm not crying," his mother said hastily. Her eyes were haunted and red-rimmed, and when she smiled, the skin stretched tight over her skull, highlighting the gauntness of her cheeks. "I was just worried. You were gone for so long."

"The whole day," his father muttered.

Isla's mother shot him a look that Isla didn't fully understand, then turned back to her son. "How – how was the fishing?"

"Not good. I didn't catch any."

"Oh. Well, that's a shame, but – never mind." Her hands twisted in her apron, dark with smoke from the charcoal ovens. "Isla, dear, we're terribly busy here. Would you mind – ah—"

"Feeding Benty," his father said quickly.

Isla frowned. "Benty stinks."

"He still needs to be fed, son. Put the bowl right next to his head, will you? His front paw still isn't healed from the wolf snare."

Still scowling, but eager to make his parents forget that he'd soaked his shirt, Isla went into the kitchen that made up one of the shack's rooms and dug in the salt-box for the bits of offal, stale crusts and vegetable ends that made up Benty's diet. He had to stand on a stepstool and reach deep into the box to get at Benty's food. There were houses, he'd heard, where the food was kept on shelves on the walls and the owners paid sorcerers and witch-women to keep the cabinets cold, but such luxuries didn't exist for charcoal-burners – not when they needed to pack up and move once this thicket was cleared.

As Isla fished out bits of viscera and dropped them into Benty's dented metal bowl, the floor of the shack trembled. He straightened up and turned around to find his mother quietly unhooking a skillet from the wall.

"Dinner?" he asked. "It's still early."

His mother smiled awkwardly. "I'm thinking what to make. Your father hunted up a very good buck the other day, and we still have several cuts left of venison." She lifted the skillet, then set it on the scarred kitchen table, her movements slow and uncertain. "What would you like to eat?"

"I think..." Isla blinked. "When did father go hunting?"

"Five days ago."

"Oh. All right. I don't remember it."

"He went at night. When you were asleep."

"At night?"

"So that the deer would be sleeping."

That made sense to Isla. Sneaking up on Benty was easiest when the dog was asleep, too. "Can we have that stew you make with mushrooms and tree fruit?"

"Juniper berries? Certainly. Don't forget to take Benty his food." His mother gave him another fleeting smile and rushed from the shack.

Odd. Isla waited until she was out of sight, then tiptoed after her. He poked his head around the door. His mother was nowhere in sight, but his father still stood by the charcoal oven, arms crossed, fiercely watching the burn. Slowly he stiffened, then turned and looked straight at Isla. At once Isla darted back to the kitchen and grabbed Benty's bowl. His father was kind enough, but not above applying the strap to a pair of idle legs.

Benty was where he always was when not hunting with Isla's father: curled up on the opposite side of the shack from the charcoal ovens, luxuriating in the shade. A little pang of trepidation shot through Isla as he approached. The dog used to be his best friend, but not too long ago, he had lunged at Isla and nearly taken off Isla's leg.

Leg? Or throat? He scratched at his neck and frowned. A phantom itch ran beneath his skin. It felt like the shadow of a much larger, much deeper wound – but surely his parents wouldn't keep a dog that had injured their child.

Today at least he was safe. Benty's chain was attached to a stake in the ground, and the chain clipped firmly to the dog's collar. Isla edged forward with the bowl—

—and Benty's head came up, the teeth already bared in a snarl.

Isla froze. *No! It's okay. He's chained up.*

The closer Isla came, the flatter Benty's ears lay against his skull, until his eyes strained in their sockets and the white showed all around. Trembling, Isla inched forward. This wasn't normal dog behaviour. This was exactly the way Benty had looked before the attack—

And what happened? I don't remember. It didn't hurt – but it felt violent *– and I remember teeth and claws and fur, but no blood—*

Isla set down the bowl of offal – and in an instant Benty surged to his feet and threw himself against his chain. The collar ripped off his neck – the leather was old or weak or rotten – and then Benty was on him, snarling, snapping, his slabber hot on Isla's skin, making strange high-pitched whines. Isla screamed and thrust his hands out against the dog's chest. The surging muscle and coarse fur fought madly, and he cried for his mother and father in great screaming tears. No one heard. No one came. And Benty lunged forward again and again, each time pressing Isla's weak arms a little further aside, going always for the throat.

Metal gleamed at the corner of Isla's vision.

Sobbing, he thrust Benty to the side and flung himself desperately towards the bowl. Benty howled and hurled himself at Isla – who grabbed the metal bowl in one hand and slammed it into the side of Benty's head. Salt-glittered offal spattered against the side of the shack.

The dog staggered and dropped.

Did I kill him? On his hands and knees, Isla crawled over and looked at Benty, though he didn't dare touch him. The dog's chest rose and fell; even now, those strange whines flowed from his throat. Not killed, but stunned. Dazed with shock, Isla staggered over to the collar. Even if the leather was old, he could at least tie up Benty with a length of chain.

Except the leather wasn't broken. Isla stared at the collar, its edges new and smooth, the buckle still shiny. The collar was new, and the buckle was unbroken.

Someone had loosened Benty's collar on purpose.

That was the only conclusion that came to Isla's mind, yet he rejected it. The only people who would play such tricks were the Hungry Ladies of the Woods, but they had no reason to prowl about his family. His parents were always respectful to the hazel thickets. They made sacrifices of their hunts and left a dish of beer by the door every night. The Ladies couldn't possibly want to harm them.

It was an accident, then. Isla clung to the idea as he refastened Benty's collar and went in search of his parents. An accident was much more comforting than the idea that he or his parents had somehow offended the Ladies or their son, the Antlered Man, or unknowingly trod on a Dusk-Revenant's sleeping ground.

He crept back into the shack. Out of all his possessions, he had only one that wasn't practical or useful: a cheap little cat-shaped doll filled with rough cotton, won from a ball-toss game at a carnival last year. It was dead weight and therefore dear, for it was the one thing he owned that wasn't meant for utility. Holding it – knowing in the back of his mind that his parents treasured him so much that they allowed him to keep the doll, even as they themselves shed personal belongings to accommodate their semi-nomadic lifestyle – always calmed him down.

His mother was working at the kitchen table, back to the door. Hunks of venison lay ready-chopped in a bowl, dusted with salt and flour and ground, dried herbs, while another bowl held roughly cut potatoes still damp from scrubbing. A piney scent permeated the air and overrode the smell of raw meat. Juniper berries. His mother was preparing the night's venison stew.

Isla opened his mouth to tell her about Benty's collar, then stopped.

Her back rose and fell; her hands and arms worked furiously, grinding away with mortar and pestle, even though the meat was already covered in juniper. As Isla watched, his mother dipped a hand into her apron pocket and came out with a handful of bright-red berries. She dropped them into the mortar and continued pounding.

Holly berries. Isla recognised them at once. Attracted by their bright colour, he'd tried to taste a handful only a few months ago. His mother had snatched them out of his hand and forbidden him in no uncertain terms from ever attempting to eat them again. They wouldn't kill an adult outright, she'd said, but they were deadly to children.

So why was she mashing them up now?

Stupefied, Isla watched as his mother tipped the mortar's holly paste onto the venison. With both hands, she kneaded the paste into the meat.

Mother's trying to kill me. But why?

"Mother?" he quavered.

His mother froze for just a moment, then turned around. "Isla, is Benty fed?"

"Yes."

"He didn't give you any trouble, did he?"

There was something about her face, perhaps the worried tilt of her eyebrows or the way the corners of her mouth quivered, that made Isla take a step back. Anything he might have mentioned about the collar died in his throat. "No."

"Good. Good. I'll put the stew on the stove soon." She rinsed her hands in a bowl of water and wiped them on her apron. "Be a good boy and keep an eye on the pot. Remember, stews need constant stirring so they don't burn. I have to go talk to your father." As she passed Isla on her way out, she paused. Her hand rose slightly and trembled as if she wanted to pat him on the head; then she drew back with a smile and left.

Isla waited for ten seconds before creeping out after her. As he circled towards the charcoal ovens, he heard his father's voice, low and troubled.

"...never have gone to that witch," he rumbled.

"It's done, and we can't go back on it now," his mother said. Isla stopped. He had never heard his mother use that tone of voice before: hard and brittle, like a piece of tree-rubber stretched too thin. "We made our choice. Now we have to live with it."

"But...every time...it's so hard."

"I know. That's why we agreed to take it in turns."

His father's voice grew muffled, as if he'd buried his face in his hands. "I can't bear the thought of hurting Isla."

Isla gasped — a soft sound, yet a sound nonetheless. He drew back, but in the next moment his mother appeared around the shack. The harsh lines around her mouth smoothed over as she smiled at Isla, but her eyes remained watchful. "Is the stew all right?"

Shaking from head to toe, Isla nodded.

"Good boy. I have another job for you now. Your father will stay and watch the current burn, but I'm going to chop some more hazel for the next batch, which we'll need to start soon. I want you to come with me and make the twigs into bundles, and then we'll carry them back together."

"Yes," Isla said, trembling, "yes, I'll come with you."

★　★　★

It has to be a mistake, Isla thought as he stumbled through the trees after his mother. The empty basket on her back thumped lightly with every step. *I still have water in my ears, that's it. Father was saying something else, and I just heard wrong.*

Still, he remained quiet as his mother led him deep into the thicket. They passed the oldest trees, long ago stripped of their twigs, then moved into the more recent areas, where the trunks and branches still shone in pale spots from recent injury. Beyond them, Isla saw the scraggly outlines of trees with their twigs still intact.

"Never cut down a tree," his mother said quietly. "Why is that, Isla?"

"Because they need to keep growing," he repeated. It was a lesson learned many times over. "Cut off the twigs for charcoal today, keep the root for charcoal tomorrow, and burn the leaves as offerings to the Hungry Ladies."

"Yes." She fell silent for several minutes. "You have a good memory."

"Yes."

"You learn fast. You never make the same mistake twice."

"Yes."

They stopped at the base of a healthy tree. His mother put down the basket, took out a long knife, and began stripping the lower branches of their twigs. "Isla, dear?"

"Yes, Mother?"

"You know I love you."

"…yes."

"But I made a mistake. A terrible, costly mistake. I wanted something very much, but I asked it of the wrong person." She paused, knife raised, and Isla saw her whole arm quiver. "Isla, do you think you could forgive your poor old mother for making mistakes?"

Isla stared at her. "Mother…"

"I'm sorry. I asked for too much. Now I have to pay the price." She turned, knife still in hand. The sunlight scattering through the leaves made shining trails of the tears on her cheeks.

She did! They did! They sold me to the Hungry Ladies!

Isla screamed. He fled from his mother, crying – not for himself, but for his parents, who had sold him to the Hungry Ladies of the Wood in exchange for wealth or jewels or another child, maybe. Between the leafless, twigless hazel trees he ran, darting through slender gaps, his feet digging into the soil from the sheer panicked speed of his flight.

"Isla!" his mother shouted behind him. "Isla, I'm sorry!"

"You're not my mother!" Isla sobbed. "You're not—"

She fell upon him, one arm wrapping around his chest, and with a huge upward effort she heaved him off his feet. She was thin and frail but he was ten and even frailer, helpless against an adult. He drummed his heels against her thighs and begged her to let him go. Tremors ran through his mother's body; he felt the hard press of her forehead against the back of his skull. She was crying. With her free hand she raised the knife.

Isla caught his mother's hand as the knife plunged downwards. There was no love now, no sense of family; he twisted her hand and heard the sick crack of breaking bone. Her agonised scream resounded through his skull as she staggered, weakened with pain. In an instant Isla squirmed free and tore the knife from his mother's hand.

"Isla!" she cried. "Isla, please!"

No! He knew what happened to children sold to the Hungry Ladies. He'd heard stories, told to him by other charcoal-burners' children and in night-time tales from his own father, about how long the Ladies kept the children alive before they finally finished eating them. *No! I don't want that to happen to me!*

But only one thing could satiate the Ladies and keep them from ravaging the countryside in their anger over a broken promise.

Blood of the father.

Almost blinded by tears, Isla hurried through the thicket. He didn't know if he could, but he had to try, because even though his mother had tried to kill him for the Hungry Ladies, she was still his mother. He loved her more than life itself. He didn't want her to die and wanted even less to die himself, so he had to kill his father to keep the Hungry Ladies from killing them all.

It was a desperate flight, from hazel trees still green with leaves to trees with naked branches scrawled across the darkening sky, and finally to the shack, glowing in the light of the charcoal ovens. Benty leaped to his feet and snarled as Isla approached, but Isla skirted the dog and headed straight for the oven. The fire had to be watched closely to keep it from burning too hot and ruining the charcoal. His father never left it untended. Shaking with tears and the awful weight of his actions, Isla crept up on the ovens.

His father wasn't there.

Relief flooded Isla, then horror. The Hungry Ladies always came for their promised morsels at sundown. He had minutes before they arrived, found their meal missing, and tore apart every living creature in the area. He had to find his father.

Head humming and vision narrowing to a tiny circle, Isla advanced into the shack. The kitchen was empty, the skillet still on the table where his mother had left it – and, he realised with a sudden pang, she'd meant to use it to bash his head in. His fear redoubled. Even with the few possessions the charcoal-burners carried, there were numerous instruments of death. Knives. His father's crossbow. Chairs could be broken into stakes and bedsheets ripped into strangling rope. Isla sobbed quietly as he picked up a knife and parted the faded curtain separating the kitchen from the bedroom.

And here was his father, kneeling on the floor with his back to Isla. Isla advanced, though his blood ran cold and pooled at the bottom of his heart. He had to. There was no other choice. The Hungry Ladies were coming. *He had to.*

His father turned around. The knife fell from Isla's fingers.

In his father's hands – his broad, rough hands scarred and scorched from a lifetime tending charcoal flames – he held Isla's doll.

Tears speckled the faded cotton.

"I can't," his father said in a voice thick with old sobs. "I just can't."

"Why were you – why were you and mother—"

"We had to. We have an obligation, and we made a mistake. But I can't, Isla. Not when we have you back." Motions gentle, almost reverent, he laid the doll aside and opened his arms. "I can't do it anymore. Come here, Isla. We can be together again. I promise I'll never hurt you."

Isla's vision broke and swam with rainbows as tears poured down his cheeks. Hope filled his belly with its awful, hollow ache. Yes. He could put aside his fears. His father was tall and strong, maybe enough so to turn away the Hungry Ladies. Isla rushed forward and threw himself into his father's embrace. Those strong arms engulfed him. Isla cried as he hadn't in years, and his father cried harder than that, his entire body shaking with love for his son.

Then Isla's mother stepped into the room and buried the kitchen cleaver in Isla's head.

*   *   *

Isla's mother freed the cleaver from the boy's skull and drew back, shuddering, as thick black blood spread across the floor.

Her husband was frozen in despair. Thick black drops spattered his face and upper body; the liquid ran in rivulets down his hands and soaked into his trousers.

"You – you didn't have to…"

Grimly she cleaned the cleaver's blade on her apron. The blood was gummy and refused to come off cleanly, instead matting and catching in the folds of fabric. "It was my turn."

"It was better this time! We stopped him!"

"No. All you did was *delay* him." Isla's mother dropped the cleaver beside the body. Though her own throat ached with unshed tears and her heart turned over like a cake being flipped in the skillet, she knelt and picked up the body awkwardly with one arm, the other hanging by her side, wrist broken. He was so light, her Isla, and before this had happened, before she and her husband made her mistake, he had always been such a fair child. A charcoal-burner's son in a noble child's body. There was little left of either, now. Patches of skin were soft and white, evidence of the water's ravages. Other parts were burned from the time they had put him in the oven. If she pried open his chest, she knew she would see the broken ribs and crushed lungs, evidence of their first panicked attempt at killing their son.

Oddly enough, of the original injuries – the out-of-control horse and wagon that had trampled the first life out of Isla – there was no sign.

"We need to leave immediately," she said as she carried Isla outside. "If we stay, he'll keep coming back."

Her husband followed, his steps slow and uncertain. Ever since Isla's first death, he had lost a part of himself, and each subsequent death pushed him a little further back to childhood. Eventually, Isla's mother knew, she would have two children to contend with: the dead one as well as the living one she'd married.

"I fixed him, though," he said desperately. "You saw! He couldn't remember the previous times. He didn't try to kill us—"

"No."

"Please! I'm begging you!" – he clutched at her dangling arm, and she gasped as pain shot through her broken wrist – "don't take my son away from me!"

White-faced with pain, Isla's mother shook him off. Tears trembled in her eyes but not in her voice. "Don't you understand? We already lost him. Our boy is gone, and this thing that keeps coming back isn't him. I should never have let you seek out that witch."

"She brought our son back to life."

"She did – and she warned us there would be consequences. Well, we made our mistake. He's back, all right, but his mind has gone wrong. Every time, he tries to kill us. What would you have us do? Place the knife in his hand and lay down to accommodate his height?"

Her husband hesitated for too long before answering, "Maybe."

"No," Isla's mother snarled. "And this time, I intend to make certain that he doesn't come back."

"H-how—"

She laid Isla's body by the oven, then fetched the axe from the chopping block. Her husband went white at the sight. "Burning doesn't work," she said with a matter-of-fact manner that didn't quite match the roiling of her belly. "Water doesn't work. We don't have enough salt to surround him completely, let alone money to buy silver charms or a coffin of spell-wood. This is the only option left. I say, if he wants to come back, let him – but he won't get far with his body in pieces."

"I can't stand—"

Isla's mother hefted the axe in her one good hand. It would be difficult to do this alone. "I need your help."

Her husband backed away, the whites staring out around his irises. "He was my son. You can't ask me to watch."

"*He was my son too.*" Isla's mother took a deep breath, then shook her head. "I should have tried harder to stop you from going to that witch. That was my mistake. But *this*" – she gestured at Isla's body – "this is yours, and I have to clean it up." She froze her face into the ice that she so desperately wanted to feel in her heart. When all was said and done, this was Isla, her baby boy. "Go inside and begin packing up. We need to get as far away from here as we can before he wakes up again."

Without another word, her husband disappeared into the shack.

Isla's mother waited until he was out of sight, then turned to her boy. A single sob escaped her, the only sentiment she could allow herself to feel. And that worried her more than the revenant that came back in Isla's shape: that with each death, it became easier and easier to kill.

It had to be done. This was her mistake, and her consequence.

Raising the axe, Isla's mother began the long, heavy process of butchering her son.

THE SPACEMAN'S MEMORY BOX

Laura Mauro

There's a game you play sometimes, when dusk is falling but there's still daylight enough that your parents haven't yet called you in for the night. It's as close as you ever get to playing games in the dark together. Mina's mother lets her stay out until midnight, and Jordan's dad doesn't much care where he is at any given time, but you and the others have to be in by nightfall, and so these are your mischief hours. The almost-dark hours, when the world is on the cusp of change.

All children know that the world is not the same once the sun goes down.

(Your nan says council estates accrue their own mythology. *It's urban folklore,* she'd said once; *you pass down stories and whisper them among yourselves until they weave themselves into the fabric. Until the concrete absorbs them, and they become real, in a way they never were before. All myths were hearsay once.*)

There's a game you play, but not yet. Not while the sun lingers. There are other games to play first. Ordinary games, everyday games. Knock Down Ginger, or Knock a Door Run; as many names as there are children in the world. And the *other* game – the *special* game, the *almost-dark* game – began its life here too, burrowing larval into your collective imaginations. Bursting from that fertile cocoon one wet, fragile wing at a time, the way night-things do, for ideas like this wither and die in daylight.

But the sun is still high, and this is the time for ordinary mischief.

Jordan has a bag of marbles. You take turns to reach in, pick one out; closed tight in your fists until everyone has taken their turn, and you imagine you can guess the offending marble by touch alone. That it is heavier, or colder, or bigger, or smaller, and so it's possible to avoid it if you just pay close attention. If you just take *care.*

Whoever draws the blue marble has to knock on the Spaceman's door.

★ ★ ★

Your friends tell stories, passed down third-hand by older siblings, who know everything; snatches of conversation gleaned from their parents, whose hushed tones betray the unquestionable truth of all they say. Your friends sit together on the grass – beneath the watchful eye of the sun, which keeps you all safe – and you pass these half-stories around, form them into strange shapes. That stairwell in Middleton House that nobody likes to linger in because it's haunted. The abandoned car that someone supposedly died in, and if you touch it, you'll die too. The Flea, who came before the Spaceman; who was once the centrepiece of the cruel and tiny theatre you all called a *world*.

The Flea lived alone on the ground floor of Boucher House. Everyone called her the Flea because – *they* said, that faceless consensus from whom all the most pernicious rumours emerge – she was small and full of spite, a terrible bloodsucker of a woman. You all believed it, even though nobody had ever actually seen her for more than a few seconds. She was so small that when she answered the door – and she did, every single time – she was visible only as a pale, fragile shape in that shard of unlit hallway; a tremoring hand clutching the security chain as though it was the only thing keeping her from floating away.

(Your nan says the Flea's husband died in the war, her son in a car accident. *She's all alone in that house*, she'd told you once, and you had known this was your nan's way of scolding you; that guilt was a more potent formula than fear or shame. *Barely knows what year it is, let alone who's knocking on her door day in, day out. When you get to her age, the mind starts to wander, and if there's nobody around to show it the way home...*

She'd taken a long drag of her cigarette. Turned back to the TV.

Her memories are all she has, she'd said, after a moment. *And someday soon, they'll be gone too.*)

You'd felt guilty about Knocking Down the Flea after that. You'd tried to reason with your friends, but stories have teeth, and they'd all built the Flea up in their collective mind as this hunched little beast –

pale-eyed and withered and cruel – and so you'd gone along with it, tried extra hard to avoid that horrible blue marble.

You'd reasoned, with your eleven-year-old's trembling sense of morality, that *watching* people bully the Flea was not the same thing as bullying her yourself.

And then the Flea was dead, and it was too late to change your mind.

★   ★   ★

You are wrong about the marble.

Your heart sinks as your small fingers uncurl, revealing blue like a plucked and hateful eye; cursed colour, ugly colour, and the others cheer at the sight of their green marbles as though they've been offered a stay of execution.

Unlucky, Jordan says, in a tone that suggests genuine contrition.

Mina smiles, gap-toothed and excitable. *You have to Knock*, she says, as though you don't know the rules; as though this isn't the twentieth, fiftieth, hundredth time you've made this stupid wager. *You have to Knock Down the Spaceman.*

You have a choice, still. The marble's judgement is unequivocal. You cannot beg its forgiveness, or request a retrial, and the other kids would refuse, in any case, to relinquish the arbitrary safety afforded to them by those milky green spheres. But you can walk away. You wouldn't be the first; Grant always sulks when it's his turn, claims the game is *f-in' rigged*, and that's why nobody really likes him. You could walk away, but your heart lurches at the thought of their whispered disapproval. The looks they'd cast upon your departing shoulders. Disgust at your cowardice, and worse, your refusal to accept the marble's judgement, because rules are rules, and hadn't you all written them together?

The game sits ill with you. It always has. But the desire to be liked is all-powerful, and you are young, still. Your world is so small.

You place the marble in your pocket. Square your shoulders. *All right*, you say, and hope that the jut of your chin is enough to disguise the quiver in your voice, your frail confidence, which has always been your weakness. Turning to face the Spaceman's door, a compass attuned to the strange magnetism, the oddity of him, like a force of nature. *All right*, you say again, louder this time. *I'll do it. Just watch me.*

⋆   ⋆   ⋆

Nobody has ever seen the Spaceman.

Nobody is even sure he really exists. His flat is always dark, always silent. Nobody enters or leaves. But sometimes, just after dark, there is movement inside; papery curtains illuminated the sick yellow of streetlight, fluttering in the breeze, though the windows are shut. The hint of a shadow, as though seen in a dream.

You all call him the Spaceman because someone – Mina's brother, perhaps, or Danny's mum's physical therapist, or the old postman, who died in spring and was replaced like a missing part – once said that he'd been part of the British space programme back in the Sixties. That he'd been sent into orbit, had been pencilled in to go to the moon, but the Americans had got there first, and he'd never recovered from the disappointment.

You hadn't known there *was* a British space programme. You know the Russians sent people into space; they sent dogs too, though you know how that ended, and you don't like to think about it too hard, because it makes you feel strange and hollow inside, like something has been scooped out of you, the way they scoop out the flesh of watermelons.

(You asked your nan once why he couldn't just get over it, and she thought about it for a long moment. Placed her pencil beside her crossword puzzle, and you thought she was about to scold you; that she'd read in your question the ill intent you yourself had not yet shaped into being.

There's nothing harder to let go of than the thing you almost had, she said, soft, and she said nothing more.)

⋆   ⋆   ⋆

You approach the Spaceman's door.

From the outside, his house is unremarkable. Its state of disrepair is equalled by so many other houses on the estate that it barely registers as abnormal. Curtains the colour of old teeth, leprous window frames shedding paint in fat flakes. There is no doorbell, no knocker. Only a letterbox, rust-rimmed and unfriendly, like the mouth of something feral.

You glance over your shoulder, assessing the danger. A passer-by who catches you in the act might grass you up, and your nan would not be angry — she has never been angry, not once in all your twelve years — but she would fix you with her disappointed gaze, and the lines around her eyes would deepen, and her shattered expectations would fall around you like the ashes of something that had once been beautiful.

The estate is empty. Your friends are there, somewhere. Observing you from an unseen vantage point, peeking from behind cars, from around corners, because the act must be observed if the rite is to be fulfilled. You fill your lungs with air. He won't answer, you tell yourself; it hardly counts as disturbing him at all. He probably doesn't even hear it. Is there room for anything in his life other than the distant stars, which were denied him?

You lift the letterbox, and the door gives way.

You freeze. It isn't supposed to go like this. The tinny slap of letterbox — one, two, three, always the magic number — and then the breathless panic of retreat, the sound of plimsolls echoing on concrete, and all your friends squealing in vicious delight as they await the arrival of the Spaceman, who never comes. Whose filmy shadow is the only assurance that he exists at all.

The door creaks open half an inch. You jump back as if stung, instinctive. Your nerves fizz with adrenaline, your muscles poised to run. But there is nobody behind the door. You'd nudged it with your own scant weight, and the silent flat beyond had bid you wordless welcome.

You turn. *It's open*, you say, in bemused wonderment, addressing the hidden cabal lurking just out of sight. *The door isn't locked.*

And someone's voice calls out: *Catalogue.*

There's a moment of contemplative quiet. Then the cry picks up, like a flock of birds. A murmuration, passing back and forth against the newborn evening, echoing from unseen corners. You feel assailed by it. All around you, singsong, three wicked, dancing syllables: *Catalogue. Catalogue. Catalogue.*

The almost-dark hours have arrived.

★   ★   ★

You don't remember who invented Catalogue. It is likely of shared genesis, a collaborative mind-child; an idea spun from a word, which birthed itself, grew fat on the nectar of your imaginations.

If Knock Down Ginger is mischief, then Catalogue is malice.

In truth, you have only played Catalogue once or twice since its invention, and never to its conclusion. The objective is simple: enter the victim's home – an open window, a door left ajar, all methods of ingress are acceptable – and return with a pilfered item. The more esoteric, the better; a spoon might *technically* fit the requirements, but the spirit of the game demands a more interesting offering. Leon once took a T-shirt from someone's back garden; Danny swiped a pot plant from an unattended windowsill. But these hardly count. The heart of Catalogue lies in ingress. In invasion.

It's about going where you are not permitted to be. About observing – in the span of that inheld breath, those featherlight footsteps – what is hidden between the walls of another's private space. The offering is formal proof, but Catalogue is a test of bravery above all, and not one of you has yet risen to its challenge.

It's not a real game. The almost-dark games never truly are.

★   ★   ★

Catalogue, the other kids sing in unison, and you feel the weight of their expectation heavy on you like the air before a storm. You, the cowardly one, with your troublesome morals passed down by your meddling grandmother, and why don't you have parents like normal kids do, anyway? *Catalogue, Catalogue,* like a tribal ritual, a rite of passage. And you realise that if you succeed – if you retrieve some oddity from the Spaceman's house – you will set a precedent such that they cannot ever accuse you of cowardice again.

In your heart, you understand that it is the worst possible precedent to set. Children escalate. They push boundaries. What happens when the thrill of theft becomes mundane? Where then will you turn in pursuit of excitement?

You push the door inwards. It opens without resistance, sliding back to reveal a strip of darkened corridor. The scent of dust. You call out, tentative: *hello?* Just loud enough that anyone inside would hear you;

quiet enough that your friends, scattered around the periphery, cannot. If the Spaceman comes, you can't be blamed for failure – the point of the game is not to be seen, after all, and you can hide behind the plausible deniability of the open door, an act of neighbourly goodwill: *your door was ajar. I thought you should know.*

But nobody answers. And you realise, as you take a step inside, that there is no sound at all. No distant chatter of television through the walls. No creak of disturbed floorboards. No ambient hum of fridge. In fact – another step, your small body engulfed by the unlit corridor – the flat seems to swallow sound, so that even the passing cars and murmuring birds just beyond the walls are completely absent. Your own flat is paper-thin, draughty; it seems sometimes that you can hear every sound on the estate.

The silence unnerves you in a way the darkness does not.

You have never seen a dead body, but you are filled with a slow dread, the certainty that, when you turn the corner into the living room – the mirror image of your own flat, flipped sideways, the strange within the familiar – you will find in there the dried and ancient husk of the Spaceman. Perhaps he'd fallen asleep on the sofa one bright afternoon, and never woken up again. Perhaps he'll be wrapped in blankets, an Egyptian mummy in cheap cotton. What a lonely death that would be, you think, as you hesitate outside the room; how sad, to die in silence, in darkness. To be discovered months later by a child who shouldn't even be here. Who would leave with some stolen object and say nothing of the dead man on the couch, because then you'd have to report it, and to report it would be to admit your trespass.

You wonder if the Spaceman has any family.

Inhaling, you turn towards the living room. There are no objects of any kind save for the curtains, long and pale and heavy. There is nothing in this room to Catalogue.

You turn back to the corridor. Beyond this point lie the bedrooms, the bathroom. Private spaces. If the Spaceman is here – dead, or alive, or at some stage in-between – he'll probably be in one of those rooms. You baulk at the scent of sterile dust, the sheer weight of the place, which seems to increase with each step you take; thick, like moving through liquid. Like amniotic fluid in a chambered womb.

Glancing down the hallway. At home, these walls are covered in pictures. Photographs taken a long time ago: Polaroids bleached sepia by the sun, fuzzy pictures snapped with a throwaway camera, in which you are very small, and your parents are alive, still. The cliffs in Antalya, where your father was born. Jewel-blue sea. Your nan, before she was weathered. Before she was sad.

It might as well be another child in those photos, for all you remember.

The Spaceman's walls are empty. The floor underfoot is bare board. Each step sends a cloud of grey dust swirling around your ankles. And you realise, as you tiptoe, that the flat is getting colder. Not a gradual cooling, the way the moon leaches all the warmth from the world at night, but sharp, like plunging into a pool of cold water.

From the furthest bedroom, a faint humming sound emerges. You freeze momentarily, afraid that the Spaceman has awoken; readying your body to bolt at the first indication of motion, Catalogue be damned. But as you stand there – back pressed against the bare-plaster wall, breathing bird-rapid, teeth clenched tight – the sound holds steady, low-pitched and unchanging. It isn't a person, you realise. A person would have to stop for breath.

You think of the way the boiler hums when your nan deigns to switch it on, because heating is expensive, and you only have so much money on the meter. You feel the hum in the floorboards, gently trembling, and the dust rises in response, each mote dancing in the scant light of the half-closed front door. The walls shiver with it. Your feet move in time with a rhythm so indistinct only your body can decipher it; automated, a gentle hypnosis, tilting your head backwards, eyes slipping shut. For a moment, you feel weightless. You feel peace.

By the time you reach the door at the end of the hall, you cannot remember ever taking a single step.

The room *sings*, a low melody like whalesong, like the winter wind howling mournful at the windows. It sings inside your head, and you put a hand out to steady yourself, press the other to your skull. The wall is reassuringly solid; a patina of loose plaster crumbles beneath your palm. The flat is real. You are real. You can still leave, you tell yourself. Aren't there worse things in the world than cowardice? Things like ghosts, and curses. Things like haunted corridors and death-cars and the black, vacant mouths of flats gutted by fire. Like lonely old women who have forgotten that they are alive.

You can still leave.

*   *   *

In your nan's room there is a box. It's not a special box, at least not to look at. Plain wood, unvarnished; the logo of some imported rum printed messily on the side. It's not a special box, but it lives on the top shelf of her wardrobe, where you cannot reach it. You shouldn't even know about it. But sometimes – in the dark, when you can't sleep – you walk the corridor like a ghost, your footsteps swallowed by threadbare carpet. You've seen her sitting with that box on her lap, staring into it so intently that you wonder if there's another world contained within.

You don't remember your parents dying. You don't remember them living, either. You have the vague recollection that they were once there, that they existed, in some other space, some other time. They must have been important, but you understand this second-hand, the way you understand that the war was terrible, and that your nan was beautiful once.

The photographs prove that they were real. You wouldn't be sure, otherwise.

The box sits in your nan's wardrobe like an unuttered promise. Once, when she was out, you dragged a chair in from the kitchen, clambered up so that you could see the box clearly. And you'd expected that box to call to you. You'd expected to feel *something*. Your history, calling from inside. The secrets of your parentage begging to be understood. But you hadn't felt anything. Not even when you'd laid your palms atop the lid, and there was no lock to stop you, nobody to tell you *no*.

Sometimes, a box is only a box.

*   *   *

The door hums.

You glance left, then right. An empty bedroom. A bare-bones bathroom; sink, toilet and bath rising crooked from the floorboards like teeth in a mildewed mouth. This is not a house anyone lives in, and yet the floor beneath you pulses like blood beneath the skin.

Sometimes, a room is only a room. Isn't it?

You could leave, but you have to *know*. The room calls you in a way the box never did. And it isn't that you're not afraid – your body is a cut wire, sparking adrenaline, you coward, you fearful little creature – but you can no more turn away from the door than you can undo your trespass. You broke into the Spaceman's home, and here is your reward. Here is your Catalogue.

The light is waning. It will be dark soon. Perhaps your friends have already left. Perhaps they have grown bored of this game. Perhaps they think you've been caught, that the Spaceman is on the phone to the police, have cleared the area so you can't drag them down with you. You are not the only coward.

You lay your palm flat against the door. Slow heartbeat, like a sleeping animal. Like something enormous, and silent, and alive. You breathe deep. Push the door open. Step inside, into the frozen dark, and feel your body drift weightlessly towards the ceiling.

★　　★　　★

Her memories are all she has, your nan had said once – a long time ago, now – *and someday soon, they'll be gone too.*

Will you remember any of this when you are old? Will you keep a wooden box full of memories in your wardrobe, fill it with the things you hope never to forget?

You have already forgotten so much.

★　　★　　★

The Spaceman looks up as you drift towards him. Curled up, foetal; silver-white spacesuit, the broad glassy dome of his helmet, in which you can only see your own face, your look of wide-eyed surprise. The air is so cold; it seems to crackle in your lungs, exit on a plume of shimmering ice crystals.

You shouldn't be here, the Spaceman says.

You kick your legs, ineffectual; your body turns a slow circle, and you realise, as you spin, that you are no longer sure which way up the ceiling is, if there is even a ceiling at all. *I thought you might be dead*, you say, which is only partly a lie.

Dead, the Spaceman repeats. Uncurling limb by limb, the careful stretch of arms which have not moved in a very long time, legs which mourn solid ground. He is tall. Proud-postured, despite his containment. *I should like very much to die, I think.*

Are you old?

His laughter is muffled by the helmet, but you recognise it all the same. *Must I be*, he asks, *to die?*

Maybe. Once, when you were younger, your nan took you to Ireland, where her sisters lived, and one night you'd driven by a lough so black and so still that when you'd stepped out of the car and onto the shore, it seemed that every single star in the sky had found its double in that mirror-smooth water. And as you squint into the infinite distance – helplessly floating, untethered – you wonder if this is how it would feel to drown in that lough.

What is this place? you ask.

I don't know, the Spaceman says. Solemn, now. He doesn't sound old, you think. He sounds lost, and sad. *I think...I must have brought a little of it back with me. When I came back down to Earth.*

Do you miss space?

He turns his head, slow, towards the empty horizon. The black glass of his visor is a single, unblinking eye. *It's the only place I've ever belonged*, he says. *The beauty of it. The silence. Perfect chaos, and perfect order.*

You follow his gaze. *But there's nothing there.*

Nothing?

You shake your head. *It's empty*, you say. *Like all the other rooms.*

For a long moment, the Spaceman is still. *Nothing*, he repeats, in grave wonderment. And then he moves. Propels himself into motion, the slow drift of outstretched limbs. A silvery fish in midnight seas, riding the currents until he is there, beside you, taking off his helmet. Fixing you with bleached-blue eyes, so pale they are almost colourless. You marvel at his gaunt skull, his grey pallor. You sense his fragility as he holds out his hands, and the spacesuit hangs from his bones like old skin.

You take the helmet. Despite its size, it too is weightless, smooth and round, marble-glassy in your palms, but warm, like an animal. You feel its pulse the way you did the door, and you understand that this is the centre of it all. This thing that you hold is the reason. It is the answer.

Tell me what you see, he says.

So you do.

*   *   *

If you don't eat that quickly, it'll melt.

You look up. The woman beside you looks so much like your nan that you think it must be her, for a moment, until you realise that she's at least thirty years too young; red-haired, shielding freckled skin from the sun with a pale green parasol. Rivulets of ice cream run down your knuckles. You lap melted strawberry from your fingers. Squint out at the sea, impossibly turquoise. Jut of pale cliffs at the far end of the beach, scrubby vegetation and honey-coloured rock.

(what's wrong with this picture?)

You've got your dad's skin, the woman says, with something like envy. *You won't burn in this heat. But we should put some sun cream on, just in case.*

I don't like sun cream, you hear yourself say. You don't sound like you. You sound like a child. Petulant and small.

Nobody likes sun cream, she says. *But if you don't use it, you'll look like Judith Chalmers by the time you're eighteen.*

Who's that?

The woman laughs. *Finish your ice cream*, she says, gazing back out at the sea. *Daddy will be here soon. Don't you want to go swimming with him?*

(no, you think, in some faraway part of you; my dad is dead. He's been dead for a long time)

You dig your toes into the hot sand. *Yeah!* you say, in that voice that is not your own, and the woman smiles fondly. The ice cream is sweet and cold. You don't like strawberry. You can't remember ever liking strawberry. The sea whispers in the distance, jewel-bright and gleaming, and you don't remember any of this, you don't remember, you don't

*   *   *

You pull the helmet off.

The Spaceman's pale eyes meet yours, entreating you to share. You pause, catch your breath; your heart is racing, and you can still hear the sea, still taste strawberry sweet and cloying in the back of your throat.

I saw the sea, you say.

The sea. He nods. *And did it make you happy?*

It didn't make me feel anything, you say, which is the truth. As the alien sensations dissipate into the winter dark, you are left only with the vague discomfort of exposure, like too much sun. This dead memory. Voices you were never supposed to hear again.

He frowns. *Didn't it capture something perfect?*

Cold glass against your skin, humming quietly. A snowglobe, you think; a moment frozen in time. *But it isn't real,* you say. Your own face, staring back at you in black glass. You look nothing like your mother. You never did. *It's just moving pictures. That's all.*

The Spaceman's frown deepens. He is neither young nor old, you realise; the stasis of the helmet has preserved him at the exact moment of orbit, living the same few hours over and over, but his heart is old. His bones are fragile. He has been dreaming for so long that he exists outside of time, outside of space. This empty room. This nothing-place. The almost-dark.

Here. You hold the helmet out in your hands. *I have to go back home now.*

He looks at the helmet for a long moment. Take it, you think, with growing impatience. You want to feel solid ground beneath your feet again. You want to breathe air that doesn't make your lungs ache. But he lifts his head. Blinks, as though seeing the emptiness all around him for the first time.

You came here for something, didn't you? Drifting away again. Without the imposing bulk of his helmet, he seems very small. *Take it.*

But don't you—

It's all right, he says. Smiling, now; growing distant, though his eyes are so pale, still, so bright. *I think it's time I went home, too.*

★   ★   ★

When you come back down to earth and find yourself again in that silent corridor, in that empty flat, the memory you'd felt so vividly begins to scatter. You let it go, feel it dissipate, the way dandelion seeds float away on the spring wind. Someday soon, you won't recall any of it.

The helmet in your arms is heavy, awkward. You realise, as you lower it to the ground, that it is no longer humming. It is a cold, inert object, a functional item that does not belong here, in this flat, on this estate. It is a wooden box on the top shelf.

It isn't alive. Perhaps it never was.

You leave it there, at the Spaceman's door. You could Catalogue it. You could be the marvel of your friends – the one who met the Spaceman, the one who was brave – but you sense their approval would be short-lived. Maybe it's time to stop all these games, you think, as you walk towards the front door. The sliver of waning light peeling in from the scant gap. The sound of cars on the main road, a dog barking somewhere far away. Maybe it's time to grow up.

BAGS

Steve Rasnic Tem

Hank's father insisted he take the waste out after dark because he was embarrassed. That's what he called it: the garbage and the trash and the miscellanea, everything he'd kept too long and now was keen to dispose of. The man had lived life poorly and this was the visible evidence. But it made no difference. In the morning, the bags and the boxes would be sitting in the alley for the entire world to witness.

Hank hated carrying these discards out at night. Their floodlight had shorted out years ago, so he only had the moon and the arc lamp above a distant street corner to guide him. Deep shadow made him uneasy. Anyone might be watching.

He was halfway through the back yard with the last bloated bags when he stopped, thinking he heard his father call him. A weather front was coming in. It sounded like distant applause.

He turned and stared at the back of the house. He'd hauled a wealth of junk from this small, unimpressive mid-Thirties bungalow. You buy, you throw away, and then you buy some more. The "regurgitating economy," Dad called it. Dad was as bad as everyone else in this regard, but at least he recognised the problem. Hank heard him coughing in the dining room. He waited for any choking sounds but hearing none decided he needn't rush.

The dark squares of window screen bulged, the porch stuffed with Dad's belongings staged for disposal or donation, the old man didn't care which. Dad said he wanted to throw away everything before he died so Hank might have a fresh start. This might have been true, and Hank didn't want Dad's shabby things, but the mania with which he'd purged himself of possessions this past year was scary.

The silhouette of the house was humped, the roof altered during his grandfather's time to add an attic room. The amateur remodel resulted in leaks, which had been causing damage for decades. How could he get a fresh start in something so ruined?

His arms began to tremble. One bag dripped as if perspiring. It felt awful brushing against his bare legs. He reeled off balance toward the alley. The area along their fence was already crowded with bags and spoiled bedding, junk-filled cartons and a few pieces of furniture in such poor shape the thrift stores wouldn't take them. A scavenger would grab what the trash service didn't haul away.

His father wanted all this material expunged, he didn't care how, but he didn't want to hear any details about thrift stores or junk men or pickers or recyclers. More than once, he'd referred to them as ghouls.

The front was cold and punishing when it arrived. The plastic bags made a rapid snapping sound in the wind. Dad never bought good bags. He never bought good anything. Hank was ashamed – it was an uncharitable thought about a dying old man who loved him.

Their neighbours' unsecured trash cans rolled down the sloping alley and gathered in the street below. They'd be blocks away by morning. Hank would have gone after them, but he couldn't leave his dad alone for long. He noticed an unfamiliar black pickup truck tucked away beneath the trees near the street. It was an aged model, so battered he couldn't be positive about the brand.

An unusually lean figure slipped from the shadows by the truck and entered the street, picked up each trash can with ease and peered inside, tossing them away as if they weighed nothing.

The sight disturbed him but he could not look away. Trash pickers had always worked this neighbourhood, scavenging items they could use, repair, or sell, but they came early in the morning before the garbage trucks ran. Hank knew many, and sometimes waited with coffee and an offer to help load their trucks. He had never seen one working the alley at night.

The dark figure picked up another can, hovered over it, then paused, and Hank could have sworn it grew taller, and broader, its head expanding to fill the opening. It tilted its head back and lifted the can, upending it as if to drink the contents. All at once the slim silhouette grew fuller, its torso swelling so quickly it drunkenly staggered back.

The murky apparition twirled around and shuffled toward the truck. Hank's insides went liquid.

Hank's perceptions were unreliable. It was dark and he was stressed – Dad was dying. Yet he couldn't bear the thought of this creature looking at him. The wind intensified, pulling at his clothes. A nearby tree bent over crazily. He grabbed the stretchy cords attached to the chain-link fence and tried to secure the bags he'd just brought out beside the others. He didn't know what was in them – his father had filled them a few months ago before this last illness. The older bags were more grey than black, layered in dust and the openings secured with those old-fashioned wire twisty ties. One bag split under the cord and something sour dribbled from the wound and down the taut skin. Dad would hate that, but he would never know.

★　　★　　★

The moment Hank entered the house he heard his dad talking. "Did you get all the bags of smelly garbage? Make sure you got them all!" His father's voice turned harsh and wheezy when he was anxious. These days he was anxious most of the time. That was okay. It showed he was still engaged.

"It's okay, Dad! I got them all!" Hank hated raising his voice.

"Then why does the house still smell like garbage?"

He didn't want to tell him he was smelling his own recurring stink. He hurried down the hall, dodging wobbly stacks of boxes overflowing with mess. There was something deeply unpleasant about brushing against dry cardboard. He had no time to process the disturbing whispers which resulted. "You've got to give it some time, Dad," said loudly to drown out the unidentifiable muttering. "I just now took them out."

Our bodies are three-fourths water, our slipcases of skin little better than leaking bags. This was painfully true in his father's case. The elderly man, lying shirtless on a rented hospital bed in the dining room, dripped, oozed, and sweated. Hank had moved in a TV for him, a bedside table full of books and magazines which had so far been ignored, framed photos of family members which his father also ignored, but insisted they be where he could see them just the same.

No eating took place in this dining room. Food smells made his father ill. His dad derived nourishment from a creamy liquid in a hanging bag via a tube plunged into his chest. Another tube delivered medicine into the back of his hand. Chemo had rendered him mostly bald, leaving a few thin strokes, a dream of hair. Pale lids capped sunken eyes. If they hadn't just been talking, Hank would have thought him asleep.

They'd sold the dining room furnishings: the good dining set, a couple of antique sideboards. Their absence left a large, tattered hole in the faded rug showing extensive floor damage. Dark spots speckled the boards, mildew, or black mould, he supposed, but he didn't know the difference, nor did he want to. He could cover it with another rug.

His father opened his eyes. They moved around, pale and filmy. Hank wondered how much he could see. Dad refused to wear glasses anymore.

The darkness outside the window changed. Hank stared, waiting for movement, looking for a face or figure, something, but could not find them.

"What took you so long anyway?"

"It's dark. I was trying to be careful. Remember, there's no light out there."

Dad grunted. "How's the bag?"

Hank glanced at the feeding bag on the pole. "At least a third full. You're not feeling hungry, are you?"

His father snorted. "If I were hungry, I wouldn't need that thing. The *piss* bag, Hank."

Hank lifted the sheet hanging off the side of the bed and examined the drainage bag attached to the frame. "I'll need to empty it in a while."

"Is Sue coming over tonight?"

"Not tonight." Hank paused. "I think she has other plans."

"You don't know for sure? Call her. Invite her over. But make sure you dump the bag before she gets here. Remember to pull my sheet up too. She seems to think she has to say hello every time she comes over, and I don't want to scare her away with this big gross belly."

"I don't think she cares, Dad. But I will, if she comes over, but I really don't think she is." The abdomen looked painful, swollen like a tick, decorated with stretched and distorted surgical scars. His dad had spread thick cream all over it with his free hand, partly for comfort, but mainly because he was afraid of insect bites. He'd developed a terror of insects crawling or landing on him. A half dozen nasty yellow sticky fly strips hung from the dining room ceiling, each jewelled with insect carcasses. Whenever the nurses visited, they complained about these strips, and how the cream got all over the IV tubing and the bandages, but Dad refused any changes to his self-prescribed precautions.

I will not end up this way, Hank thought, and immediately felt disrespectful. He'd die before he reached Dad's age. He wasn't that healthy.

"You make the appointment for the belly tap?"

"It's Thursday afternoon."

"You couldn't get me in sooner? I feel like I'm going to burst."

"I know it's uncomfortable, but that's the soonest I could get an appointment."

His father grunted and closed his eyes again. Ever since his last stay in the hospital he kept his eyes closed most of the time, in embarrassment, or so he couldn't see what was happening to him, answering the doctors' or the nurses' intimate questions with mumbles and head movements.

"You two should get married, you know," Dad said, eyes still closed. "Don't make my mistake."

"Maybe Mom was always going to leave. People do that."

"I didn't pay her enough attention. I was too busy with my own projects. Now those projects are in trash bags, and I haven't seen her in years. I'm sorry I did that to you."

"She could have called me or written. I'm her only child. She didn't. I know nothing about her. You stayed, Dad."

"Don't wait until I'm gone. Don't screw this up." Hank knew he was a disappointment. The fact he'd become Dad's caretaker was proof Hank had nothing better to do.

His dad raised his head and stared as if he'd been struck. "You have to lock down this relationship *now*, while you still look halfway decent. Trust me, you don't want to grow old alone." He fell back onto the pillow and closed his eyes. "Make sure the doors are locked," he whispered. "If somebody tries to break in—"

"Nobody's breaking in, Dad." But Hank was no longer sure.

"I said *if*. I can't stop them. People see stuff coming out of here, they might think we have something worth taking. How's it going with the back room?"

The back room was the biggest room in the house, packed wall-to-wall with furniture, trunks overflowing with his mother's belongings, projects his dad abandoned. Hank had no idea what most of it was, just that it had filled the room thirty years or more with an inaccessible, impenetrable accumulation.

"I think I found a junk dealer who'll take it all, maybe even pay you a little for it."

"I *don't* want to know the details. I don't want to watch – have them come through the back door. I can't be thinking about strangers pawing over my stuff. But that's good. It'll make a nice size bedroom for you two. Sue will have an empty house to make her own. She won't say no to marriage if you can offer her this house without me in it."

Hank didn't reply. There was no point. He watched a mayfly land on his dad's belly and struggle in the ointment, stuck fast. He grabbed a tissue and snatched the bug, leaning over and kissing Dad on the forehead to disguise what he was doing. His dad's eyes sprang open in confusion.

"Goodnight, Dad." The eyes moved around as if searching for something, then closed again.

At some point he would have to tell him that he and Sue broke up weeks ago. If his dad died before then it would save them both a painful conversation, but he wanted his dad to live as long as possible. Hank just didn't want to see the disappointment in his face.

With surprising strength Dad grabbed him by the back of the neck and pulled him within inches of his mouth. "Keep the ones you love close," he whispered hoarsely. "They're all you have in the end. To the rest of the world, you're food."

★   ★   ★

Trips to the hospital meant unhooking everything and getting him into sweatpants and a shirt, sitting him up on the edge of the bed, and a short but difficult transfer into the wheelchair. Dad struggled to help but he had little strength left.

He was slippery. His dad was always wet. The massive belly made a sloshing sound and the shift in gravity made the move tough to control. Hank hadn't dropped him yet, but he was afraid every time.

The hospital admitted them through the emergency entrance and provided a bed in an alcove some distance from the other patients. Dad wasn't happy about it. He said going through those Emergency doors made him feel like he was dying. Hank did not remind him that he was.

Hank didn't want to watch, but Dad said he needed him there. They sat Hank in a heavy steel chair a couple of yards from the plastic paracentesis canisters. The clinicians required at least five for his dad, but several more were ready if necessary. Hank always turned away as the large needle went into his dad's belly but felt a morbid fascination as he witnessed canister after canister fill with the straw-coloured liquid. This fluid would be analysed but they already knew it was full of cancer cells.

It was called ascitic fluid, and despite the fancy containers it was biomedical waste and had to be eliminated. Hank had no idea how they did it; he assumed they couldn't put it out with the regular garbage.

He was surprised the belly didn't shrink more given the amount they drained. Dad contained an endless supply. With each visit Hank felt a little sorrier for the old man.

An observation window stretched behind the surgical table, with doors opening and closing as workers moved carts and gurneys around, removing canisters and other materials and bringing in fresh supplies. Hank didn't pay much attention until a towering figure in dingy, stained scrubs wheeled in a filthy metal cart. He was alarmed such an unclean presence might be permitted in a hospital. The individual wore a voluminous surgical cap and a duckbill mask so Hank couldn't see the face. This masked worker bent awkwardly as if its waistline were misplaced. It slinked around the room examining the equipment as if unfamiliar with the environment.

The figure lifted a canister full of ascitic fluid, sniffed it, and held it up to the overhead lights. Hank was so convinced it was going to take a sip he turned away and shuddered. He stood up to warn the clinicians. One turned and said, "Sir! You need to sit down!" Hank pointed at the window, but the area behind the window was empty.

★   ★   ★

Trips to the hospital exhausted Dad and he slept for hours afterwards. Hank took advantage and made arrangements in advance with a local junk dealer, who arrived with two trucks and a crew. Hank closed the multi-paned French doors to the dining room and the workers carried bags, boxes, and loose items from the back room out both the front and back doors. Some were curious and stared through the glass doors at his dad and the festooned tubing. Some neighbours gathered outside to watch. Hank paid attention to what was coming from the back room; much he couldn't remember having seen before. He supposed the day provided entertainment for everyone.

Some big men worked on the junk man's crew, broad men and tall men, one so incredibly tall and of such unlikely strength Hank felt compelled to follow him around. They all wore dust masks. Maybe Hank should have been wearing a mask every day while living in this house.

He supposed he should ask them to slow down and let him peek into those containers. There might be some valuable objects leaving their home. But the goal was to get rid of it all, and his dad wasn't going to sleep forever. Besides, downsizing and making space felt as if Hank were accomplishing something.

He vaguely recognised his mother's hats and dresses, a favourite painting, a jewellery box, a vase. There were cartons full of correspondence – some might be letters from his mother – he didn't know. Heavy furniture requiring four men to carry, water-damaged antiques good for nothing but firewood. Bags of art supplies from when his dad wanted to be a painter. But if there had been paintings Hank never saw them. Bags of jottings and notebooks from when his dad wanted to be a writer, but as far as Hank knew he'd never finished anything. He felt some regret, but he wasn't going to stop them. Better to be done with the job and have all this gone.

When they finished the junk man gave him a small check. Hank didn't feel cheated. Clearing the room had been the goal. It was what his dad wanted. The junk man said, angrily it seemed, "There's something I want to show you," and walked back into the room. Hank followed.

With the room emptied he was alarmed by the scars and cracks in walls and woodwork. He knew something was odd the moment he walked in. He felt a slope in the floor, and it bewildered him, as if he'd strolled into a funhouse. A shuddering sensation passed through his feet as he tried to find some balance.

"You can feel the instability, right?" the man said. "Look over here at the baseboard." At least a three-inch gap yawned between the baseboard and the floor along one wall. The junk man walked toward the far corner but stopped well short. "It's worse over here. I came close to pulling my people out. Do you have a wet basement by any chance?"

"Sometimes." Seepage had ruined everything in the basement more than a few times over the years. He rarely went down there due to the stench.

"I'm guessing you have a few rotted posts. You need to get an engineer in here; this house might not even be safe to live in. I've seen it before – the skin of the house is intact, but the bones are gone. The hoard filling this room might have been the only thing holding the house up."

★　　★　　★

Hank wouldn't be calling anyone. There was no money for it. It was hard to believe in upcoming catastrophes beyond the disaster which was already here. He couldn't see the point in worrying his dad further, who still slept soundly. He should check on him, he thought, but what could he do if there was something wrong? Things were already as wrong as possible for his father. Hank retreated to his own bedroom to lie down and think.

Unlike the rest of the house, Hank's room was a study in minimalism, open and clutter free. Forced to live with the tangle of his father's possessions made him intolerant of mess in his own space. The ability to stretch out and roll around on the floor like a child, staring at the ceiling and imagining stars, was priceless.

Today he could see the cracks spreading through that firmament, and where the corners and door and window frames misaligned. He'd stared at those surfaces countless times before, seeing what he'd wanted to see.

He heard footsteps in the hall and for a brief, impossible moment thought Dad might be up and looking for him. He opened the door and saw through the French doors a towering figure in faded scrubs leaning over Dad's bed. Visiting nurses sent by the care service had come into the house unannounced before, but Hank still considered it unacceptable. The nurse turned, but due to some distortion in the glass panes she or he had no profile. "I'll be right with you," Hank said. He went back into the bedroom to change clothes.

Slipping into fresh jeans he kicked over the pillowcase holding some clothing and other things Sue had left behind, spilling them everywhere. He didn't know if she wanted them, but he couldn't bring himself to throw them out with the trash. He scrambled to gather them back into the case.

He'd never seen a person as tall as today's nurse. He or she was new. These services had a tough time keeping personnel. He hoped this one had been properly vetted.

Hank rushed from the bedroom. The nurse was no longer in view. He jerked open the doors and ran to his father, who lay crumpled to one side, small and deflated within his over-abundant skin.

★ ★ ★

As strange as his father's last moments had been, Hank found it even stranger how quickly a life is wrapped up, packaged neatly, and the process of erasure begins. Everything had been prepaid. As per Dad's instructions he called the funeral home and two young men looking uncomfortable in their old-fashioned black suits came to pick up the body. Another phone call to the medical supplier resulted in the removal of all rented medical equipment within the day. A week later a man delivered the ashes in a burgundy-coloured plastic container slightly bigger than a cigar box. Everything his father had been weighed less than five pounds in Hank's hands. The awkward gentleman unhelpfully explained the cremains were bone fragments processed down to resemble ashes.

Hank had no idea what to do with these ashes or bones or whatever they were. He had an unreasonable fear of accidentally throwing them away with the remaining trash.

He spent the next week hauling everything left out to the alley and the fence. The city service wouldn't take it all and he wondered if he might be fined. The pickers would be grateful for the bonanza. He worked all day every day with short breaks, stopping in early evening because he didn't want to be out there at night. Without his father to goad him the timetable was his own.

On what he planned to be the final clean out day he ran late. It was past twilight, and the shadows flowed in. He kept thinking how relieved he would be when the job was finished. He had the last items in the back yard, boxes of housewares, and bag after bag of miscellanea, mostly those bags Dad filled ages ago.

He could barely distinguish one rough shape from another. The backyard was almost full, and he couldn't imagine how he was going to manage it all.

A tumult erupted from the alley, cats screeching and dogs barking, heavy movements in the gravel between the alley pavement and their yard. He was hesitant to walk out there, but eager to be done with this final chore.

It began to rain. The soft beginnings of it, landing on the bags, sounded like beating moth wings, of which he'd seen many when dragging stuff from the rooms. A rapid metallic tapping began, and Hank turned around and looked at the house, the rain hitting the metal flashing and the gutters, pouring off the sides because they hadn't been cleaned out in years, leaves and twigs and fragmented roof shingles clogging the openings into the downspouts. He glanced up at the roof itself, saw the gaps where shingles had been torn away, and couldn't understand why he'd never noticed this damage before. He felt irresponsible, like a neglectful parent.

Waterfalls began to pour here and there from the cracks between the board siding, tearing away bits and pieces of the house. Hank knew little about construction, but assumed water was getting in from the damaged roof and down behind the sheathing. He looked around, finding fallen plaster and crumbling brick. Cracks spread through the limestone foundation stones. There appeared to be a definite lean to the back porch, the lines no longer true, the entire structure beginning to separate from the rest of the house.

He heard a muffled groan and a cracking noise. A portion of the roof line suddenly complicated itself, breaking into several additional angles.

Hank held his place in the thundering downpour until it stopped, the world gone quiet again except for the gentle dripping of the bags. He shivered within his soggy clothes. Furious with himself and with his father, he grabbed bags and carried them to the alley, threw them on the others and went back for more. He made several such trips before pausing to rest, collapsing against the fence.

The storm advanced the night prematurely. Streetlights came on. He heard distant traffic, but no cars moved on the nearby streets. He heard a damp shifting noise, and a bag moved. He assumed it was the contents settling, when one side stretched out, and the entire bag began to distort. The plastic near the top ripped, and something climbed out of the bag, but it was too dark to tell what it was. After a moment of stillness, it scampered away. Perhaps a squirrel or some other varmint had gotten inside while the bags sat in the yard. Hank approached the piles and nudged each bag with his foot, waited for some movement, and went on to the next. None of the other bags responded.

Something crawled across his arm, and he shook it off. He probed deeper into the layers of bags, their stench rising around him now the rain had ended. He wasn't sure what he was looking for, but he couldn't stop.

A few insects scrambled from the small openings where the bags were tied, then a larger number, and then a flood. Soon the dark plastic skins were thick with them, the bugs pouring off the bags and into the alley as if frantic to escape.

Hank heard scraping trash cans, and gazing down the alley saw the angular silhouette progressing brokenly from can to can, leaning over the dark mouths then standing up larger, swollen head and swollen chest, swollen belly then thin again, rapidly processing everything it had eaten.

It turned its body and shambled toward him, to the next garbage can, close enough that Hank could see the vague rot along its profile, its edges deteriorating from all the waste consumed.

Hank was faint with dread, legs too weak to support him. He'd been holding himself together so well, but he was so tired. The house was empty, and Dad was gone.

He felt himself settle into his skin and dropped to the ground between the high black plastic walls, as if he were hiding inside a large bag of his own making.

When his turn came and the creature peered inside, its small eyes seemed impossibly far away, and yet its immense mouth so very close.

RISE UP TOGETHER

Adam L.G. Nevill

After emerging from a dark forest bearding the main road, I entered the seaside town where Mike had lived for the past five years. The dregs of natural light had almost disappeared but the road and street lighting remained dark. Resorting to high beams, I found myself willing the town's lights to come on. They never did.

Tired after a five-hour drive to the coast, my concentration during the final leg of the journey was scant. I barely looked further than the SatNav or the road directly ahead, so my first impression of the town amounted to little more than a sense of endless rows of neat houses, dully glowing like marble at night. All of the buildings were white and crammed along the coast, bringing to mind a vast Victorian cemetery festooned with sepulchres. A town long and narrow, a harbour in the middle and an interminable A-road hemming the inland side.

At the southern tip of the town, around eight, I parked outside the white house that belonged to Mike; a three-bed molar embedded within a curving jawline of identical buildings. I hadn't seen Mike since he left the city, half a decade before. And like many old friends, we immediately broke into sheepish grins and pitched a few comments back and forth. Mike was inside the porch. I was on the drive, shaking cramp out of my back and joints. But my relief at no longer being inside the car unspooled into an uncomfortable surprise. I felt that specific awkwardness when confronted by unexpected alterations in the appearance of a familiar person, caused by illness or age.

Mike was only forty-one, the same age as me. And, to my knowledge, he hadn't suffered an upheaval in his personal life. He certainly hadn't mentioned anything in the handful of emails we exchanged each year. And as he didn't participate in social media he wasn't easy to keep up with. His correspondence had also grown scarce, a little abrupt, and light on content during the intervening years. A gulf had grown between us, one enforced by physical distance. That was the cause. Or so I'd assumed.

His hair was grey and thinning. It hadn't been the last time I'd seen him, and I can't understand why men suffering hair loss allow their remaining hair to grow thick at the sides, whilst vainly attempting to fashion the meagre strands on top into a semblance of cover. A practice that only adds years to the face. If there is no hair style in a man's future, remove the remains or take it right down. Not Mike. He seemed determined to make himself appear much older than he actually was, and ridiculous, with an arrangement of combed wisps swept backwards.

The divergence of his wardrobe from fashionable to a style far beyond his years only worsened the presentation of his head. He was also uncharacteristically overweight and there was a putty-like texture to his visible flesh, save his eyelids and cheeks. Those were pink and shiny with eczema. Pale, round-shouldered and bulgy, his paunch was unwisely emphasised by the taupe slacks he wore too high and belted tightly. Schoolish lace-up shoes and a formal shirt completed the ensemble, the latter tucked deep below the waistline. A biro was clipped to a chest pocket.

On the colour spectrum he was now grey and beige and washed-out. I could have passed him in the street without a flicker of recognition. And yet from my first sighting of him at university and until we met for his farewell drinks, Mike had been a peacock and a compulsive user of the gym. This was prior to his move to the seaside to take a job for a corporation that maintained retirement villages. A middle-management position as nondescript as his current apparel. He now looked like a man who still lived with his parents and dressed like the elderly father. But Mike had no family. No partner had been mentioned either.

The analogy of a man remaining too long in the family home, I extend to his actual home. Cosy but regimentally tidy. Clinically clean yet fussy and furnished in a style I'd not associate with anyone shy of seventy years of age, who wasn't female and pathologically house-proud. A woman from our parents' generation. I might have accepted his surroundings if he'd been renting a furnished property, but he owned the house.

Spotless walls, brass and glass lightshades in the hall, a pristine kitchen equipped with a tea cosy and checked tea-towels upon a wooden rack. Floral crockery. Even a bloody spice rack. A dry-wipe board for shopping lists. A calendar of improbably colourful pastoral scenes. A line of hardback cookbooks and, seemingly, the complete works of Delia Smith.

I only stopped gaping to remove my shoes, as bid by my old friend, and padded into an overly-lit living room with the curtains drawn. Therein a coffee table, one bookcase, a television, an easy chair and matching sofa with tasselled cushions. And not much else. No stereo. The Mike I once knew loved indie music and could wall a room with his vintage vinyl collection. Perhaps they were in another room.

When I peered over my shoulder to make some quip about the massive improvements in his housekeeping since our student days, I caught him deftly placing my shoes together before repositioning my bag against a wall. He then straightened the skewed mat. The latter fussing executed with irritation.

When seen in bright light, the man who settled heavily in the lounge was also bone-tired. If Mike's mouth struggled to support a smile, his eyes couldn't summon the strength to attempt one. Nor did mine when I spotted the heraldic symbolism printed upon the sides of the tea cups that he'd carried into the living room. *A royalist too now?*

When I mentioned that I could kill a beer, Mike muttered that he only had sherry. So I stuck to the watery, unsweetened tea he'd provided. Was it Earl Grey or ash that I could taste? There was something oddly fragrant yet charred about the brew, and when I set it down after two sips, Mike, with the speedy reactions of a first-class slips fielder, managed to rise from the sofa and insert a coaster beneath the mug before its base touched the polished surface of the table.

"Oh. Yeah. Sorry," I murmured.

I was then barely able to find the will to contribute to the wretched small talk he tossed my way – *How was the journey? Should brighten up tomorrow. Take a stroll along the seafront while I'm at work. Chambers does a fine cream tea* – without him once looking me in the eye.

I was once made redundant by a company that had been most unscrupulous in its use of me. As the head of human resources had slipped a white envelope across the boardroom table to me, he'd looked just like Mike. Guilty, furtive, ashamed, eager for the meeting to conclude. Mike wasn't going to sack me but he was deeply mithered by something, and I suspected he'd returned to the preoccupied state of mind that I'd interrupted on arrival.

The ceiling light and an anodyne print behind his head of a cornfield seemed of more interest to him than his newly arrived friend who he'd not seen in years. During the first twenty minutes, he even checked the sensible watch on his thick forearm several times as if I was keeping him from something vital. He didn't listen to my answers. There were too many silences.

During one uncomfortable pause in what served for conversation, I noticed the thick drapes that concealed the garden; velvet with pelmets and braided cords of gold. A mocha wall of fabric that sealed the windows and walls to the floor. They conjured an unintended theatrical effect and had they been opened and I confronted with a bored audience wearing evening dress, watching us from rows of upholstered chairs, I might not have been as surprised as I should have been.

Our mutual discomfort endured until the hour approached nine.

When Mike consulted his watch for a third time in quick succession, as if he were timing a sporting event, I could no longer hold back. "Mate. What's up? Something on your mind? It's been a while but I remember that look."

"No. No. Nothing. Absolutely fine. Never been better. Just tired. Early start. Work." He didn't smile and his yawn, I am sure, was fake. His eyes also flitted to the wall behind his seat. He hadn't been able to relax since my arrival but at the sight of the wall, his anxiety ratcheted sufficiently to make him paler, even breathless. Mike muttered something to himself, then bit his bottom lip. "We should think about turning in. I'll show you your room."

"If this isn't a good time, you should have said—"

"No. No. No. Nothing like that. Not used to guests. You're the first in...how long? Not sure." He couldn't meet my eye and peered at his shoes, the curtains, the light, the ceiling, the door, his watch again. Then stood up fast. "You must be shattered. Long drive."

"I'm all right. First night. I thought we might have a couple of drinks."

Mike swept up the crockery and ferried it into the kitchen before returning with a damp cloth to wipe down the coasters. To actually wipe down the coasters. That's when I began to laugh.

Mirth I cut off at the sight of his fidgety expression; the mind behind it entrapped by an absorption that detached his awareness from me, the room, the present and drew it inwards. Into what must have been a maelstrom of fretting. I pitied him. And dumbfounded, I mutely stared at him. So reduced. Cowed, restless and antsy. The long weekend of sinking ale, swimming, wolfing gourmet burgers and fresh fish that I'd envisaged, no longer felt remote but impossible.

"Is there a pub? We can chew the fat over—"

"No! Noooo. Noo, noo, noo," he mooed pitifully. The tone silly enough to incite the first prickle of irritation along my nape. "Nah. Knackered," he went on. "Busy, busy, busy. At work. Need to turn in." He faked another yawn and paced about my chair like a waiter looking to close up. His restless hands meaninglessly rearranged the television handsets. Again, he glanced at his watch and seemed to wither at what he saw recorded there. "An early one won't kill us—"

Before he could finish another weak and unconvincing excuse for his odd behaviour, the wall behind his head was thumped hard. From the other side.

I started. "What the hell?"

Mike flinched so hard his feet nearly left the silvery carpet. He resembled a man who'd just suffered a shock; some awful news about his health or loved ones. Or, this was a man who'd been threatened. I couldn't decide. But his hovering beside my chair developed a desperate impatience; a suggestion of his mind's growing insistence that he act urgently. His chubby hands made a feeble upwards motion as if he were directing me to stand up. "We better," he said, and the wafting of his hands increased as he angered.

"Mike?"

"Come on! Let's go! We need to—"

And then the wall was thumped again, even harder than before, from the other side. A sudden, violent provocation from the neighbouring property.

"Jesus. Who is that?"

Mike swallowed to find his voice. Constructing a feeble grin, he muttered, "Bit sensitive to noise." He rolled his eyes and tried to enlist me in an understanding of the neighbours' concern. "You know how people get."

"Not really. Not when it's not even nine. When we're only talking. At a reasonable volume. In your home."

But Mike was already dousing the lights. And to avoid being shut inside a pitch-black living room, because he was inching the door closed before I even got to my feet, I followed him into the hall. Where he swept up my holdall, killed the lights and jogged up the stairs to a first floor that reeked of lavender.

Upstairs, he became embarrassed and tried to snigger his way out of explaining the reason for our speedy evacuation from downstairs. But he never mentioned the two thumps against his living room wall. "Bathroom's there," he said instead, pointing at a closet-sized space that glimmered like a sterilised surgery, its array of fancy soaps and lotions arranged upon a glass shelf. "You won't need a glass of water, or anything, will you?" he asked and fearfully peered at the darkened staircase. "'Cus…" But he never finished.

"No," I replied, my voice like my spirits, leaden with disappointment, as I dutifully trudged into the spare room to placate him.

His relief was evident. Delighted at his success at driving me up those stairs and into the spare room, he appeared near euphoric as if some dire psychological need had been assuaged.

The door of the spare room was shut tightly and pushed into the frame until the catch clicked. "See you in the morning!" he called through solid wood.

I half expected to hear the sound of a bolt, to ensure that I never came back out of the room. Baffled, I sat on a hard mattress and fussy duvet in the dull, featureless room in which I had been billeted. A home office. A white self-assembly desk filled one wall. That and the home computer on top were entirely dust free. A chair was tucked neatly beneath the desk. A bookcase supported manuals and folders. A brief perusal of their plastic spines connected them to business management and accounting. There was nothing else inside the space beside some pressed flowers in wooden frames, on the wall at the end of the bed.

The white walls glared. A cell with windows screened by another set of heavy, imprisoning curtains. They dropped to the floor as if to eradicate any sight of the outside world.

"What the fuck?" I asked myself. "What the actual fuck?"

Beyond the room, not a single sound arose. The residual tone in my ears hummed loudly.

"Fuck it." I undressed to my underwear and shirt. Killed the light. Pulled back the duvet. Seeking air, I fumbled in total darkness at the side of the bed near the windows and their imprisoning acres of drapery. The house was too warm, airless and fragrant. I slept poorly without an open window.

By the time I'd fought through the swaddling cascades of the curtains and shoved a small window ajar, I realised that the streetlights still hadn't been switched on. The road Mike lived in was obliterated by darkness and not a chink of light escaped any of the neighbouring buildings. I was too irritable to fathom why.

I dozed then woke with a horrible lurch and wasn't sure which way was up or down around the bed. Nor did I know where I was for a few disorienting seconds.

The second time I found myself half-awake I understood that I had been awoken. By footsteps outside. Slow footsteps, a shuffling, as if a group of people was quietly passing the house.

By the time I'd sat up and blinked meaninglessly, in the sensory deprivation that Mike's spare room enforced upon a guest, and had pulled aside the curtain, I saw nothing but a greater darkness, chilly with night and extending away from a window frame I could not even see.

The footsteps had passed. There may have been evidence of a muted voice further along the street, or not.

I lay down and turned over. Then turned over again, this way and that, until I noticed the sound of traffic. In the near distance. I checked my watch. Not even two. But from the main road that hugged the back of the town, there swished a regular sound of tyres upon tarmac.

A little later I heard the sound of a battery humming. This was outside and accompanied by the sound of wheels rolling across cement. And then another group of slowly moving pedestrians with low voices crossed the end of Mike's street. A procession that seemed to go on and on. Then fade away.

Hot, unrefreshed and stifled, my skin damp, I gave up on sleep at five and read the book I'd brought with me. But I'd not progressed far when I heard Mike shuffling about on the landing, then tinkling and tinkering in the tiny bathroom. Minutes later, I detected his careful attempts not to wake me as he descended the stairs. I dressed and went down.

To say he was more like his old self that morning would have been a vast exaggeration but at least he was more at ease than he'd been the night before. His conversation, sadly, hadn't improved. "Up early? I always get up early. Good breakfast then off to work. Help yourself to cereal and toast. Jam and stuff in the fridge. I won't. Friday, so I treat myself to a bagel and pastry. Pick 'em up from a small place close to the office. Tea?" It went on for some time. Cheery yet forced, devoid of any real content; all driven, I felt, by a lingering residue of the immense relief he'd felt last night on the landing outside the spare room.

To dam the stream of his drivel, I said, "Dark place, this. No streetlights. What's that all about?"

"Cutbacks. Social care for the elderly consumes the entire council tax budget and nigh on all the money from central government."

"I thought this place was wealthy."

"Oh, it is. Money they've got down here. Most expensive bit of coastline in the country. But the average age is pushing eighty and the burden on social care is immense." He seemed to want to say more but held back, then changed the conversation. "I won't be home until five. What you gonna do with yourself today?"

When I mentioned that I'd check out the seafront, he nodded vigorously. "Cool. Good call. Good, good." He gave me laborious directions to the best car park that were pointless after the first right turn 'up a dog leg', so I stopped paying attention.

"I thought," I interjected, "that we might go out and get something to eat later. And—"

"No chance. You have to book and as Saturday is the biggest night of the year here, everything was hoovered up weeks ago for the entire weekend. And nothing's open past eight anyway."

"You're kidding me. Eight?"

His head bobbed up and down, which made his extra chin quiver like a goitre and the muffs of hair at the side of his head sway like sea creatures. "Start of the season! Air Show. Steam trains. Regatta. County show. Farmers' markets. Starts this weekend."

"Takeaway?"

"Don't worry about all that. I've got plenty in." And then he made haste to leave. "Left you a spare key. Don't lose it. Oh, and can I ask a massive favour?" he said, while sweeping up his car keys and a leather wallet that contained the work he must bring home to diligently fuss over in the home office.

"Shoot."

"I leave the curtains closed. Never open them at the back. Or the windows. Back is kinda…out of bounds. So please don't open them."

I stared, and awaited the reasoning behind the unusual request.

"Yeah? They stay shut." He emphasised the instruction in an anxious tone similar to the one he'd adopted to encourage me to go to bed at nine.

I nodded. "Before you take off, can I get your Wi-Fi code, mate."

"Ah! Slight problemo. Only comes on between seven and eight."

I stared. And stared some more.

"It's…complicated," he said. "But, later, yeah. Gotta fly. There's a bacon, sausage, double cheese, hash brown bagel out there with my name on it!"

I waited for the sound of his little car to hum away, then strode into the living room and heaved aside the heavy curtains.

To find myself confronted by a wooden fence.

Close to the glass, a wall of panels separated by concrete posts stretched at least twelve feet high. It had been constructed with new timber. Between the fence and the back of Mike's house, a spotless gravel trench, a foot wide, ran along the rear of the entire property.

I unlocked one half of his French windows and pushed the door until the edge struck the fence. I squeezed myself through the gap and stepped out and into the gravel trench. As I pondered the enigma of a fence erected so close to Mike's house, I puffed on my electronic cigarette.

When the first cloud of exhaled vapour drifted over the fence, a door on the neighbours' side was thrust open. Followed by a hurried scuffing of feet across gravel, then grass. In the gaps between the fence panels, a small figure wearing a red cagoule, that I saw in glimpses, raced along the barrier. A shrill voice, breathless with outrage, shattered the early morning silence. "You! You're smoking!"

After my shock receded, I managed, "I'm not."

"I can see it! Smell it! My husband has a respiratory condition! You should have been told!" The fabric of the woman's coat scraped the fence as she searched for a slot through which to peer. A flash of white hair whisked across the gaps and a small fist struck wood and made me jump. "You cannot be out here!" The woman was furious.

"What?" I asked, shocked, and embarrassed by how intimidated I felt.

"It's not to be opened! This is *ours!*"

"This bit of gravel?" I managed. "On Mike's side of the bloody fence?"

"You cannot! You will not! Set one foot further than the threshold!" The little figure in the red coat was now spitting with rage. Polyester swished as she stalked backwards and forwards like a predatory cat behind bars. "The curtains! The door!" she screamed when a bloodshot eye finally found a peephole. An eye wild and wet that fixed upon me and drilled its madness at me. "You cannot set one foot further than the threshold! This is *ours!*"

From somewhere behind the woman, another elderly voice barked. Male, husky with age and exhaustion, that raised itself admonishingly. "Go back inside the house! Get inside! How dare you! We will have our privacy!"

"It's not even your—" I cut myself off when I recalled the ardour with which Mike's instructions were imparted and how his apprehension had ascended to real fear the night before. The thumps on the wall were a signal. A signal indicating that he must go to bed, initiated by this pair. They were his neighbours. Not mine. His problem. This was supposed to be a relaxing weekend reunion with an old friend, beside the sea, so I stepped away, telling myself that I wasn't going to make an awful situation worse for Mike. The fact that the confrontation had shaken me enough to feel craven, I suppressed for the sake of my own self-esteem. The intensity of the neighbours' rage was astonishing and the confrontation went some way to explaining why my old friend had been so nervous the night before. My ignorance of the rules had put him on edge.

I slipped back inside his house and slammed the door.

The neighbours continued to shout at me from behind the fence but I couldn't hear them properly through the double glazing. Struggling to order my thoughts, I took a seat and continued to puff away at my ecig.

Why allow a pair of rude old bastards get away with this? They must have fenced off his back garden. Appropriated it. The idea made me smile, grimly. It was absurd. Because surely his house had come with a rear garden? And even the little gravel trench on his meagre side was also out of bounds to him? Surely not? And I could only assume that he wasn't *allowed* to open his curtains, or windows, at the back, nor cross 'the threshold'. *It's complicated*. It certainly appeared to be.

The spite and fury in the silly old creature's voice became trapped inside my skull like an echo and when clarity returned, I realised I'd had enough. The visit was a write-off. I'd scoot around the seafront, say cheerio to Mike when he got home, then take off to salvage the rest of my short break from work. Back on home turf. I didn't want to witness any more of what Mike had become, nor the awful arrangements he endured with his vile neighbours. And his living in a town where everything closed at eight! I'd seen nothing of the place, as it had been caped in darkness the night before, but I already loathed it.

I let myself out the front and drove to the ring-road to find a sign that would lead me to the town and seafront. And passed through the labyrinthine monoculture of housing painted a brilliant white. Every garden was immaculate, symmetrical, exploding with floral colour, the edges of each drive and front lawn worthy of the regimental parade ground. The properties varied in size, from vast mansions to tidy maisonettes, but I'd never seen such uniformity, precision and order in any town or city suburb before.

Residents were occasionally glimpsed but only within front gardens bordering the starkly clean streets. They all appeared to be fussing over their hedges and flowers and ornamental trees. Up ladders and trimming, mowing, weeding and plucking, and hosing down pristine paving with jet washers. All boomers, or older.

Every third house had the curtains drawn or shuttered against the day. And I didn't see a single old car, either stationary or mobile. The private cars were new. Four-wheeled-drives and performance vehicles were favoured here. The few that were mobile were driven by an assortment of grey and white heads; some forms so shrunken they could barely see over the dashboard. Wizened passengers were often sunken into the murk of the rear seats; figures as small as children wearing dark glasses.

I quickly grew weary of the Union Jack flag and Cross of St. George, displayed at every opportunity to enforce some prideful sense of belonging to a culture and place where only the blind might have suffered confusion about their whereabouts.

The traffic moved slowly and wound thickly in a progression to and from the satellite retail estates, lining the inland side of the town like a castle's outer walls. I passed half a dozen of these enormous operations that were surrounded by oceans of tarmac gridded with white lines. DIY stores, garden centres, warehouses the size of airports selling pet supplies, cafés, bakeries, mall-sized supermarkets. Traffic islands, neat verges and dual carriageways necklaced the retail estates. At every set of traffic lights, a complex array of signage listed attractions: botanical gardens, zoological gardens, a steam railway, seafront.

I picked up the signs to the sea. My need to see a wide expanse of water was equal to my desire to escape the interminable roads and glaring white buildings and the compulsive order of the gardens and streets, the combed grass and polished gravel. Pretty, no doubt, yet ostentatious and stifling in its conservatism and uniformity. I found it ghastly and failed to understand its attraction for Mike, though the town threw light upon Mike's wardrobe and his fussy little house and its fragrant interior. That terrible particle-board desk stored in a chintzy spare room... It all began to make more sense in daylight, as if he'd become overwhelmed and transformed by the presiding status quo.

Perhaps he'd felt obliged, even coerced, to conform to the prevailing consensus. Even more alarming, there was a servile and timid air to my old friend, whose pitiful existence seemed to revolve around his labours for retirement villages. His entire being seemed to have been engulfed by the aged, their culture, values and needs. Precipitating his premature aging.

After thirty minutes in the town's suburbs and outskirts, I longed to see a young face. The first I encountered was working on the seafront. She wore a green apron and served coffee in one of the countless tearooms and cafés that thronged streets and lanes winding from the idyllic town centre to the shoreline. Many of her peers performed similar tasks; waiting upon tables, pushing wheelchairs, picking up litter, emerging from public toilets with a mop and bucket, carrying cases into hotels, while aged guests shuffled behind, prodding with canes and gesticulating to emphasise arrangements that were to be followed.

The service industry workers struck me as cowed, put-upon, unnaturally silent and morose. They reminded me of Mike. Though his fretting and pettiness possessed a sharper edge of despair.

Maintaining the standards of the suburbs, the seafront and streets of the town were Singapore-immaculate. Probably washed daily, and I experienced a horrible deference when placing my feet upon them. Not a single bin overflowed. The buildings were painted the pastel of seaside ice creams. Iron awnings and fences gleamed onyx. Knightsbridge, Mayfair and Marylebone came to mind. Hanging baskets drew the eye, their bouquets as vivid as still-life paintings. Not a single storefront was dark. Each was filled with light and colour and plump with tastefully arranged merchandise.

There were no tattoo parlours, betting shops, fried chicken takeaways, pizzerias, sports clothing shops. My efforts to find a vaping shop were made in vain. Not even the area outside the train station – a universally grubby quarter on my many travels – had been marred by a blob of chewing gum, or lozenge of dog mess. And it was a pity I needed nicotine liquid and not what was being sold in one of several gourmet butchers, florists, fishmongers, mobility scooter showrooms, estate agents, golf stores, delicatessens, or assisted living agencies.

At least there were three independent bookshops, though one only sold cookbooks and a second was hopelessly swamped with mass market thrillers, suspense-with-romance novels, puzzle books, Sudoku and confectionery. The third was marred by a lifesize cut-out of a popular gardening celebrity, as well as a promotional poster for the biography of a motor sports celebrity. I couldn't make myself go inside.

Beyond the town, I found the effect of the sun upon the glittering sea and deep red sands so arresting that I became disoriented. And the long, ethereal sweep of coastline, undulating over valleys into the far misted distance on either side of a harbour packed with huge white yachts, made me feel tearful. I'd not seen anything so beauteous in years. It didn't seem part of England but of an imagined idyll. I was surprised I'd never seen a picture of the vista. How had it escaped stampedes of holiday makers and travel writers and bales of Sunday supplements?

I also failed to observe one infant, or a single pushchair in the town or seafront. No children played on the sands. No mums and nannies strolled and laid down picnic blankets. Later in the day, no pupils from local schools trudged home, even after I'd lingered until well past four. No youths kicked footballs or sat upon walls prodding phone screens. With the exception of the uniformed staff, I saw no one but the aged. And they were everywhere.

Ravenous by lunchtime, I'd planned to sit down, eat my pasty and drink a coffee in one of the Victorian shelters facing the sea, or on one of the many benches, but this proved impossible. Each was filled with massed lines of elderly residents, who sat joylessly and confronted the eternity of water. Others faced the sea in an infinity of expensive cars parked on every section of kerb beyond the beach huts. My hellos went unanswered. My nods were unreturned. It wasn't easy to tell but I fancied I was being watched with disdain, even suspicion.

Walking beyond the harbour, about two miles out of town to where the villas with sea views dwindled, I found a strip of headland studded with more wooden benches. And I sat before the fence of a gargantuan golf course. As it vanished into the southern distance, the manicured grounds seemed to exceed the coastal length of the town. A few thin, colourful figures hobbled across the shorn grass and swung away between the distant mounds. Beyond them the course was empty, and barren.

The bench I'd selected had an elaborate floral arrangement tied to the armrest and a brass plaque drilled into the backrest. Idly, after unwrapping my pasty, I surveyed the first memorial.

Always in our hearts. Cherished wife. Beloved Mother. Adored Grandmother. Respected Great Grandmother. Friend to all. June Hazzard, 1903–2021.

I required all of my fingers to establish the preposterous lifespan of the woman my seat was dedicated to.

Once I'd finished eating, I moved along the perimeter of the golf course. It wasn't possible to walk anywhere else; the golf club's coastal boundary was protected by an unnecessarily menacing wire fence and allowed a few feet of earth for those who walked the public land of the coastal path. And as the steel barrier shimmered into the distance, the path either disappeared beneath the wire, or the fence suggested itself liable to push a walker off the cliffs.

The next bench, dedicated to the 'loving memory of Richard M.T. Cord, MajGen', listed his birth date as 1900 and his death in 2015. Its neighbour celebrated the memory of a Margaret 'Babs' Forester who'd also lived some way past one hundred. I walked to the end of the course and only stopped calculating the monumental lifespans of the locals, bench by bench, when I, at last, discovered a plaque remembering a chap who'd only made it as far as ninety-eight. 'Taken by the sea he'd sailed his whole life' was the explanation given, suggesting he'd not expired through old age and one of its many infirmities. A sailing ship was engraved below the text.

After the previous night's restlessness, I napped for a while. By the time I returned to the seafront in late afternoon, it was emptying. A shading of dusk and the easterly breeze skimming off the tranquil sea was sufficient to drive the populace inland.

I made my way back to Mike's in light traffic. Rush hour didn't amount to much. A few service vehicles. Builders, gardeners and pet groomers, and the odd slowly driven performance vehicle. When I pulled up outside his house, I presumed it was the woman from next door, who'd shouted at me for opening the back door, who was now on her knees and pointlessly digging a trowel into a showpiece of a flower-bed beneath Mike's kitchen window. Her thin, scowling mouth was visible beneath the brim of a large straw hat.

Her husband stood ramrod straight, his back to me, before the hedge that divided the properties, and administered secateurs to a plane of privet that any spirit level would have judged perfectly flat. Neither of them acknowledged me.

I let myself in.

Mike was waiting for me. And Mike wasn't happy.

As well as angry, he'd been crying and was genuinely shaken. The only relief he seemed able to achieve, from this tormented state, was by scolding me; though only after coaxing me to the rear of the living room and away, I felt, from the kitchen windows at the front, through which the neighbours were visible.

I felt like a child, or a henpecked husband in a Seventies sitcom, chastised for coming home from the allotments smelling of beer. He paced and twisted his fingers about his fat hands but struggled to look me in the eye. His voice never managed more than a whisper. "I told you. Last thing I fucking said! Don't open the bloody curtains. Or door at the back. One simple thing. Godammit, what were you thinking?" I let him continue until he was repeating himself as well as experiencing some difficulty breathing.

"Mike," I said. "What are you doing here?"

"It's complicated."

"Not to me it's not. You live next door to a pair of horrible cunts—"

"No! Stop!" He tried to push the words back inside my mouth, one clammy hand actually closing over my nose and mouth. I pushed him away.

"In a sterile, cultureless desert of unfeasibly ancient people—"

"You musn't!" His soap-reeking hands fell upon my face again.

"Fuck off!" I roared at him and shoved him hard, against his ridiculous wall of curtain.

We then stood in silence for a while. Each of us panting. Delirious with emotion. Until Mike sat on the floor. He sobbed twice, then abruptly stopped when he seemed to remember some foolishly neglected concern. He glanced fearfully at the light-fitting and shot to his feet. "Can you see if they've gone," he whispered like a frightened child and pointed towards the kitchen.

I checked but only after I'd snapped myself from a timidity that was contagious around him, inside his horrid perfumed house.

The neighbours had cleared off and I felt disproportionately relieved to find the front lawn empty. "You let them walk all over your front lawn like that?"

"They make the garden nice."

"But it's intrusive."

"The front's theirs. As well."

"I don't understand. You only own the house? Why would you buy a house when you don't own the front and back gardens? And don't say it's complicated or I'm going to take a shit through their letterbox."

Mike visibly shuddered. "I signed them over. Front and back. Couldn't take it anymore. Squabbling about the border. Was for the best. If you lived here, you'd understand." He checked his watch. "Come on. We've time." He raced for the front door. Then paused, one hand on the latch, to whisper, "Keep your bloody voice down. Even outside."

This air of conspiracy seduced me enough to comply; the anticipation of secrets soon to be disclosed was too great a temptation. I'd grown desperate for some kind of explanation for his preposterous situation, perhaps for the very town he had chosen for a home.

I followed him into the street.

Head down, he scurried a few feet ahead of me, up a hill between a canyon of gardens worthy of Babylon and houses as polished as imperial tombs, until we reached a small park fronting what looked like an old primary school.

Inside the park, Mike indicated that I should follow him to a spot beneath the branches of an oak tree as if he meant to conceal us when out in the open.

"Thank fuck," I said, nodding at the school. "So there are some children here. I bet the town can just about scrape enough of them together to fill that one small building."

"Volume," he said and pressed one finger to his lips.

"We're outside. No one can hear us. Don't be ridiculous."

"Please. And it's not a school. Not anymore. It's a care home. Converted. The people here…"

"Are all old."

"The ones you are seeing." Mike sighed and closed his eyes. "They are the children."

"Come again?"

"All of them. The people, residents. The ones you've seen. Are the children. These are the young ones that you are seeing. Their parents are still alive."

"Hang on. Hang on. Not possible. And what has happened to you? We're hiding under a tree and you're…" I recalled the plaques on the benches, the wizened, mummified heads I'd spotted in the rear of passing cars.

Mike's forehead glistened with sweat. "The parents and grandparents run everything. Make every decision. Or, rather, they execute the will of the mayor. It's passed on, passed down. The workers arrive by train and road. From outlying, inland towns. Places that are not so nice."

"Did you just say grandparents?"

"Oh yeah. Lots of them are still alive."

"Never. That would make them…" My maths failed.

"It's not uncommon in this town to still have living parents when you hit a hundred."

"Never."

"Or grandparents."

I sniggered. "So where are they?"

"They won't be seen by day. They don't look so good. What's left of their old eyes can't cope with much light, particularly sunlight. Most are in care homes, retirement villages, or live with their children. And they don't sleep well at night." He seemed to draw into himself then, become absorbed again by his cyclic preoccupations, his mania.

"You are absolutely fucking with me."

"Alas. I am not."

I thought back to my restless night and the sound of cars, of groups shuffling through the streets in the early hours, the whir of a mobility scooter. "How? How is it possible?"

"The keys."

"What?" I kept my voice down so as not to agitate him further. He was ill and had quickly adopted the swivel-eyed aspect of a conspiracy nut. Soon exasperated, as if I'd forced him to explain algebra to an infant, he searched for analogies, metaphors, similes with which to make his revelations simpler for me to grasp. He must have then dismissed them all before checking his watch and gazing at the sky.

"Mike?"

"Remember," he muttered, looking past me. "That TV show? *Benny Cadabra*. We're the same age. Think we even talked about it once when we were stoned. Early Seventies. Creepy as fuck."

"Fuck's that gotta do with anything?"

Mike gently raised a finger to his lips to shush me. "Benny used to read the kids' minds on his show and then give them what they wanted? Toys and crap. He knew what they were thinking. What they wanted. Always. Everyone assumed he'd been told what the kids wanted, by their parents. But a few in the industry always claimed that he was genuinely psychic. All I'm saying is, there is a lot of *that* in this town. Particularly acute next door, I might add. But it wouldn't matter where I lived in this place. It's a common trait. An ability. You remember Benny Cadabra's magic carpet? Used to float it about the TV studio. You could see the wires. How we all laughed! But he didn't need them. The wires were a ruse to disguise the fact that he could...really do that. *Float*."

I turned away. Had given up. It was that time: bag, car keys, hit the road. Sometime within the last five years, my old friend's mind had blown like a fuse. For some inexplicable reason, as we stood beneath the branches of a tree in an empty park, so that no one could overhear us, he was now rambling about a disgraced children's entertainer we'd seen on TV when we were in primary school. An alleged sex offender. I seemed to remember that the testimony of his juvenile accusers was discredited but the taint had ruined his public life. I'd assumed he'd died in exile. It wouldn't have been unreasonable for anyone who even remembered the freak to have assumed the same.

Mike exhaled and seemed to deflate as his chest fell. "Benny Cadabra. Also known as Benny Tench. His real name. He's the mayor here. All on the Q.T. Low profile."

I paused. "He was in his sixties when we were in nursery. That would make him…"

"One hundred and nine years old. And still running the council. Through intermediaries. A chairman if you will. He found a neglected community of retirees here. When this place was a rundown seaside resort. As I understand it, Cadabra was part of a movement that had existed since the 1800s. With some strange fucking ideas. A cult, if you must. They were like freemasons. Ran charities, the usual stuff. Smokescreens before they seeped into politics. When Benny showed up here, with the tabloids chasing his fat arse for kiddie fiddling, he made inroads at the council. Way back. All long before my time. But back then, he used *the movement's* keys to take over. His influence spread. Like a virus."

Mike's mind drifted. "You know, the hospital is the town's biggest employer. It's almost as big as the town itself. Considered to be a temple. It sustains. Recycles. Lengthens lifespans. And it's not just medicine that they practise there. Oh no." He paused, as if struggling to continue with this disjointed rambling, until a compulsion forced him to blurt, "We don't count. You and me. Not meaningfully. Too young. None of the workers. Utterly disempowered. Lot of us. Broken. Indentured servants. Me too. You know, the Brexit vote was higher here than anywhere in the UK. Only radical Tory candidates even stand here. The other parties tried to establish a foothold once or twice. Last time, their combined votes were 134 out of a potential fifty thousand. And those, I think, were mistakes in the voting booths. Down here, their eyes aren't so good." Mike paused and checked his watch. "I need to eat something and it's getting on."

It couldn't have been much past seven but I followed the hunched and beaten figure back to his dismal, isolated, fenced-off house.

The two meals he served on trays had been microwaved; a Lancashire hotpot for me, shepherd's pie for Mike. And yet it'd taken him half an hour to fumble two cartons in and out of a machine and to pour the steaming contents onto plates. "Sherry?" he asked, absentmindedly.

I demurred.

"Bit of telly?"

I demurred again.

"Wi-Fi is up if you need it? Well, there's fifteen minutes left."

"Out of your hour," I said automatically, though my interest in anything he had to say had dipped since we'd returned from the park.

"Privilege." Mike pointed his fork at the wall and spoke around the revolving mulch of mince flopping between his bulging cheeks. "Sometimes they take it down completely."

"The people who stole your garden and tell you to go to bed at nine?"

Mike nodded and tucked into his pie.

"Do they buy your clothes too?" I said and experienced an urge to simply scream with laughter.

Mike nodded, his face expressionless. "She lays them out for me. They've house keys."

"What?"

"Searches. She spends more time in here than me. Looking. Mooching. Bank account, that too. He manages my finances. Gives me pocket money." Mike shook his head and sighed. "How it works here. Top down."

I felt cold and stiff upon my velvet chair.

"You have *the keys*. Or you don't," he muttered.

Now it was my turn to look at my watch. "Mike. Mate. I'm off first thing. Cutting it short. Sorry, I'm done. Too much. To take in. And seeing you like this...makes me very uncomfortable." I'd have left as soon as I'd finished eating but didn't fancy driving in the dark, for hours. I'd have struggled to stay awake. But if we were to go to bed at nine, at least I'd be on the road before six.

He smiled at that. "Totally understand. Don't blame you at all."

"Why even invite me down?"

"Was going to ask you to be my best man. It's been arranged."

"What?"

"She's eighty-eight. Claims she's eighty-three. But I'm not fooled."

He glanced at his watch. "Getting late." He collected our plates. "Gimme a knock in the morning before you take off."

The neighbours' bang against the living room was particularly fearsome that evening. They must have used an implement. And it wasn't even half eight. They were displeased.

I turned out the lights on my way upstairs.

Bereft of alternatives, I sat up in bed and read for a couple of hours until my head began to drop. With the light turned off, I was instantly swallowed by darkness and fell asleep within minutes.

As the night progressed, I must have risen from the depths of sleep in stages. Around midnight, though mostly unconscious, I possessed a vague peripheral awareness of the house around me and the street outside. And through my dreaming mind, I heard a car engine grumble to life and I became aware of traffic. The noise must have been travelling from the ring-road.

And there was distant applause. I think. Closer to the house. Raised voices came and went continuously, in and out of my sleep, yet failed to fully wake me. Perhaps this went on for hours, or mere minutes; I have no way of knowing. But the ambient sounds were incorporated into my dreams of a long parade, shuffling through an endless darkness, and of a motorcade of wheelchairs whirring, of near mummified brides carried on litters by terrified migrant workers, of tiny elderly men propped up like proud generals inside pushchairs, of houses that were marble inside. And I heard a furtive bumping of glass...then something dry and sharp prodded at my mouth, before feeling my face.

That woke me and the soft thumps against glass continued into my full awakening.

"Mike," I said, twice, but wasn't answered. I could see nothing and slapped about for the bedside lamp. And never found it. Nor my phone. It was hopeless. I was forced to stumble, bent over and terrified of collisions, towards a memory of where the door must be.

And as I raked my hands through the air, seeking the wall and the light switch that it must contain, the fumbling upon the windows persisted. And increased, as if whatever was on the other side had become excited by the idea of movement within the room.

Something out there began to make firmer contact with the glass too, like a full hand or head, gently bumping. And as I reached the light switch, I heard the swish of the curtains across the window I had left open.

My breathing steadying and dizziness subsiding, I investigated the commotion against the house's exterior. But with the curtains open and ceiling light on, the glass was a mirror and I saw little of whatever had finally ceased in its bumping to flap upwards, as if to escape the glare. I only glimpsed the tail of a garment made from a pale cloth.

I killed the light and allowed my eyes to accustom themselves to the darkness, then returned to the windows. Something that I will wish, for the rest of my life, that I had not done.

Several of them were outside, hanging in darkness.

Sat up cross-legged, or just floating upon their fronts as if upon water.

In expectation, their insubstantial heads were turned towards the open window. Excitement was expressed in that frail cooing and the papery muttering of dry mouths.

One of the old things of the air must have awoken me by reaching through to touch my face. At the mere thought of them getting inside, I seized the latch and slammed shut the window.

I could do nothing then but stare, and pant as if from some great physical exertion. And I watched the thin forms sway and hover nearer and paw their lumpy extremities at the window panes. Their little mouths moved and gaped but I heard nothing from them once the window was sealed. But beneath the wizened and elderly figures drifting in empty space, a small crowd had gathered and stood upon the pavement below. They were little more than silhouettes with their arms either raised above their heads or engaged in the soft applause I'd heard in my sleep. I had a sense that the group on the ground were both congratulating and encouraging these sticklike and barely living things that levitated beyond my window.

Across the road and over the immaculate hedges and lawns, the curtains of two homes were also open. The front rooms were dimly lit with soft light and inside those ordinary but horribly homely spaces, I saw more of the town's elderly, crawling around the ceilings like infants. Their ancient children and shrunken grandchildren sat on chairs and sofas below them and clapped their elders.

I shut the curtains and looked for my bag and clothes.

They'd gone.

"Mike!" I fled the room and threw open the door to my host's room to find an unoccupied bed, meticulously made. The master bedroom resembled another spare room, little used by occasional guests. Not a trace of Mike's personality had been allowed to exist within his own home.

And again, in that bedroom, came a soft, insistent bumping against the glass from outside. I knocked off the light and tore the curtains aside.

Another two of the elderly forms hovered beyond the window panes. Like newly made insects, they appeared constructed more of cartilage than flesh; of the latter there was little, and it resembled cured leather, threaded with black blood vessels. The gender of the pair was indistinguishable but the head that wore a knitted skull cap was showing teeth best suited to a donkey's mouth. What served for eyes were hidden behind the black lenses of small, round glasses, such as the blind wear to conceal disfigurement. With the exception of the hat, the thing was naked and ribbed and too angular about the pelvis. There was no genitalia and the skeletal legs drifted uselessly like a paralysed tail.

The second figure was crying and scratching at a few remaining threads of hair upon a stained scalp. It drifted haplessly and turned in a horizontal circle.

Beneath them, Mike's odious neighbours slow-clapped the airborne frolic and showed white teeth within stretched grimaces that might have been smiles.

Across the fences and hedgerows, at roof-height, other frail forms glimmered in the ambient light falling from open back doors. They drifted like haggard kites in insufficient wind. Occasional shrieks of euphoria, from the celebrants on the ground, pierced the double glazing.

I fell more than walked down the stairs.

And lit up the empty house room by room. A glance between the kitchen blinds confirmed that my car was missing, though Mike's remained on the drive. And I didn't linger by that window, dropping the blinds when the spiny back of something wearing a shiny grey wig became visible. It was bent over as if searching the flower bed for something lost; perhaps the very purpose for it even being there.

A dull clatter of applause sounded from the street.

Distant traffic ran like a full river.

Upon the coffee table I found Mike's note.

Once a month they all go up together. The community. Them with the keys. They disport before those of us who remain keyless. And sorry, mate. I feel like a heel leaving like this. But you were my only chance to get out. I've done my bit. Five bloody years! And I've waited four just to be granted a guest.

I couldn't leave. There was no point trying after the first couple of attempts. What they did to me... Let's just say, I'm surprised I ever recovered. Maybe I didn't. You've no idea how long twenty-four hours truly is, when shut inside a lightless house with the most senior in this community bumping around the ceiling. And they bite. I was on antibiotics for six months to get rid of the infection in my leg.

The only saving grace from all of this is that I never had to do any gardening.

My car's out of petrol and I don't know how long you'll be here but while you are in residence, don't smoke/vape in the house or open the curtains, windows or the back door. I'd recommend keeping the TV on setting 14 too. Or there will be hell to pay.

I'm still not sure how they do it but they can hear everything that you think inside the house. And where I work. Maybe inside the car too. And some of them are bloody nosey. They don't have much else to do besides gardening and pottering and complaining. I never wrote you those emails either. SHE did, next door.

As I said, I am really, really, really sorry. In the end I couldn't even look at your Instagram page during the Wi-Fi privilege periods. And you're a bit of a smug cunt, if truth be told. But I hope that one day you can forgive me.

Mike

P.S. Once I'm done with them, I'll leave your clothes and car outside your flat.

I waited until morning. When all had returned to what passed for normal in that place, I slipped away on the train. As promised, I found the car, my belongings in the boot, outside my flat. Though their presence filled me with no confidence that Mike ever managed to escape the town.

The interior of the car was cleaner than it had ever been since I'd owned it and all of the seat covers were new. The clothes inside my bag had been dry-cleaned, except for one shirt and a jacket that were missing. I'd worn them the day before Mike fled. I could only assume that he'd worn them to disguise himself as me, but they'd become too soiled even for dry-cleaning.

He never made contact with me again.

I spent a few days processing the experience and composing a report that I'd intended to make to the authorities. But no matter how many times I redrafted a timeline and my observations, what I recorded was too outlandish and deranged for the rational to take seriously. Though that wasn't the sole reason I never contacted the police.

Upon the very day that I'd decided to visit the local police station, I became aware of an awful smell in my meticulously scrubbed and valeted car. The origin of the stench of putrefaction took some finding too. And only with the use of my steel barbeque tongs was I able to ferret out and retrieve the source of the smell.

Though bloated and blackening, two human fingers and a thumb had been stuffed between the driver's side seat and backrest. And the removal of these digits from a hand had not been made cleanly. I'd guess that two were bitten through at the first knuckle. The third, the thumb, had been wrenched from the hand to which it had once belonged.

A warning, and one that I took seriously, while reclining upon my new seat covers and waiting for the blood to return to my face.

Try as I might to forget the town, I never will. Despite its natural advantages and pristine presentation, it continues to maintain a discreet public profile. Nothing within the place, save the advertised private retirement facilities, intended for the affluent, ever encourages anyone to visit.

Despite that, the town's black heart still thumps like an unwelcome and intrusive hand upon a living room wall. The worm at the heart of the community is all but forgotten in the public domain, yet still the parasite writhes, unpunished and all but forgotten.

And yet I do suspect that the nearly dead become lonely. With lifetimes of dissatisfaction to express, and with so much time to fill, they occasionally delight in tormenting the odd outsider and scapegoat. Like poor Mike.

BIOGRAPHIES

Jenn Ashworth was born in 1982 in Preston. Her first novel, *A Kind of Intimacy*, was published in 2009 and won a Betty Trask Award. On the publication of her second, *Cold Light* (Sceptre, 2011), she was featured on the BBC's *The Culture Show* as one of the UK's twelve best new writers. Her third novel *The Friday Gospels* (2013) and her fourth *Fell* (2016) are also published by Sceptre. Ashworth has also published short fiction and won an award for her blog, *Every Day I Lie a Little*. In 2019 she published a memoir-in-essays about reading, writing and sickness called *Notes Made While Falling* which was a New Statesman Book of the Year and shortlisted for the Gordon Burn Prize. Her latest novel is *Ghosted: A Love Story*. She lives in Lancashire, is a Fellow of the Royal Society of Literature and is a Professor of Writing at Lancaster University.

Ramsey Campbell has been given more awards than any other writer in the field, including the Grand Master Award of the World Horror Convention, the Lifetime Achievement Award of the Horror Writers Association, the Living Legend Award of the International Horror Guild and the World Fantasy Lifetime Achievement Award. In 2015 he was made an Honorary Fellow of Liverpool John Moores University for outstanding services to literature. Among his novels are *The Face That Must Die*, *Incarnate*, *Midnight Sun*, *The Count of Eleven*, *The Darkest Part of the Woods*, *The Overnight*, *Secret Story*, *The Grin of the Dark*, *Thieving Fear*, *Creatures of the Pool*, *The Seven Days of Cain*, *Ghosts Know*, *The Kind Folk*, *Think Yourself Lucky*, *Thirteen Days by Sunset Beach*, *The Wise Friend*, *Somebody's Voice* and *Fellstones*. His Brichester Mythos trilogy consists of *The Searching Dead*, *Born to the Dark* and *The Way of the Worm*. His collections include *Waking Nightmares*, *Ghosts and Grisly Things*, *Told by the Dead*, *Just Behind You*, *Holes for Faces*, *By the Light of My Skull* and a two-volume retrospective roundup (*Phantasmagorical Stories*) as well as *The Village Killings and Other Novellas*. His non-fiction is collected as *Ramsey Campbell, Probably* and *Ramsey Campbell, Certainly*, while *Ramsey's Rambles* collects his video reviews, and he is working on a book-length study of the Three Stooges, *Six Stooges and Counting*. *Limericks of the Alarming and Phantasmal* is a history of horror fiction in the form of fifty limericks. His novels *The Nameless*, *Pact of the Fathers* and *The Influence* have been filmed in Spain, where a television series based on *The Nameless* is in development. He is the President of the Society of Fantastic Films. He was born in Liverpool in 1946 and still lives on Merseyside with his wife Jenny. His pleasures include classical music, good food and wine. His website is ramseycampbell.com.

Philip Fracassi is the author of the award-winning story collection, *Behold the Void*, which won Best Collection of the Year from *This Is Horror* and *Strange Aeons Magazine*. His newest collection, *Beneath a Pale Sky*, was published in 2021 by Lethe Press. It received a starred review from *Library Journal* and was named Best Collection of the Year by *Rue Morgue Magazine*. His debut novel, *Boys in the Valley*, was published on Halloween 2021 by Earthling Publications. His upcoming releases include the novels *A Child Alone with Strangers* (Aug 2022) and *Gothic* (Feb 2023). Philip's books have been translated into multiple languages, and his stories have been published in numerous magazines and anthologies, including *Best Horror of the Year*, *Nightmare Magazine*, *Black Static*, *Dark Discoveries*, and *Cemetery Dance*. As a screenwriter, his feature films have been distributed by Disney Entertainment and Lifetime Television. He currently has several stories under option for film/TV adaptation. For more information, visit his website at pfracassi.com. He also has active profiles on Facebook, Instagram (pfracassi) and Twitter (@philipfracassi). Philip lives in Los Angeles, California, and is represented by Elizabeth Copps at Copps Literary Services (info@coppsliterary.com).

Sharon Gosling is the author of multiple middle-grade historical adventure books for children, including *The Diamond Thief*, *The Golden Butterfly*, *The House of Hidden Wonders* and *The Extraordinary Voyage of Katy Willacott*. She is also the author of YA Scandi horror *FIR* and writes adult fiction for Simon & Schuster, including *The House Beneath the Cliffs* and *The Lighthouse Bookshop*. Having started her career as an entertainment journalist, she still also occasionally writes non-fiction making-of books about television and film. Titles include *Tomb Raider: The Art and Making of the Film*, *The Art and Making of Penny Dreadful* and *Wonder Woman: The Art and Making of the Film*. She is a big fan of folk horror, and has published several short horror stories in anthologies such as *The Mammoth Book of Halloween Stories* and *The Alchemy Press Book of Horrors 2*. She lives with her husband in a small village on the side of a fell in the far north of Cumbria, a place best known for being the home of one of the UK's earliest vampire legends. She's currently working on a literary retelling of this story.

Muriel Gray was born in Glasgow. She is a BA honours graduate of The Glasgow School of Art in graphic design and illustration and worked as a professional illustrator before joining the National Museum of Antiquities in Edinburgh as assistant head of design. She then moved into broadcasting, starting as a presenter on Channel 4's seminal music programme *The Tube*, which she presented with Jools Holland and the late Paula Yates, whilst still retaining her post at the museum. A full-time career spanning over three decades in the media followed; in 1987 she founded her own production company, which grew into the largest in Scotland and sold to RDF Media in 2005. She is also known as an opinion writer in many publications, such as *Time Out Magazine*, *The Sunday Correspondent*, *The Sunday Mirror*, *Scotland on Sunday*, *The Sunday Herald* and many others. She has won several prizes for journalism, including columnist of the year at the Scottish press awards. She is the author of three bestselling novels, *The Trickster*, *Furnace* and *The Ancient*, which Stephen King described as 'scary and unputdownable', two non-fiction books, including the definitive history of Kelvingrove Museum, and many short stories and essays published in anthologies. She has written plays for live theatre and radio. She was the chair of the judges for the 2007 Orange Prize for Fiction. Muriel is a former rector of Edinburgh University, chair of the board of trustees of The Glasgow School of Art and is currently joint deputy chair of the board of governors of the British Museum and a non-executive director on the board of the BBC. She continues to live in Glasgow, is married and has three children. She likes trees and amphibians and being up mountains.

Charlie Hughes has been writing dark suspense and horror stories from his home in south London since 2015. His short stories have been published by *Ellery Queen Mystery Magazine*, *Mystery Weekly* and in various anthologies. His horror short story 'The Box' won the 2016 Ruth Rendell Short Story Competition. His stories have been performed on the *NoSleep Podcast* and *Creepy Podcast*. Charlie has a novelette slated to appear in a forthcoming issue of *The Magazine of Fantasy and Science Fiction* and 'The Riverman' will appear in *Horror Library, Volume 7*. You can find out more at charliehugheswriting.blogspot.com.

Jonathan Janz is the author of more than a dozen novels. He is represented for film and TV by Ryan Lewis (executive producer of *Bird Box*). His work has been championed by authors like Josh Malerman, Caroline Kepnes, Stephen Graham Jones, Joe R. Lansdale, and Brian Keene. His ghost story *The Siren and the Specter* was selected as a Goodreads Choice nominee for Best Horror. Additionally, his novels *Children of the Dark* and *The Dark Game* were chosen by Booklist and *Library Journal* as Top Ten Horror Books of the Year. He also teaches high school Film Literature, Creative Writing, and English. Jonathan's main interests are his wonderful wife and his three amazing children.

Scottish writer **Carole Johnstone**'s award-winning short fiction has been reprinted in many annual *Best of* anthologies in the UK and US. Her debut novel, *Mirrorland*, was published in 2021 by Borough Press/HarperCollins in the UK and Scribner/Simon & Schuster in the US and Canada. Translation rights have been sold to thirteen other territories and it has been optioned for television. Her second novel, *The Blackhouse*, an unusual murder-mystery set in the Outer Hebrides, was published in 2022. She lives in Argyll & Bute, Scotland, with her husband. More information on the author can be found at carolejohnstone.com.

Brian Keene writes novels, comic books, short stories and non-fiction. He is the author of over fifty books, mostly in the horror, crime and fantasy genres. His work has been translated into over a dozen languages and has won numerous awards. Among his novels are *The Rising* and its sequels, the *Earthworm Gods* series, the *Clickers* series, and many more.

Several of his novels and stories have been adapted for film, including *Ghoul*, *The Naughty List*, *The Ties That Bind* and *Fast Zombies Suck*. He has also written for such media properties as *Doctor Who*, *Thor*, *Aliens*, *The X-Files*, *Hellboy* and *Superman*. The father of two sons, Keene lives in rural Pennsylvania with author Mary SanGiovanni.

Stephen Laws is an award-winning horror novelist whose work has been published all over the world. Among his many titles are *Ghost Train*, *Spectre*, *The Wyrm*, *The Frighteners*, *Chasm* and *Ferocity*. Peter Cushing loved his novels, but hated the bad language therein. Horror actress Ingrid Pitt organised a team search of his hotel room, concentrating on a 'haunted sock drawer'. Roger Corman bought him a pizza. He made Christopher Lee cry in public. He won second prize in a 1963 'Name the Sugar Puff Bear' competition. His son has a famous godfather in the genre. He plays piano, and one of his compositions was performed with full orchestra on a pre-Civil War Yugoslav television 'variety' programme. This is all true.

Alison Littlewood's first book, *A Cold Season*, was selected for the Richard and Judy Book Club and described as 'perfect reading for a dark winter's night'. Other titles include *Mistletoe*, *The Hidden People*, *The Crow Garden*, *Path of Needles* and *The Unquiet House*. She also wrote *The Cottingley Cuckoo,* as A.J. Elwood. Alison's short stories have been picked for a number of Year's Best anthologies and published in her collections *Quieter Paths* and *Five Feathered Tales*. She has won the Shirley Jackson Award for Short Fiction. Alison lives with her partner Fergus in Yorkshire, in a house of creaking doors and crooked walls. She loves exploring the hills and dales with her two hugely enthusiastic Dalmatians and has a penchant for books on folklore and weird history, Earl Grey tea, fountain pens and semicolons.

Laura Mauro was born and raised in London and now lives in Oxfordshire. Her short story 'Looking for Laika' won the British Fantasy Award for Best Short Fiction in 2018, and 'Sun Dogs' was shortlisted for the 2017 Shirley Jackson Award in the Novelette category. Her debut collection *Sing Your Sadness Deep* won the 2020 British Fantasy Award for Best Collection, and her short story 'The Pain-Eater's Daughter' won the 2020 British Fantasy Award for Best Short Fiction. She blogs sporadically at lauramauro.com.

Seanan McGuire is a writer, filker, fan, and a resident of the perpetually dampened Pacific Northwest. She is the recipient of the Hugo Award, the Nebula Award, the Locus Award, the Alex Award, the Pegasus Award, and the Astounding Award. She has been a nominee for the Philip K. Dick Award. She is very uncomfortable listing awards like they're Pokémon, and would be happier listing Pokémon. Publications include the novels *Middlegame*, *Every Heart a Doorway*, and *Rosemary and Rue*, as well as works released under her pen name, Mira Grant, including *Feed*, *Parasite*, and *Into the Drowning Deep*. Seanan collects Magic cards, My Little Ponies, and excuses to wander into the nearest swamp, hopefully never to be seen again. Find her online at seananmcguire.com.

Alison Moore's short stories have been published in various magazines, journals and anthologies, including *Best British Short Stories*, *Best British Horror* and *Best New Horror*, and broadcast on BBC Radio. The title story of her first collection, *The Pre-War House*, won the New Writer Novella Prize. Her debut novel, *The Lighthouse*, was shortlisted for the Man Booker Prize and the National Book Awards, winning the McKitterick Prize. She recently published her fifth novel, *The Retreat*, and a trilogy for children, beginning with *Sunny and the Ghosts*. A second collection, *Eastmouth and Other Stories*, will be published in October 2022. Her website is alison-moore.com.

Mark Morris (Editor) has written and edited almost forty novels, novellas, short story collections and anthologies. His script work includes audio dramas for *Doctor Who*, *Jago & Litefoot* and the *Hammer Chillers* series. Mark's recent work includes the official movie tie-in novelisations of *The Great Wall* and (co-written with Christopher Golden) *The Predator*, the Obsidian Heart trilogy, and the anthologies *New Fears* (winner of the British Fantasy Award for Best Anthology) and *New Fears 2* as editor. He's also written award-winning audio adaptations of the classic 1971 horror movie *Blood on Satan's Claw* and the M.R. James ghost story 'A View from a Hill'.

Adam L.G. Nevill was born in Birmingham, England, in 1969 and grew up in England and New Zealand. Of his novels, *The Ritual, Last Days, No One Gets Out Alive* and *The Reddening* were all winners of the August Derleth Award for Best Horror Novel. He has also published three collections of short stories, with *Some Will Not Sleep* winning the British Fantasy Award for Best Collection in 2017. Imaginarium adapted *The Ritual* and *No One Gets Out Alive* into feature films and more of his work is currently in development for the screen. The author lives in Devon, England. More information about the author and his books is available at adamlgnevill.com.

Carl Tait is a software engineer, classical pianist, and writer. His work has appeared in *After Dinner Conversation* (Pushcart Prize nominee), the *Eunoia Review*, the *Literary Hatchet*, the *Dillydoun Review,* and others. Carl grew up in Atlanta and currently lives in New York City with his wife and twin daughters. For more information, visit carltait.com.

Steve Rasnic Tem, a past winner of the Bram Stoker, World Fantasy, and British Fantasy Awards, has published 470+ short stories. Recent collections include *The Night Doctor & Other Tales* (Centipede) and *Thanatrauma: Stories* (Valancourt). Valancourt has also published a volume of his selected stories, *Figures Unseen*. His novel *Ubo* is a dark science fictional tale about violence and its origins, featuring such viewpoint characters as Jack the Ripper and Stalin. You can visit his home on the web at stevetem.com.

Born and raised in Houston, Texas, **Evelyn Teng** spends her time reading, writing, and baking more cookies than can be comfortably eaten by one person. She draws inspiration for her stories from video games, the outdoors, and tabletop gaming sessions with friends. She studied English and Psychology as a dual degree at Texas A&M University and currently works as a legal writer at an immigration law firm.

Conrad Williams is the author of the novels *Head Injuries, London Revenant, The Unblemished* (winner of the International Horror Guild Award), *One* (winner of the August Derleth Award), *Decay Inevitable, Loss of Separation* and *One Who Was With Me*. He has also written a crime trilogy (*Dust and Desire, Sonata of the Dead* and *Hell is Empty*). He is the author of four novellas: *Nearly People, Game, The Scalding Rooms* (winner of the British Fantasy Award) and *Rain*. His short stories are collected in *Use Once Then Destroy, Born With Teeth* and *I Will Surround You*. He is working on a new novel called *The Backs*.

Rio Youers is the British Fantasy and Sunburst Award–nominated author of *Westlake Soul* and *Lola on Fire*. His 2017 thriller, *The Forgotten Girl*, was a finalist for the Arthur Ellis Award for Best Crime Novel. He is the writer of *Refrigerator Full of Heads,* a six-issue comic series from DC Comics, and *Sleeping Beauties*, based on the bestselling novel by Stephen King and Owen King. Rio's latest novel, *No Second Chances*, was published by William Morrow in February 2022.

FLAME TREE PRESS
FICTION WITHOUT FRONTIERS
Award-Winning Authors & Original Voices

Flame Tree Press is the trade fiction imprint of Flame Tree Publishing, focusing on excellent writing in horror and the supernatural, crime and mystery, science fiction and fantasy. Our aim is to explore beyond the boundaries of the everyday, with tales from both award-winning authors and original voices.

•

Other titles in this series:
After Sundown
Beyond the Veil

Other horror and suspense titles available include:
Snowball by Gregory Bastianelli
Fellstones by Ramsey Campbell
Somebody's Voice by Ramsey Campbell
The Queen of the Cicadas by V. Castro
The Haunting of Henderson Close by Catherine Cavendish
In Darkness, Shadows Breathe by Catherine Cavendish
Five Deaths for Seven Songbirds by John Everson
Voodoo Heart by John Everson
Sins of the Father by JG Faherty
The Wakening by JG Faherty
Boy in the Box by Marc E. Fitch
One by One by D.W. Gillespie
Black Wings by Megan Hart
Stoker's Wilde by Steven Hopstaken & Melissa Prusi
Demon Dagger by Russell James
The Dark Game by Jonathan Janz
The Raven by Jonathan Janz
We Are Monsters by Brian Kirk
Hearthstone Cottage by Frazer Lee
Those Who Came Before by J.H. Moncrieff
August's Eyes by Glenn Rolfe
Creature by Hunter Shea
Misfits by Hunter Shea
Screams from the Void by Anne Tibbets
We Will Rise by Tim Waggoner

•

Join our mailing list for free short stories, new release details, news about our authors and special promotions:

flametreepress.com